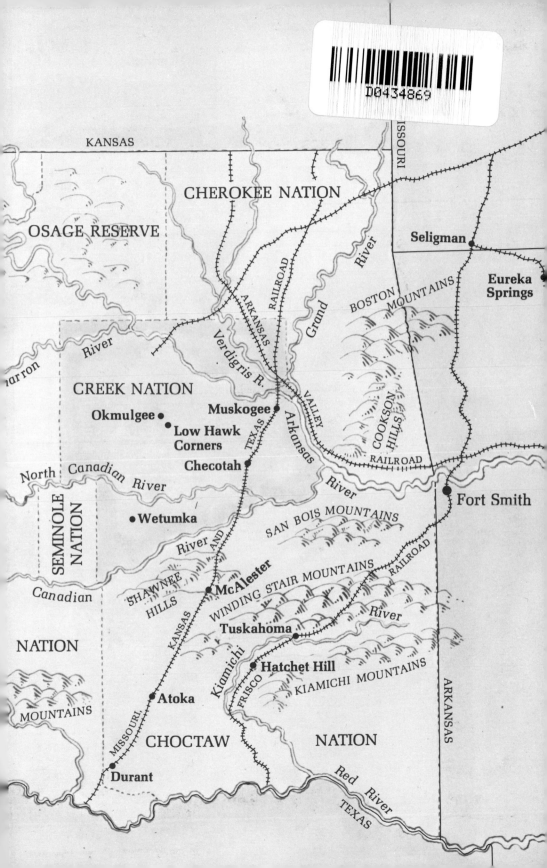

KANSAS

CHEROKEE NATION

OSAGE RESERVE

Seligman

Eureka
Springs

MISSOURI

ARKANSAS RAILROAD

Grand River

BOSTON MOUNTAINS

Verdigris R.

River

Cimarron River

CREEK NATION

Okmulgee

Low Hawk
Corners

Muskogee

Checotah

COOKSON HILLS

VALLEY

Arkansas

TEXAS

RAILROAD

North Canadian River

River

Arkansas River

Fort Smith

SEMINOLE NATION

Wetumka

SAN BOIS MOUNTAINS

Canadian

River

KANSAS AND

SHAWNEE HILLS

McAlester

WINDING STAIR MOUNTAINS

River

RAILROAD

NATION

Tuskahoma

MOUNTAINS

Kiamichi

FRISCO

Hatchet Hill

KIAMICHI MOUNTAINS

ARKANSAS

MISSOURI

Atoka

CHOCTAW

NATION

Durant

Red River

TEXAS

Winding Stair

Other Books by Douglas C. Jones

WINDING STAIR

Douglas C. Jones

Holt, Rinehart and Winston
New York

Published by Holt, Rinehart and Winston,
383 Madison Avenue, New York, New York
10017.
Published simultaneously in Canada by
Holt, Rinehart and Winston of Canada,
Limited.

Library of Congress Cataloging in
Publication Data

Jones, Douglas C
Winding stair.

    I. Title.
PZ4.J7534Wi   [PS3560.O478]   813'.5'4
    79-4195
ISBN: 0-03-050936-X

FIRST EDITION

Designer: Joy Chu
Endpaper maps by David Lindroth

Printed in the United States of America
10 9 8 7 6 5 4 3 2 1

Author's Note

This story is not a historical chronicle of the Rufus Buck gang, all five of whom went to the gallows in Fort Smith, Arkansas, on July 1, 1896, and with the exception of Judge Isaac C. Parker and George Maledon, all its characters are fictitious. But the narrative does describe the kinds of crimes for which the Buck gang and others were tried in the Federal Court for the Western District of Arkansas in the last quarter of the nineteenth century. It is dedicated to the good and decent people—red, white, and black—of the Indian Nations, now eastern Oklahoma, who once suffered the ravages brought on by the complexities of national expansion.

Winding Stair

FROM THE PLATFORM UNDER the gallows beam, where the ropes were placed on execution day, you could stand and look out beyond the confluence of the Poteau and Arkansas rivers. You could see between the Ouachita Mountains on the south and the Ozark Plateau to the north, along the flat floodplain extending westward through the Indian country. It was a land given the tribes that had been removed from their farms east of the Mississippi River in the 1830s, given them as their own various sovereign domains and known thereafter as The Nations.

It seemed to me the first time I stood there that no place could be more desolate. In that country across the rivers, terrible things had begun and many had ended here, on the gallows tree. When the condemned fell through the trap, they did not face the land they had savaged but rather the courthouse that had once been an army officers' barracks, and beyond that the frontier city of Fort Smith, its frame-and-brick and stone buildings like sharp-edged beads strung irregularly along Garrison Avenue, eastward from the river for more than half a mile to the Catholic church.

When one looked on this city of 11,000 people going about the usual business of civilization in 1890, there was about it some sensation fascinating and repelling at the same time, improbable of explanation but impossible to forget. I

1

have tried many times to describe it. But if the soul and texture of old Fort Smith remain indefinable, at least some of the facts of which I am aware can be set down. Unfortunately, what I observed was at the lowest level of social endeavor, dealing as it did with crimes almost unimaginable—and their punishment.

A part of the atmosphere came undoubtedly from the reputation of the man who sat on the federal bench there, Isaac Parker. His was a jurisdiction primarily concerned with law in the Indian Territory. He was called the Hanging Judge in most eastern newspapers, and with some justification. He came to the bench in Fort Smith in 1875, and during the first fifteen years of his office he sentenced more than a hundred men to hang. Of these, some were killed trying to escape; some died of disease in the jail; a few were pardoned by the President of the United States. All the others—eight blacks, nine Indians, and forty-seven white men—were executed.

From a distance, the scaffold looked like a bandshell. It sat at the southwestern end of what had been the old army fort compound, a city block or more surrounded by a six-foot stone wall. Within that larger enclosure a wooden fence large enough for perhaps a hundred spectators had been built around the gallows itself. Once inside the smaller fence, the nature of the structure became apparent. There were the thirteen steps rising ten feet above the ground to the platform that extended twenty paces under a slanted roof and back wall. A trap ran the entire length of the platform, directly beneath the massive oak beam on which it was said eight people could be hanged at one time. By June of 1890, the largest harvest on a single drop had been six.

Local citizens called it the Government Suspender.

One

THE INCIDENT CAME TO BE KNOWN AS THE WINDING STAIR Massacre. On a warm spring morning in the mountains of the Choctaw Nation, I beheld the first of its victims when one of our possemen drew back a wagon sheet from the naked body of Mrs. Eagle John. She had been a reasonably attractive woman of about forty, but what she had been seemed of little consequence now. She was lying in the sassafras thicket of an old fallow field among the pines, her cotton-stockinged legs spread, her hair in disarray on the blackened ground. Her cheeks were puffed from internal bleeding although no marks of a beating showed on the dark waxy skin of her face. One eye was open in an expression of surprise and disbelief. Her throat had been slashed, the wound gaping like a cleavered slab of pork, open to the cervical.

With the first shock of seeing that butchered body, it seemed incomprehensible that only four hours before I had been in my Fort Smith hotel room drawing maps of the city and of The Nations. I had arrived from Saint Louis a few days previously to work as clerk and investigator for Mr. William Evans, prosecuting attorney in Parker's federal court, with the promise that soon I would be assigned to one of the deputy marshals on investigation of criminal cases. After I'd completed my degree at the University of Illinois and read law for a year in my father's office, it had been decided that I should become acquainted with law enforcement. Father said if I was bent on becoming a prosecutor, which I was, then I'd best learn something about how the state provided defendants to prosecute. His friendship of many years' standing with Isaac Parker made my appointment to the Fort Smith court possible. Now, in order to better explain the confused and often contradictory nature of the court and its function, I purposed to make maps for my father so that in my letters the terrain would be clear to him.

The maps were a device to overcome boredom as well. Evans kept me occupied during the day, but nights quickly became insufferable, with no friends or outside interests in the city. The thought had come to mind of attending Henryetta's Frisco Hotel and Billiard Parlor, one of the bordellos near the railyards. But I had little desire for such commercial

3

and sweaty coupling within the smell of river fish along the Fort Smith waterfront. Nor did the Garrison Avenue saloons, well accoutered as many were, hold any fascination. No matter the loneliness and boredom, I was determined not to spend each night becoming sotted in some barroom.

I was struggling with straightedge and India ink at the desk in my room—the Farmers' Federal Bank clock had just struck midnight—when Joe Mountain came.

The Main Hotel was a good one with elevators, electric lights, and a rotating fan in the ceiling of each room. Even though it was relatively new, the hallway floors squeaked when anyone walked along them. But on that night I heard no sound of anyone until there was a sudden banging on my door. Before I could cross the room, the door swung open and there filling it was a large man wearing a Texas hat and a yellow duster that hung away from his legs like an unpegged tent. In the dim hallway light his teeth showed in a wide grin. He moved into the room silently as a large spider and I stepped back, reaching behind me for something heavy on the desk. His smile stretched across a wide, high-cheeked face, the eyeteeth fully a quarter-inch longer than the rest. It gave him the appearance of a smiling wolf.

"You Eben Pay?" he asked. His voice was deep, and although it had a soft guttural quality it filled the room.

"Yes. What do you want?"

"Cap'n says you come along with me. We're goin' to The Nations," he said, eyes and teeth shining in the light from my desk lamp. Framing his massive Indian head was a shock of black hair falling straight across his ears to his shoulders. Along his left cheek was a line of blue dots, tattooed from eyebrow to jawbone.

"Captain who?" I asked, still moving away from him. He had brought into the room a heavy odor of cooked meat and tobacco, a pungent but not unpleasant smell that I had never experienced before.

"Cap'n Oscar Schiller. He and you and me and my little brother Blue Foot are goin' to The Nations tonight. Me and Blue Foot track for the Cap'n. We're Osage. I'm Joe Mountain. You got any boots?"

"Who in hell is Oscar Schiller?" I asked.

"He's a marshal. One of Parker's marshals. Best one around. He says

4

you come with me. We got a big murder. Old Billy Evans, he told the Cap'n to take you along. Ain't that what you're here for?"

"That's part of it," I said.

"Well, you better get dressed. When the Cap'n gets after somebody that's done murder, he don't like to stand around."

"Wait outside. I'll be ready in a minute."

He made no move to leave as I opened my trunk and started pulling out field gear.

"We're gonna catch the late-night Texas freight," he said. "What's your first name, Eben Pay?"

"That's all the name I've got. It was my father's name. Still is."

He laughed without changing expression. HIs wolf-teeth showed constantly in his dark face.

"It's a good name. I like it. Does it mean anything?"

"No, it's just a name."

My hands shook as I laced my boots, partly from the Indian's unexpected entry, also because I was getting into The Nations. I had the feeling as Joe Mountain watched me dress that he disapproved my field gear, most especially the narrow-brimmed hat and the lace boots. He was wearing elaborately beaded and fringed moccasins.

"I bet you never would have thought I was Osage," he said, grinning. "With my hair like this. Us Osage, we used to wear it roached, but nowadays we just let it grow. Except for my little brother Blue Foot. He's young, but he's an old-fashioned Osage. He roaches his. You'll see."

Joe Mountain led me down the back fire-stairs and into an alley, explaining that the hotel people raised hell when an Indian came parading through their lobby, even an Indian on government work. We hurried out to Garrison Avenue and along the dark street. All the gas jet streetlamps had been extinguished, as they were each night before ten. We could see a few saloon lights and I heard a player piano in a barely recognizable rendition of "Willie We Have Missed You." We passed the American Express office and the Anheuser-Busch brewery with its stables facing on the street, each of the high arched doorways crowned with a brass eagle.

"What's happened in The Nations?" I asked, panting as I tried to keep up.

5

"Hell, Eben Pay, I don't know. Cap'n, he'll tell us all that when he feels like it."

"Why do you call him Captain?"

"Because, that's what he wants to be called," Joe Mountain said and laughed. "The Cap'n generally gets what he wants."

As he spoke, I began to realize that he was not constantly grinning, as had first appeared. Rather, his teeth were too large for his mouth, so that his lips were always parted. Although he was as large as any man I had even known, he walked with a flowing rhythm and grace that reminded me of a full-foliaged black locust tree bending in a hard breeze, the leaves in fluid motion.

We came to the Frisco station at the foot of Garrison Avenue, where I had detrained only four nights before, and turned north along the tracks. To the west was the Arkansas River, dark and unseen now, and beyond that The Nations. We passed along the fronts of long warehouses and a number of old hotels, where lights were showing. Joe Mountain said something about whores and pointed toward one of the lighted buildings.

"That's Henryetta's place," he said. "You ever been in there?"

"No."

"Me neither, except sometimes when I go with the Cap'n on official business." He waved an arm off into the darkness. "Down a little farther is Big Tooth Betty's. You ever been in there?"

"No, I haven't been in any of them."

"They say she runs a fine whorehouse. They won't let me in there, either."

The night was warm and above us stars were out. But across the river, the sky darkened and The Nations seemed swallowed in a black void with only occasional lightning to mark the western horizon. The flare of blue-white light would run along the edge of the world, silent and distant, looking cold and ominous.

"I don't like that lightning," Joe Mountain said, and I supposed it was some savage superstition. But he sensed what I was thinking and laughed. "It means we may get our ass wet before this is over."

Switch engines were working the yards, their lights blinding us as we moved to the mainline spur. There, headed by a big road-locomotive that dwarfed the yard engines, stood a long line of boxcars. The firebox sent dancing patterns of flame-red color across the tracks.

At the caboose, beside the tracks, was a group of men. One was an Indian dressed like Joe Mountain, except that he wore no hat. I could see his long roach hanging from the top of his head like black corn silks sprouting from a smooth melon. He held a heavy rifle in each hand. With him was a small white man in a palmetto hat holding saddlebags draped over one arm, and a little apart a brakeman and conductor were waiting impatiently.

The man in the palmetto moved toward us, his hand extended. Oscar Schiller was everything I would have expected a federal peace officer not to be. He was small to the point of frailness and wore thick steel-rimmed spectacles that gleamed in the lights from the working engines. He was clean-shaven, and when he spoke his thin lips moved only slightly. As he introduced himself, I could see his eyes were pale blue and that he seldom blinked.

"Mr. Pay. Sorry to roust you out so late, but Mr. Evans said you might be interested in the investigation of a case in The Nations."

"I was hoping for it," I said, taking his small fingers in my hand. Like the Osages, he wore a long duster over cotton duck trousers and jacket.

"We've got a little killing down in the Choctaw. Indian woman, a widow."

"I thought jurisdiction in Indian cases belonged to the Indian courts."

"They do. But not if there's whites in it. There's a white in this. Had a wire, Choctaw police at Hatchet Hill. Found the body last night. This train'll get us there by daybreak."

His conversation was clipped and blunt, somewhat rude. His voice was rough, like sandstones rubbing together. From the start, I disliked him.

Abruptly, he turned and mounted the steps of the caboose and I heard him use a phrase I would come to associate with him as time passed.

"Let's get to business."

The train-crew quarters were at the front of the caboose, but in back were two facing pairs of passenger seats. Oscar Schiller and Blue Foot took one of these, Joe Mountain and I the one across the aisle. Blue Foot had not uttered a word and now sat staring at me. He was smaller than his brother, but he had the same flat, high-cheeked face and black eyes. His fingers were slender, almost delicate as he held the rifles between his legs, butts resting on the floor.

Schiller took a newspaper from his saddlebags and began to read, ignoring the rest of us. He produced peanuts from a pocket of his duster and ate them as he read, dropping the shells on the floor.

"Where is Hatchet Hill?" I asked Joe Mountain.

"Down on Kiamichi River, south of Winding Stair Mountains," he said. "You gonna like this case, Eben Pay. Murder's the best kind. The Cap'n takes in after anybody who does murder and he don't let up until he's got 'em."

We jerked to a start, the big engine up ahead driving forward, popping each coupling tight along the line of cars. The brakeman passed down the aisle, then the conductor. Schiller handed him some red tickets and Joe Mountain laughed.

"Railroad passes," he said. "The Cap'n got enough railroad passes in them saddlebags to choke a mule."

"Where does he get railroad passes?"

The big Osage looked at me as though he thought me a complete idiot.

"From the railroads. The railroads give passes to newspaper writers because they like to have good stuff wrote about their trains. They give passes to the Cap'n because if they didn't, he'd arrest half the men working on their lines for going into The Nations without a proper permit."

By treaty with the tribes of The Nations, whites were allowed into their territory only if they married into a tribe or if they had a work permit from the federal government. The railroads had been building through that country for years, and they were run almost exclusively by whites. I knew from my short term in Evans's office that many whites were honestly employed in The Nations without a permit, a situation generally ignored by the authorities. But there were others who were there specifically because Indian courts and police had no jurisdiction over them and there was no normal system of state law to control their conduct. These were engaged in pursuits generally neither honest nor admirable. Even so, I could develop little respect for Schiller's extortion of the railroads by way of tacit threat to itinerant workers whom they needed but who had no legal papers.

We rolled past the Frisco passenger station, picking up speed southward along the banks of the Poteau River. The tracks turned west then, and as the lights of Fort Smith disappeared behind us I knew we were in the Choctaw Nation. There was a long stretch of flat country before we started into the hills. The train was a through freight and we passed all the hamlets without slowing. The light of kerosene lamps shone in the buildings, parading past our window like faint orange puffballs against the dusty glass. As the night wore on, we saw only occasional lights and the rest was darkness. But Joe Mountain made sure I knew where we were.

"San Bois Mountains over there," he said, pointing into the night. And later, "We're almost to the Winding Stair."

I had been led to believe that all Indians were a stoic and untalkative people. Yet Joe Mountain was as garrulous as any man I ever knew. Long after Oscar Schiller had dropped his newspaper among the peanut hulls on the floor and gone to sleep, Joe Mountain talked.

He told me how he had grown up on the Osage reservation, learning to read and write at the agency mission school. He had even taught there for a while, before his father died and he returned to the family to help his mother raise the younger children. Many hours were spent with Blue Foot, he said, along the Arkansas River west of Pawhuska. He had taught his brother how to track and to shoot and had told him the tribal history.

"We don't write our history down like you white people do," he said. "Even if we have learned to write. We pass it along from one man to the next by telling it."

In that way, Blue Foot had learned of the old days and how the Cherokees had first come, early in the nineteenth century, and how the Osage had fought them until the army finally established a fort at Belle Point called Fort Smith, just to keep them apart. And there had been stories of the fights with Kiowas, to the west on the Great Plains, where the Osage went each year to hunt buffalo. And stories, too, of tribes

9

coming from far away to obtain the Osage orangewood for making bows.

"The Ozark Mountains," Joe Mountain said. "My people call it Place of the Bows because of that wood."

As he talked, I could not help but stare at the line of blue dots along one side of his face. After a long time, he laughed and touched his cheek with his fingertips.

"My granddaddy give me a tattooing needle," he said. "He told me his daddy got it from the French, when they was tradin' along the rivers and before your people came into our country. My granddaddy's daddy traded a Pawnee boy for the needle. Did you know the Osage used to catch people and sell them to the French?"

"No," I said. I had heard somewhere in one of my University of Illinois history courses that the French had used North American Indians as slave labor in their Indies sugar fields, but had never wondered how they came by those Indians.

"Well, we did. We ain't too proud of it now. But times have changed. You know how long ago that was, when my people went out on slave raids for the French?"

"I have no idea."

"Me neither. But it was a long time ago. And times have changed."

From beneath his duster he pulled a long-handled tomahawk. The head was pointed like a cake knife, with elaborate sworls etched into the bright metal and a lacework of tiny holes.

"This came from the French, too, a long time ago," he said, and quickly slipped it back under the duster. "Cap'n says I got no business with such a savage weapon. You see those rifles Blue Foot's got? Them's what the Cap'n says is good for government work. Winchester .38–40s. Good for deer or men either."

As we passed through the town of Poteau, all dark, and started into higher country, the engine began to labor. Joe Mountain said we were in pine timber country now, and even if there were farms with lights still on, they'd be hidden back in the woods. At times, the train moved so slowly on steep grades that a man running alongside could have stayed abreast. I was sleepy but Joe Mountain's stream of conversation on Osage history and local terrain kept me wide awake.

We labored through the Winding Stair Mountains, the tracks seeking low passes. Going down into Kiamichi Valley, we gained speed. With Tuskahoma, the Choctaw capital, behind us, we came to the river, crossed a steel trestle bridge, and squealed to a stop at Hatchet Hill.

The village was strung along the valley, set between sharply rising slopes that even in the darkness looked tropic green. It was only a scattering of squat, square buildings along one side of the tracks, like a set of poker dice carelessly tossed and caught suddenly against the felt cushions of a billiard table. The only light glowed faintly from the open door of a small general store. The Kiamichi Mountains were to the south, behind the town. Across the tracks and the river were the rising slopes of the Winding Stair. As we stepped down from the caboose, the brakeman waiting impatiently to wave the train on to Texas, it was approaching dawn, but still dark. I could smell pine trees and cinders and hear behind us the river running between steep banks.

In the headlight of the engine, just before the train pulled away, I saw a large group of men and horses. One of the men walked out to shake hands with Oscar Schiller, then the two moved off to talk by themselves. Joe Mountain said the man's name was George Moon and that he was police chief in these parts. He was a small man with the inevitable big hat and canvas jacket. He was wearing a large revolver and a star on his shirtfront.

Joe Mountain also said that "the other white man" in the crowd was the veterinarian from Tuskahoma who had been brought down to Hatchet Hill while we were making the trip from Fort Smith. I saw no one I could recognize as a white man.

"What's the vet for?" I asked.

"I ain't sure," Joe Mountain said. "But he's the only white doctor they got around here."

Two Choctaw women came from the store with a wicker basket of corn muffins and a crock of buttermilk. As we ate—the milk cold and good, taken by each of us in turn from a dipper to wash down the dry breakfast—we could see George Moon and Oscar Schiller move over to the group of men, the marshal's yellow duster and palmetto hat marking him even in the dark. He went among the Indians, shaking hands and addressing them.

"Cap'n likes to mix right in with these Choctaws," Joe Mountain said, and Blue Foot made a grunt, his first sound since I'd laid eyes on him. "We don't much cotton to 'em," Joe Mountain added. I recalled Evans saying something about old enmities dying hard.

"Are all those people policemen?" I asked.

"They likely are now," Joe Mountain said. "Goerge Moon pins a badge on everybody in sight when trouble starts."

The sky in the east had begun to pale as the women moved off with their milk and cornbread. The two Osages and I remained apart from the others, silently watching as the night faded away. Finally, Schiller came back to us and the Choctaws followed him, pulling their horses. Mounts were being brought to us as well, led by Indian boys who wore the same Texas hats as their fathers.

"We'll be riding a ways," Schiller said. "So you'd best do your business now."

He and the two Osages faced the railroad track and started unbuttoning their pants. I joined them, hoping the women were by now back inside the store. Some of the Choctaw policemen came over and positioned themselves a little apart, though all in line along the track, as if it was some kind of ritual. Joe Mountain continued longer than anyone else, splashing down a goodly number of railroad ties.

My horse was a dapple gray mare and she grunted when I went up to the saddle. I'd never before ridden a work rig, and the high fork and cantle seemed awkward. The stirrups were too large and I resolved right then to buy a pair of those high-heel boots as soon as I got back to Fort Smith, to avoid having a foot slip completely through the bows.

By now, the sawtooth ridges heavy with pine had appeared against the sky. The water of the river shown farther along the valley as it twisted between the hills and caught the light of the coming dawn. Now that the train and its soot and cinders were gone, the valley smelled of a fresh spring day, clean and crisp. Joe Mountain edged his horse close to mine and again I could see his teeth under the wide hat brim.

George Moon came from the store leading a small Negro boy. He boosted the lad up behind one of the Choctaw policemen and mounted himself to lead us across the tracks to a wooden bridge. On the far side of the river we were immediately in the pines. The road began to pitch up sharply, trees crowded close on either side, and once more it was

12

completely dark. I allowed the mare to pick her own way, following Moon and the policeman with the boy, Schiller and the white veterinarian. The two Osages were riding beside me, and a short distance behind came the rest of the Choctaws.

At irregular intervals along the road were mountain farms where the land had been cleared of timber. There were a few houses and barn lots near the road. As the light grew, we began to see people doing their morning chores, slopping hogs or carrying buckets of milk from the cow sheds. Each of them stopped and looked at us as we passed, but none made any greeting.

About thirty minutes out of Hatchet Hill, with daylight full upon us, we came to a cleared field on one side of the road, a field that had gone fallow years before and was now overgrown with small dogwood and sassafras trees. In the road was a small wagon, standing with trace chains and a singletree lying before it. Around a small fire across the road from the clearing was a group of men and horses.

"More Choctaw police," Joe Mountain said.

The Osages and I remained mounted as the column came up and turned off into the trees around the fire. Schiller was there, talking with the men, and the black boy was there, too. After only a few moments, the marshal came back to us.

"Here's what we got," he said. "A Choctaw woman named Mrs. Eagle John. Widow woman. Got caught here last evening by parties unknown. That nigger boy over there was with her. She owns a farm up the road, was on her way to visit relatives in the valley somewhere. The Choctaws got here after dark, too late to track. So Blue Foot, I want you to cut for sign in case they left the road. There ought to be about five or six horses. You other two, get down and let's get to business."

Joe Mountain and I dismounted and followed Schiller and George Moon into the old field, pushing back the low-hanging sassafras branches. A number of Choctaw policemen moved ahead of us. One of the Choctaws pointed to an empty whiskey bottle and Schiller nodded as though he had expected it to be there.

A few paces from the road, the scrub trees thinned. We were in a space covered with last year's growth of weeds and some of them had burrs that clung to our trousers. At the center of this clearing there was a large tarpaulin spread over a form I recognized as a human body. I felt the corn muffins turning in my stomach. We grouped ourselves around the form and stood there looking down until Schiller spoke impatiently.

"All right. Let's look."

One of Moon's policemen pulled back the tarp. No one spoke for a long time. The only sounds were the harsh buzzing of flies, and from the ridge behind us crows cawing. Beside the naked form, tied in a neat bundle, was her clothing, secured in a large sunbonnet.

"You know her, then?" Schiller asked, his voice grating.

"That's old Eagle John's wife, all right," Moon said. "She lived about a mile up the road here, with that nigger boy."

"They did a hell of a job on her, didn't they?"

"They must have held her until she was dead," George Moon said. "It don't look like she done any thrashing around when they cut her."

The vet had come with us and now he squatted between the woman's legs, opening a little black bag. I felt the corn muffins start up and staggered out of the clearing and into the pines alongside the road. Leaning against a tree trunk, I threw up. The cornmeal clogged my nose like wet sand. It took a long time to finish.

Back on the road, the others had assembled around the wagon. Everyone made an elaborate effort not to look at me as I blew my nose and stood behind Oscar Schiller. There was no talk while we waited for the vet to come out of the clearing. When he did, he said the woman had been raped.

"Enough semen to float a catfish boat, Marshal."

"All right, let's get the boy over here," Schiller said, then he turned and looked at me. "You feel better?"

"Yes." I started to say that coming on such a scene, regardless of knowing pretty much what would be found, was a shock. But Schiller had turned away and I said nothing.

George Moon brought the Negro boy from the group still around the fire. He said the boy's name was Emmitt and he'd lived with Mrs. John all his life, and that he was eight years old. The boy turned under Moon's hand to avoid looking at the wagon. He stared at the thin column of smoke rising from the fire into the high pine treetops.

"Son, we want you to tell us what you saw here," Schiller said. The boy swallowed twice before he spoke, and his expression did not change, his eyes still on the Choctaw fire.

"Miz John and me was goin' for a visit with the Otubees, who is Miz John's in-laws, she says. We come along here yesterday late, and these men come out from the woods over there." He pointed to the trees behind the fire. "They stopped Ole Blue . . ."

"Is Ole Blue the horse, Emmitt?" George Moon asked.

"Yes suh. They stopped Ole Blue and Miz John say get out the way. They jus' laugh. They laugh all the time. They drinkin' whiskey out'n them big bottles and laughin'."

"How many was there, Emmitt?" George Moon asked.

"They was five. One white man in dandy clothes. He come over and start puttin' his hand on Miz John here," and he reached up and touched his chest. "She try to whup him with her fly switch but he take it away from her and keep on laughin' and tearin' her clothes."

"What did the others look like?"

"I never seed any of 'em around here before. They was one nigger. He was drunk and yellin' and watchin' that white man pull at Miz John. They was another man sit back on his horse and jus' watch and not doin' nothin' but laughin'. He jus' sit on his horse. He was a dark-skin man, too, but I think he was Indian. They was two others I know was Indians. I never seed them before, either. One of 'em commenced to help the white man pull Miz John off the wagon into the road. The other one, he got up on the wagon seat and throwed me down on the groun'. He found Miz John's purse under the seat. He had one eye all white."

I felt the skin on the back of my neck move. The man Emmitt described had been on the station platform the night I arrived in Fort Smith. He had passed near me and I had seen his puffy Indian face and the eye with a cataract, a short and stocky man with close-cropped black hair and thick lips turned down bitterly at the corners. But now wasn't the time to interrupt and I said nothing.

"Man with that bad eye, he take some stuff out'n the purse, then throw the purse over to the man on the horse still yet. Man on the horse didn't even look in it, just stuff it in a saddlebag."

"Emmitt, did you see what the man with the bad eye took out of the purse?" Schiller asked.

"I dunno. He taken a little watch and some money."

"Was it hard money?" George Moon asked.

"Yes suh. It was silver money."

"Would you know that watch again if you saw it?" Schiller asked.

"I reckon. It was jus' a watch, a little watch."

"All right, what happened then, Emmitt?"

"The man with the bad eye jump off the wagon and him and them others drag Miz John off into the bushes. She hittin' at 'em and yellin'. I see her clothes tore almost off her. Then they had her back in them bushes and I couldn't see, but she was yellin' like no yellin' I ever hear before."

Four Indian policemen were bringing the body back to the road, wrapped in the tarpaulin like a mummy. Only the high-button shoes were showing. The boy was facing away from them as they pushed the long bundle into the wagon bed. He started crying silently, the tears running down his cheeks and along his jawbone. His expression did not change, but the tears ran down his face, wetting his collar. Without prompting this time, he went on.

"That man who jus' sit on his horse all the time. He ride over close to me and look down and he's got a big pistol in his belt. I thought he'd shoot me. He jus' grin and then he got off and started unhitchin' Ole Blue. I was layin' in the road. And so when he started unhitchin' Ole Blue, I jumped up and run off. I run into them woods and he shot at me but didn't hit nothin'. So I kept on runnin', all the way to Hatchet Hill."

"You didn't see any of them again?" George Moon asked.

"No suh. I run through the woods. I stayed off the road so's they wouldn't catch me. I run all the way to Hatchet Hill in the woods. For a long time, I was runnin' and I could hear Miz John yellin'."

"What was she yelling?" Schiller asked.

"Jus' yellin' for somebody come help her."

The tears ran down his face as he looked at the smoke rising from the fire to the high treetops.

Now Schiller squatted beside the boy and laid a hand on his shoulder. Emmitt did not move away but neither did he look at the marshal.

"Now son, when we catch these men, will you be able to tell us if we've got the right ones?"

16

The boy frowned. He rubbed his eyes with his fists and shook his head.

"They cut my guts out."

"No. They won't. We're going to leave you with one of these policemen, in his house at Hatchet Hill, and nobody will bother you. But when we catch 'em, we'll need you to tell us if they're the right men."

"You gonna catch 'em?"

"Yes. We are."

"Well, I reckon I could tell you if you got the right ones."

"Good," Schiller said. He dug into his pocket and gave the boy a dime. "You can buy some ice cream. And later, when you come to Fort Smith, you can have lots of ice cream."

For the first time, the boy looked up at Schiller.

"I'm comin' to Fort Smith?"

"Yes. When we catch 'em. There's lots of ice cream in Fort Smith."

The tight knot of men around the boy began to break up then. One of the policemen took Emmitt away while two others were hitching a saddle horse to the wagon. Blue Foot had appeared, waiting to one side until the boy was finished. Now he came forward and spoke to Schiller, the first time I had heard his voice. His English was not as good as Joe Mountain's.

"Six horses, one without rider," he said, pointing off into the woods. "They goin' up the mountain."

"I figured," Schiller said. "They'd want to stay off the road after this. How old is the trail?"

"Last night. About dark," Blue Foot said.

Before the marshal could turn to his horse, I touched his arm and he turned to me, his eyes cold and unblinking.

"I think I've seen this man with a bad eye. A cataract, from what the boy said."

"Where?" Schiller snapped.

"In Fort Smith at the train station. The first night I was in town. He met another man who'd been on the train with me."

"What other man?"

"A white man. And he was wearing expensive clothes. I think they're the same two Emmitt was talking about here."

"I'd bet on it. Describe this white man."

17

"He was a good-looking man, about my age, tall. Blond hair, blue eyes."

Schiller frowned and shook his head.

"Could be anybody. But we know the other one, don't we, Joe?"

Joe Mountain laughed. "You bet. It's Milk Eye."

"Milk Eye Rufus Deer. He's a Yuchi Indian. Hangs out in the Creek Nation mostly. I never knew him to get this far south."

"Then we know who we're after?" I asked.

"We know one of 'em anyway. But finding him may not be so easy. He stays pretty well hid out. Now and again he shows up at one of these straightaway horse races they have over here in The Nations. He's a betting man. He's been in minor trouble for years, but he's busted his ax this time. Well, let's get to business."

Some of the Choctaw officers would return to Hatchet Hill with the body and the boy. The rest of us, under Schiller's direction, would start the hunt.

We moved off into the timber, Blue Foot riding some distance up front, Joe Mountain just behind him, a Winchester across his lap. Blue Foot watched the ground for sign, but Joe Mountain looked ahead into the pines.

The experience had shaken me badly. Reading of murder and rape in Evans's office and seeing it lying naked and blood-soaked on the ground were very different matters. The sight of human flesh laid open by a blade was, I felt at the time, something that would haunt my sleep forever. I was to learn that even the most ghastly scenes soon pale in memory.

I had seen a violently killed person only once before. In Saint Louis when I was a small boy, my father and I had come onto a man lying in the street who had just been struck and killed by a beam that had fallen from a building under construction. Father moved away quickly, saying I should not stare at the man because it would embarrass him to be seen lying helpless and formless and bloody in the street. Perhaps that was the worst part of what we had just seen, even worse than the assault itself on Mrs. John—her inability to avoid lying naked under the eyes of men, lifeless and stripped of all dignity.

Through all of this horror, Oscar Schiller had shown no emotion, no

18

change in mood. He went about his business as though it were the most routine labor, like cutting lumber or plowing a cornfield. His cold, unblinking eyes took photographic images of everything, like a box camera, impersonally and without passion. When he gave the boy Emmitt a dime, his face was the same as it had been when the tarpaulin came off Mrs. John's body. I began to wonder if he perspired like other men, or if he was ever hungry or had ever been in love with a woman. I began to hate him a little.

We had ridden only a short distance when I realized Joe Mountain's companionship and conversation were badly missed. It had suddenly become important that the big Osage like me, even though we had met only a few hours before. The marshal said nothing more to me as the day wore on and we moved deeper into the pine woods of the Winding Stair.

Two

OUR COLUMN PROCEEDED THROUGH THE PINES WITHOUT A sound except for the whisper of horses' hooves on the carpet of needles and the occasional squeak of leather or tinkle of bit chains. Jays called harshly and among the cedars we passed were pairs of bluebirds and redheaded woodpeckers showing their garish black, white, and red markings against the greens and blues of foliage. At first, the ground sloped upward gently but this soon gave way to steep ridges. We came to stands of hardwood and here the underbrush was thick and tangled. Sometimes the trail led around these groves of hickory and oak but many we plowed through, the branches of saplings slashing us across the face. The pace was set by Blue Foot's speed as he moved ahead, reading the sign left by the men who had done rape and murder.

At the head of the column, Blue Foot and Joe Mountain were generally out of sight in the trees, but Oscar Schiller and the Choctaw police chief George Moon were always there. Now and then, Schiller turned to look back along the line of march, and his gaze always sought me out as though he expected to see that I had fallen off my mare and disappeared into some brushy canyon. His features were set in that stony, hard-lipped expression. Sometimes, I saw him chewing a matchstick.

Once, we stopped to dismount and tighten our saddle cinches. Some of the Choctaws looked at me from under hat brims suspecting that I had no idea how to perform such a task. But although the saddle was strange to me, horses were not. Along the way, I caught a number of the Indians regarding my small hat and city boots with some dismay, as though they had never seen such things before. Perhaps, too, they found it odd that here among men so obviously well armed I would have no weapon. But then, neither did Schiller, at least no visible weapon.

The Choctaws smoked constantly, rolling their own cigarettes with tobacco from soggy-looking bags. To avoid setting the woods on fire, they pinched out the hot coals just before the cigarettes were smoked all the way down to their lips, afterward rubbing their fingers on saddle horns to ease the heat's sting.

Twice we rode past discarded and empty whiskey bottles. The

Choctaws would point them out wordlessly, apparently thinking me incapable of seeing them.

It was past noon when we stopped to rest the horses. As I sat against a tree trunk, painfully aware of the blisters along my thighs, Oscar Schiller walked over and gave me a can of sardines and two baking soda biscuits. He said nothing but went back to squat with George Moon. There was no key on the sardine can but I was determined not to ask Schiller for an opener, no matter that I was famished after losing my breakfast. Joe Mountain came back from his forward position, grinning, and opened the can with that outlandish French trade hatchet.

"You gotta eat, Eben Pay. This chase has barely started."

He had sardines and biscuits, too, and we sat together eating, sopping the oil with the dry biscuits. It had begun to cloud over, and without the sun the woods turned cool and gloomy. The birds had also disappeared, except for crows that always seemed to be on the next ridge setting up their infernal racket.

Joe Mountain looked up through the trees and said, "I told you we gonna get our ass wet."

Oscar Schiller and George Moon had finished their meal and were talking about the case. They were near enough to overhear.

"They're going straight to something," Schiller said. "They didn't stop for the night, or if they did it wasn't for long. Blue Foot says the trail isn't getting any fresher."

"Yes," Moon said. "They're headed for someplace."

"There's not many farms around here, are there?"

"A few miles ahead, if the trail don't change, we come back to the road where it comes up over these ridges and heads out for McAlester. There's farms along that road."

"I think it means one of two things. They've got a farm where they'll hole up, or else they're out for more harm."

"They don't come from around here," Moon said. "Not that anyone knows of, so it's unlikely they'd have a place to hole up. I think they may be out for harm."

"Well, I don't like it. They put me in mind of a Comanche war party. Anything gets in the way is in for trouble. I think they've let the wolf loose. Out on a hell-raising drunk. They've had enough liquor to be doing that. Too drunk to have any sense and not drunk enough to pass out."

We rode on throughout most of the afternoon, the hills less rugged now and the timber thinning. We passed old logging roads, most of them abandoned long ago, and a few fields that had been left and were overgrown with small trees. From some of these, we could look out across the mountains to the west and see rain falling, like a thin blue-gray veil shrouding the ridgelines. Joe Mountain had been right. We were going to get our ass wet.

As the timber thinned, Blue Foot began to speed up his lead and sometimes we had to put our mounts to a trot to keep pace. It was difficult to read any sign in the pine needles, even after the horses ahead had passed, except that now and then there were droppings. At least, I found I could tell the difference between the fresh ones and those dropped by the horses of the men we were hunting.

One of the Choctaws moved his horse up alongside and rode for a long time without saying anything. He offered me his sack of tobacco and a pack of thin cigarette papers, and I managed to roll a smoke as I rode, letting the mare follow the horses ahead on her own. When he did speak, it was quietly, as though he had no desire to break the continuing silence of the column's movement.

"I'm Charley. You a deputy, like the Cap'n?"

"No. I work out of the federal court in Fort Smith."

"Ah," he said and smiled. "Judge Parker, sure. You work for Judge Parker, like the Cap'n. That's good."

I handed him the tobacco sack and thanked him. The taste of the smoke was good in my mouth, still oily from the sardines.

"Got a gun?" he asked. When I said I did not, he pulled out a heavy Colt single-action and offered it to me, but I told him I hoped I wouldn't need it.

"You oughta carry a good gun," he said, but shrugged and slipped the weapon out of sight again under his coat.

That ended it and he allowed his horse to drift back away from me, but I could hear him talking in Choctaw to his companions, probably telling them everything he'd learned about me.

It was turning dark and there was the smell of rain in the air when the two Osage scouts rode back through the trees to hold a conference with Oscar Schiller and George Moon. The rest of the party sat well back, watching. After a few moments, the scouts reined their horses away and rode off in different directions at a gallop. Schiller waved us up alongside and said we were coming to the Hatchet Hill–McAlester road again and that there was a farm just ahead. He told us the trail of the men we had been following apparently led to this farmstead. Choctaw policemen all around me began pulling Winchesters from saddle boots and checking the loads in Colt revolvers, spinning the cylinders. None that I could see showed any expression, but my own heart was pounding. We moved for perhaps three hundred yards, seeing ahead the thinning trees. Schiller stopped us again, well back in the trees, and the Choctaws fanned out, forming a long line. I moved my horse close in behind Schiller and waited with the rest, the soreness in my legs forgotten.

Blue Foot came up to us suddenly from the trees on one flank, and he was breathing hard as he pulled in beside Schiller and Moon.

"They been there, maybe," he said. "But nobody now. No horses around, at the house or in the barn lot. There's a man tied to the well curbing."

"Let's get to business," Schiller shouted and dug his heels into his horse's flanks. It was what I imagined a cavalry charge to be. We swept from the line of trees at a run. Leaving the woods, we could see a long cleared space down the slope before us, and the buildings of the farmstead. The house was a long, single-story building with porches on both sides running the entire length and a breezeway or dogtrot through the middle, separating the rooms at either end. Beyond that was a barn and other outbuildings, then the road marked by a rail fence. It ran off in either direction from the ridge on which the house stood, disappearing into heavily wooded valleys. The yard around the house was flat and broom-swept, and scattered across it were a number of dead chickens, lying like puffed feather pillows.

Choctaw policemen were already going into the house, weapons ready, when Schiller and Moon pulled up in a cloud of dust and dismounted at the well in one corner of the yard. Joe Mountain came riding up from the outbuildings. Tied to the high stone well curbing was a man, leaning crazily to one side, his head cut horribly and his beard

23

crusted with blood. He was barefooted and nothing covered his body but long flannel underwear.

"That's Thomas Thrasher," George Moon said. "He owns this place."

"Well, he's dead," Schiller said. They cut the rope holding the body to the curbing and it collapsed onto the ground, sliding down sideways in a sitting position, gone partly stiff. There were deep cuts through the underwear under the arms, into the rib cage, and the collarbone thrust up through a vicious wound in the shoulder like a celery stalk snapped in half.

"There's your murder weapon," Schiller said, pointing to a single-bitted ax that lay a few feet away covered from haft to blade with blood. "Let's get him on the porch."

It had started to rain. The air in the yard was still, like a vacuum, the large drops falling straight to the ground like lead pellets in a shot silo. High above, the wind was roaring.

One of the Choctaw policemen came from the barn with a wagon canvas. We laid Thrasher's body at one end of the porch and covered it. Somehow, looking at it had not been so bad as seeing the woman in early morning, although the mutilation was much worse.

We were on the porch, under cover from the rain, when Blue Foot came up from the outbuildings, waving his Winchester.

"Cap'n! Another dead man in the pigsty. Them pigs been at his face."

A number of men ran to the pigpen, shouting and waving back the hogs bunched along one fence row. From the sty they lifted a form, limp and completely naked. When they carried it to the house, I moved away to the far end of the porch. They put it beside the other body and some of them bent over what was left of the face.

"One of the hired help, I'd guess," George Moon said. "But I can't tell which one, the way he's been chewed. Mr. Thrasher had two Choctaws working for him here."

Somebody said, "This one's shot through the back. See that lump on his chest? See that? That there's the bullet, Cap'n."

"I want that slug," Oscar Schiller said. "Gimme your knife, George."

Inside the house, Choctaw policemen were going through the rooms.

I would have joined them except for my apprehension over what I might see there, so I stood on the porch, away from everyone, looking down across the yard where the rain was beginning to slant before a growing wind. The dead chickens had become sodden lumps of feathers, as though they had just been scalded and waited to be plucked. When Oscar Schiller touched my arm, I jumped. He was holding a flattened bullet in the palm of one hand.

"You see that, Mr. Pay?" he asked. "That's what a slug looks like that's gone through a man. But the base is intact. It's a .45." He put it in a pocket and wiped his hand on his duster. He acted as though he enjoyed all of this.

He was starting to say something else when there was a shout from the rear of the house. We ran to the backyard through the rain. There was a long line of hollyhocks bordering a path from the back porch to an unpainted privy. Blossoms had already begun on the tall stalks, but now the rain was beating them off, leaving petals strewn across the wet ground like red and white quilt pieces. At the privy there were half a dozen Choctaws, holding the door open.

It was a two-holer and sitting on one hole was a young Indian man, his pants and drawers around his ankles. He sat slouched against one wall, his eyes staring out into the rain. His front was covered with congealed blood and the toilet seat was slick with it. I saw then the riddled door, each bullet hole with fresh, raw splinters showing harshly against the weathered wood. Schiller and Moon bent over the man, looking closely at his face.

"You know this one, George?"

"Yes, it's Oshutubee. He was a carpenter apprentice to Mr. Thrasher. They did contract work for the Nation in Tuskahoma. That means the one we found in the pigpen was Price. A farmhand. Both of them were Choctaws."

"Get him with the others," Schiller said. "At least this one hasn't got a mess in his pants."

As the policemen carried the body around to the front porch, I walked toward the house with Schiller and Moon, drenched to the skin and resolved that as soon as I got back to Fort Smith I would buy a slicker to go with the high-heeled boots.

"Contract work, you said?"

"Yes," George Moon said. "Mr. Thrasher was a carpenter. He came to The Nations and married one of our women about twelve years ago."

"So he's part of the Choctaw Nation."

"Yes, but still a white man. When he came here he had a child with him. From some marriage before, over in Arkansas I guess. A little girl about six years old. She's about eighteen now I guess."

They stopped and looked at one another, the rain running off their hat brims.

"And Mrs. Thrasher? Is she still alive?"

They stood there in the rain for a long moment, looking at one another.

"She was the last I heard," George Moon said. "But right now I wouldn't bet on anything."

"Then we've got two women somewhere in this."

"Afraid so. Somewhere."

We had moved to the back porch when Joe Mountain rode up, his face wet with the rain, his teeth shining.

"Bunch of horses, Cap'n. Maybe ten. Went off down the field behind the barn to the McAlester road. It looks like they split up there and some went both ways. But I can't tell for certain. This rain has raised hell with tracks."

"All right. Get under cover. Pass the word along. I think we're in for a twister blow."

To emphasize his words, a sudden gust of wind drove the rain across the porch and we moved quickly into the breezeway. Choctaw policemen were already there and George Moon started talking with them in words I couldn't understand. Schiller motioned me into the house.

The kitchen had been badly used. Part of a ham was in a roasting pan on the cold stove, and there were dirty dishes on the table, along with a platter of baked sweet potatoes, some partly eaten. The coffeepot was empty and Schiller filled it from a bucket on a small stand near the door. As he moved around to get the fire started again, his feet kicked through debris on the floor. There were three empty whiskey bottles, some broken plates, and bits of food. Lying brightly among the litter were several empty cartridge cases. When he had the stove going, the damper wide open and the grate door as well, Schiller picked them up and looked at them.

"Here's .45 cases," he said. He looked through the rear window at the privy, almost hidden now in the driving gray rain. "Well, Mr. Pay. We might as well bed in for the night."

So for the time being the hunt was over. It was something I hadn't expected. But whoever had done these things was hours ahead of us, in which direction we didn't know, and moving on rainswept roads. Perhaps by now even out of this storm.

We moved into the parlor. Chairs were overturned and some of the upholstered furniture had been ripped open with a knife. I thought of Mrs. John's throat.

"Cap'n," George Moon said from the door. "There ain't no sign of the women. We looked through the house and the outbuildings. There ain't no sign. We found a dead dog under the porch. Shot dead, an old hound dog."

"All right," Schiller said. "Get your men under cover."

After George Moon had gone, Schiller turned to me and shook his head.

"Not much to be done now," he said. "As far ahead of us as they are, we'd not do much except get wet if we went out thrashing around in this weather."

"What about those women, Marshal?"

"There's three selections. They may not have been here when that bunch rode in. Off visiting someplace. Or, they may have run off to hide in the woods. Or, they're in some ditch now, beyond our help."

"They could've been carried off."

He shook his head, still bouncing the brass cartridges in his hand. "I doubt it. They were traveling fast and likely didn't want extra baggage. I'll admit, Mr. Pay, two of the selections don't set too well with me. I just hope to God they weren't even here. But I feel like George Moon. I wouldn't bet a dime on it. And if they ran off into the woods, why aren't they back? Maybe they're out there now, watching us, afraid to come in, not knowing who we are. And if they were here and caught, why weren't they treated like Mrs. John? Used and slaughtered? The bunch that rode in here had time to get good and horny again after they left Hatchet Hill road, so why would they have waited and carried the women off someplace else to use them?''

It was the longest speech he had made to me. He turned back to the kitchen where I could smell the coffee beginning to work. I knew he had no expectation of response to his questions, even if I'd had answers, which I didn't. Someone was telling him the dead chickens in the yard had all been shot. Everything had moved so fast, what had happened to those chickens had never occurred to me. But they'd been shot, like the men. Everything had been shot except the hogs.

Above the sounds of the growing storm, there was shouting from the front of the house that the canvas had blown off the bodies. They lay face up, the water running off the cheeks that already had begun to look sunken and wasted like old candle wax burned out from the inside. Choctaws ran about the yard, one in pursuit of the canvas, others searching for large stones to anchor it in place. The thought crossed my mind of some kind of hysterical Easter egg hunt under a darkening sky gone berserk.

Hail began to slant against the walls and windows of the house. More water fell with it, and the lightning that we had watched through much of the afternoon was over us now, so close the crash of thunder came immediately with the flashing brilliance. Everything, the whole day, was a swirling kaleidoscope of changing blood-red forms, shapeless and wet, and now the blinding blue-white light. The wind blew the dead chickens across the yard.

"Get under cover," Oscar Schiller was yelling. "There's a root cellar in the kitchen."

Some of the Choctaws and Joe Mountain were running through the kitchen. Someone lit a lamp and Schiller was holding open a slanted door at the far end of the room, a door I had not noticed. It revealed wooden steps into the cellar and we stumbled down to find places among the food scattered across the earthen floor, apples and potatoes and flour. The gang had rifled this place, too. It smelled of damp burlap and rotting wood beams and bacon rind.

"Blow out that light," Schiller said. "It's killing the air."

We sat there in total darkness, listening to the howl of the storm overhead. The wind and rain and hail beat against the house, and once I heard glass shattering. Joe Mountain was squatting beside me in the dark and he pressed something into my hand, round and hard.

"Apple," he said, and I heard him bite into one of his own.

There was a strange detachment from reality sitting there with no light. Like a vacuum in time and space, or an absence of gravity, where a man had to hold his hand to the floor beneath him now and again to keep from rolling over on his side like one of those ball-bottom dolls children play with. When Schiller and Moon began to talk, their voices came out of the void, disembodied, causing my mind to reshape the structure of their faces from the sounds alone. The sandstone rasp of Schiller's voice made him seem larger than I knew he was, and George Moon's slurred speech created the image in my mind of a flat, high-cheeked face, dark and with one milk-white eye.

"George, this looks like more than just turning the wolf loose," Schiller said. "Did Thrasher keep money here?"

"Not that anyone around here ever heard of," George Moon said. "He made a little each year contractin', but mostly spent it as he made it. He traded a little corn each year with the store in Hatchet Hill, for tobacco and dress cloth. He may have made a little bettin' on races. But I don't think they were after money, except what was layin' around loose."

"What was it, then?"

"It was the horse," Moon said.

From beside me, Joe Mountain spoke, his mouth full of apple. "There ain't a horse left on the place now. There ain't no stock. There's a milk cow in the barn, been shot half a dozen times, and dead."

"He had a few beef cattle," Moon said. "They'd be up in the woods now, in some of those old clearings, out on spring graze."

"They ain't no cattle tracks out of here," Joe Mountain said.

"What horse are you talking about, George?" Schiller asked.

"He's a black racer. A stallion Mr. Thrasher bought in Texas a few years back. All black except for stockings on the rear hocks. Thrasher had some ordinary farm stock, but the black was a racer. Never bred to harness, Cap'n. Just a racer. Mr. Thrasher branded him with a T on the left flank, but it was hid by the saddle fender when he was rigged up. Mr. Thrasher didn't want no brand that showed on his hide in races, because

29

I guess he didn't want to mark up that black coat at all."

There was a long silence while the storm raged above us. Then Schiller spoke again.

"All right. The racer's gone. And the two women. What about the women, George. Tell me about the women."

Once more, a long silence. Listening to the rattle of hail on the house, I wondered where the other Choctaw policemen and Blue Foot had taken refuge from the storm. Then George Moon spoke again.

"Well, Cap'n, Mrs. Thrasher was a barren woman but a rich one. Not money rich, but land rich. She's got family off down south of McAlester somewhere. But she owned this place, her and her first husband. They had no young 'uns either. But she got this place when her daddy died, him as had come from Mississippi when he was a boy and took up this land."

"Choctaws."

"Sure. When Mr. Thrasher married, he got hisself a well-to-do woman."

"Did she gad around?"

"Hell no. She was a comely woman but a homebody. She visited a little here on the mountain, but that's about all."

It suddenly occurred to me that they were speaking of this woman in the past tense, as though she were already gone. Sitting there in the dark, it was not a comforting thought.

"All right, George. Now about the girl."

"A real pretty little thing," he said. "Blonde hair and blue eyes. Jennie is what they called her."

"Any beaus?"

"None I know of. Mr. Thrasher watched over her pretty close. He had a wagon fitted out for sleeping and cooking so when he went to races in different places, he'd take Jennie along and she'd make his meals and they'd live in the wagon. Sometimes on contract jobs, too."

Above us, the storm seemed to be blowing over. But no one made any move to leave the cellar. Joe Mountain was eating another apple, his teeth grinding in the dark.

Somebody started speaking Choctaw and George Moon said a few words, too. I could tell they were questions.

"Charley Oskogee here lives down the road a ways," George Moon said. "Sometimes he hires out to help Mr. Thrasher slaughter hogs or crib corn. His woman comes up now and again. He says there ain't many people come up this way. He says there ain't nobody courtin' on Miss Jennie. Charley Oskogee, he's one of my policemen."

There was no need to point out that the man with this information was a Choctaw policeman, but George Moon did it as a binding seal to what had been said, like a notary public's imprint.

"Charley says in the last few weeks there's been some whiskey peddlers in the hills, sellin' their winter makin's."

"What kind of peddlers? What did they look like?"

"Just peddlers. Charley says there ain't nothin' he can remember about any of 'em. Just down here in the hills peddlin' their winter makin's."

"You don't remember any special ones, nosing around?"

"Charley says no, he don't."

The talk stopped and we sat listening to the wind and rain. The howling storm had moved off to the east, into the Ouachita Mountains of Arkansas. The hail driving against the sides of the house was finished and now there was only the sodden roar of water falling on the roof. Climbing back to the kitchen, we could see shards of glass from a shattered window mixed with the other debris on the floor.

George Moon went out to see to his men and Oscar Schiller began questioning the one called Charley. It wasn't his real name, I knew. Many of The Nations people took up such names at least for their commerce with whites because tribal names were too often completely unpronounceable to English-speaking people, most of whom were not interested in learning Indian words, anyway.

The two of them walked through the house, Schiller pressing the Choctaw for anything he might remember having seen before that was missing now. Charley said he could think of nothing. Except maybe Mr. Thrasher's pearl hat. He said Thrasher always wore a black hat with a large mother-of-pearl button sewn on the front of the crown. He said they were always expensive hats, bought in Texas when Thrasher went there to race or on business. Schiller wrote it all down in his little book. Since we'd been at the Thrashers', Schiller had been writing in a book, which he'd taken from the store of goods he carried in his saddlebags.

Standing in the parlor, staring mutely at the ripped furniture, he

31

took a small silver can from his pocket, not much larger than a thimble, that was filled with a light brown powder. He sucked on a wooden match until it was wet and dipped it into the powder. Deliberately recapping the can and slipping it inside his jacket, he put the matchstick back in his mouth and chewed on it. Father had told me there are many vices, women being one under certain circumstances. Hard spirits and black cigars, he'd said, would ferment the soul. But snuff dipping was just plain nasty. At least, it explained the musty sweet odor I'd noticed about Schiller.

One thing was not explained. When he had a match, chewing it between his taut lips, his eyes were brighter and he moved more quickly. He was more talkative, too, for a man so naturally taciturn.

Joe Mountain had the ham back in the oven. He had kicked up the fire again and the kitchen was warm and smelling of food. It was hard to reconcile that aura with all we had found in this place. He went into the root cellar and brought up a hatful of potatoes. Without bothering to brush the dust off, he put them in the oven.

Some of the men were still in the barn and others squatted along the walls under the porch roofs, smoking. It had grown dark, and the tips of their cigarettes made hot little points of red light. The yard was a muddy pool, the lamps we had lighted inside making shining reflections across it. I wandered through the house, tired, leg-sore and hungry, all of that forgotten when the excitement was at high pitch.

Back in the kitchen, I found Joe Mountain carefully placing a number of bottles in Schiller's saddlebags. He looked at me and grinned.

"Found these in the cellar hid under the potatoes," he said. "Old Thrasher made his own whiskey, I reckon."

"What are you doing with it?"

"We confiscate whiskey," he said, and laughed. "You can sell this kind of whiskey in Fort Smith for maybe fifty cents a bottle."

"Sell it?"

"Sure, Eben Pay. Sell it. Nobody here gonna need it. We confiscate lots of whiskey in The Nations and sell it in Fort Smith. A little extra money don't never hurt nobody."

"Does Marshal Schiller know you're doing that?"

Joe Mountain laughed again. The tattooed dots along his cheek were deep blue in the lamplight. "Hell, whose saddlebags you think these are?"

There in the kitchen with Joe Mountain, I sat and tried to let it all leave my mind. This farm, suddenly depopulated by some savage bunch of drunks, a good farm probably going back to weeds now like so many of those deserted fields we'd passed in the woods crossing the mountains. I thought about the people moved here by force, into a land new and hard, already claimed by someone else. And I thought of how the vices of all men, no matter what color, seem to multiply as old social orders break down and new ones try to establish themselves.

"How could they murder three men just for a horse," I said, and it startled me that I'd said it aloud. Joe Mountain looked at me with that long-toothed grin that was no grin at all.

"We had one a spell back, up in the Cherokee Nation," he said. "Traveler just passing through killed a man and his little son with a sledgehammer for a pair of button shoes."

I started to protest the senseless brutality, and the seemingly blind acceptance of such a way of life by everyone concerned. But at that moment someone ran from the other end of the house into the breezeway and along it to the front porch where George Moon and Schiller were talking.

"Cap'n!" the man shouted. "You better come. There's somebody in the bedroom attic. We just heard 'em."

"Damn," I heard George Moon exclaim. "I should have thought of an attic."

Three

WITH THE FIRST CRY THAT SOMEONE WAS HIDING IN THE HOUSE, men came with weapons up and cocked, but Schiller pushed among them, knocking down the gun muzzles. He went up onto a chiffonier like a monkey, awkward but effective, his pale eyes shining behind the steel-rimmed glasses as he found the attic hatch and pushed it aside. Charley Oskogee went up with him, his pistol ready. But there was no need for it. In a moment the two of them were pulling a girl from her hiding place. She was slack-lipped and wide-eyed, limp with shock, her long blonde hair hanging over her face. They handed her down, a slender form that seemed childlike. But as we carried her to the walnut four-poster bed, her cotton dress plastered to her body with sweat, it was obvious that she was no child but a young woman full-blooming.

Someone spread a heavy comforter over her and Charley Oskogee bent close, pushing her hair back from her face. He spoke softly to her, but even though she had known him as a neighbor and seen him many times, there was no sign of recognition on her face.

Oscar Schiller took a lamp into the attic but was back almost at once.

"Well, that's one of them anyway," he said to George Moon. "But there's no sign of the other one up there."

"This is Jennie," George Moon said. "I better send Charley Oskogee for his wife. We need a woman here now. It don't look to me like you'll get much from this girl tonight, Cap'n."

"No, I don't think so either. But don't send Charley. He ought to be here with the girl, because she knows him. Send one of your other boys."

The girl stared at us blankly, her eyes blue above pronounced cheekbones. I was struck by the long neck and delicately small head as she lay with her hair on the pillow framing her face. She reminded me of a print I had seen of Bronzino's *Lucrezia*, even to the length of her straight nose and the finely sculpted upper lip, all so much admired by the Florentine artists. Such a face in this wilderness seemed a startling contradiction, and if from that moment I was not actually in love with Jennie Thrasher, most certainly I was at least infatuated by her face.

Schiller quickly moved everyone out of the room excepting me and Charley Oskogee, myself because I was white, I supposed, and near the girl's age. We tried to comfort her, telling her we were friends and she had nothing to fear, but she obviously didn't hear a word we said. Once, as Schiller bent over her, she seemed to shrink back from the unblinking stare, and seeing that, he made no attempt to question her.

Joe Mountain came in with a white enamel chamber pot. "She been up in that attic a long time, I bet, Cap'n," he said. "I found this slop jar in another room for her."

"All right," Schiller said impatiently. "Put it down, Joe. When the woman gets here that can be taken care of."

We sat around the bed, watching her, the rain pounding on the roof as it came straight down. Twice, her eyes went from one of us to the other, but it was a long time before she spoke. We could hardly hear her when she did.

"Where's my papa?" she whispered. "What happened to my papa?"

"He's gone, missy," Schiller said in his sandstone voice. Her eyes seemed to draw back from him. "We're here to find who would do such a thing. I'm the law and these men are friends."

Her expression did not change as she turned her head toward the dark window where the faces of Choctaw policemen looked in.

"I knew that was it," she said, more loudly now. "I knew that was it when they did all that shooting."

"What shooting, missy?" Schiller asked, bending over her. But the urgency in his voice had no effect and she said nothing more. Finally he turned away from the bed and shrugged.

She did not cry, her expression did not change, as she became aware for the first time of her father's death. She appeared strangely detached, or perhaps resigned to it, as though she not only expected such a thing just then but had been expecting it for a long time. She lay with her pale Florentine features, staring without seeing toward the Indians at the window, their faces as expressionless as her own.

Charley Osgokee's wife came in finally, having ridden from her farm with one of the Choctaws, her shawl and long gingham dress plastered to her fat body from shoulders to knees. She was wearing a wide-brimmed man's hat which she threw into a corner, taking us all in with one quick sweep of her black eyes, saying nothing. She shooed us out like a flock of reluctant chickens and closed the door behind. In a moment, she opened it again and said something to her husband in Choctaw. Charley Oskogee hurried into the kitchen for hot coffee and meat gravy from the ham.

Oscar Schiller drew me along the breezeway to the front porch and we stood close together in the dark where the rain made a thick dampness in the air.

"Mr. Pay, come morning, me and these men are going to see if we can find anybody who might have seen the ones we're after," he said. "I don't think people are going to say much at this point, but we need to try. I want you to stay here with that girl."

"Stay here?"

"Yes, and when she gets some sleep and some food and feels safe again, she'll begin to talk. You find out what you can. What she saw. I don't know what happened here, and I don't know what might have happened to her. Not much, I'd suspect. Else that bunch wouldn't have left her alive. I doubt they knew she was here."

"She doesn't seem very talkative," I said.

"You just be around when she gets talkative." We stood silently for a long time, my legs aching. I was very tired. Schiller may have sensed it. "You get some sleep, too," he said. "We'll be back in a day or so, and whether we catch anybody or not, we'll all head back to Fort Smith. I'll send a few of these men back to Hatchet Hill with those three bodies. And I'll have one of them get a telegraph off to the marshal's office to pass the word all through The Nations to be on the lookout for Milk Eye, and for that black horse."

He turned, leaving me standing there, but stopped and looked back. I thought I detected a smile.

"I'll leave a couple of the men here, too, in case they come back."

The thought that the marauders might return had not entered my mind until then. I doubted that Schiller thought they would, but if his purpose was to make the night more chilling than it already was for me, he had succeeded.

We heard no more from the Choctaw woman in Jennie Thrasher's room that night except once when she handed out the chamber pot and Charley Oskogee carried it off into the rain. After he brought it back, he looked inside the door for a moment but his wife closed it again. He said Miss Jennie was sleeping. Policemen by then were sleeping on the porches and all over the house, except in the kitchen, where Oscar Schiller sat with his hat off, studying what he'd written in the little book. I had not seen him before without the palmetto and his hair was straight and strawlike, cut short around the ears and neck. He was graying, but the gray was hard to detect because, one way or the other, it was nearly colorless. He looked like some schoolboy, intense of mind, bent over his forms.

I found a place in the breezeway and was shivering with cold when Joe Mountain appeared with a thick cotton quilt. He squatted beside me, eating a baked potato, hull and all. I was too tired to accept a bite when he offered it. Rolling myself into the quilt, it occurred to me that only a few hours before I would have found my situation incongruous. Here I was in the wilds of Choctaw country, at the scene of a brutal murder, wrapped in a homemade quilt and refusing to eat when asked, not because the offer came from a man my friends in Saint Louis would have considered a heathen savage, but because I wanted sleep more than food. My mind stumbled through the events of the day, a day such as I had never spent before in all my life, but sleep came quickly with the warmth of the cover and the knowledge that the big Osage was there beside me in the night.

Sometime during the dark hours before dawn, I woke to a sound other than the monotonous drumming of rain. It was a quavering wail, high-pitched for a moment before dropping into deep guttural moanings. It came from somewhere beyond the house and cut through the rain to the senses like a knife blade passed along the finger, unnoticed for a few seconds until the sting begins. I sat up, the quilt falling off my shoulders, the chills starting up my back.

"What in God's name?" I asked. Beside me, Joe Mountain laughed softly.

"That's Blue Foot, down in the barn," he said. "He's singing an old Osage death chant, for them men out there." I knew he meant the three under the wagon canvas on the porch, grown stiff by now.

"Why's he doing that?" I said. "I didn't think he even liked Choctaws, and two of those are Choctaws."

"He don't like Choctaws," Joe Mountain said. "But Blue Foot's strong on all the old tribal stuff. He figures it's his duty to send off the dead right, no matter who they are. My granddaddy taught me that chant and I taught Blue Foot. He does it pretty good, don't he?"

"I've no means of comparison."

"He does it pretty good. It's an old chant, Eben Pay. From a long time back. So Blue Foot, he's sharing it with the Choctaws because the dead deserve it, and because it shows the Choctaws some of our old stuff that we had before they even came. And maybe he just wants to keep a few of them awake."

Once it was known, I found it soothing. I could not go back to sleep with it because although there was some of the rain's same monotony about the chant, there was a stirring quality as well that demanded attention. There was a sad yet joyful feeling to it, and a sense of finality, the last good punctuation to a man's life. As the eastern sky at the end of the breezeway began to turn pale, the song ended and I was sleeping again before Oscar Schiller and his posse were up and off into a new, wet day.

Charley Oskogee's wife had not slept. When I went into the kitchen there was fresh bread baking and a pot of boiling turnips, also coffee and a glass canning jar of hominy opened and ready to be fried. Without a word, she made me a breakfast of eggs and pork sausage heavily seasoned with black pepper and sage, and although the taste was almost as good as the smell of it cooking, it left a solid lump in my stomach for most of the day.

Jennie Thrasher was wearing a clean dress and her hair had been braided into long plaits and rolled in two spirals above and behind each ear. She was lying on top of the bedcovers and her feet looked tiny in their black button shoes. She watched me as I came in and drew a chair over close to the bed.

"What's your name," she said.

I told her, and when she waited for me to say more, I explained that I was from Saint Louis, a very large city.

"I remember you from last night. Have you got any chewing gum?"

When I told her I did not, she said she usually chewed paraffin but that was always in the fall, when her stepmother was canning. With that she lay there staring at me, and after an embarrassing moment of silence I began to tell her about Saint Louis. She became animated when I mentioned the zoo and sat up in the middle of the bed, drawing her legs back under her skirt.

"Do they have tigers?"

When she talked, she tilted her small dainty head to one side, emphasizing the long neck. I could see the tiny blue blood veins running along it like faint pencil marks. She somehow looked older now than she had when we'd taken her from the attic.

She was not reluctant to talk with me, and I suspected that on this hill farm she had few opportunities to see a white man her own age. After a while, I brought up the subject of the raid, and what she had seen or heard. As Schiller had supposed, it wasn't much.

She had been in the kitchen churning when the raiders appeared. She had seen none of them. Her father had run in and pulled her into the bedroom and told her to stay in the attic until he came for her, no matter what happened. He had been very excited, but he told her nothing about who might be coming into the yard or whether he knew any of them. I made a mental note to tell Oscar Schiller that Thrasher had apparently known someone in the group, and feared them.

Jennie said she didn't know where her stepmother had been at the time but later she heard her talking. There had been a great deal of talking and laughing in the yard, and then she heard them come into the house. She had been terrified, and the sequence of events seemed blurred in her thinking. There had been shooting, later, in the back and in the front yard. She said she thought she heard her papa cry out once, but she couldn't be sure. Another time, she heard men's voices and her stepmother's as well in one of the rooms below her attic hiding place. But she couldn't recall anything that was said except now and then loud cursing and swearing and taking the Lord's name in vain.

After a while it grew quiet, and she waited for her papa to come for her. Then there were other men running through the house and it started raining on the roof just above her head. I knew that was when we'd come. She said she was afraid the storm would blow the roof off.

"You didn't recognize any of the voices?"

She stared at me a long time, her eyes wide and her lips parted enough for me to see her tiny teeth set in perfect rows like sweet corn.

"No," she said. "I was too scared, and besides, up in that attic I couldn't hear good. Listen, why don't you make a cigarette and smoke it. I like to smell cigarette smoke."

Charley Oskogee was on the back porch with a rifle, watching the wood lines around the farm. My hands were shaking for some reason, and he smiled and rolled a cigarette for me. Passing back through the breezeway to the bedroom, I could see Joe Mountain on the front porch, a heavy Winchester cradled in one arm. It struck me that he looked intent, like a cat watching a mouse, and very deadly, as he stared across the rainy clearing.

I sat beside Jennie Thrasher for much of that day, smoking because she enjoyed watching me. But from time to time she ignored me, either sitting on the bed or lying back on the high pillows, smoothing her skirt down along her thighs with both hands. Once, when the Indian woman was out of the room and we could hear her rattling pans in the kitchen, Jennie sat up and leaned close to me. I was holding a cigarette between thumb and forefinger and she reached down and took my hand in hers and lifted it to her mouth. I could feel the soft warmth of her lips as she drew deeply on the cigarette, twice, inhaling like a man.

"You sure got soft fingers," she said. "I bet you don't hoe much corn or anything like that."

"No, not much," I said, my chest heaving as she gently released my hand. She lay back and closed her eyes. I tried to compose myself, but looking at her there on the bed, it was difficult. I finally left the room and went to the front porch and stood watching the rain, feeling the heat of the cigarette on my fingers where she had touched me. I put the cigarette to my mouth and felt the wetness of her lips on it. My heart continued to thump, and for a while I forgot all the killing and blood and the disfigured bodies and the milk-eyed man. My mind was spinning with thoughts of other things.

Later in the day, one of George Moon's men rode back in to see if Jennie Thrasher had said anything that might be useful. I told him what she'd said as he stuffed food into his mouth, and then he was off again into the rain, riding down to the road and east toward McAlester. Joe Mountain came up to me and we stood watching the rain fall. It was slackening enough so that in the distance we could see the pale gray outlines of far mountain ridges.

"That's a pretty little girl, ain't she?" he asked and he was grinning at me. I could feel my face reddening and I changed the subject before it went any further.

"You think those men will come back here?"

"No. If they do, that'll be the end of the case," he said, and laughed. He pointed the muzzle of the Winchester toward the wood line where we had appeared the day before. "How many men you think I could hit with this rifle if they was to ride out of those trees and come down on us? How many before they got to us?"

"Where do you think they went, Joe?"

"Holed up someplace. I'd bet a far piece from here. This rain likely cooled 'em off some. They was about to run their full course anyways, as much as they'd been drinking. But I don't worry about that. I let the Cap'n worry about it."

Jennie Thrasher came out of her room only once that day. She stood in the breezeway leaning against the wall, watching the rain. In that light, her eyes turned as gray as the far mountains.

On the next day, Oscar Schiller and his posse came back. That was the day Jennie told me about the whiskey peddler. We were in her room, she in a rocker by the window.

"Has anyone been visiting through here the past few weeks?" I asked. George Moon had said he believed the men who came here were strangers to the area, yet somehow they had known about the horse, or whatever else it was they were looking for.

"In the spring, there's always a few come by," she said, rocking and looking out through the thin white curtain that framed the window. "Whiskey peddlers mostly, with their winter mix."

"I suppose they just wander through. I don't suppose you know many of them."

"No. They just come. In the spring. There was one came by two maybe three weeks back, the only one so far this year. Papa never bought any whiskey from any of them. He always makes his own." She paused and sat silently a moment. "He always made his own."

I didn't want her drawing back into a shell, thinking about what had happened to her father, so I asked her the obvious question.

"Did you know this one who came by—two, maybe three weeks ago?"

"No. Papa said he was a Creek. He came along the road from McAlester on a horse and leading a mule. He said he wanted to get to the Frisco railroad along the Kiamichi because there were lots of people along there who might want whiskey. They sat out on the edge of the porch and talked because Papa liked to jaw with whoever came along. They got talking about horse racing and the man said he'd heard Papa had a good racer and Papa said he did and took the man down to look at Tar Baby."

"Tar Baby?"

"That's Papa's racer. A black stallion."

I recalled the night before, in the parlor. In that room were a number of books and one was Joel Chandler Harris's *Uncle Remus*. It and the Bible there looked well used. I wondered if Thrasher had ever read the stories aloud to the girl, back when they'd first come into this wild country to live and become Choctaws.

"Then they came back and drank a few sips of Papa's whiskey. The man said he didn't like traveling the roads because the Choctaw lighthorse might catch him and arrest him for the whiskey he was carrying on the mule. So Papa told him he could get to Hatchet Hill going along the ridgelines, through the woods."

There it was! A man interested in looking at a racehorse and finding a back route into this place, off the roads. It didn't matter now if I did scare her off, I had to ask the next question. I tried to sound calm.

"What did this man look like?"

She knew at once what I was driving at then, and she stared at me for a long time.

"Just a little man with a brown face," she said. "Just a Creek."

"Would you know him again if you saw him?"

"Yes. Mama and me were in the parlor, cutting quilt pieces, and I was at the window over the porch where him and Papa were talking. I was close enough to spit on him."

"His voice, Jennie. When you were up in the attic, did you hear anyone who sounded like this whiskey peddler?"

"No," she said and abruptly rose from the rocker and went to the bed. "I'm tired now. If you aren't going to smoke anymore, I'm going to take a nap."

That was the end of it, but it was enough. I was elated, and even her pouting mouth could not detract from the moment. I got out and let her have her nap, although I was sure she had no intention of sleeping. She would lie there on that bed thinking about what we'd talked about, and about that Creek whiskey peddler.

When Schiller and his posse rode in, they were wet and tired and muddy. He listened to me without comment, then went into the kitchen and wrote everything down in his little book. He took some railroad passes from his always-ready saddlebags and handed them to me.

"Mr. Pay, I want you to take Miss Thrasher back to Fort Smith. And pick up that nigger kid Emmitt in Hatchet Hill. Evans will want to place both of 'em in protective custody. George Moon has to go in anyway, to testify in another case, so he'll ride along with you back to the railroad and then on into town. Me and these other men are going down to Charley Oskogee's to get fresh horses. We're not finished nosing around yet. I think I'll drift up into the Creek Nation. I've got other business there anyway. All we can do now is wait." He added as though to himself, "They're all stupid and taken to drink, so that black horse can't stay hid long. There's more to it than a horse, but I don't know what. Yet."

He wasted no time about it. He had his posse mounted and filing out of the yard toward Charley Oskogee's farm within a few minutes. Joe Mountain waved to me and grinned as he rode off, but Schiller lagged behind, sitting in his saddle and looking at me and George Moon as we stood on the porch.

"George, you look out for this young gentleman," he said, meaning me. "And Mr. Pay, you see the U.S. commissioner in Fort Smith and get us some John Doe warrants for murder and rape. Four of them. And one on Milk Eye Rufus Deer. We'll be needing them." He still sat there looking at us with those unblinking eyes, as though he wanted to say more but didn't know how. Then he said, "And you take good care of that Miss Thrasher. You hadn't ought to mind that, I suspect." For the first time since I'd known him, I saw him smile openly, only it was more like a leer, showing snuff-stained teeth. He reined away and called back. "I'll see you in a few days in Fort Smith."

Actually, it would be two weeks.

Four

IN THE COMPOUND OF WHAT HAD ONCE BEEN THE ARMY POST at Fort Smith, all the buildings had been razed except for a commissary and the officers' quarters, which now housed the Federal Court for the Western District of Arkansas. These and the gallows were the only structures within the enclosure of the former fort walls, and the commissary was used only for storage now, although when he first arrived, Judge Parker and his family had taken up residence there. The officers' quarters was a typical two-story military sandstone of the Jacksonian era with a gabled roof that ran the length of the building and high verandas at front and rear of a central hall. On one side of this passage was the courtroom, and on the other the judge's chambers and the offices of the United States attorney and other officials of the court.

Originally the jail had been in the basement of the courthouse but recently an addition had been patched onto the south end of the structure for this purpose. There, the cathedral windows with one-inch iron bars looked out onto the compound. Each window was three stories high and behind them, inside the shell of the outer walls, was a birdcage of cells rising in tiers above the floor.

I had become only vaguely aware of these physical surroundings on my initial arrival in Fort Smith, having been more concerned with personalities than with sandstone and oak beams. On the first day, I had paid my respects to Judge Parker and had given him my father's best wishes. Most men encountering Isaac Parker for the first time did so with some trepidation in light of his reputation. I found him to be a gentle and genial man. He was fifty-two at that time but looked much older, his large head of hair and close-cropped beard laced with white. He had asked after my father and recalled for me the times the two of them had argued cases in the federal court at Saint Joseph. But his heavy work load had not allowed for more than a few moments of casual conversation and he sent me along to the prosecutor's office with my father's letter of introduction in hand.

William Evans knew the details of my coming and he had greeted me as though I were his long-lost nephew. He was an older man than Parker but looked younger. His beard was long but well kept and he had the habit of peeping over his pince-nez when he talked, all the while fingering the gold watch chain that draped across his massive belly. From it were suspended a number of small badges indicating his fraternal affiliations and academic achievements. After his effusive greeting, he had set me immediately to work among the files and briefs and documents attendant to the function of his office.

All that had been interrupted by the midnight train ride to Kiamichi River and my introduction to violent crime as it sometimes occurred in the Indian country.

When I returned from the Choctaw Nation with a retinue of Indian policemen and our two witnesses, Evans took charge personally, housing Jennie Thrasher and Emmitt in the women's section of the jail. There were no inmates at the time and the cells located on the top floor of the courthouse building proper were adequate if not elaborate. Both Jennie and the boy were allowed to come and go as they pleased, but for their own safety could not leave the courthouse without being accompanied by a jailer or a deputy marshal.

I had hoped Evans would include me in his interrogation of witnesses in the Winding Stair case, but apparently he had reason not to. He told me nothing afterward of what either Jennie or Emmitt had said, and I could only suppose that I had already heard anything they had to tell. But he was anxious that I spend some time with the girl, in the event she might recall some detail important to the case. Each time I saw her, I reported dutifully to Evans what had been said. Or at least, most of it.

During this time I had not a word from Oscar Schiller. I imagined him to be roaming The Nations, confiscating whiskey from honest farmers for his own private sale in Fort Smith. But my low opinion of him was not shared by Evans.

"One of our best men," he said. "When he brings in a prisoner, we're always sure of conviction." Evans told me that Schiller had gone off to join the Third Arkansas Infantry during the war, a boy of barely fourteen. I had noticed that at a distance, Schiller looked young, perhaps no more than thirty, but at close range, it became clearly apparent that he was older, and Evans's remarks assured me the marshal was at least in his early forties.

"Why do his people call him Captain?" I asked.

Evans laughed, puffing a large cigar and peering at me over his glasses.

"Schiller came home from the war something of a hero. Badly wounded at the Wilderness. In that same fight he killed a Yankee artillery captain and brought back his saber as a trophy. He spent a great deal of his time going from one saloon to the next along Garrison Avenue, telling the story. His drinking companions began calling him Captain, although he had been discharged out of the army a private."

"I can't imagine him telling stories," I said.

"A frenzy of purging himself, I suspect, after all he'd seen in the war. He left Fort Smith for about ten years, then came back and worked in the marshal's office for a while before he got his commission. I'm afraid somewhere along the way, he became a bluenose. Never drinks."

Evans had me at work among his other assistants. There was little to remind me of the Winding Stair case except for my daily talks with Jennie Thrasher in the fort compound or among the gravestones of the National Cemetery on the banks of the Poteau River.

The walks began the day after we returned from The Nations and continued throughout those two weeks when the weather turned warm and muggy, promise of the humid, sweltering times ahead along the river bottoms. Before noon each day I left Evans's office and bought a lunch of chicken or meatloaf sandwiches and small cakes, all neatly stacked in what the locals called a poke—a brown paper bag. Lunch in hand, I would return to the courthouse and ascend the steep stairs to the women's cells above the main rooms and extend my greetings to Zelda Mores, who had special charge of Jennie Thrasher.

Zelda was a lady jailer. She was very heavy, well into her fifties, with a small bun of graying hair at the back of her head and the trace of a black mustache across her upper lip. She always accompanied Jennie when the girl left her cell. On those days when we went to the cemetery for lunch, Zelda would be some paces behind, watching, always keeping us within range of the .45 British Webley revolver she carried. Zelda had become a legend in Fort Smith after the time an escaping prisoner had made a dash for the compound wall in broad daylight. The lady jailer fired one shot with her awkward-looking pistol and so severely wounded the man that he died in jail awaiting trial. The casual manner of that story's telling in the Garrison Avenue saloons had appalled me at first, but such stories were beginning to be routine.

Jennie and I usually walked from the south gate of the compound and the cemetery to a stand of large elm trees where the ground sloped down to the Poteau. There we ate and talked of weather and racehorses and tigers. Among the gravestones were meadowlarks and the branches overhead were generally aswarm with sparrows and jays. Jennie began to call one of the elms our tree and insisted that I cut her initials into its bark. I explained that such a thing was likely against the law, it being a tree in a national cemetery and therefore government property.

My infatuation for her increased. Sometimes I rolled a cigarette and let her smoke it and each day I brought chewing gum. Zelda disapproved of both. She would frown at us, standing in the shade of an elm some distance off, her feet planted wide apart and holding her purse in her left hand, ready, I presumed, to draw the Webley with the right should the situation require it. The thought at such times that Jennie might be attacked for what she knew never entered my mind. I felt her to be as safe with Zelda as I would have with Joe Mountain and his Winchester.

Jennie treated me as though I might be some longtime friend for whom she had considerable affection. I was astonished at first with her familiarity. As though we had grown up together and knew one another's secrets and barn-loft escapades. Yet, looking back, I realize there was an intense reserve that she held up between us, impenetrable as a box hedge.

She never spoke of her childhood, or of her days in the Winding Stair. Whenever I turned the subject in that direction she impatiently walked away or stood throwing stones toward the river, pouting and silent. On the other hand, she seemed fascinated with anything I might tell her about the city or my own life.

"Tell me about your mama," she said once. "I never knew mine. She died when I was little."

I explained how my mother's people emigrated from Georgia before the Civil War. "They started farming up in the Ozarks, about a hundred miles from here," I said. "It wasn't very good farmland. Then, when the war started, all the men went off to join the army and left the women to tend the hogs and cornfields. Mother and her brother and my grandmother were alone."

"I hate it when I'm left alone," Jennie said.

I remembered what Mother had told me about those times, how the two armies came together almost in Grandmother's front yard, and fought the battle of Pea Ridge. "Down here in the South they call it Elkhorn Tavern," I said.

"I never heard about it."

"It wasn't so bad, according to Mother. There was a lot of noise, and some bullets hit the house. But after the armies had gone, then the bad times started."

"What kind of bad times, Eben?"

"Partisan bands started raiding through that hill country. They claimed to be fighting for one side or the other, but actually they were out for loot and plunder."

"Plunder?"

"Anything they could lay hands on. Livestock especially. Mother said they were always after food. They'd even scrape the salt from the smokehouse floors where it had dripped off the meat."

"And your folks were alone through all that?"

"Actually, not quite. For almost a year after the battle they were nursing a wounded Union soldier they'd found on Pea Ridge. When he left, he took my mother with him. That was my father." And I recounted how the wounded Union soldier had eventually married the young girl who had helped nurse him back to health. They had gone off to Missouri, where a few years later I was born to them and given my father's name, Eben Pay.

"I like that story, Eben," Jennie said. "And now your mama's people are still in the Ozarks."

"Yes. A few, I suppose. The war broke up the family. But there are some here. Father took us back only once, when I was very young. All I can recall of it is an old lady who kept wanting to kiss me because she said I looked like some relative in Georgia. She had white whiskers on her chin that scratched me."

Jennie laughed. She suddenly took one of my hands and placed it against her cheek.

"See, Eben, I've got white whiskers, too."

Her skin was warm under my fingers, with a hint of dampness from the heat. At that moment Zelda Mores called down the slope that it was time to go, and laughing, Jennie jumped up and ran back toward the courthouse compound. As Jennie went past her, the old mustached bitch fell in behind her like an escort of cavalry.

Even so, it had been a good day. Sometimes Jennie's mood would change abruptly, suddenly and darkly, and she would stop laughing and talking. I had no idea why. Only once in that time did she mention anything remotely to do with the murders at the Thrasher farm. We were walking across the courthouse compound, she close against my side, when she spoke.

"Eben, you know my papa always said things look worse than they really are. Maybe that's how this all is, too."

I recalled in one of my literature courses at Illinois, someone had said—a great philosopher he was—that there was no crime he could think of that he was not himself capable of committing. That thought and what Jennie said troubled me very much.

By the end of the two weeks, the Winding Stair case had faded. My father had always said that if a criminal is not caught within a few hours of the commission of the crime, he likely will never be caught at all. I had begun to think the murders and rape in the Choctaw Nation would simply slip into the archives of the court as an unsolved atrocity. But then Oscar Schiller returned, and once more the excitement came and the eager anticipation of being back on the trail, as though I really were one of Parker's men.

OUR PRIVATE RECOLLECTION OF men we have known is often at variance with public judgment of them. Much of what my peers in later years knew of Judge Isaac Parker came not from personal contact nor the serious and studious biographer, but from the sensational columns of newspapers.

Parker was himself a victim of federal government reaction to a siege of lawlessness in the Indian Territory, and of misunderstanding and apathy. He was overseer of a land mostly ignored by those with power to change it, except when the news of a multiple hanging burst upon the pages of the eastern press. He was the boy crying wolf, and the wolf was always there! Yet nobody listened until the judge's pronouncement of sentence on some violent felon, and then for only a moment of horror before all of it was pushed from the mind again.

When he took the bench in Fort Smith, capital crimes and their punishment were proscribed by law, a fact seldom remarked upon in print or on the floors of Congress. In pronouncing death sentences, Parker often explained to the condemned that the letter of the law, which he was bound to observe, left him no alternative.

The harshness of that law was in keeping with those times. And more, it was apparently the only means that Congress had taken time to devise for assisting the Indian courts in maintaining

order in their own countries. Ironically, Parker himself knew as well as any man the genesis and evolution of the condition. He outlined it for me in those first weeks I spent working for his court in Fort Smith.

Long ago, before the first white men came, the Osage were there. There were others as well, but largely, the Osage held domain. Early in the nineteenth century, other tribes, powerful tribes, began to arrive from the southeast. At first they came of their own accord, and in small numbers, but later they were being forcibly removed by the United States government, under pressure from white citizens who coveted the Indian farms in the eastern mountains and the Deep South. These displaced persons were called the Five Civilized Tribes and they were herded into the country west of the place where the Poteau and Arkansas rivers flow together. They established societies in the new land that were self-governing and self-contained. They were the Choctaw, Chickasaw, Seminole, Creek, and Cherokee.

But in the original treaties with the United States that gave them the land forever was a serious disclaimer. Their laws and police and courts were only for their own people. They had no jurisdiction over white men.

At first, this seemed of little consequence. They tilled their fields and ran their legislatures and punished their own lawbreakers. But when the Civil War came, many fought for the South and afterward, because of this, large tracts of their land were taken from them to be used as reserves for other tribes. Only the eastern portion of what had been called Indian Territory remained. The Nations.

Into all of this vast area both east and west, the Indians of North America were moved as the expanding nation pressed outward into open spaces and inward upon itself. They came from everywhere. There were the Seneca, the Mohawk, the Shawnee, the Erie. The Chippawa, the Kickapoo, the Ottawa. The Pawnee, the Comanche, the Cheyenne, the Tonkawa, the Kaw, Modoc, Sac, and Fox and many more. Strangers, old friends, old enemies—all placed near one another without regard for cultural differences, without regard for hopes or fears, aspirations or despairs.

And there were also, after the war, the black peoples who had been slaves to the various Civilized Tribes, freed now and made a part of the tribes of which they had once been mere property.

By 1889, the western part of what had been the original Indian Territory was opened to white settlement by land run. The first one came in the Unassigned Lands, almost dead center of the old Territory and just west of the Civilized Tribes' Nations. The whites came and claimed the land and a new city sprang up overnight. It was called Guthrie, this new capital of the new white Territory of Oklahoma. And rather quickly, the Indian lands became white lands, by run or lottery or sealed bid. But there was still The Nations, bordering on Arkansas to the east. Still sovereign, with the one important disclaimer.

By now, railroads and stage routes were being run through the lands of the Civilized Tribes, and with these came whites in growing numbers. And with these came the scum and the renegade rabble from all the dwindling frontier, because the Indian courts had no power over them, and the Indian police were restrained from controlling them. These came to escape the law of established states and territories, and they were a brutish and mindless breed.

They brought all the things that destroy a struggling young community. They brought violence and a monumental disregard for human life and property. They brought larceny and prostitution and whiskey. Whereas before there had been the occasional flaring of old tribal enmities between the displaced red men and those who were already there, there now came the white marauders who pillaged, raped, and murdered under the assumption that they were in safe-haven. And worse, under their influence, and from loss of an old settled order among many of the tribesmen, some of the red men became like them. The dregs of white society had come and inevitably attracted the weak and despondent of the red.

The federal court at Fort Smith was established partly to respond to all of this. The task was a thankless and impossible one.

"We have been damned by many," Judge Parker once told me. "But this is a ruthless land. Ruthless because our handling of it has made it so. But I say this to you: We have pride in what we do. When in a community there is the promise of quick justice fulfilled, and it is sure under the law, then in that community there will be no lynch mobs. Eben, let me point out, there are no such mobs in The Nations. Under circumstances in which they live, this is credit to them, and a little to us as well."

The day was near when many territorial courts would be formed throughout The Nations to maintain some semblance of civilized society there. But when I knew him, Judge Isaac Parker and his deputy marshals carried that burden alone.

Five

HENRYETTA'S FRISCO HOTEL AND BILLIARD PARLOR WAS almost deserted that Wednesday afternoon, June 25, 1890. I sat in the big downstairs barroom reading the Fort Smith newspapers, waiting for Oscar Schiller. Not having heard from him since he rode off into the rain from the Thrasher farm, I had received a note to join him in the infamous railyard brothel. It had to do with the Winding Stair Massacre, as all the newspapers were calling it.

For some time, the story of the Thrasher-John murders had been circulated in print. Bloody details were abundant, provided undoubtedly by some Choctaw policeman willing to talk with an enterprising reporter. But nothing had been written about Milk Eye Rufus Deer. The crimes were variously attributed to badmen and gangs who had been known to operate in The Nations.

I had obtained warrants from the United States commissioner in Fort Smith for the arrest of Deer and four John Does for the unidentified killers. The commissioner was a mousy little man named Mitchell who held sway in a small office near the courthouse. Although he was not impressive in his person, his position was important. He was in fact a federal magistrate who tried misdemeanors, issued subpoenas and warrants, and held hearings on accused felons to determine if they should be held over for the grand jury. Without him, the volume of work in Parker's court would have been unbearable.

Oscar Schiller had never called for the warrants nor sent anyone for them. I had begun to wonder about this apparent lack of interest when I got his note, left on my desk in Evans's office by some unknown emissary.

"Mr. Pay," Schiller wrote. "Meet me the afternoon of 25th instant at Henryetta's to interview informant on Thrasher-John. Schiller."

Evans had studied the pencil scrawl and complained that he expected me to finish some of his case notes that day, but in the end allowed that I should meet the marshal.

"Schiller sometimes thinks he runs this goddamned court," he said.

After my lunch with Jennie that day, I returned to my hotel room and got into my field gear because one never knew with Schiller where one might end up. I had bought the things Winding Stair had shown me to be useful. A slicker, cotton jacket and pants, a wide-brimmed hat to keep off sun and rain, and heeled boots. I found the boots difficult for a time and had been wearing them around the room at night, learning how to walk.

Evans had given me a letter identifying me as an investigator out of the prosecutor's office, and with this badge I finally decided to arm myself. I bought a small Smith and Wesson breakdown revolver chambered for .38 shorts. One of the older deputy marshals who acted as court bailiff and was always around the courthouse suggested I drill holes in the ends of the slugs because, as he said, hollow points were very persuasive. I ignored the advice and, in fact, hoped I would never have to use the nasty-looking thing.

Walking along Garrison with the pistol in a shoulder holster under my jacket I had felt conspicuous as a bald woman and was sure each passing pedestrian was aware that I carried a concealed weapon and would soon put the local police on me.

Henryetta's bar-parlor was like any upper-middle-class living room of that age. There was an abundance of overstuffed chairs covered in red velvet, highly polished cuspidors placed strategically about the room, peacock feathers sprouting from white enamel urns in each corner, and a number of bad oil paintings. Most of these showed naked women running about, pursued by hairy satyrs. The place smelled of perfume and talcum powder and on busy days of cigar smoke and tobacco juice, I supposed. But on this Wednesday afternoon, I was the only person in the place except Henryetta, her upstairs girls, and Big Rachael.

Henryetta was a large overdressed woman with red paint smeared somewhat crookedly across her mouth. She had more gold teeth than the Frisco baggagemaster and her fingers were almost immobile with glassy rings. As I sat reading my paper, she watched me. When I looked toward her, she smiled, showing her dazzling but crooked teeth.

Big Rachael was cook and bouncer. He was larger even than Joe Mountain, with a small head attached to an enormous body with no visible neck. His arms were longer than those I had seen on apes in the Saint Louis Zoo. He was obviously a gentle soul, but his reputation for brute strength and loyalty to Henryetta was legend in Fort Smith, as was his German potato salad and fried pork steak.

Although I was of limited experience in such matters, it seemed to me that Henryetta's was a refined and well-operated whorehouse. I asked for lemonade laced with an ounce of gin and explained to Big Rachael and the madam that I was there to meet someone. I was left alone and none of the girls from upstairs came down to market their wares. After a second lemonade, Big Rachael acted as though I had always been there, and although even with the gin I did not feel exactly like a regular customer, the place was comfortable.

When Oscar Schiller came in he glared at me once and went directly to Henryetta. They conversed in low tones for a moment and then the marshal indicated that I should follow him into one of the small alcove-like rooms where the open doors were hung with strings of colored beads. They made a small crystal tinkling as we pushed them aside and sat at a table before a bay window overlooking the Frisco yards. Schiller dipped into his snuff can with a match and stared at me, unblinking.

"Mr. Pay."

"Marshal."

"How have you been?"

"Busy," I said.

"That's the best way to be. What we've got here is an informant. A whore who thinks she's heard something. She has a child in Memphis and she goes there now and again, and I've been able to help her in that."

I thought of the railroad passes he always carried and wondered if the Frisco officials ever imagined their free tickets were being used in such a way.

"Where's Joe Mountain and Blue Foot?" I asked.

"Over in the Osage reservation, I guess."

He said nothing more and I sat watching the small switch engines working the cars in the Frisco yards. Beyond them, a stern-wheeler was pushing a barge along the river toward the Fort Smith docks. In the larger room, Henryetta was still leaning against the bar, half-dozing, one fat elbow hooked on the polished mahogany. Big Rachael was swatting at June flies. Neither of them paid any attention when a young woman appeared at the stairs and came toward us, brushing the beaded curtain aside with a flourish.

She was small, but not so small as Jennie Thrasher. Though her flame-red hair was piled in curls on top of her head, she was not yet painted for the night's work, and she wore a simple cotton dress with long sleeves and high neck. She sat sideways at the table, her legs in my view, and deliberately yanked up her dress so I could see her ankles, above black patent leather shoes.

"Who's this good-looking young devil?" she asked. Her lips were full and sensuous but when her teeth showed, the whole effect was ruined. Between each tooth was a charcoal black mark of decay. It was like the mouth of a child who had eaten too much candy.

"This is Mr. Pay," Schiller said. "He's here to help me listen to this story of yours."

"I talk better with a gin drink," she said, smiling at me.

Big Rachael was already bringing a water glass filled with pink liquid. He spilled some of it as he placed it on the table before her.

"Do you like sloe gin, Mr. Pay?"

Schiller gave me no chance to reply. "All right, Lila, let's start with it."

After a few sips of sloe gin, Lila told us she had a special lover who came to Henryetta's each time he was in Fort Smith.

"He's a real ladies' man," she said. "A handsome boy, almost as handsome as you, Mr. Pay. He's always bragging about the women he's humped. He says I ought to pay him, he's so good." She laughed, showing the bad teeth. "He always says he's going to hump every woman in The Nations before he's finished, and a few in Arkansas besides."

She sipped her drink, watching me as Oscar Schiller chewed on his matchstick and looked at the tabletop, no expression on his face.

"Well, he was in here one night about a week ago. Maybe a little more. Maybe ten days ago. Anyway, he says he's been over in The Nations and he'd been boozing bad. He asked for me, of course, I'm the only one he ever asks for. After another customer, I had him up to the room for the night. He's always got the ten dollars for a whole night. He likes to talk, just lay there and talk."

"Get on with it, Lila," Schiller said.

"That night, he was nervous as a feist dog in heat. He asked me to get him some newspapers and he read those. He got a bottle of rye from the bar and drank most of it and then tried to do me, but couldn't, but it didn't seem to bother him much. He just wanted to loll around and talk. He was silly drunk after a while. He started telling me all the things he done and what a bad mean man he is. He said he'd just got even with this son of a bitch in The Nations who'd done him dirt. He showed me a knife he had. It wasn't no hunting knife but you had to pull the blade out of the handle. It was a big mean-looking knife. He said nobody was gonna put anything over on him, and then he blabbed on about all the women he'd humped."

She gave another laugh, and it had no mirth in it. She seemed to drop it into the conversation absentmindedly, like a stone falling into a pool of water, making a quick circle of motion, and then disappearing. I couldn't help thinking that although she was foulmouthed, if it hadn't been for the bad teeth, she would have been a beautiful woman.

"Then he said something about this same son of a bitch trying to hide himself down in the Winding Stair Mountains with his little china-doll daughter but him and his friends had found this son of a bitch anyway. That's when I started getting interested because I'd seen all that stuff in the papers about the massacre and the things done to that Choctaw woman and all the blood. I asked him who this man was, but he just laughed and started telling about the time he was a little kid and he was playing with another little kid who made him mad. So he poured coal oil on this other kid and set him on fire. He said his daddy had lots of money and could get him out of anything he might get into anyway. Then he started bragging again that there was no son of a bitch who could keep him from humping anybody he wanted to, just layin' there on the bed naked, excuse the expression Mr. Pay, and bragging about how all the women loved him."

The blood had begun to pump through me and I was so absorbed in what Lila was saying I hardly noticed as Big Rachael came in and placed another gin-lemonade in front of me.

"This boyfriend, Miss Lila?" I said. "Who is he?"

She tilted her head back and glanced at Oscar Schiller, who seemed unaware of anything that had been said.

"Well, I can't just throw out his name without no deal first, can I?" she said.

"Tell the rest of it," Schiller said harshly.

"There ain't any more to tell. He just kept saying him and his friends in The Nations would show anybody who turned out to be a son of a bitch what a mean bunch they was. He said they was worse than the Daltons and the James boys up in Missouri years ago. He said they didn't even bother robbing banks and trains but just went around when they felt like it, looking for pussy and livestock. You'll pardon the expression, Mr. Pay, but that's the way he said it." She laughed and winked at me.

"Do you know any of his friends?"

"Not his friends in The Nations. We don't let Indians in here and even them whites in The Nations are more Indian than the Indians. And outside The Nations, I bet he hasn't got any friends. Not men friends. He knows how to make a woman feel good when he's sober, but men don't seem to take to him much."

"You never saw him come in here with another man?"

"No, I never. Most men come here in bunches and half-drunk by the time they get here, like it was to get up the nerve to do it. But my boyfriend never comes with anybody. He got drunk one night upstairs and started crying about not having any friends and no brother or anything, and I said like a joke, 'Well, if you did, you just set 'em on fire,' and he slapped me real hard a few times."

"He cried?"

"Not the time I'm telling you about. That was awhile ago. When he was drunk. Lots of men cry when they get drunk sometimes, don't they?"

"What else did he say about the Winding Stair Mountains?"

"Nothing. Just what I told already. I thought about it and read those newspapers again and talked to Henryetta. She said I'd best tell the Cap'n or else he might get displeased and come troopin' in here sometime with a whole flock of local laws and start to—"

"All right," Schiller cut in, a dangerous edge to his voice. "He's not interested in that part of it."

"I was just sayin' what happened is all. We decided I better tell. So we sent Big Rachael over to the courthouse with a note to the Cap'n here, for him to come see us when he got back from wherever he was. So that's what happened. And here you are, Mr. Pay. Why ain't I ever seen you in here before?"

"Let's get to business," Schiller said, leaning across the table toward her. "Who is this boyfriend, Lila?"

"How much?"

"Don't step on my toes, Lila."

"Cap'n, you know what he'd do to me if he ever found out I'd talked with you about this. He'd do something terrible."

"I might do something terrible myself if you don't tell us his name," Schiller said.

"You got money for these things, haven't you? I can't tell his name without some money."

Schiller looked at me. "You think we might come up with some money out of Evans's office?"

"Not for what we've heard this far," I said. "But if we get the man's name . . ."

We both watched her closely. Now, showing me her legs was forgotten. She toyed with the glass before her, frowning.

"Well," she said. "Well, I'd want twenty dollars."

"Five is more like it," Schiller said.

"Five? Five? Jesus Christ, I'm takin' my life in my hands right now, and if I tell you that . . ."

"I could arrest you for withholding evidence. I could get your butt on the witness stand and if you refused then, Parker'd give you six months in the federal jail for contempt. And if you lied about it, he'd give you six years in Detroit for perjury."

"Oh, Jesus Christ," Lila said. Concern was plain on her face, and the laugh was no longer there. She leaned across the table toward Schiller and lay a hand on his, and when she spoke she whined like a child about to be spanked.

"Jesus Christ, Cap'n. Don't be mean to me now. I told you all this, and you know I could use the money. I'm just a girl trying to make a living. Jesus Christ, Cap'n."

"Make it ten," I said. Schiller glanced at me, pulling his hands away from Lila's. He shrugged.

"All right," he said. "Ten. That's all. Ten dollars."

"Well," Lila said. "Can I have another drink of sloe gin?"

"Why not? Henryetta's paying for it."

Big Rachael brought her another full glass. This one she took in long swallows. I could hear the switch-engine bells clanging. It had grown dark, and their headlamps were turned on.

"Well?" Schiller said impatiently.

"Johnny Boins," she blurted out, as though if she said it fast enough and had it over with, no one could be sure she'd said it.

"Johnny Boins? Do I know him?"

"He's nice and tall, like Mr. Pay here, and with blond hair and blue eyes with them long lashes."

"I know that name," Schiller said as I sat there with the hair standing on the back of my neck. It was the man I'd seen with Milk Eye, I was sure of it. The man on the Frisco depot platform the night I arrived in Fort Smith. He had been on the car with me during part of that journey, and I tried to recall where he had boarded the train. But it was unclear in my mind. I had hardly noticed him until he and the small man with the puffed brown face and the white eye had passed me as I waited for my baggage.

"He ain't from around here. But he's been in trouble a couple times in Parker's court for whiskey in The Nations. But he never has been convicted. He hangs out over in the Creek Nation."

"He live there?"

"No. He lives in Eureka Springs, up in Carroll County, Arkansas. Up in that wild mountain country."

Schiller leaned back in his chair with a sigh. He looked at me and was almost smiling.

"Give her the money, Mr. Pay," he said. I hesitated, watching Lila.

"Miss Lila," I said. "Would you be willing to go before a grand jury and tell them what you've told us?"

"Jesus Christ! No, I won't tell nobody a thing. You send me off to jail if you want to, but that's better than gettin' my head caved in."

"Give her the money," Schiller said.

Outside, the evening breeze was coming off the river and I was aware of my damp shirt. My hands were shaking with excitement.

"She'll be on the first train to Memphis," Schiller said. We started back along the tracks toward Garrison Avenue.

"What about Johnny Boins?"

"We're going after him. Tonight. There's a Frisco freight later on, we'll take that to Seligman and change to the North Arkansas line and ride right into Eureka. Be there before noon tomorrow. Now, you get over to the commissioner's office and have him issue a warrant for Boins' arrest. Tell him what we've heard. But don't get a murder warrant. I want a little time with this Johnny Boins before he really knows what we've got him for. Get a warrant for being in Indian country without a permit."

"That's a misdemeanor."

"Yes, but it'll never be tried. Once we get him here, that nigger kid can identify him and then we'll hold him for a hearing with the commissioner and I suspect he'll be bound over for the grand jury. We'll just hold him until we catch those other four."

"We could get a murder warrant now, I'd bet."

"No. I want a little time with him. Until we've got an identification on him that will hold in court, we don't even know if he's one of our men. This may be a wild-goose chase."

"No it isn't," I said. "I'll bet my life he's the one I saw on the Frisco station platform with Milk Eye that night."

I had hoped my revelation would stun him, shake him somehow. But he kept walking, the streetlights shining against his glasses, his frail body hunched forward as we walked. I might as well have commented on the weather.

"I figured that's who it might be," he said. "And get a search warrant, too."

"On a misdemeanor?"

"The commissioner will do it. You tell him what we're up to. If this is one of our men, we'll want a search warrant."

"It's our man," I said. "I'd bet my life on it."

"Let's hope you don't have to."

Six

SUMMER TOURISTS ARRIVED IN EUREKA SPRINGS ON THE NORTH Arkansas railroad, leaving the cars at the deep valley station in the north end of town where the mountains pitched up sharply on every side. The June hardwood foliage was like a jungle, and through the leaves of trees standing in thick ranks up all the slopes showed the fine Victorian houses and hotels and the peaked roofs of grottoes built around the many springs. The streets were so narrow and winding that barely two wagons could pass, and all along the sidewalks were stone benches where pedestrians making the steep ascent to hotel row could rest and admire the spectacle of houses built almost on top of one another up the shoulders of surrounding hills.

The Carroll County courthouse and jail was only a few hundred yards along the valley from the railroad station. There, Oscar Schiller and I made ourselves known to the sheriff's chief deputy. The sheriff, we were told, was seldom there.

The deputy was also jailkeeper. He was a genial man of such mild disposition and unimposing manner that he left little impression on us. Within five minutes of having met him, neither Oscar Schiller nor I could recall his name. He was willing to take us as guests of the county under the façade of a vagrancy charge so that we might sleep in his cells and eat at no expense to ourselves. At the same time this gave him the opportunity to skim off the few pennies profit a jailer of those times could make on the allowance paid for feeding overnight prisoners.

Johnny Boins was a well-known figure in the town. He had been variously involved with misdemeanors since old enough to walk. Once, his parents had sent him to a private school in Missouri where he vandalized the headmaster's library and assaulted another student twice his size and age with a paring knife from the academy kitchen. Lila's story of the playmate doused with kerosene and set fire was confirmed. The deputy said we might see that victim at any time on the streets of Eureka Springs, a twenty-year-old man now but still with the burn scars across his face. Johnny Boins, the deputy said, had always been a high-spirited boy. A genuine hell-raiser. During his tenure as town terror, he had knocked out the plate-glass windows in most of the stores along Main and Spring streets at different times. As he grew older, his tastes changed. He had been threatened a number of times with shotguns by irate fathers whose daughters he had dishonored and one he had allegedly impregnated.

"I don't reckon Johnny ever felt the sting of a willow switch," the deputy said. "He was the Boins' only child, and they never could bring theirselves to whup him. He'd get in trouble and they'd pay his way out of it or later, get theirselves a good lawyer."

It was an exceptional situation in this deep mountain country, where the young were expected generally to toe the line or suffer the physically painful consequences. But because the Boinses were held in high regard in the community, and because they had the money to spend on him, Johnny was never in serious trouble with the law.

"His punishments run to strawberry shortcake and cream in his mother's kitchen," the deputy said. "Far as I know, he ain't ever been whupped or convicted of a crime."

We were closemouthed about the real reason for wanting Johnny Boins. The deputy was cooperative and promised to keep our presence in town to himself. It would be an easy matter to lose ourselves amongst all the flood of tourists when we needed to get out on the streets.

Our first day was given over to an examination of the town so a decision could be made on where Johnny Boins might be arrested. The deputy told us that in winter, when the tourists were not there, Johnny was usually away. But in summer he always returned. He worked part-time in his father's hardware store. Mornings he spent along hotel row, playing croquet with the girls who were in the Ozarks with their parents to enjoy the scenery and take the waters. In the evenings, he played poker with some of the young men tourists and sometimes caroused along the streets with them singing songs unfit for decent ears. And each day, too, after a morning session on the croquet courts and before taking his place among the nails and screwdrivers, he had a bath at the Olympia Bath House, located up the mountainside between the courthouse and hotel row.

Oscar Schiller gave no hint of what he was thinking as we strolled along the streets, but I knew he was figuring where best to arrest Johnny Boins. Too many of his colleagues had been shot to death trying to take a fugitive without planning ahead.

Moving along the steep sidewalks, we paused frequently at one of the benches and sat watching the people pass. The Boins hardware store was not difficult to find and we stationed ourselves across from it at about the time the deputy said Johnny Boins would come in to work. I had no way of knowing whether I would recognize him, having seen him only that one time. For some time, I had been trying to recall the features of both men, but as so often happens, the more I tried to picture them in my mind, the muddier became my memory of their faces.

It was half-past one when Oscar Schiller and I began our vigil across the street from the Boins store. We waited almost an hour. When Johnny Boins finally walked around the corner of the winding street and along the sidewalk toward his father's store, I recognized him at once. He was dressed in a tailored, vested suit and wore a small straw hat fashionable among the tourists and much unlike the one I had seen him wearing before. He had a smile on his face, showing fine white teeth, and he tipped his hat to all the passing ladies. Even from across the street, I could hear the metal taps on the heels of his patent leather pumps.

"There he is," I said.

Schiller fixed his stare on the tall figure across the street. I found it somehow disappointing that he showed none of the excitement that made my own chest pound. He said nothing until after Johnny Boins had disappeared into the hardware store.

"Are you sure?"

"Yes. It's him."

"He's some dandy, ain't he?"

"He's the one I saw with Milk Eye on the station platform."

Abruptly, Schiller rose. "All right. Let's see about that bathhouse."

The Olympia Bath House looked like a Moorish mosque. Like so many of the buildings here, it was constructed of native limestone. There were columns in front along the sidewalk, and a huge dome above, plated with brass, turned green now and aswarm with pigeons and sparrows. Inside was a lavish waiting room or lobby with a desk at the rear beside a wide door that led back into the baths. The clerk explained that there were immersion baths with cold, warm, and hot water, a Turkish section, a massage parlor, and a sun deck in back for lounging. Immediately behind the reception desk was a long room, lockers built along either wall and padded dressing benches down the center aisle. The fee was fifty cents including a towel, each additional one costing a dime. Oscar Schiller allowed me to pay for both of us, explaining that I could submit a voucher to Evans for reimbursement.

In the locker room, we undressed, wrapping ourselves in the towels. In the instant I saw Schiller's body the impression of a frail, bony child came to mind. His ribs showed and the joints of his spine pressed against his pale skin like the knobby stalks of the hollyhocks we had seen in the Thrashers' backyard. Along his right side was an ugly scar, and I remembered Evans's story of his Civil War exploits. He kept his back to me as he pulled the towel around his hips, as though ashamed to be seen naked.

We did not bathe, but passed through all the rooms with their white enamel tubs, brass fittings, massage tables like long chopping blocks. There were at least two dozen men there, relaxing in the steamy rooms, taking the sun in wicker chairs where it streamed through high cathedral windows. Oscar Schiller looked at everything, mentally marking each door and window and alcove. By the time we had returned to the locker room, damp from the steam, I knew he had everything stenciled in his mind, like the blueprint of a floor plan.

"Everything comes back through this room," he said while we dressed. "And it's least crowded, too. I don't want a lot of other people around in case there's shooting. Killing innocent bystanders can be embarrassing. We'll take him here, when he comes out, naked. A man caught without his clothes isn't in any frame of mind to resist."

It rained during the night and by morning the streets were clean and fresh-smelling. The honey locust was blooming up the hillside above the courthouse, the blossoms like popcorn balls, delicate and sending their sweet smell through the town. By midmorning, I was out of the courthouse and wandering the streets. I bought a china dog for Jennie, white with the words *Eureka Springs, Arkansas, 1890* printed along one flank. In a small bookstore I bought a copy of Blackmore's *Lorna Doone* although I had a copy in my room at the hotel in Fort Smith. Well before noon, I was at the spring across the street from the Olympia Bath House. Within a few moments after I took a seat and began to pretend reading, Oscar Schiller showed himself at the corner of the bank building, as we had planned.

I could imagine Johnny Boins, on hotel row, playing his morning game of croquet with the young ladies all dressed in bright cotton frocks and undoubtedly wearing bonnets to avoid freckling in the warm spring sun. People passed along the street, many of them walking and some stopping at my spring to drink the water from one of the many public cups sitting in neat rows along the ledges of the bluff where the water came out. I waited, the sweat beginning to run down through the hair on the back of my neck. The sun rose higher, warming as it did. At exactly noon, I heard the click of Johnny Boins's heels along the sidewalk from up the ridge.

He was smiling as he came into view. For an instant, his eyes fixed on me and my throat closed. But he gave no sign that he had ever seen me. I sat with my head lowered, my wide hat brim shading my eyes. I could hear his heels tapping toward me, then crossing the street toward the bathhouse. I looked again and he was going into the Olympia, his head up, his back straight like a drum major passing in review. I allowed a few moments before I rose, my knees wobbly. Oscar Schiller was watching me from the corner of the bank. Even at that distance, I could feel his eyes on me. I walked across the street and into the lobby of the bathhouse.

Johnny Boins had disappeared into the locker room. I sat down in one of the lobby's overstuffed chairs, and waited long enough for him to undress and move back to the baths. I could feel the weight of the pistol in my shoulder holster and for a moment wondered if I could hit anything with it. I promised myself that once back in Fort Smith I would go down to the river each day and practice on bottles and cans. The palms of my hands were moist with sweat.

The locker room was deserted when I went in. I found an empty stall midway in the room and slowly undressed, placing my clothes carefully on the shelf with the Smith and Wesson hidden beneath, its butt easily at hand. I sat for what seemed an eternity before Schiller came in and started taking off his clothes. I could feel the warrant, under the folds of my towel, becoming damp from my hand.

We waited. Time seemed to stand still. I tried to put my mind on other things. At the University of Illinois, I could recall at examinations waiting for the professor to arrive with the forms. Always, when the papers were placed before us, the minutes would speed past. But the waiting beforehand was forever.

Bathers passed through the room, conversation swelled, and laughter. They spoke of the bass and other fish to be caught in the local streams. They talked of the excellent string quartet at the Basin Hotel. They talked of the overwhelming scent of honeysuckle along the sidewalks of the town where the vines clung to the dry walls and latticework of homes.

Suddenly, he was there. He walked from the baths wiping his hair with a towel. Another bather was passing him on the way in and they spoke, Johnny Boins smiling. He came along the room, naked, toweling his head and humming. I found myself thinking that Lila was right. He was a handsome man. He paused at his locker a few feet from mine, looked at me and nodded. Before he could reach for his clothes, I was up, thrusting out the warrant.

"Mr. Boins, I'm from the United States attorney's office in Fort Smith. I have a warrant for your arrest."

His head jerked around and his mouth opened for an instant as he stared at me and the paper I held out to him. His lips went tight and he was moving, so fast it took me unawares. He heaved up one of the dressing benches, throwing it against my side. A wooden bucket for used towels was in his hand as I staggered back against the line of lockers, stunned by the heavy bench, the warrant fallen to the floor. He raised the heavy bucket to strike.

From the corner of my vision there came a spidery form, white and frail. Oscar Schiller, moving soundlessly with bare feet on the stone floor, leaped in close to Johnny Boins as the bucket went up. His arm whipped back and down like the quick stroke of a scythe and I saw a heavy pistol in his hand slam hard against Johnny Boins's head. Boins fell against a locker and collapsed back into the middle of the floor, knocking over a second dressing bench. I stumbled to my own locker and drew out the pistol, cocking it and pointing it at Johnny Boins's form. He

69

was sitting up, his face bloody. Over him, looking absurd in his nakedness, stood Oscar Schiller, his revolver cocked and thrust into Johnny Boins's face. It was the largest revolver I had ever seen, jutting out from the tiny hand, but it did not waver.

"My God, you've killed me," Johnny Boins gasped.

"Johnny, if you try anything serious again, I'll shoot you," Schiller said as though he were speaking of the bass or the honeysuckle.

A number of men had run into the room, watching us with wide eyes. I could imagine the impression we made—three naked men, one bleeding on the floor, the other two with cocked pistols over him.

"My God, that's a heavy pistol you've got there, mister."

"My name's Schiller. I'm a deputy marshal out of Parker's court. You've heard of that haven't you, Johnny?"

Johnny Boins looked at us, his eyes clear despite the blow he had taken. He held one hand to his head and the blood ran through his fingers. Then, incredibly, he laughed.

"What the hell is this all about?"

"Like Mr. Pay said. We got a warrant for you."

"What charge?"

"Trespass in the Indian Nations."

Johnny Boins stared at Oscar Schiller incredulously.

"Trespass?" he said. And he bent over on the floor, laughing.

It was the most lasting impression I would have of Johnny Boins. That he could laugh, now. I imagined him laughing when he set fire to his playmate and when he helped pull Mrs. John from the wagon seat on the slopes above Hatchet Hill. Or when he made love to the women he had seduced. The same laughter, for killing or love.

"Get into your clothes, and quick," Oscar Schiller said. "Or I'll dent your head again."

"No, don't hit me again with that cannon, Marshal," Johnny Boins said, rising and leaning against the lockers. The blood ran down his chest. "That's some weapon you've got. I'm in hardware myself."

"I've heard as much."

"I'd say that's a .38-40 on a .45 frame, single-action Colt."

"Get into your clothes, Johnny."

And so on that calm spring day, we took the first of the Winding

Stair Five, as I had come to think of them. And it gave me a deeper insight to Oscar Schiller, who could coldly manage people as though they were dominoes, compensating for his physical frailty with intense purpose and planning. Someone had said to me once in my college years, "If you ever get into a fistfight, try to stand uphill from the other man." In that Eureka Springs bathhouse, I began to realize that Oscar Schiller always stood uphill.

Our work was a long way from finished. After we had Johnny Boins dressed and handcuffed and had dressed ourselves, there was a moment of apprehension that among the crowd of bystanders there might be some one of his friends who would try to break him away. But apparently we overestimated Johnny Boins's esteem among those who knew him. As we passed through the crowd toward the street, one young man called out.

"I hope you've got him good, this time."

"Go to hell, Carl," Johnny Boins said, holding a towel to his bleeding head. In the street he turned to me and spoke as though in great confidence. "That Carl's a jealous bastard. We went to school together once. I whipped his ass every day. I'll do it again, too, when I get out of this little scrap. Whatever it is."

To avoid going along the front of the Boins store, we passed down one of the many flights of stone steps that led from one street level to another. Oscar Schiller pushed along at a fast pace, shoving Johnny Boins before him. When people saw us coming, our prisoner with the bloody towel to his head, they moved quickly off the sidewalk. As for Johnny Boins, he talked all the way to the jail. He asked us both what our first names were, and addressed us by them constantly. It was as though he thought we were newfound friends, casually taking a stroll.

It became Oscar Schiller's sorry lot to return to the Boins store with our search warrant for his parents' home and apprise them of what had happened to their son. I stayed at the jail with Johnny Boins and he continued to talk. He seemed impelled to explain to me all the good things about his life, and even after I told him that whatever he said to me might be used against him in court, he went on, lighthearted and cheerful, yet his words serious enough.

He told me how hard his father had worked through the years to establish the best hardware business in the county. His mother had always worked in the store alongside his father—even when Johnny was still a toddler—leaving him to play each day in the back room among the plowshares and coiled ropes. There had been various tutors, after he had shown that the public schools did not, as he put it, fulfill his requirements. Somewhere along the way, he had become a well-educated man. I had known college men ready for their final forms before graduation who could not express themselves so well. He obviously had great respect for his parents, to whom he gave credit for anything he had ever accomplished. His mother had read aloud to him from the time he could talk and had stopped only recently. He was twenty-six years old, a confirmed bachelor, and he said his mother had always been disappointed that he had never found a nice young lady for his wife.

I found it difficult not to like him, even though there was a towering conceit just below the surface of anything he said. From what we suspected he had done in the Choctaw Nation, I had expected a brutal, unfeeling wretch. But he was far from that, although given to foul language from time to time. It became increasingly difficult to imagine him among murderers and rapists in those rain-swept mountains south of Fort Smith. I even began to doubt that he was our man, wondering whether Lila and the deputy sheriff had their own motives for painting such a lurid picture of him.

Oscar Schiller dispelled all such notions when he returned a short time before dark. He took off his glasses and hat and wiped the sweat from his face as we stood in the deputy's office, Johnny Boins safely locked in the cells behind.

"Mr. Pay, that's a hard chore," he said. "I don't think those people believe to this minute that their boy has ever done anything except be misunderstood. They'll be close behind us with a good lawyer, I suspect."

"Did you find anything?"

"A lot of love letters from women up north," he said. "Some old *Police Gazettes* and postcards with pictures of women in tights. And this." From his pocket he brought a long clasp knife. He pulled out the blade and it was six inches long.

"A lot of people have those," I said.

"With a blade like that? Well, it doesn't matter. There's this, too."

He handed me a dirty, crumpled envelope and from it I took a ragged piece of lined tablet paper. It was a letter, written in a crude pencil scrawl.

"I told you these people were a stupid lot," Schiller said. "Leaving something like that laying around to be picked up."

The note read:

"J.B. A man named C found the place. Horse and girl. Meet me F.S. on 3 day of next month."

At the bottom of the page was a drawn symbol:

My hand shook a little as I pointed to the drawing.

"What's that?"

"It's a signature. You see a lot of those in The Nations. I'd say it was a deer's head. I'd say it means Milk Eye Rufus Deer."

The envelope was addressed to John Boins Esq., Eureka Springs, Arkansas, and postmarked on the Missouri, Kansas and Texas railroad in Muskogee, I.T., May 21, 1890.

I knew what I held in my hand was a summons. For Johnny Boins to meet Milk Eye Rufus Deer in Fort Smith on the exact day I had seen them there together on the Frisco station platform.

And I knew something else besides. My throat constricted at the thought. The horse in the note was Tar Baby. And surely the girl was Jennie Thrasher. Oscar Schiller, with his usual uncanny perception of what was on my mind, shrugged as he took the letter and replaced it in his coat pocket.

He said, "I told you there was more to it than the horse."

Seven

ON THE MORNING AFTER WE RETURNED TO FORT SMITH, UNITED States Commissioner Mitchell held a hearing in his chambers, a small room in an old warehouse across Rogers Avenue from the federal courthouse. Oscar Schiller and I escorted Johnny Boins, who clanked along awkwardly in handcuffs and leg-irons. He was still cheerful and jocular, and when Emmitt was led into the magistrate's court by one of the federal jailers, our prisoner indicated no sign of recognition or apprehension.

Evans was there to present the government's case. First I told of having seen a man fitting the description of Milk Eye Rufus Deer with Johnny Boins on the Fort Smith railroad station platform. Oscar Schiller presented the clasp knife and the letter with the deer-head signature. Emmitt without hesitation identified Johnny Boins as the white man in the group that had attacked Mrs. John on the Hatchet Hill road, and retold in detail the story of that terrible day.

Johnny Boins waived counsel, his parents not having yet arrived in town, nor their attorney from Little Rock. In his own defense, he said he had come to Fort Smith in early June for social reasons. He said he did not know anyone named Milk Eye Rufus Deer, nor anyone fitting that description, and claimed the letter had obviously been placed in his quarters by parties unknown, because he had never seen it before. He said he had not been in The Nations since November 1889, when he visited Choteau to attend a horse race.

The commissioner ordered Johnny Boins bound over for grand jury investigation on suspicion of murder and rape. The entire proceedings lasted about fifteen minutes.

There was a federal grand jury sitting in Fort Smith on a permanent basis, each panel serving for a year before a new one was drawn. Oscar Schiller and Evans hoped the threat of going before that body would give Johnny Boins the incentive to identify his companions during the drunken spree in the Choctaw Nation. But Boins laughed at any such notion and continued to claim he knew no such people and that he had not been in The Nations at the time. Besides, he said, there had never been any need to resort to rape to get all he wanted.

Oscar Schiller's scheme of withholding from Johnny Boins our real reasons for keeping him in custody had proved fruitless. Boins had told us nothing. Now, the possibility of an indictment by the grand jury had no better results. We knew no more than we had known about the people involved in the Winding Stair Massacre, except that one might have a name beginning with C. It didn't seem to bother Schiller, who said something to Evans about other irons in the fire.

I was anxious to see Jennie Thrasher, but Evans sent me off to the city jail on another case, to take a deposition from a prisoner there. The day was cloudy and high winds were whipping in from the west. There was talk of a possible tornado, one of the perennial spring and summer dangers along the flat valley of the Arkansas. The city's sparrows were staying close to the ground and the few redwings and chimney swifts aloft were hurtled along before the wind like black cinders before a bellows. It was at least ten degrees warmer than it had been in the mountains, and by the time I hurried back to the courthouse my shirt was damp with sweat.

Jennie Thrasher and Zelda Mores were not in the women's section of the jail, but I knew where I might find them. I started toward the National Cemetery, across an almost deserted compound. I wondered for a time why there were not the usual groups of men talking, chewing tobacco, and horse trading. It was likely the threat of a storm, but then I remembered that while we had been in Eureka Springs, two men had been hanged for murder in the Chickasaw Nation. Evans had told me that after hangings, which were well-advertised public gatherings, people generally stayed away from the gallows compound for a few days.

She was standing far down the slope toward the Poteau River, on a large rock that thrust up from the well-kept turf, her hair down and blowing in the wind. Zelda Mores was a few paces away, her purse held ready, mustached face glaring as I came near. When I stepped up to the rock on which Jennie Thrasher stood, her face on a level with mine, I could see she had been crying, the tears blown back along her cheeks. I started to give her the little china dog, but seeing her drawn features I thought better of it. She looked at me, saying nothing. There was no display of relief or pleasure that I was back, and in fact she acted as though I had never been gone. It was a hard disappointment.

"Hello, Jennie," I said. She looked past me toward the river and I was conscious of the cotton dress pressing her breasts in the wind, and her long neck with the tiny blue veins. "What is it? Why have you been crying?"

"I'm not crying," she said. She lowered her head and rubbed her cheeks with her fingertips. Her hands were long and well shaped, but the nails were badly bitten, almost to the quick. It gave her fingers a chunky, blunt look.

"Listen, I've been in the mountains," I said. "But not the kind of mountains you know. A wonderful place I can tell you about, where the houses look like stacks of blocks . . ."

"They want me to talk about it," she broke in. "They want me to talk about all those bad things. What happened to my papa. You told me I wouldn't have to talk about that."

"Who wants you to talk about it?"

"That mean old bastard with the long beard," she said, her voice bitter.

"Evans? Evans talked to you again?"

She nodded. "Just awhile ago. He's a mean man, Eben."

"He's trying to find the ones who did all those bad things."

"I don't know nothing about it. I was up in that attic. I don't know nothing about it. You believe me, don't you? Don't you?"

Suddenly she lifted her hands and took my face between her fingers. She bent to me and her lips pressed against mine, firm and warm for a long moment. I felt her hair blowing around my face, and as she drew back some of the yellow strands clung to my cheeks. I reached to take her in my arms, but she pulled back and turned, running across the cemetery through the gravestones.

"Good-bye, Eben," she called, and ran past Zelda Mores, who looked as startled as I must have.

"What in God's name," I said and started after her, but Zelda stood before me threateningly.

"You'd better leave her alone now, Mr. Pay," she said.

"What's going on here?"

"Mr. Evans. He showed her Johnny Boins in the split room." The split room was a small alcove at one end of the men's jail, divided by a partition, where witnesses could identify suspects standing on the other side of a screened window. "She went all to pieces when she seen him."

"He did *what*? For God's sake, why didn't he tell me . . ."

Zelda turned after Jennie, who was already disappearing into the compound gate. The bile was rising in my throat and I could feel my good disposition going to hell. Oscar Schiller's words were in my mind: "There's more to it than the horse." I despised him for having said what was now becoming obvious to me.

By the time I reached the courthouse compound, Jennie and Zelda Mores were already inside. I ran past the gallows, where a deputy marshal was leaning against one wall with a Winchester, watching a prisoner scrub the platform with lye water. As I rushed up the steps to the courthouse, a crowd of people met me coming out and I pushed through them. Court was in recess, and that meant I would find Evans in his office.

I opened his door without knocking and caught him before his desk, his hands full of documents. As he turned to me, I shouted at him.

"What did you do with that girl?" The color came suddenly to his cheeks above the beard. He yanked off his pince-nez and threw them on his cluttered desk.

"I assume, young man, you're speaking of Jennie Thrasher?"

"Of course I'm speaking of Jennie Thrasher. She's been crying."

"I wouldn't be surprised." He sighed, shaking his head and gaining control of his own temper. He moved behind the desk and sat down. "I did what had to be done."

"You took her to look at that man without taking me. And all along I've been her closest friend since what happened to her, and with your approval and encouragement."

"I didn't want you there."

"God dammit . . ."

"Look here, son," he said quietly. "Don't come in here raving about that girl, or how I'm running this case. Are you afraid we might find out more about her than you want us to know?"

"I hope you're not implying that I know anything I haven't told you."

"Of course not."

"She's told you what she knows," I said, still panting. "She's told you that. And she knows nothing. She was up in that attic, terrified. Why in God's name are you badgering her?"

"Oh hell," he said, leaning back in his chair and closing his eyes. "She knows Johnny Boins, Eben. She knows him but won't admit it."

"But she said . . ."

"I know what she said. But after a while in this business you can tell. When she saw him she almost jumped out of her hide. It was like I'd hit her in the belly with a stick of stovewood. He never saw her, of course, behind that screen, but it didn't matter. I can promise you, she knows him."

I was so furious, the implications of what he said failed to penetrate. All I could think of was her drawn face and the painful twist of her mouth.

"I thought we were supposed to be her friends."

"You don't have any friends in this business. You try to find the truth."

"Truth, hell! What you're trying to find is a conviction, no matter what, and you . . ."

Abruptly he was up, slamming his fist down so hard on the desk the typewriter bell rang.

"You listen," he roared. "The truth so far is you've got too close to that girl. You're blind to what might have gone on in this case. Think, for God's sake! That letter. What girl do you think they were talking about in that letter?"

With a little encouragement, I could have strangled him. Yet at that moment, I knew he was right. It had been a thing in the back of my mind from the time we'd heard Lila's story. Johnny Boins bragging about women and getting even with someone in The Nations, and now the letter. If we had arrested the right man, surely Jennie Thrasher was the girl Milk Eye said he'd found. But until Evans threw it at me, I had been unable to face it.

"Did she say anything else? About the case?" I asked, choking and hardly recognizing my own voice.

Evans sat down again, replacing his pince-nez. Deliberately he unwrapped one of his fat cigars and struck a match to it. I knew he was taking his time to allow my temper to cool, but it only made me indignant, to be treated like a child.

"Nothing. She said nothing more. But I warn you, Eben, she likely knows a great deal. I told her that someday she'd be on the witness stand and would have no choice but to tell. You know what she said when I mentioned perjury?"

He looked at me through the dense blue smoke, peering over his pince-nez, and beneath his beard I thought there was the beginning of a smile.

"How would I know?" I said sarcastically. "Not having been invited to listen."

"She said I could go to hell!"

The whole thing was falling down around me. The enthusiasm I had felt just a short time ago at the prospect of seeing her again had gone sour. And I could still feel the caress of her hair against my face. I took the china dog from my pocket and put it on his desk.

"Would you have someone take this up to her?"

"Yes. If you don't want to do it yourself."

"From what you've just said, I assume you want me clear of this whole case and everything to do with it."

The remark infuriated him. He was up again, banging his desk with a clenched fist, red-faced and the cigar almost aflame from his puffing.

"God dammit, Eben, I don't want you clear of this case. But you still haven't grasped the kinds of things we deal with here. Hell's fire, haven't you learned anything about this business yet?"

He slammed the cigar into a tortoiseshell ashtray and spun around toward his dusty window, looking out onto the compound as he tried to regain control. The back of his neck was still red when he spoke softly, but with great emphasis.

"Whiskey! Greed! Lechery! God knows what else. It's tearing that country apart. Do you know how many men we've got out as deputy marshals at any one time? About two hundred! And do you know how many men we've lost in the line of duty? Shot or stabbed or clubbed and left to die in some ditch? Over fifty! Why, the things that go on make some of those old hell-raising towns like Ellsworth and Dodge look like a

79

girl's-school promenade. Do you know how many square miles we try to police from this court?"

"What's that got to do with . . ." I started, but he turned on me.

"I'm trying to make you understand something!" he shouted. "I'm trying to get it through that thick skull of yours what we have to deal with here. We can't get involved with these damned cases personally. Do you know how much territory we've got? Hell, even I don't know anymore. We started with over seventy-four-thousand square miles. That's bigger than New England. It's too big. We can't get involved. . . ."

He stopped, sweating, the beads of moisture running down his face and into his beard.

"All the goddamned predators over there in that country. Congress has whittled away parts of it and given it to other courts, but it's still too big. Hell," he said, throwing out his arms and then slapping his sides with his hands. "You've got to assume the worst and take it all as a part of the working day, Eben. Anything can pop up. Anything."

He sat down and grabbed the cigar again, stabbing at it with his hand.

"We shouldn't even be in this case. The Choctaw Nation is supposed to be under the jurisdiction now of a court in Texas, but they haven't picked it up yet, so we're still in it. And now, you've gone and got the sweetass over some pretty little thing . . ."

He let it trail off and somehow what he'd said irritated me only a little. Perhaps because it was all true.

"Then you still want me to work with Schiller on it?"

"Yes, but God dammit, don't come in here again raising hell about how I'm preparing the case."

"All right. But I'd still appreciate it if you saw she gets this stuff." I placed two packages of peppermint chewing gum on his desk beside the china dog.

"I'll do that. And I don't think I'll be needing you the rest of the afternoon. Get out and walk, or shoot some pool and forget it. You got a load of guts, Eben, but you got a generous nature, too. Don't let it blind you. Now, let's not say anything more about it."

He had already begun to arrange papers and open files lying in folders on his desk, puffing his cigar furiously. As I went out, I gave him one last bellow—"I think I'll get drunk!"—and slammed his door.

It was Frisco payroll day at Henryetta's, and the downstairs bar-parlor was crowded with railroaders. Henryetta was at her usual place against the bar, but not dozing now. Her golden smile flashed as she talked with her customers, telling bawdy stories and winking slyly. I found a small corner table, wanting to be left alone, but she came over and started a conversation which interested me not at all, even when she said that Lila had left for Memphis the day after Oscar Schiller and I had talked with her. Big Rachael brought me a lemonade and gin, but I irritably pushed it away and told him to bring me a bottle of the best house rye and a water glass.

For a moment, it appeared she might ask me to leave, what with my rudeness. Then she shrugged her fat shoulders and returned to more amiable guests. Some of the girls were working the parlor, dressed in their evening clothes. They disgusted me with their bare shoulders and garishly painted lips—all meant to titillate, I supposed. Each time I saw one of them laughing, the red mouth open in mock cheerfulness, I thought of Jennie Thrasher's pink lips and how they had felt against my own.

To hell with it all, I thought. Getting myself involved with a little Nations chippy who didn't want to get involved with me. A girl who cussed and smoked cigarettes. As the rye burned down my throat and boiled in my stomach, I goaded myself with the thought of Jennie. Evans was right, of course. All along, I'd thought the whole messy business might blow away in the wind, leaving Jennie and me as though courting in Saint Louis, me in my boater and needlepoint shoes, her in demure taffeta and lace. To hell with it all, I thought. I am going to throw myself one magnificent drunk, and then go back home where I can drown myself in civilization and good breeding.

I began to relax, looking at the crowd and at Henryetta's gold teeth, finding it all suddenly amusing and frivolous and high-spirited. Not so slowly, the liquor began to dissipate despair and self-pity.

The room was full of talk about the great event planned in just two days in celebration of the Fourth of July. There was to be a prizefight on the sandbar along the bend of the river across from Fort Smith, it being against the law to hold such a contest in the state of Arkansas. It held little interest for me at first, but as the rye took its effect everything changed. I could hardly keep from hearing all about it; because the railroaders seemed so accustomed to shouting while they worked around the noisy trains, it had become the only way they knew how to talk.

A visiting professional prizefighter from somewhere in the East would be matched against a local challenger. The challenger was Big Rachael, the overwhelming favorite. I heard it said that Dirty Jake, the professional, weighed 12 stones. Mentally, I calculated that this meant he was about 168 pounds. It occurred to me that Evans had failed to explain, in his professional role, that there were so many Anglo-Saxons working in Fort Smith. But then, it could be expected because the English had always been railroaders.

If Dirty Jake weighs 12 stones, I thought, Big Rachael would run close to 21, for he was every ounce of 300 pounds. I giggled at my own cleverness, converting old English weight to pounds. As the rye continued to dull the sting of what had happened earlier in the day and created, too, a loss of inhibition, I found myself making bets with the railroaders against the local favorite. They were laying three-to-one odds that Big Rachael would knock Dirty Jake senseless. Soon, I was at the bar, inviting bets at five-to-one that Big Rachael would not last twenty rounds.

During the course of this sporting talk, two of Henryetta's girls took my arm and explained that my money might be more enjoyably spent upstairs, but I brushed them away. Henryetta and some of the railroaders apparently thought me too abrupt with the girls, considering the nature of their business and the enterprise they displayed. I began to hear comments that I was another of these Yankee sons of bitches, like Dirty Jake, come down to Fort Smith to show off and spread my big-city money around.

My belligerence increased as the level in the bottle of rye dipped downward. By dark the place was crowded with men, some of whom eyed me with hatred. It was exhilarating. With the bravado of youth and the whiskey dulling my sense of self-preservation, I stood at the bar exclaiming on the fine art of fisticuffs and prizefighting, an endeavor I had never actually witnessed. What was worse, I began to cast asperions on those stupid enough to sweat over oily locomotives, then waste their money betting on something they were not intellectually competent to understand. I used all the fine words I could recall from the University of Illinois and various law offices, browbeating them with terms beyond their comprehension. But they got the hang of most of it.

There was a scuffle near me along the bar and I realized one of the railroaders was trying to get at me—to emphasize, I thought drunkenly, how little I knew about fighting. Henryetta was beside me then, shouting that there would be no disturbance in her place. Big Rachael, against whom I had just wagered almost fifty dollars, gently escorted me toward the door, his hand on my back like a slab of bacon. They pushed me to the door and across the veranda and down the steps into the street, a large number of whorehouse customers immediately behind. It finally came to me that I might be in for a severe beating, and at that thought I began to laugh. I kept thinking that already darkness had come on, and a good bottle of rye not yet finished. The headlights of the switchyards engines looked like dingy mothballs.

But more serious considerations overtook me as the dark forms of railroaders closed around me. There would be no chance standing among them, for they could get at me from all sides, so I somehow moved over against the wall of Henryetta's, dancing along like the drunken man I was. My hat blew off in the still-gusting wind and for an instant I thought of the little Smith and Wesson pistol back in my room. Then they were on me. I struck the first blow, happily feeling knuckles against breaking teeth. Their fists hammered me. Blood was salty in my mouth and my nose was smashed but I managed to land a few more hard punches before their weight overcame me and I was on my knees.

I tried to cover my face with both arms, expecting them to finish me in a final rush. But nothing happened. The dark forms heaved around me, grunting and cursing, and I heard then the dull thud of something solid against flesh. They were falling back, two of them thrashing about on the ground like beheaded chickens. Over me was a formless shape, crowned by a wide-brimmed hat. At first, I thought it was Big Rachael, come out to prevent homicide, but then I saw the cake-knife blade of the hatchet in his hand.

"I don't want to kill nobody here," Joe Mountain shouted, the hatchet swinging at his side like a metal snake's-head. "But you men come in here again, I'll start using the edge on you."

"You goddamned red nigger bastard," someone yelled.

Joe Mountain pulled me to my feet, still watching the group around us. They shouted insults, but no one wanted to come within striking range of the French hatchet. The two men who had gone down from blows by the flat of the blade were up on wobbly legs, moving back among their fellows, screeching at us.

"You goddamned dirty red nigger son of a bitch."

Joe Mountain pulled me toward the corner of the house, along the wall. My legs were weak as water, and he had to haul me like a limp sack of wheat grain. In the lights from the switch engines I could see his teeth shining.

We were around the house then, and there was no purpose in hurrying because the railroaders had already started back inside, still shouting their insults about Yankees and red niggers. We stumbled along through backyards, over one picket fence and through the gap in another. We came to the next block, on Commerce Street, and only then did Joe Mountain stop and look at me.

"You're bleedin' like a cut pig, Eben Pay," he said. "You can't whip the whole Frisco railroad."

"Like hell," I said, laughing. I spat a mouthful of blood onto the sidewalk and the big Osage laughed with me.

"Come on, Cap'n got a place just up the street where he stays when he's in town. We better go and get you cleaned up."

"Where the hell'd you come from, Joe?" I asked, stumbling along beside him. He held one hand under my arm to keep me from falling.

"The Osage reservation," he said.

"I mean at the damned whorehouse. Where'd you come from?"

"The Osage reservation," he repeated, grinning.

"Joe. Joe, I'm sure glad you did." I grabbed a lightpole and hung on for a moment and Joe Mountain waited, watching me bend over and throw up.

"Eben Pay, you puke more'n any man I know," he said.

Eight

ALONG COMMERCE STREET THERE WERE A NUMBER OF BOARD-inghouses, some of them new, others from before the war and now dilapidated and unpainted. In one of these, Oscar Schiller shared the basement room with a furnace, stacks of empty cardboard boxes, and worn-out bedsprings. It was a large room and the light from a single kerosene lamp on the night table beside Schiller's bed left deep shadows in all the corners and behind the furnace that squatted like a concrete-coated toad at one end. There were old ladder-back straight chairs discarded at various times by the people who lived above, and in addition to Schiller's bed, covered by a homemade quilt cover, there were two bare mattresses on the floor with rumpled blankets.

In the shadows of one corner, leaning back in a chair tilted against the wall, was a well-dressed black man, his dark hat set at a jaunty angle over one eye. From beneath his coat I could see the butt of a large pistol and on his vest a metal star large as a Mason jar lid. He watched me with an even stare, seeming not at all surprised to see my bloody face and red-stained clothes.

Oscar Schiller was sitting on his bed, his shirt off and the long flannel underwear showing dampness under the arms as he bent over the night table. There, arranged in neat rows, were five snuff cans, a box of snuff, and a sheet of paper. On the paper was a mound of white powder that looked like sugar. He was mixing snuff and the white powder in the snuff cans. I knew it was cocaine, the powerful stimulant so popular among much of Saint Louis high society. I had never tried it, but I knew it was expensive. Also on the night table was a cup of hot tea, and into this Schiller sprinkled a spoonful of the narcotic, stirred it, and took a long sip before looking up at me.

"I see you found him," he said.

"He was at Henryetta's," Joe Mountain said. "Trying to stomp a bunch of railroad men."

"Is the local law looking for him?"

"No, it was just a friendly fight."

It began to dawn on my befuddled mind that the big Osage had not appeared at the whorehouse by accident. Schiller had had him out looking for me. I was infuriated.

"I don't need you to change my pants," I said.

"Evans told me you might need some watching," he said, spooning his snuff and cocaine into the little cans. "When Joe came in from The Nations this afternoon, I sent him looking for you, Mr. Pay."

"I don't need you to change my pants," I repeated. "And I'm sick and tired of this 'Mr. Pay' foolishness. 'Mr. Pay' this, 'Mr. Pay' that! You're old enough to be my father. Even my grandfather, maybe."

Schiller watched me swaying, with Joe Mountain's hand under one of my arms to keep me from falling. In my mouth was the sour taste of vomit and blood.

"What would you like to be called?"

"Well, hell," I said. My mind shot off on another tangent. "Why the hell do you use that stuff?"

"Cocaine? I don't see it does me any harm. It's not against the law. You know I don't do things against the law."

From the corner, the black man laughed softly.

"Well, there's another damned thing," I said, defensively. "I don't want anything more to do with all this crooked horseshit. All this confiscating Nations whiskey to sell here. And those damned railroad passes you get by threatening people and then selling them. I don't want any more of that horseshit. When we go someplace from now on, I'll pay my own way, I don't want any more of that railroad pass horseshit."

Oscar Schiller sipped his tea and the corners of his thin mouth twitched and for a moment I thought he might smile.

"He's rambunctious, ain't he, Cap'n?" Joe Mountain said.

"He's drunk and disorderly," Schiller said. "But that's all right. From here on, we'll call you Eben, if that's what you want. And next time we take a train somewheres, you can pay your own way. I'll even sell you the tickets for half price."

Joe Mountain and the black man laughed. Although I suspected Schiller might be serious, the situation suddenly struck me as ludicrous and I laughed, too. It hurt my swollen lips.

"This here is Burris Garret," Schiller said, waving a hand toward the man in the corner. "He's a deputy marshal. He works out of Okmulgee, in the Creek Nation. Burris, take a look at that nose."

Garret came over and shook my hand. He was almost as tall as I, a broad-shouldered man with a strong neck and a well-shaped head. He wore a close-trimmed beard that formed a black frame around his full-lipped mouth.

"Why don't you lay down over here?" he said. Joe Mountain led me to one of the mattresses and I managed to get down on it without falling. I lay there faceup and Garret bent over me, feeling my nose. His face was the color of drugstore chocolate syrup, glistening in the lamplight. The room was spinning and I held fast to the mattress with both hands. But then my head began to clear, and one of those moments of abrupt clarity came when Garret squeezed the bridge of my nose between his heavy fingers.

"You got a busted nose, Mr. Pay," he said.

"Better not call him that," Oscar Schiller said and Joe Mountain laughed again. Burris Garret chuckled and it sounded like air bubbles coming up from the bottom of a full rain-barrel. He took a handkerchief from his pocket and ripped off one corner, rolling it like a cigarette. He pushed the cloth cylinder under my upper lip, pressing it hard against my gums. What was left of the handkerchief he took to a dry sink near the furnace, wet it in a water bucket there, and placed it across the bridge of my nose.

Joe Mountain was telling Schiller about looking along Garrison Avenue for me and finding me at Henryetta's. He had watched through the windows as my little escapade developed, not being allowed inside.

"Eben Pay was making bets on the prizefight," he said. "I could hear him from outside. Was pretty noisy about it. He was betting against Big Rachael. Them railroad men was mad as wet yellow-jackets."

"Well, Joe, I suspect maybe you and me ought to go down there and show some displeasure about one of our men being rough-handled," Oscar Schiller said. He rose and came over to me, pulling on a shirt. I was still hanging on to the bed, but in the whirling room I could see the marshal's face over me. Joe Mountain and Burris Garret walked outside the door and I could hear their voices as Schiller stood above me, buttoning his shirt.

"You sober enough to understand something needs saying?"

I mumbled that I was. He had his jacket then, and after slipping into it he took a handful of peanuts from a pocket and began to hull them, tossing the meats into his mouth and chewing. It was a long spiel, and I struggled to hear it all in my alcohol haze.

"Do you know how much money I make? Because I'm a district chief deputy, I get a hundred dollars a year flat rate. But other than that, I get paid like all the other deputies out of Parker's court. I get two dollars for every prisoner I bring in alive. He may be mean and try to shoot my ass off, but I get two dollars for him. If my posse has to kill him, I don't get a dime, and I have to pay for burying him. For each witness I bring to court, I get fifty cents. I get ten cents a mile travel. If I'm traveling with a prisoner, I get ten cents apiece for each one, the same for my scouts. That covers transportation and eats and lodging. The marshal of Parker's court gets thirty-five percent of everything I make, just like he does for all the deputies.

"Sometimes I get a reward on a prisoner convicted, paid by one of the railroads or a bank or even a community. I've got to gouge out all I can get otherwise. You may think a lot of what I do is dishonest. But let me tell you, in my day, before I joined Parker, I did a lot of things worse than what I do now. The Wyoming Cattleman's Association got a reward out for my hide right now. There are at least two counties in Texas would like nothing better than to get me in front of one of their jake-leg courts for appropriating various horses. I haven't had to kill a man since the war, but I've done about everything else.

"Most of the men who ride for Parker are no better than me. Some are a lot worse."

Throughout all of this he had been looking down at me with those unblinking eyes shining behind his glasses, chewing slowly. Now he turned away and moved to an old trunk and took out the big nickel-plated revolver I'd seen in his hand in Eureka Springs. He slid it under his coat and started for the door, but he wasn't finished.

"That's one reason I hate these little pop-head no-accounts we're after now. Most of the people I chase are just like that. They haven't robbed any train or bank, they don't have any reward posted on 'em, so if we bring all of them in, I'll make about enough to buy a new pair of boots. Provided I don't get killed in the process."

"Well, why the hell do you do it, then?" I asked.

"It's the best way I know to stay out of the pen or off the gallows," he said. "Hell, Eben, if I wasn't doing this I'd probably be robbing banks myself. So don't begrudge me a dollar here and there. And don't start that holier-than-thou business with me again. This isn't your high society Saint Louis you're involved with. The people we chase ain't no band of angels. And neither are we."

At the door, he spoke to Burris Garret.

"Why don't you tell him what we've got planned?" he said. "Come on, Joe, let's get to business."

"If I'm with the Cap'n," Joe Mountain called through the door, "they'll let me in that whorehouse." I could see his wolf's teeth shining.

Burris Garret pulled up a ladder-back beside my mattress and sat backward in the chair, resting his arms across the back. He felt my nose again and I winced, feeling cartilage grind under the skin.

"Old Schiller thinks you're a good man," Garret said.

I lay with my eyes closed, sobering fast, attributable likely to the disgorging of rye under the streetlamp. I began to feel the bruises, along my ribs and under my eyes against the cheekbones. But it felt good. The hurts and the long talk Schiller had made, all of it felt good.

"I've been looking for your friend Milk Eye over in the Creek Nation," Burris Garret said. "No luck yet."

He spoke with a strange accent, but he had been well schooled in English. I supposed him at first to be from the North or perhaps from one of the British West Indies. Neither was the case.

"You work the Creek Nation?" I mumbled, fighting sleep now.

"That's right. I know all that country. Born there. Grew up there. My folks were Creek slaves, then after the Treaty of 1866 they were Creek citizens. I went to one of the Creek boys' academies. They got some good ones. Then I joined the Creek lighthorse. The Creek police. About three years ago, I got my commission as a deputy marshal out of Parker's court. We'll be working together on this case. It's winding down to the Creek country."

His chocolate-colored face swam before my eyes.

"I never knew there were any . . ." I started to say, then stopped. He chuckled.

"Black marshals? Sure, there are a few. Parker doesn't care what you are, so long as you can marshal."

He pulled the wad of cotton cloth from my mouth and stared intently into my nose.

"Looks like the bleeding stopped."

"What about Schiller? Will he stay on this case?"

"Sure, it's his case. But we'll all be together now. We're going over to that prizefight across the river day after tomorrow."

"What for?"

"We got a lead. I arrested a whiskey peddler this morning and brought him in from the Creek Nation. On the way, he fell off his horse a lot." Garret laughed. I realized his gentle manner might be deceptive. "After a while, he got tired falling off his horse and banging up his head. He told me there were rumors some of the Winding Stair bunch might come in for the betting."

He swabbed my face with a damp cloth and I caught my breath when he touched the bridge of my nose.

"Whiskey peddlers are good sources. They're scared of what's going to happen to them in Parker's court. And they know most of the people in The Nations and what they do for pleasure."

"You mean there are people over there who might know who we're after?"

"I suspect so."

"And they won't come forward? They won't help bring in these killers?"

Burris Garret looked at me a long time before he answered, as though he wanted to think carefully about his words.

"No," he said. "Oh, some will, but a lot of them have done things themselves that make them leery of the law. Some are scared to talk. And there are a lot of good people there who don't like the idea of turning their own kind over to a court outside their country. They all know that when a man gets to Fort Smith, he'll get tried by a white jury."

I remembered what Evans had said once about the men hanged since 1875, when Judge Parker arrived.

"But Judge Parker's hanged more white men than Indians, by a hell of a sight."

"Sure. And it's the white ones people in The Nations are most afraid of. You take a Cherokee killer. His own people are reluctant to inform on him and send him to a white man's court. But if the killer is a white man, they're usually afraid to inform on him.'"

"But why?" I asked, and knew it was a stupid question even as I said it. Garret laughed, more at me than because it was funny, I suspected.

"Bad things can happen in the night," he said.

"Well, it looks like we've already got the white man in this case," I said.

"That's right. So you see why my whiskey peddler had to fall off his horse so much before he told me anything at all. He's a Creek, and the Yuchi are almost family to the Creeks sometimes."

"You think Milk Eye might come?"

"He's a betting man, no doubt about that. And there'll be chicken fights later, after dark. And Milk Eye does like chicken fights. But I don't expect him. He may not be too smart but he's smart enough to stay hidden a while longer."

"Do you know Milk Eye?"

"He and I grew up together," Garret said. "He's a tough little Yuchi. His people are good folks. But they work hard and never have anything. They scratch corn and sorghum on a little patch of ground not far from Okmulgee. Poor as bald-headed whores."

Garret stood up and hitched at his pants. The butt of the pistol thrust out black and deadly from beneath his coat.

"You get some sleep now," he said. "Think I'll walk down to Henryetta's myself."

He left the lamp burning and I lay watching the cobwebs moving gently among the rafters. I could still taste blood and sourness in my mouth. Before sleep came, my mind staggered from one thought to the next. It had been a day that would stay in memory for a long time, each detail. I had been cut down a few pegs. First, that bastard Evans. Then Schiller. Not the railroaders, though. I had won that one. Maybe I had won them all. I felt a little older and I congratulated myself on the wisdom of my father for sending me here. Perhaps I had purchased a little wisdom myself, at the expense of a punctured self-esteem and a broken nose.

Something else filtered through my hazy thinking. At this moment, three very intimidating men were at Henryetta's, letting everyone know I was a part of the Parker court. I had come to know these men, and other deputies who worked for Parker, and they were good peace officers each in his own way. But Oscar Schiller was good because people were afraid of him, and it made me feel good that I wasn't.

As I fell finally into a deep sleep, the last thing I heard was the late-night Texas freight road engine whistling in the yards before pulling out to the south for Winding Stair and Kiamachi Valley.

I N THE FLAT OF AN ANVIL, THERE
is a small hole that on proper
occasions of celebration, when filled
with black powder and correctly
fused, will explode like a howitzer. The
process is called Shooting the Anvil. In
Fort Smith on that 1890 Fourth of July, it
was everyone's favorite firecracker. The
advantages of shooting an anvil were
apparent. The heavy metal itself was not
damaged, and after each shot, it could be
recharged and blown again, each time
making the same defiant roar and lifting a
dense cloud of white smoke into the clear,
windless sky.

During most of the war, Fort Smith
had been occupied by federal troops. That
and the influence of the border country
made it less a southern city than an
amalgam of many regions. On Independence Day, everyone turned out for the
Garrison Avenue parade and the cere-
monies in National Cemetery, where men
clad in their old uniforms of blue or gray
placed flags on the graves and the city
band played the marches of both armies,
all typical of the place as a part of
Arkansas, which had seceded from the
Union and then from time to time threatened to secede from the Confederacy as
well.

When the grand and glorious day
arrived in 1890, there were speeches, too,
at the new pilings on the Arkansas side of
the river where Jay Gould was building a
railroad bridge, just south of the foot of

Garrison Avenue. In the yard of the new Belle Grove School, there was a band concert, with lemonade served by the volunteer firemen. Open house was held at Saint John's Hospital, where visitors might expect to see the chairman of the board of governors, Judge Isaac Parker.

Along Rogers Avenue, the German and Jewish restaurateurs sold chocolate and coconut cakes on the sidewalks. Saloons were open all day, many offering drinks at half price and free lunches ranging from prime roast beef to pan-fried catfish. The city's chili vendors pushed their carts among the crowds, serving their hot stew in tiny pie shells. All the streetcars were decorated in red, white, and blue bunting, and bursts of firecrackers and Roman candles were set off by mobs of yowling boys along the sidewalks.

On The Nations side of the river, people gathered for the prizefight, and the barges and ferries crossed back and forth from early morning until well into the night. The madams from along railyard row came in surreys, their ladies gathered about them and all carrying parasols. They stayed well back from the mob around the ring, watching from a distance as the local gladiator attempted to maul the invader from the North. The area was a white field of shirt-sleeved men, arm garters garish and multicolored, most of them with large hats to shade against the sun. The Fort Smith newspapers would say that more than two thousand people attended the affair, and perhaps that many more tried to see what was happening on the sand flats at the bend of the Arkansas, watching from the high banks across the river.

In that sea of faces, one came to realize how cosmopolitan this little frontier city had become. The Irish and English from the barges and the railroads, the German brewery workers and the Jewish shopkeepers. Gas well drillers and cotton farmers, the hill people and the flatlands garden farmers, the blacks who worked in the city and the ones across the river who were now part of various Indian tribes. And the tribesmen themselves. The Choctaw, Creek, and Seminole. And the Cherokee, on whose land the spectacle was being waged. Walking through the crowds, one could hear two dozen different languages, see all shades of skin pigmentation, all manner and texture of hair, all color and shape of eyes. It was a seething, writhing human stew, set off here along the border of the last continental Indian frontier, a place never passaged by the old pioneer wagon routes to the west or the newer railroads building toward the Pacific. A backwater in time, with a surging energy and life all its own, unique among all places as it celebrated the one hundred and fourteenth year of national independence.

Nine

THE FIGHT WAS A COMPLETE DEBACLE FOR THE FORT SMITH favorite.

Big Rachael's long arms and massive fists were of little use against the smaller, quick-footed Dirty Jake, who pummeled the bigger man almost at will, sending him down again and again. Big Rachael would rise, spitting blood, and stagger to his corner where seconds dashed water in his face and swabbed off his mouth and nose. Before the minute expired, he would be back at center ring, toeing the mark as required in the rules of the prize ring.

They fought bare-knuckle, and after the third round each time Dirty Jake slammed his fist into Big Rachael's face, there was a sodden plop and blood flew out in the bright sunlight like the juice from an exploding watermelon. My own broken nose began to hurt from watching it, and after a while I moved back through the crowd—away from the ring, away from the sounds of it. But somehow, there was a dreadful fascination about it, and standing near the wagons and rigs drawn up at the edges of the mob, I turned back and saw the rest.

After the twenty-ninth knockdown, Big Rachael did not return to his corner but went directly to the ring ropes and between them. He passed through the crowd as they gave way before him, everyone staring at his mangled face and the red-stained sweatshirt and tights. He was crying by the time he reached Henryetta's surrey, and the crowd stood silently listening to the big man.

"I couldn't catch the little bastard, Miss Henryetta," he blubbered. "I just couldn't catch him."

"It's all right, Rachael. You done the best you knew how. Get on back of the wagon."

After he had climbed up behind the rear seat and sat with his legs dangling, she whipped her team off toward the ferry slip. It was not a pleasant scene, the giant leaving a blood-splattered ring and begging his mistress for forgiveness. There were few in the crowd who did not know that Henryetta had bet her money on the Yankee.

Oscar Schiller came over beside me then and we watched the surrey going down toward the river, other vehicles following close behind. There had been a great deal of shouting from the crowd at first, but when the nature of the contest had become clear, they quieted, and they were mostly silent now as they dispersed.

"I don't suppose you've seen anyone we might be wanting," Schiller said.

"I don't even know what I'm looking for. Where's Garret and Joe Mountain?"

"Other side of the crowd. Let's go to the barn. You ever see a chicken fight?"

"No. But I hope it's not as bad as the one I just saw."

"It's a helluva lot worse."

But I was to be spared the sight of more blood that day. Garret and the Osage found us, and with them was a Creek policeman wearing what appeared to be an old army thigh-length coat. The garment struck me as incongruous in the July heat.

"This here is Moma July," Garret said. "He's got something to tell us."

Moma July was much like many of the The Nations Indians I had seen, only running a little more to middle-age overweight. His skin was darker than most, darker than Burris Garret's. It was the color of old pine bark, with a trace of yellow in it. He wore the usual large hat over close-cropped hair, and it settled so far down on his head there was the impression that his ears were holding it up. Around his thick neck was a yellowed bone necklace.

"Since you Fort Smith men sent us all them details on the Winding Stair killings, I been watchin' out," he said. "Three days ago I was on the north fork of the Canadian, lookin' in on a man we caught a few times sellin' whiskey. Name Skitty Cornkiller. I never found no whiskey this time, but when I was ridin' off, I seen something else. There was this colored man hoeing in a garden behind the house. He's a man works for Skitty Cornkiller. And he was wearin' this hat. Big hat, black with a button on the front."

Oscar Schiller glanced at me and I nodded, recalling what Charley Oskogee had told us about Thrasher's pearl hat. I felt the excitement lifting in me, but Schiller's expression did not change, as though this were something he had expected.

"Who's the colored man?"

"I don't know much about him. He's been with Skitty for years."

"Well, we'd best get to business, then." Schiller looked at me again. "You'll have to miss those chicken fights."

A number of enterprising Cherokees had dug fire pits near the cotton barn and were roasting pigs. We stocked up on a mess of this greasy fare and headed west into the growing evening. Of course Schiller had his saddlebags, well stocked with sardines and hard biscuits, but I preferred the pork. Yet like most of the food in this country, it was heavy on the stomach. Within a few hours of traveling, moving slowly along dusty roads with the Creek leading, the old saddle bruises along my thighs revived, and when we camped for the first night, I slept on my back with my legs apart. My nose ached, but when I touched it I could feel the swelling almost gone.

The land was turning gray with the dawn as we waited in the brakes along a bend of the Canadian River's north fork a few miles south of Checotah, Creek Nation. From about a mile away, we could hear a Missouri, Kansas and Texas freight moving toward the Choctaw Nation, the sound carried by a gentle wind that rustled the reeds and brush around us. In the near distance, toward the west, was a line of honey locusts, mostly old and twisted trees that waved and bobbed majestically in the wind, their masses of tiny leaves changing color as they danced and fluttered, catching the light of a new day.

Beyond the trees was a small, dilapidated farmhouse, the eaves drooping like rumpled covers from the corners of an unmade bed. Along with a few outbuildings, it sat in the midst of cleared ground, mostly uncultivated. We could see a clutter of trash scattered about the yard, and as the light increased, a few chickens began to move about pecking at the debris. We heard a rooster crow, but so far as we could determine, there was no dog.

The outlines of Skitty Cornkiller's farm came more clearly to view with the approach of the sun. I jumped when a mockingbird started his program of calls from a hackberry bush close behind us. Joe Mountain grinned at me and winked. From farther up the flats, where timber stood in uneven lines, a cock cardinal began his morning challenge, his notes fluid and precise as a symphony flute.

Moma July had told us that Skitty Cornkiller was half Creek: his father was an Indian, his mother a white woman, gone years ago to her people in Kansas. Left to himself, Cornkiller had turned to whiskey smuggling and let the farm go to ruin, although the black man tried to raise a little garden truck. We could see, close behind the house, the drooping turfs of radishes and a few green onions, some already gone to seed.

"It's light enough now so you can shoot, Joe, if you have to," Schiller said. The Osage nodded, his lips stretched across his big eyeeteeth. "All right. Let's get in fast."

We mounted and started pushing our way through the brakes toward the farmyard. Joe Mountain had his Winchester up and Moma July was holding a sawed-off ten-gauge shotgun. Neither of the marshals had drawn a weapon. The horses picked their way through the honey locusts. We could see clearly now a litter of tin cans and broken glass, a rusted plowshare, some old wooden crates, and a number of barrel rims, like children's rolling hoops left discarded haphazardly across the grass-less yard.

Moving quickly, we went down from the saddle, the two Indians before us. There was the frame of a screen door but no screen in it, otherwise the opening was unobstructed. Joe Mountain ducked in first, Moma July close behind, and we all followed. Burris Garret pulled a single-action pistol from his belt and cocked it, and I thought at the time that it was strange these Fort Smith marshals seemed to prefer the old singles over the pistols of more recent years.

There were two rooms. In the first were items of furniture that had the mark of quality about them, but like the house they had gone badly to pot. A large Rhode Island red hen was perched on the back of an ancient and scarred settee, and another walked calmly across a cold cookstove. In the other room was a four-poster bed and on that a bare mattress and on the mattress a sleeping man. He lay on his back, mouth open, undisturbed by our silent entry or by the many flies that had already begun to buzz about the room like tiny aerial whipsaws. On one of the bedposts was a cartridge belt and holstered pistol. Moma July lifted it quickly and handed it back to me, never taking his eyes off the sleeping man. We gathered about the bed as though it were an open casket of some departed relative and looked down at the man in his long flannel underwear. He had an erection.

Moma July jabbed the sleeping man with the muzzle of the shotgun.

"Skitty, wake up. You got company," he said.

Skitty Cornkiller grunted and rolled over against the wall, drawing his legs up so his knees almost touched his chest. He was slender and from my first impression I supposed him to be in his midtwenties. His hair was jet black and cut short. Although his skin was as fair as my own, he had pronounced cheekbones and a wide, thick-lipped mouth. Moma July punched him in the kidney with the shotgun, harder this time.

Cornkiller gasped and sat up, saying something explosive in Creek. His eyes were bloodshot, and as he tried to focus he sat there jerking his head back and forth, looking at each of us in turn.

"Wake up, whiskey peddler," Burris Garret said, and he reached over to take a handful of flannel underwear at the throat and yank Skitty Cornkiller to the edge of the bed.

The sleep was going quickly from the young Creek's eyes, and he stared at the big badge on the black man bending over him.

"God damn, mister, what's the matter?" he said, his voice thick with sleep. "What you men want?"

"We want to talk, Skitty," Oscar Schiller said. Garret pulled the Creek to his feet. He stood half-bent, the front of his underwear still standing out stiffly.

"God damn, mister. I gotta go outside. I gotta piss."

"Not yet you're not," Garret said. "Where's that colored man works for you?"

Cornkiller blinked, still stooped, staring at the cocked pistol in the black marshal's hand.

"God damn. What is it you men want?"

"Where's that hired man?" Moma July said, slamming the muzzle of the shotgun into Skitty Cornkiller's side. The young Creek drew back, his breath hissing through his clenched teeth, his eyes suddenly gone savage. He sputtered a string of unintelligible words, each one snapping out like popcorn from a hot pan.

"God damn, mister, don't poke me again with that thing. My man's out the barn. He sleeps the barn."

"All right. Joe, you and Officer July go get him," Schiller said. "Come on you, we'll get you outside."

They pushed Skitty Cornkiller out the front door, Burris Garret still holding the gun in one hand as he shoved the young Creek with the other. Cornkiller stumbled to the edge of the porch, fumbling with the buttons on his underwear. He turned away from us as though embarrassed to have us watch him relieve himself. Before he was completely finished, Burris Garret had him by the small of the back, pulling him inside.

The black marshal snapped handcuffs on one of Cornkiller's wrists, locking the other ring to the frame of the bed. By the time we moved to the back porch, Joe Mountain and the Creek policeman were coming toward the house, before them a black man pulling suspenders up over his shoulders. He was barefooted but on his head was a black Texas hat, and even from across the yard I could see the button on the crown.

"Stupid bastard," Oscar Schiller said softly. Then he turned to me and spoke vehemently. "Don't ever forget this, Eben. It's the stupid ones who are dangerous. They haven't got the sense to think ahead and they'll kill you quick as a snake strikes. A smart one always thinks twice about it."

"What is it you gentlemens want?" the man asked. They pulled him over, sat him down on the porch, and manacled his arms around one of the roof posts. He was smiling, showing widely spaced teeth, two of which were gold-capped. His face was scarred on either cheek and I thought at first it was some kind of crude tattooing. Thick bushy hair that had started to gray hung below his hat. He was a powerful man, the muscles of his arms and shoulders showing through the thin blue cotton shirt he wore. I judged him to be about forty-five.

"Joe, go in and watch that man we got chained to the bed and send Burris out here. I want him here."

We waited for Burris Garret to come out, Schiller dipping into his can of snuff and cocaine with a matchstick. When the black marshal stepped out, our prisoner's grin widened.

"Howdy, Marshal," he said. "I sure glad to see you here. I thought these men come to rob us. Why they got these things on me?"

He rattled the handcuffs against the porch post. Garret stepped before him and now the pistol was out of sight under his coat.

"We need to ask you some questions, old man, and we don't want you runnin' off."

"I ain't gonna run nowhere."

"What's your name, old man?"

"Nason Grube."

"You a citizen of the Creek Nation?"

"No sir, I ain't," he said. The sweat had begun to roll down the sides of his face, and as he spoke he flicked his lips with a long, pink tongue and looked around at us, a question in his muddy brown eyes. "Is you men after me, Marshal?"

"You just answer the questions, don't ask any," Garret said. "If you're not a citizen of the Creek Nation, what are you doin' here?"

"I works for Mr. Cornkiller on this ole farm. I come down here from Missouri and worked on the construction when they was buildin' the KATY line. I had me a permit onct. But I ain't no more. I guess you caught me out on that, Marshal, but I ain't gonna run off nowheres."

"So you're an illegal?"

"Yes sir, Marshal. I never was a Creek. I was a free Missouri nigger come to work the railroad, and I was legal then, but now I'm not."

"Where'd you get those marks on your face?"

He laughed. "I bet you thought they was like them marks on that Osage's face you got with you, that big man. But they ain't." His pink tongue flicked across his lips in a quick, darting movement. "Mr. Cornkiller sometimes gets mad with me and hits me with a stick of stovewood. He don't mean no harm. He's always sorry after he sobers up."

Garret glanced at Oscar Schiller and moved back. The white marshal, chewing his matchstick, stepped off the porch, moving close to Nason Grube.

"Where'd you get that hat, Nason?"

"Mr. Cornkiller give it to me. My ole hat 'bout wore out. So he give me this one."

"Where'd he get it?"

"He never said. I guess in Okmulgee or Muskogee, maybe."

"You sell whiskey with Mr. Cornkiller, don't you, Nason?"

"No sir, I never done that." He seemed to realize only then that we were on more serious business than rousting out illegals in The Nations. He sat with his legs over the edge of the porch, his large feet far apart, the toes splayed in the dust. As Oscar Schiller continued, Nason Grube stopped looking at any of us and let his eyes wander across the yard to his little garden patch, as though he expected some kind of help from his wilted plants.

"You went off to the Choctaw Nation not long ago, didn't you? You went down there and got yourself into some trouble, didn't you?"

Almost imperceptibly, Nason Grube pulled back against the manacles, knowing now that our business wasn't bootlegging, either.

"No sir, I never done that."

Schiller pulled the hat off the man's head, causing him to start violently. He handed it to me, and the red silk lining shone in the rising sun.

"Keep that safe in a saddlebag. We'll need it in Fort Smith."

"I ain't done nothin' to go to Fort Smith," Nason Grube said, his voice quavering. He was still contemplating his garden.

"Nason, I'm serving a warrant on you for murder and rape in the Choctaw Nation. You got one of them John Does, Eben?"

An expression of disbelief crossed the man's face and he pulled back against his cuffs. With the hat off, he looked older, his head covered with a graying mat of curly hair.

"No! I ain't never done no such of a thing," he said. "I ain't never in my whole life done no such of a thing."

I read him enough of the warrant to ensure that he understood why he was being arrested. All of it seemed incomprehensible to him. He sat there stunned, his mouth open, the pink tongue flicking out and the sweat running down the sides of his coal-black face.

"Officer July, you'd best keep a watch on Nason here," Schiller said. "Now, we better get to Cornkiller."

103

Before we went inside, Schiller said to me, "You remember that note we found in Johnny Boins' room?"

"I've been thinking about it ever since July told us Cornkiller's name," I said. "They had a man called C looking for that horse. You think it was Cornkiller?"

"You're damned right," Schiller said. "And that Creek whiskey peddler the girl said come through their farm, interested in the racehorse. All the same man. You're damned right."

At the thought of Jennie Thrasher, my throat tightened and I said nothing more. Oscar Schiller must have sensed my feeling because he turned away from me and looked at Nason Grube chained to the roof post. When he spoke, it was almost to himself.

"And that poor dumb bastard is a good bet for the nigger that kid told us about."

Nason Grube sat there, still, his arms pulled taut against the restraining handcuffs, looking into his garden. Moma July rolled a cigarette, lit it, and put it between the black man's slack lips. At first, Grube let it hang there, and then seeming to realize what it was, began to puff furiously, his eyes squinted against the smoke.

"He doesn't look much like a murderer now," I said.

"No, but he'd look a lot different with a belly full of whiskey. Before we get to Cornkiller, let me see that gun of his."

The cartridge belt was still slung across my shoulder and Oscar Schiller slipped out the small revolver. He swore softly.

"Hell's fire, this thing is a popgun," he said. "A Colt .32 double. Most of those wounds we saw at Thrasher's were bigger stuff."

"If he was there, it doesn't much matter who pulled the trigger," I said.

"Well, you're the lawyer," Schiller said as we turned into the house.

When we reappeared, Skitty Cornkiller leaped up awkwardly, one hand fastened to the bedframe. He began to yell that he hadn't done anything and he wanted to know who the hell we thought we were coming on his farm waving guns around. Schiller moved in close to him and with a sudden, vicious jab, his fingers extended, he caught the young Creek just under the ribs. I could hear the breath explode out of Cornkiller's lungs and he fell back onto the bed, doubled over, his short hair bristling out from the top of his head like spines on a chestnut burr.

Schiller drew up a chair close to the bed, and when Garret came in he was on the other side, pressing in, too, as though they were squeezing the young Creek between them. After a few moments, Cornkiller began to straighten and I could see a flicker of cold light deep in his eyes. He glared at Schiller and bared his teeth.

"God damn, mister, why'd you do that?"

"I want you to understand what serious trouble you're in, Skitty."

"I ain't in no trouble. I ain't sold any whiskey for a long spell. They ain't a drop on the place. God damn, you ain't got no call doin' all this pushin' and shovin'. I ain't done nothin'."

"You sell whiskey all over The Nations, and everybody knows it," Garret said. "You've been fined once and spent time in Fort Smith Jail once for it. Don't try to horseshit us, Skitty."

"I ain't sold a drop since you caught me last time, Garret."

"You were in the Choctaw Nation less than a month ago, with a mule loaded with whiskey," Schiller said. Cornkiller's head jerked back and forth as each marshal shot his questions. "We know all about it."

"God damn, mister, I ain't been in no Choctaw Nation."

"You were in there with a man named Johnny Boins," Schiller said. There was that quick light in the depths of Cornkiller's eyes, quickly shut off.

"I don't know nobody by that name."

"You're a big bettin' man, Skitty," Garret said, bending close to him. "You ever see a racer called Tar Baby?"

"I never heard of him."

"I didn't say the horse was a stallion. How'd you know that horse ain't a mare?"

"I never said he wasn't."

"You said *him*! You said you never heard of *him*!"

Cornkiller lowered his head. "I never heard of him."

Schiller reached over and with the cup of his hand under the young Creek's chin, lifted his face. The eyes were defiant.

"We like looking at men we talk to," Schiller said. "Now, Skitty, you were in Choctaw Nation with a man named Milk Eye Rufus Deer, not long ago, wasn't you?" Again that instant flash of light in his eyes.

"I never heard of no such man."

"I said don't horseshit us," Garret snapped. "Everybody in Creek Nation has heard of Milk Eye."

"God damn, Garret, I heard of him. But I never knowed him and I never been no place with him, not in Choctaw Nation nor no place else."

"Yes you were," Schiller said. "You killed a Choctaw woman down there, after you raped her."

"I never done no such a thing," Cornkiller yelled, spittle forming at the corners of his mouth. His eyes were like an animal's, caught in a steel trap. Close to his face, Schiller's glasses gleamed malevolently.

"You killed a Choctaw woman, and then you killed a man named Thrasher and his two hired hands, and then you raped his wife. And you killed her, too."

"I never, either," Cornkiller screamed, pulling against the cuffs on his wrist.

"You killed the first one, then you killed Mrs. Thrasher, too," Schiller roared and he leaped up, kicking back the chair. Suddenly the nickel-plated revolver was out, the muzzle pressed hard into Cornkiller's throat. The young Creek gagged, trying to pull back as Schiller pushed the gun muzzle into his neck. "I ought to blow your goddamned lying throat out right here."

Cornkiller's eyes bugged and he choked as Schiller rolled back the hammer to full cock. For an instant, I was sure he was going to kill the Indian.

"Nobody killed that Thrasher woman, she got loose . . ." He stopped, still gagging. The realization of what he'd said spread across his face like a blush. For a moment only, Schiller kept the pressure on Cornkiller's throat, and then as suddenly as it had appeared, the big pistol was back beneath the marshal's duck jacket. Skitty Cornkiller sat there, tears running down his cheeks, coughing, his eyes rolling.

"Oh God damn, mister, that hurt me," he sobbed. "You really hurt me, mister. Oh God damn, God damn."

If he knew what he was saying, the significance of it was obvious to us all. We had been waiting for the Choctaw police to report that they'd found the woman's body, but apparently she was alive, still in hiding, afraid to come out. If she could be found to bear witness . . .

"All right, Skitty," Schiller said softly, almost gently. "That's about all for now. Except you might tell us who did kill those people, if you didn't."

Cornkiller spoke without lifting his head.

"I don't know nothin' about it. I don't know nothin' about no killin'. I ain't gone talk to you no more, mister. God damn you."

"Well, it don't matter. Eben, you got another one of those warrants?"

I handed him a John Doe. Schiller slapped it on the bed beside the young Creek.

"Can you read, Skitty?" Cornkiller shook his head. "I'll read it all to you, then. We don't want you to make any mistake about this. You're arrested for rape and murder in the Choctaw Nation."

"We'll just take you down and turn you over to the Choctaw police," Garret said.

Skitty Cornkiller's head snapped back up and he looked wildly at the two men before him.

"God damn, Garret, you can't turn me over to no Indian police. You gotta take me to Fort Smith. That Thrasher was white. . . ." He knew as he said it that he'd made a second mistake.

"You don't like them Indian courts too much, do you?" Garret said. "They'll convict your ass in a hurry and tie you to a tree and shoot you to death, won't they?"

Schiller bent over him, still speaking softly. "Skitty, how'd you know he was white?"

"Well, God damn," Cornkiller stammered. "Well, God damn. It's in all the newspapers."

"You just said you can't read."

"Well, God damn. Somebody told me about it."

"You're under arrest, Skitty. But we aren't taking you to the Choctaw lighthorse. We're taking you to Fort Smith." Schiller read him the warrant. The whole episode left a hard metallic taste in my mouth. But I was confident Skitty Cornkiller was one of the Winding Stair bunch. I wasn't so sure about the black man.

In the barn, we found more evidence. There was a mule and a broken-down mare with the hair worn off her gaskins from trace chains. She had been as badly used as the rest of this farm. But there were two other horses, both good stock and showing signs of having been well kept. One was a bay gelding, the other a blue roan stallion, strong but past his time for prime breeding. The bay had a T brand on one flank.

"I'd say this is a Thrasher horse," Oscar Schiller said, running his hand along the withers of the bay. "He ain't Tar Baby, though, sure as hell. That roan, he looks like he might be called Ole Blue. Better take these two to Fort Smith. You might find somebody to recognize 'em, along with Skitty Cornkiller."

He was thinking of the black boy Emmitt, but he was thinking of Jennie Thrasher as well, and I saw the trace of a smile on his thin lips. I felt my anger rising, choking my words.

"What has to be done is pretty obvious, Marshal."

"Turn these other two nags out. From the looks of it, open range graze will be better than anything they've had here."

"They'll sure as hell eat Grube's garden," I said. "Why don't you take them in and sell them?"

His cold eyes turned on me for a moment, but then the smile was back, only a twitch but undeniable.

"There's no market for stock like this, or I would," he said. "And for Grube's garden, he's not going to be needing it anyway."

We shackled our prisoners together and sat them on the floor in the room where Joe Mountain worked over the cookstove, making breakfast. The two men were subdued now, almost resigned, and they told the Osage where he could find salt pork and flour for gravy. We gave them coffee while we waited for the food and twice Moma July rolled a cigarette for the black, though he refused to do so for Skitty Cornkiller.

There obviously existed a strange bond between our two men. It was as though the younger was father to the older. Like a child, Grube constantly watched Skitty Cornkiller's face as if trying to catch some unspoken thought, waiting for the opportunity to support or encourage the young Creek. And the Indian treated Nason Grube as he might a young girl, his expression guarded, his manner gentle. They spoke infrequently to one another, and then in Creek so that only Moma July and Garret understood what passed. I found it somehow typical of this place that an old uneducated black man had learned in his years in The Nations how to converse in another tongue. A number of times, they looked at one another silently. It was like a hunter and his well-trained dog looking at each other, the one with fondness, the other waiting command.

Neither of the marshals asked further questions of the two. Burris Garret sat in a chair tilted against one wall, watching the Osage scrambling eggs. Oscar Schiller had gone into the bedroom and sat there with the palmetto off, writing notes in his little book, his hair hanging damply across his forehead.

The prisoners ate awkwardly, their hands still cuffed. The rest of us made fast work of the greasy meal, Schiller insisting on moving out of there quickly.

When our little cavalcade reached the railroad tracks, Schiller pulled up and sat thinking, chewing on his matchstick for a long time before he spoke, staring out across the rolling country of the Canadian River bottoms, lush and green under the July sun. He was trying to make some kind of decision, I knew, and a great part of it was whether he would tell us what he planned. Finally, he motioned the black marshal and me away from the others, leaving Joe Mountain and Moma July with the prisoners.

"I been thinking ever since Cornkiller said that woman in Choctaw Nation had got loose," he said, and I knew he was speaking about Mrs. Thrasher. "If that's true, we ought to find her."

He turned squarely toward me, twisting in his saddle, his eyes cold.

"Eben. You're the lawyer on this chase. What's our chances for a conviction on the Thrasher killings with what we got now?"

"Not a strong case," I said, and because he was now including me in his thinking, my resentment once more began to disappear. "We can put them on Hatchet Hill road with that boy's testimony. But all we've got to put them at the Thrasher farm is that we tracked them there. Maybe . . . just maybe . . . Cornkiller can be identified as the whiskey runner out scouting for the racehorse. We've got what appears to be a Thrasher animal, and we've got the button hat, but both could have been bought from somebody else. And that note Johnny Boins forgot to burn, that doesn't prove much either. And the whore's story would be shaky."

Oscar Schiller grunted and looked off across the countryside again, nodding his head just enough to make the wide brim of the palmetto quiver.

"That's how I figured it," he said. "I've seen Parker juries convict on less, but I'd like to be sure, dead sure. We could hang 'em all on the Hatchet Hill thing, but that depends on whether we ever get that kid to telling his tale on a witness stand."

"Why wouldn't he?"

Burris Garret laughed.

"I want these people on the Thrasher thing," Schiller said. "If Cornkiller was right, and that woman is still alive, maybe she saw enough to put the whole lot of them at the scene. When the killings were done."

He spat the chewed matchstick off to one side and turned to me again.

"Now we've got a couple more of these bastards, the woman might not be afraid to show herself."

"We haven't got Milk Eye," Burris Garret said.

"I've got to try it anyway. Don't noise around what I'm up to. I'll ride up here to Checotah and take a KATY train and catch up with you later in Fort Smith."

He reined his horse away from us, glancing back toward the two prisoners.

"Take them two on in. And for God's sake, watch 'em close because if they do anything foolish, the Creek will cut 'em in half with that shotgun and we don't make any profit on dead prisoners."

We watched him as he kicked his horse along the railroad tracks, riding awkwardly as though his legs were too short for his feet to seat in the stirrups.

The day was turning muggy and hot, and a short time after we left the railroad embankment, Burris Garret and I shed our jackets. The Creek policeman kept his army coat on, but Garret and I were sweating our shirts damp.

At one point, we paused under some large sycamore trees to rest the horses and have some water, and I heard Nason Grube and Skitty Cornkiller break their silence with a few words in Creek.

"What are they saying?" I asked Moma July.

"The colored man, he says, 'What they gone do with us, Mr. Cornkiller?'"

"Yeah, and what did Cornkiller say?"

"Cornkiller says, 'They gone try and hang us, old man.'"

Ten

DURING OUR RIDE TO FORT SMITH, BURRIS GARRET TALKED WITH
the two prisoners as though we were all farmers going to market our
hogs. Nason Grube responded at once, smiling and flicking his long, pink
tongue across his lips, and after a while Skitty Cornkiller was talking,
too, with all the casualness of any good citizen not remotely concerned
with being accused of capital crimes. They spoke of crops and horses and
the weather and how The Nations had changed for the worse since the
railroads had started building through the country.

Moma July never joined in any of this. He rode or sat at the campfire
with hooded eyes, watching, holding that vicious short gun across his
lap. Oscar Schiller had been right. He was anxious for an excuse to use it.

It was incomprehensible that these two prisoners, wearing our steel
bracelets and suspected of rape, could speak so easily in our presence.
And it was equally unfathomable that Burris Garret could be so amiable
with two people into whose faces he had only a few hours before thrust a
cocked .45.

I came to know a great deal about the black marshal on that trip. He
was a truly gentle man, and a gentleman besides. When he was in school,
he told me, he had become interested in Creek law, but had finally given
it up. He reckoned that soon The Nations would become a part of some
United States territory and anything he might know about Creek law
would be of little use in white man's court. He was a great deal like Joe
Mountain, speaking of white man's government, white man's greed,
white man's encroachment on Indian country, doing it without any
embarrassment or excuse.

"Of course, white men haven't got a corner on that market," he said.
"Only thing is, they're better at it."

His straightforwardness and honesty were rare.

On the second night, Garret and I were drinking coffee while Joe
Mountain and the Creek policeman slept, soon to be wakened for their
turn at standing guard. Neither of our prisoners had given any indication
they might try to escape, but Garret insisted on two being awake to watch

112

them at all times. Of course, when we camped, we chained them to a tree. We had been amused at Moma July's snoring, and spoke of how the racket scared the night birds away. Then Garret turned serious, staring into the fire and sipping his coffee from the collapsible tin cup he always carried.

"I'll be glad when it comes," he said. "Making The Nations a territory. Since the war, people like me, black people who came here slaves and were freed, or the ones born here since, we've all been part of some tribe. I'm supposed to be a Creek. But hell, anybody can look at me and tell I'm no Creek." He laughed, his hat tilted back and the firelight showing on his high forehead. "Most of us don't really feel like we belong to The Nations, even though we belong to the land. I think we'd be better off if this was all a territory. I'd feel better about it anyway."

But later, lying with my legs apart still from the saddle soreness, I watched the brilliant sky with its pinpoint of July stars, and I wondered. Here was a black man, legally a red one, anxious to go from the society that had nurtured him. I could understand why he'd feel he didn't belong in the red culture, but I wasn't sure he'd find it any different when he became a part of the white one. There was an uncertainty in the man standing now with one foot in either, not satisfied with his lot among the Creeks and unsure of his future with the whites.

It was early morning when we came to the Arkansas River ferry. Halfway across the river, we could smell the fresh bread just coming from the ovens in the town's bakeries. Along the Fort Smith shore there were a number of people who somehow knew of our coming. It was a large group, mostly men and boys, and at first I was apprehensive. But they caused no trouble, wanting only to have a look at our prisoners. They gave way before Joe Mountain and Moma July, leading our handcuffed pair off the slip and along the street. Burris Garret and I followed with the horses.

"That's two of the sons a bitches," someone shouted. But other than that, the crowd was silent. For a moment I recalled what Judge Parker had said about quick justice and mobs.

Once we had our prisoners turned over to the deputies at the federal jail, Burris Garret and Moma July said good-bye. They were going directly back to the Creek Nation.

"That Milk Eye man can't hide out forever," Garret said. "Take care of that nose."

Moma July shook hands solemnly without speaking. I hated to see them go. Joe Mountain said he was going to the Choctaw Strip, a small slice of land on the Fort Smith side of the river just south of the federal compound on Belle Point and the site of the original fort. It was now a collection of ramshackle shanties.

"You need me, you send any of these Indians who hang around, Eben Pay." His grin widened. "They'll know where to find me." I had the suspicion that although he still harbored a lingering animosity against the Choctaws, he didn't let that get in the way of socializing with some of their women.

I went directly to Evans's office, hoping to catch him after his regular morning session with his assistants. There was a strong temptation to go up to the women's section of the jail, but I wanted some time before seeing Jennie Thrasher. Evans's morning meeting was apparently a busy one. He didn't come for two hours. In that time, I occupied myself with a flyswatter and read the various Fort Smith newspapers always scattered about the prosecutor's office. One story explained why local citizens had met us at the ferry slip. An account of the Creek Nation arrest was printed, with all the details, and for the first time Rufus Deer was named as a suspect in the Winding Stair Massacre.

When Evans came in, face flushed with the heat, I waved one of the newspapers before him.

"Look at this," I said. "Where'd they get all this?"

He threw a stack of papers onto the desk and slipped off his coat. His shirt was drenched with sweat.

"Well, I see you're back, and still with that sweet disposition," he said. He stared at my face over his pince-nez. "And I see all my informants were correct. Your nose is crooked as a dog's hind leg. How is it?"

"It's just fine, thank you," I said, still holding out the newspaper. "How did they get this?"

"It's all true, isn't it?"

114

"For once, yes. Of course, there are the usual misspellings of names." The newspapers persisted in naming me Eban.

"Oscar Schiller gave it all to the telegraph operator in Checotah the day you caught them," Evans said.

"For God's sake, didn't he know that was like coming right in with it to these newspaper offices? All these telegraphers are stringers."

"Oscar Schiller generally knows exactly what he's doing, wouldn't you say?"

"This is all over The Nations by now, just like it's all over Fort Smith. If Milk Eye didn't know before that we were after him, he sure as hell does now."

Evans sat down and flamed up one of his fat cigars, and when he looked at me I saw he was slipping into his professorial role.

"Milk Eye has undoubtedly known all along," he said. "Now, everyone else has the same advantage." He rummaged through the clutter on his desk and finally pulled forth a yellow telegraph paper and tossed it to me. It was a dispatch from Okmulgee, capital of the Creek Nation, signed by Governor Legus Perryman. It offered a $500 reward for the capture and conviction of one Rufus Deer, citizen of the Creek Nation. "You see, that's something that never would have happened if Schiller hadn't spread the word. With that reward out, there are a lot of people who might be tempted to help us a little."

"I can see the other side of it, too," I said. "A reward can make money for Deputy Marshal Oscar Schiller."

"That, too," he said, squinting at me through the smoke and holding both arms out to the side to catch some of the air circulated by the large ceiling fan. "But if it helps bring the son of a bitch in, more power to him."

I tossed the wire back onto the desk.

"All right, I can accept that, but not with very much grace."

He was twisting his head from side to side, staring at my nose, taking it in from all angles. In that massive beard, I suspected there was a smile.

"You know, I think that nose looks better on you now."

"If Joe Mountain hadn't pulled me out of that place, it would look a great deal worse."

"Yes, I know all about it. Everybody in town knows about it. How

115

you took on the whole Frisco railroad and how Oscar Schiller sent the Osage down to . . . well, let us say, to assist you."

"After I'd sobered up, I was grateful for it, but I don't take that with very good grace, either."

"You're a hardheaded man, Eben," Evans said. "Now, tell me your program."

I stood there gaping at him for a moment. It was difficult to believe that Evans was giving me any leeway. "I suppose we need to get a hearing set up with the commissioner, and get these two new ones over there, along with . . ."

He waited, but I wasn't ready to say it. Finally he nodded, and I was glad he was no longer smiling.

"Yes. Along with the colored boy and the Thrasher girl. You'll need to show them the horses first, over in the federal stable. If they identify those, that would be enough for the commissioner to bind them over for the grand jury. So no need for showing them the prisoners until the hearing. If they recognize the horses."

From Evans's knowledge of the details, I knew the wire Oscar Schiller had sent from Checotah had been to the prosecutor's office.

"I'll handle the presentation of the government's case. Let me know when the details are taken care of." He was going through one of his drawers and finally pulled forth a thick, folded paper and a badge. He laid them before me on the desk. "I almost forgot this. It came over from the marshal's office yesterday."

The badge was a six-pointed star imprinted with the words *United States Deputy Marhsal* and it seemed to weigh two pounds. The paper was a document prepared in the marshal's office and signed by Judge Parker making me a temporary special deputy assigned to the prosecutor's office in the case of the Winding Stair killings. I was completely dumbfounded.

"Now, this doesn't mean you're to hang a lot of iron on your belt and start running around The Nations arresting people," Evans said. "We'd have a hell of a time explaining to your father if you went and got your ears shot off. But with that, you can do a great deal more around here, with authority that is more than word of mouth. It'll take some load off me and the deputies."

Evans rose from his chair and lifted his right hand shoulder-high.

"Raise your hand. Do you, Eben Pay, swear and affirm that you will, to the best of your ability, perform the duties of special United States deputy marshal for the government and for this court, taking no fees other than those due you, so help you God?"

"I do," I said, feeling foolish.

"Sign the last page and leave it here," he said, and sat back down, yanking his chair close under the desk. He began to leaf through the stacks of papers lying there.

"So for now, go on, and let me know what you're doing from time to time. I've got my own work to do."

"I really don't understand this," I said.

Once more he peered over his pince-nez, a little impatiently.

"Oscar Schiller recommended it, and I approved," he said. "Now go, Eben."

That son of a bitch Schiller, I thought, but with the badge in my hand, I was in no mood for sour grapes. It was just a chunk of metal and a scrap of paper, I said to myself, yet there was about it an exhilaration beyond anything I'd yet known. It was better even than having the people of this court save me from my drunken brawls. I could only hope that someday I'd feel as good about passing my bar examinations. Outside Evans's office, I pinned on the star but got no further than the compound before taking it off and slipping it into my pocket. It made me feel as conspicuous as a naked man.

Commissioner Mitchell said he could take our hearing in two days, on Monday, though it would mean setting aside less serious cases. He asked me how soon Evans was going to the grand jury with the case and I told him we hoped to have all the members of the gang in custody before we presented it. He then congratulated me on becoming a special deputy and once more I was reminded that in Fort Smith the Parker court had few secrets.

"By the way," Mitchell said. "Johnny Boins' parents are in town. Staying at your hotel, they say. Hired a lawyer from Little Rock to defend their boy. The man says he'll ask the court to appoint him counsel for any of the other defendants in the case who haven't got a lawyer. Says it's all a put-up deal, by Oscar Schiller and the other officers of the court.

117

He's been in town once, while you were in The Nations, telling that story. Name's Merriweather McRoy. He's one damned fine lawyer.''

It didn't make me feel any easier about the case. Except for the black boy's testimony, everything we had was circumstantial. But I was too busy to worry with it then. I arranged to have Emmitt taken to the stables and look at the blue roan, and regardless of what Evans had said, I set up a window-room confrontation so the boy could get a look at Skitty Cornkiller and Nason Grube before the hearing. I held off on Jennie Thrasher. Let her see them first in the magistrate's court, when she was under oath, I thought, brutal as that might be.

At midafternoon, I went to the hotel to get out of my crusty field gear and take a bath. The high-heeled boots had put knots in my calves that hurt with each step. In the hotel saloon, the coolest place in Fort Smith with its open tubs of cracked ice behind the bar, I drank beer and had liver and bacon. The waiter seemed more attentive to my needs than usual. When I went to the cashier, he called me marshal and said there was no charge. I paid him anyway, embarrassed but trying to carry it off as casually as possible. I tossed two silver dollars on the counter and touched the brim of my hat with two fingers as I sauntered to the elevator. All pretense of calm disappeared when I walked into my room again. Jennie Thrasher was sitting on the bed.

"Hello, Eben," she said.

In the faint light from the window she was like a porcelain doll, cool and detached in this sweltering room, a smile sculpted on her full mouth, her hands lying in her lap. Her blouse was unbuttoned partway down the front and I could see the lacy top of a cotton chemise covering the hollow between her breasts. She looked altogether breathtaking.

She was up quickly, moving across the room and pressing against me as she threw her arms around my waist. Her eyes and mouth turned up to my face in open invitation, and I started to take her in my arms and carry her to the bed, to hell with Evans and Schiller and this whole case. But with a willowy movement she was away from me, laughing, teasing me with the rhythm of her body.

"Are you glad to see me?"

"Damn it, Jennie," I said, suddenly furious with the illusion she purposely gave, had always given, of some delicious feast just out of reach, and with no more substance than a fistful of July breeze. "What are you doing here?"

"My God. What happened to your nose, Eben?" She reached up and touched it lightly and I drew away from her impatiently.

"Never mind my nose. I ran into a Frisco locomotive. Now what in God's name are you doing here?"

"I wanted to see you," she said, her head tilted to one side in the way she had, and I realized she was a coquette beyond all the talent of any young woman I had ever found in Saint Louis society. The kind of woman I had always despised. But I did not despise Jennie Thrasher, and the contradiction made me more furious than ever, because it bewildered me.

"I got tired of that hot jail," she said, doing a little half-turn dance step, holding her skirt out to either side. "That old baggage Zelda Mores drinks a bucket of beer each afternoon when it's hot, and I just waited until she went to the privy and I slipped out. She's likely still sitting over there sweating and fanning her fat neck and not even knowing I'm gone."

"You can't do this," I said, slapping my hat down on the desk, where all my maps for father were still undone. "How'd you get up here? How'd you get in this room?"

"You were eating when I came in, and I told one of those nice men downstairs that you'd asked me to come over on official business, because now you're a marshal, and he sent a boy up here with a key because I told him we shouldn't disturb your dinnertime."

"Just like that, you told them I'd sent for you and they let you in, just like that?"

"Sure. I smiled at him." And she laughed.

There was the urge to charge across the room like a rutting bull and grab her before she could move that laughing, moist mouth out of my reach, to take her face between my hands and hurt her. But Evans's words, not to get involved, were stark and irrefutable in my mind. Jennie herself broke the spell, turning away from me and sitting on the bed once more, with an expression of complete detachment. Her face and mood were as mobile and intractable as a summer storm blowing in from The Nations, and it left me defenseless and miserable.

"Come let's talk, and give me a cigarette," she said. "I've missed our little talks."

I gave her a tailor-made cigarette and lit it for her and she puffed it a number of times, inhaling deeply and with a satisfied sigh. She patted my shoulder as though I were some pet dog or horse, but it felt good to have her touch me, even in that way. It came home to me again that the vision of a beautiful little girl, innocent and without defense—what I had seen lying on the bed at the farm in Winding Stair—was more illusion than reality. That I could sit near her and think such a thing was some sort of triumph, but I wasn't sure I liked it much.

"We've got to get you back to the courthouse. All hell's going to break loose if they find you gone."

"All right. But after I smoke."

"You haven't got any business wandering around the streets where anybody can get at you."

"I was lonesome," she said with a flash of temper, her mood shifting again. "Nobody over there at that damned jail likes me. You like me, don't you, Eben?" She didn't wait for my response, but rushed on as though afraid I might not tell her what she wanted to hear. "It's worse than the farm. Nobody to talk to and nobody who cares about me."

"That's not true, Jennie. We've got you in there because we don't want anyone to hurt you."

"Just because of the case, and you want me to talk all about it and I've already told you all about it. It's all just official, and you are, too. Sometimes you make me sick, Eben, really, you're so official."

"Listen, Jennie, we've brought in two men and a horse that may have belonged to your father and you'll have to come to the commissioner's hearing and tell us whether you can identify any of them."

"You see? You're so damned official." She puffed on the cigarette, turning it hot and red. She had switched on the ceiling fan before I arrived, but it did not stir the air enough to dissipate the smoke. "I read in the newspapers. You arrested a nigger and a Creek."

"For God's sake, don't say nigger!" It was a thing my mother had always impressed on me, but until now I had not realized how distasteful the term was.

"All right. Colored man. Colored man, is that better?" She jumped up and marched over to the window and stood there looking through the curtain at Garrison Avenue below. "Why should I know them? I told that old bastard with the beard that I didn't see anything that day. Why do you all keep bringing it up?"

I moved over behind her, close enough to smell her hair. Now was the time to tell her the best of it, something that I was sure would make her happy.

"Jennie, we think your stepmother is alive," I said quietly. "We're almost sure of it. Oscar Schiller is in the Choctaw Nation now, trying to find her."

Her back stiffened and for a long time she faced away from me, trembling. Then she whirled on me and her eyes were full.

"What? What did you say?"

"I said we think your stepmother is still alive."

With a shriek she flung herself against me, pounding at my chest with her fists. One blow struck me in the mouth and I tasted blood before I could react and pin her arms to her sides. The lighted cigarette had dropped onto the rug, filling the still room with a pungent odor of burning hair. As suddenly as her rage developed, it disappeared and she collapsed against me, sobbing.

"Oh God, my papa's dead and that bitch is still alive," she cried. "Oh God, God, God, my poor papa. What am I gonna do now?"

She was sobbing, moaning, gasping out words hardly intelligible, her tears wetting my shirt as she hung against me. Then she shuddered violently and pushed me back and sat on the bed, her head down, still crying. I had no idea what to say to her. I handed her my handkerchief.

"Here, wipe your face. Blow your nose."

"God, what am I gonna do now?" she asked softly. She snuffled into the handkerchief and looked up at me, her eyes red and her skin blotched. "I'm sorry, Eben. But me and her never got along at all. She's just an old bitch."

"But Jennie, she raised you."

"No! No, she didn't. Papa raised me. He always kept me close to him whenever he went anyplace, to races or up to Tuskahoma to build things for the Indians. He knew I never liked any of those people, and he knew I never liked that old bitch, and she didn't like me either, and he knew that, too."

I sat with her and she let me put my arm around her shoulders and

121

hold her near. For a long time she said nothing, wiping at her face with the handkerchief.

"Papa never sent me to the Choctaw school, the only one around," she said. "He took it on himself to teach me to read and to write. Sometimes in the evening we'd sit in the front room and he'd read to me out of his books. Then he'd go off to bed with that old bitch who was always fussing about me not doing enough around the house. Mostly, I stayed with Papa or the hands, in the barn or in the fields or the blacksmith shed. Papa let me because he knew I didn't like her."

"But she never mistreated you, did she?"

"Papa wouldn't let her do that. But she'd look at me with those black Indian eyes and I knew she hated me." She drew back then and looked at me a long time and touched my cheek with her fingertips. They felt cool and dry. "Let's go," she said.

"Yes. Button your blouse."

I was glad Joe Mountain had shown me the rear stairwell. Holding Jennie's arm, I moved her out into the alley and onto Rogers Avenue and along it toward the federal compound. We walked in the afternoon heat without saying anything until we reached the north gate, then she stood back from me.

"I'll go on from here alone. I don't want you having trouble with Zelda Mores," she said. "And Monday, I'll say whatever you want me to say at that hearing or whatever it is."

"Jennie, I just want you to say the truth."

"Oh hell, Eben, this is all such a mess."

"In the morning, I'll ask Zelda to take your over to the stable and look at that horse. He's a bay gelding with a T brand."

"It's probably Red," she said. She was looking toward the river now, and she seemed defeated. "If she's still alive, she's probably hiding on her brother's place down close to McAlester. He's got a big farm down there and she used to visit him all the time, always nagging Papa to take her down there. That's probably where she is."

She turned to me once more and lifted her fingers to my face.

"You're a nice man, Eben Pay. And I wish you were still in Saint Louis. I wish you'd never come. You don't belong in this place." And she turned and quickly walked into the compound.

Feeling a little sick, I was inclined to agree with her.

At the Frisco depot a northbound passenger was loading out and the station was crowded. But there was no one at the telegraph window and I sent a wire to Oscar Schiller, in care of George Moon at Hatchet Hill. I suggested that he look closely at the farm of Mrs. Thrasher's brother in McAlester. If the woman was alive, that's where she would be.

For the first time in my life, I felt the need, the real need, for a stiff drink of hard liquor. Back in my room, alone, I had it and sat in the growing darkness thinking about Jennie Thrasher and what she'd said to me. And about her stepmother and her father and how life had been for them all on that farm in the mountains. The more I thought about it, the more depressing it became.

NEXT TO SUCH THINGS AS smallpox and cholera, whiskey was the most malignant and destructive force on the frontier. There had been a history of liquor traffic in Saint Louis, of which most of us were only vaguely aware. There the French and later the English voyageurs had supplied their expeditions into the wilderness. The trade whiskey had moved up the Missouri, the Kansas and Smoky Hill, the Platte and the Yellowstone, a commodity both lucrative and insidious in white intercourse with the Indians. It had moved along the Arkansas, too, beyond Fort Smith and into the western country even before Indian territory was established there, and it continued well past the tenure of the Parker court despite all efforts to stop it.

It infected not only the red man but the white as well. There was, in 1890, an alcohol problem in the frontier army, within law-enforcement agencies, and among the citizenry at large, whether in high places or low. It was debilitating or caustic, creating lethargy on the one hand, violence on the other.

To many, it was the subject of jokes, the rough humor of the taproom, where it was variously called Pop Skull or Tiger Sweat or Panther Piss. But to many it was deadly serious and for some it shrank life expectancy at an astonishing rate. Not only for those who used it and suffered its physical effects, but for those who were the victims of men besotted with it.

No one ever attempted to explain to me the nature of its hold on so many. Nor why, regardless of its obvious bad effects, there never seemed an end to those who rushed to its addiction. In Fort Smith, I began to learn from experience some measure of its attraction. Yet to this day, the power of its appeal remains a mystery to me. And to every man or woman, it had a different use.

Sometimes, it was the happiness water. It provided bleared solutions to hard problems. It was the hallucination of well-being amidst the drudgery of existence. It was escape, from whatever dreadful reality each man or woman harbored in his or her mind. It gave courage where before there had been only fear. It lent color and excitement to a life that was in fact drab and dull.

For me, it vaporized loneliness. In college and later in Saint Louis, I had known its temporary qualities in the form of high-spirited larks and sprees with classmates or city friends. But in Fort Smith, its purpose became not to brighten experience, but to erase it. To blot it out, for a few hours, until everything became bearable again.

In that weekend when we were somewhere between the start and the finish of the Winding Stair case, I knew it as gentle anesthesia. As it took hold of me, there were times when the impulse came to go down into the city, to meet strangers and treat them as friends. To go find Joe Mountain, whoring in the Choctaw Strip. To go to Evans's home or even to Parker's, and play with the children and wait for an invitation to dinner. To go back to the federal compound and take Jennie Thrasher from the jail and bring her to my room again.

But each such impulse was quickly throttled. I still had enough reason left to realize that I could hardly walk across the room, much less on the streets of Fort Smith. The thought of being arrested for drunkenness by the city police, thrown in the city jail, was both horrifying and funny at the same time. But I stayed in my room, and thought, To hell with everybody.

I recall little of those two days. But somehow my good fortune did not desert me, and unlike so many who have fallen hard into the bottle on occasion, I had no desire to return to it. I never became totally drunk again.

Eleven

ANOTHER OF THOSE VICIOUS LITTLE SUMMER THUNDERSTORMS was brewing the evening we rode into Low Hawk Corners a few miles southeast of Okmulgee in the Creek Nation. There was Moma July, who had met us at the Muskogee train depot with horses, and there was Joe Mountain and Blue Foot. We were to meet Burris Garret at the small crossroads community from which he had wired that Milk Eye Rufus Deer might be in the neighborhood. Oscar Schiller was still in the Choctaw Nation, looking for Mrs. Thrasher. It brought a certain pride to be coming to The Nations on this manhunt without the little marshal who wore eyeglasses, but it gave me an uneasy feeling not to have him there. I knew Garret was a capable man and would have plenty of help from the Creek police if we needed it. But Schiller's absence left a blind spot in my confidence, much as I hated to admit it.

There was a great deal to put us in good spirits. On Monday, July 14, just three days before, the United States commissioner had conducted a preliminary hearing that disclosed sufficient evidence to hold Skitty Cornkiller and Nason Grube for the grand jury. They were in the federal jail without bail. Emmitt had recognized the Creek whiskey peddler as one of the men who assaulted Mrs. Eagle John on Hatchet HIll road, and the roan was indeed Ole Blue. The boy had not been so positive about Nason Grube, but under Evans's intensive probing he had finally concluded that he could identify the man as a member of the gang.

The bay we found at the Cornkiller farm was her father's horse, Jennie Thrasher told us, and she was positive in her identification of Skitty Cornkiller as the whiskey man who had appeared at the Thrasher farm showing such interest in the racer Tar Baby. She said the pearl hat had been her father's, beyond a doubt.

Throughout the hearing she had been calm, even stoic. She seldom looked at me, and then only when she thought I was unaware of it. I sensed no hostility in her, only a cool detachment, and I made no effort to speak with her, knowing as I did how she must have felt about being drawn deeper into the case. I had to admire her, although she seemed to give her testimony out of a feeling of resignation. Afterward, Evans had taken me aside to comment on it.

"I don't know what you did to that girl, but whatever it was, it worked. She'll make a good witness."

Evans and I had spent considerable time in the jail's visiting rooms with Cornkiller and Grube, trying to get some sort of information out of them, but both continued to insist they knew nothing about the crimes. Skitty Cornkiller said he had bought both horses and the hat from a passing stranger. He said he had a bill of sale on the horses but had lost it when he was drunk. They refused to admit knowing Johnny Boins, and for his part Boins would not talk with us at all. Merriweather McRoy, the Little Rock lawyer, had been with him a number of times by then, and any possibility of cooperation from the tall, handsome man had become a forlorn hope.

Low Hawk Corners was a settlement of less than a dozen buildings, the principal one being the store of Louie Low Hawk, a Creek who operated a general merchandising business and had for a long time been confidant and aid to the Creek lighthorse police. He was a smallish man, like many Creeks I had seen, but otherwise bore no resemblance to the common conception of Indian. His hair was brown, his eyes gray, and his complexion fair as my own. He was highly respected among his own people, I learned, having served a number of terms in their legislature. When I met him he was a member of the Creek school board, which handled the not inconsiderable task of administering the educational system in the tribe. He and Burris Garret met us as we rode up and directed us to the large barn only a few yards behind the store, where we stabled our horses. A number of mounts were in the stalls and I assumed correctly that Creek policemen had gathered there ahead of us.

It was growing dark and beginning to spatter a few drops of rain as we went to the store, a building typical of structures in that country— long and low with wide porches front and rear. Had there been a breezeway through the center of the place, it could have passed almost exactly for the Thrasher farm in the Winding Stair. Incredible as it seemed, the rainy night I had first spent at the farm was little more than a month before, yet the events compressed into that short time had affected me more profoundly than all the prior happenings of my entire life.

As we came up I could see an old Creek woman in a rocking chair at one end of the back porch. She watched us with black eyes in a face that was much the same in shape, color, and texture as a black walnut shell. Her features were etched, it seemed, in some hard substance, the lines and ridges so sharply drawn that one might not touch them without being cut. She wore an ankle-length calico dress, a ragged shawl, and a wide-brimmed man's hat over gray and thinning hair. As she rocked, watching us, she puffed slowly on a corncob pipe.

The inside of the store was no different from any other of its kind. Living quarters at one end, the rest of the building taken over by a long counter with a coffee grinder and hand-crank cash register, shelves and boxes and barrels, a cold potbellied stove, leather and metal gear suspended from pegs all along each wall, and two tables with chairs and benches for hangers-on. Along the rear wall, looking out onto the barren backyard and barn, were two large windows. A number of men were lounging about, watching us quietly with dark eyes. Most wore the canvas duck jackets and trousers so popular in this land, and in their drab immobility they reminded me of a tintype photograph, suspended in time on a metal plate. Some wore badges and all were heavily armed.

Burris Garret drew me to one of the tables and Louie Low Hawk brought tin cups of apple cider and bowls of chili. Moma July joined us, but he appeared tense and ate very little. Joe Mountain and Blue Foot, leaning against the wall in a space not occupied by any of the Creek policemen, ate standing, their rifles leaning against the wall behind them. A few customers came and went, mostly women and young girls, and each time Louie Low Hawk cranked the cash register it made a loud clanging like an aged fire engine.

"This is called a posse base of operations," Burris Garret said around a mouthful of chili. "You've never been involved in one of these, have you?"

"No. But it doesn't appear to be too clandestine."

He laughed. "Hell no, everybody knows we're here. But that's a thing can't be avoided. We can hope they aren't guessing correctly why we're here."

"We been tellin' around that we're after the horse thieves been stealing stock south of here," Moma July said. He had begun to smoke brownhusk-paper cigarettes, one after the other.

"Not even those policemen over there know why we're here or which direction we might ride out. Dawn tomorrow, we'll take a ride, and if we're lucky we might catch our friend Rufus Deer."

"We use Low Hawk's place a lot for this," Moma July said. "He's my cousin."

"What makes you think Milk Eye will be around here? If I were in his place, I'd be in Mexico or at least Colorado."

"He gets homesick. It's what I'm counting on," Garret said. He had finished his meal and took a gold-plated toothpick from his vest pocket and began to scratch at his teeth with it. "We've got an informant. White man, runs a brick kiln a few miles from here. Name's Orthro Smith. He calls his place Smith's Furnace. He's got a man who's been working for him off and on lately named Smoker Chubee. Now this Chubee has been seen from time to time with Rufus Deer, and he let slip the other day that Rufus was showing up at the Furnace. It's a hangout for a lot of these local studs. I think Smith sells whiskey up there, but we don't bother him as long as he keeps telling us things we need to know. So that's where we'll ride first tomorrow. If Rufus isn't there, we'll swing over past his folks' farm."

"The Deer farm?"

"Yes. Where Rufus lives with his folks when he's not out in The Nations someplace getting into mischief. Did you see that old woman on the back porch when you came in?"

"In the rocking chair, yes."

"Well, that's the old lady. That's Rufus Deer's mother."

"For God's sake, what's she doing here?" I asked.

"She and the old man, Old Man Deer, they rode into the Corners this afternoon in a wagon to buy some wire or something," Garret said, picking at his teeth. "With the storm coming up, they decided not to try and get home tonight. The old man is at one of the houses down the road. The old lady asked Louie Low Hawk if she could stay on his porch to keep from getting wet."

"She's done it before," Moma July said. "She just sleeps in that chair."

"She can't be blind," I said. "She sure as hell knows we're here."

"Of course. But likely she isn't sure what for. If she does, she's right where we want her to be. If she stays the night here, we'll get to her farm before she can in the morning. In case that's where Rufus is."

"But the old man . . ."

"One of my men is with him," Moma July said. "They're all playin' cards and likely drunk by now. The old man ain't goin' nowhere. He don't care what happens to Rufus anyway."

It all seemed pretty slipshod to me, but I could only assume these men were dealing with people they knew. Louie Low Hawk had brought a box of dominoes and we started to play, a coal-oil lamp on the table. There was a hard yellow cheese made from goat's milk and we chewed on that and listened to the rain and the coming of thunder from the west. I tried to concentrate on the game to dispel an uneasy feeling I had about the whole thing. The Creek policemen standing back against the wall watching us with those still black eyes did little to calm my nerves.

When it became clear that we would spend the night here, Joe Mountain came over and said he and his little brother would go find a bed in the barn.

"Joe, why don't you get some blankets from Mr. Lou Hawk and sleep on the back porch," I said. "I'd like it if you kept an eye on that old woman out there."

"That old lady in the rocker?" he asked, grinning.

"That's the one. If she leaves, I want to know about it right off."

"All right, Eben Pay. You want us to stop her if she tries to go someplace?"

"No. Just let me know right off if she does."

The two Osages left and Burris Garret laughed.

"That old woman won't go out in this wet."

"You told me you'd known her son for a long time," I said.

"Rufus? Sure, since we grew up together north of here. Rufus wasn't a bad kid. But he was always tough, making up for being such a runt. His mother was always a nice old woman, too. She used to make us sweet cornbread muffins."

"What happened to his eye?"

"He was born that way. You know, his own old man gave him that name. Milk Eye. The old man was just an uneducated Yuchi trying to rake out a living on a little farm. He was always ashamed of Rufus because of the eye. I think he felt like he was responsible for it somehow, and his own bitterness turned him against the boy."

"Rufus was always mean, but smart, too," Moma July said. "But he didn't go to much school."

"You've known him a long time, too?" I asked.

"Sure. He stole one of my daddy's horses when he was just a kid. We got the horse back when he tried to sell it in Okmulgee. The Indian court had him whipped. That was the first time he had any trouble with the law."

Burris Garret laughed, his gold toothpick still between his lips, sticking out through his beard like a tiny spike.

"Rufus was a little wild, even then," he said. "He and I used to go over to the Seminole Nation and raise hell. We stole a pig over there once. Roasted it on a sandbar of the Wewoka River and ate about half of it in one night. Got sick as pups. We must have been all of twelve years old."

"He got meaner every year," Moma July said. "He was carryin' guns everywhere he went when he was still a young 'un. But he always went to church with his mama."

"Rufus got interested in horse racing and chicken fights and all kinds of gambling," Garret said. "He always had plenty of money when most of us were still dead broke going through the academy."

"I never went to the academy," Moma July said.

"No, and you didn't get into all kinds of trouble, either. Rufus was suspect in a lot of the bad things going on around here. And I suspect he's been accused of doing more than he did. But he stole a few horses, and he was in on some penny-ante holdups over in Cherokee Nation. He started hanging out with some of the wild ones who were coming into the Territory in the seventies. Him still a kid. He got a reputation for visiting you at night if he didn't like you, killing your chickens or setting fire to your barn. People around here have been a little afraid of him for as long as I can remember."

"Does he still attend church?" I asked.

"Before this Winding Stair thing he did. He's a testifying Baptist. There was a white Baptist mission preacher a few years ago thought he had Rufus talking in tongues one night. But all Rufus was doing was confessing a few of his sins in Yuchi dialect."

It was still early when everyone began to stretch out on the floor for sleep. Louie Low Hawk brought bedding for Garret and me. We moved the table back and made pallets under one of the rear windows. The lightning was closer now, and after the lamps were out its light illuminated the windows in brilliant blue-white squares, coming sometimes slowly and flickering to full intensity only after what seemed a long time. Sometimes it crossed the entire horizon, running along like artillery fire in volley from west to east.

Before I slept, I went to the backyard privy and returned to the porch running through the rain. I paused for a moment to smoke with the two Osages. In the flashes of light from the lowering clouds, I could see them sitting against the wall, their rifles across their laps, and I knew they would sleep that way, if they slept at all. At the far end of the porch, the old woman rocked, and I was sure she watched us with those brittle eyes in the hard, wrinkled face.

"I wonder what she's thinking," I said softly.

"Maybe about her son, and us after him," Joe Mountain said, drawing on a cigarette until the red glow lighted his face and made pinpoints in his eyes.

Looking at her, I wondered what it was like to have a son facing the hangman in Fort Smith. The thought made me shudder, and Joe Mountain laughed.

"You better get in the house, Eben Pay. You act like you're cold."

During the night, the lightning came intermittently, sometimes waking me with the noise of thunder. The rain lulled me back into an uneasy sleep. The room was hot and I slipped off my jacket and boots and laid the shoulder holster and pistol beside my pallet. The floor was hard and the Creek policemen in the room were snoring in every discordant tone imaginable. It was well past midnight when I woke from a fitful sleep and sat up on the pallet, aware of some new sound.

In the dim flashes of lightning, I could see Burris Garret at one of the windows, looking out. As thunder rolled away, more distant now than earlier in the night, I heard a voice calling from the darkness beyond the back porch.

"Garret! Marshal Garret! Burris Garret!"

"What's that?" I whispered, but Garret hushed me with a hissing sound. I felt more than saw him moving across the room to the open door, and I scrambled up and followed him, hearing that voice calling once more.

"Garret. Hey, Burris Garret, come out."

I reached the porch behind him, and in the total darkness could see nothing. Rain dripped from the eaves, making a loud staccato rattle on the hardpan surface of the yard. In the next quivering light, coming from the east as the storm moved away, I saw the forms of Joe Mountain and Blue Foot crouched at one end of the porch, the barrels of their rifles silver. Garret stood at the edge of the porch in stocking feet, and I could see the heavy pistol in his hand, raised and cocked. As the light faded once more, dimly at the far end of the porch was the outline of the old woman in the rocking chair, moving gently back and forth.

The call came once more. "Garret? Is that you?"

I moved close behind the black marshal and he sensed me there and reached out a hand to shove me away from him, even as the next lightning flash spread the yard before us and the barn beyond, black and square, and at one corner a dark movement.

"Get back," Garret hissed. "Get back away from me."

I moved along the wall toward the Osage scouts, trying to see, and then with unexpected fury, the shooting started. The crash of gunfire cut jarringly across the faint blue glow of lightning and the sound of distant thunder, slamming against my ears, and I saw at the edge of the barn the brilliant orange slashes of black-powder guns. The window behind me shattered and there was the soft, moist splat of bullets striking the wall around me. I fell to the porch, remembering only then that my own weapon was back inside beside the pallet, and as I went down, Burris Garret began to shoot, and the two Osages, pumping long fingers of muzzle flash toward the barn. The din of it rattled my teeth, Garret's pistol making a hollow roar and the two Winchesters barking in harder, sharper tones. The guns made quick, hot blossoms of light, outlining the figures bent forward for only an instant.

I lay there panting, my heart pounding so hard against my ribs I thought at first I was hit. Then as suddenly as it had begun, it was over, and once more the only sound was the rumbling of thunder far away and the splatter of rain falling from the eaves in long, ditching lines along the edge of the porch. When the next lightning came, the first thing I saw was

Joe Mountain and his brother at the far end of the porch, their rifles still up, motionless and waiting. Looking quickly to the barn, I saw that whatever or whoever had been at one corner was gone and now there was only the square, stark building in the pale shimmering light.

Burris Garret was down, on his face in the yard at the edge of the porch, one arm flung out to the side, the pistol still in his hand. His stocking feet were on the porch, as though hanging there by the toes, and in the same glance I saw the rocking chair, swinging back and forth, back and forth, and empty now.

Scrambling toward the fallen marshal I shouted, and in the blackness after the fading lightning I slammed into a porch roof post and fell into the muddy yard. Men were coming out of the store, their weapons ready. Kneeling beside Burris Garret was Moma July. From the eastern horizon the storm flared up again, giving us enough light to see for a moment. Joe Mountain was there, thumbing ammunition into the magazine of his Winchester.

"I think they gone now, Eben Pay," he said. Across the yard, Blue Foot was running toward the barn and Joe Mountain followed him, splashing through the mud, running with long strides.

"Let's get the marshal inside," I yelled, and a number of Creek policemen helped me lift him, still facedown, and carry him back across the porch and into the store. Someone kicked over a sack of dried beans in the darkness, and they rattled across the wooden floor like shod mice. Louie Low Hawk struck a match and soon there were lamps lighting the faces of the Indian men bending over the wet and muddy form. I could see no wounds at first, but when we turned him over there was an ugly hole in his shirtfront and the blood was running out, staining the fabric a deep red, spreading across his chest and stomach.

"Get his clothes off," I said, my hands shaking as I fumbled with the buckle on his belt. "Somebody get a doctor. Is there a doctor around here?"

Louie Low Hawk, holding a lamp, his eyes puffed with sleep, shook his head.

"Nearest one's at Okmulgee."

"I'll go," Moma July said, and his voice had a strange, hard rattle.

"No wait. I want you here. Send someone else," I said. "Mr. Low

Hawk, get some towels and sheets, we need to make a compress."

There were three wounds. One in the ankle and another in the left arm, both with bones broken, but these were not as serious as the one in his lower left rib cage. The slug had apparently hit a rib and slanted upward through a lung and was still lodged somewhere in his body. Burris Garret lay with eyes open, a calm expression on his face, but when I tried to speak to him he gave no indication that he heard. A red froth was forming at the corners of his mouth.

Joe Mountain was in the door then, asking for a lantern.

"They gone, Eben Pay," he said. "But I think we hit something."

"You'll make a fine target out there hauling a lantern around."

"They gone now," he said, his teeth showing for an instant before he was gone again, pausing on the porch to light the lantern Louie Low Hawk bad given him.

The rain had begun to slacken off and the lightning was fading into the east toward Cherokee Nation, as though it had remained only long enough to illuminate the fight. I worked frantically on the body wound, but could not stop the bleeding. Louie Low Hawk brought cotton stuffing from a comforter ripped apart and I packed the wound and bound it tightly, wrapping a sheet around the body. Two Creek policemen had immobilized the other wounds with splints made from ax handles and bound with strips of cotton bolt cloth. Through it all, Burris Garret lay without any sound except a deep, gurgling rasp in his breathing, his eyes still open. Low Hawk wiped the blood from his lips with a handkerchief that quickly became crimson. There was no sign of pain on Garret's face, but the color of his skin had begun to change, the rich brown turning a pasty gray.

We could do nothing now but wait. Joe Mountain appeared again, without the lantern, and I knew Blue Foot had it somewhere out there in the night.

"Eben Pay, you better come look," he said. "We found something."

My socks were wet but I pulled boots on over them anyway and slipped into my shoulder holster and jacket. Louie Low Hawk handed me another lighted lantern. As we crossed the muddy yard, I could hear Moma July and a number of his policemen behind me. The rain had stopped.

At the edge of the barn where I thought I had seen movement just before the shooting started, the lantern light glistened on empty brass shells scattered on the ground. I stopped to pick them up and saw from the base of one shell that they were Winchester Center Fire .44-40s. We passed around the barn and into a lane set off on either side by a snake-rail fence. A few yards along the lane, I could see the glow of another lantern and Blue Foot beside it, his roach wet and clinging to his bald pate. He was squatting beside a huge form that I realized was a dead horse. I had never seen a dead horse before, and the thing looked monstrously big and grotesque.

It is difficult in lantern light to distinguish colors, but this was a very dark horse with stockings on both hind feet, and he was a stallion. My heart began to pound loud enough to hear as I bent and rubbed my hand across his flank through the wet hair. There was a saddle on him and when I lifted the fender, there was the T brand showing plainly. For a moment I stared at it, then straightened and looked at Joe Mountain.

"There's your horse, Eben Pay," he said. "There's your Tar Baby."

It is impossible to recall what I was thinking then. There was a leaden core in my gut, partly from the chili and partly from premonition that this case would never be finished now.

Blue Foot had picked up a muddy rifle somewhere along the lane, and he showed me the top of the barrel where I could read the engraving. *Winchester Center Fire .44-40.* He worked the lever and the chamber and magazine were empty.

"He shot it dry," Blue Foot said.

"We got something else," Joe Mountain said. "Come on."

We followed him between the snake-rails, the lantern light shining on the fence. There were goats bleating off to one side and in the darkness their eyes reflected our passing light. We had gone only a few hundred feet when Joe Mountain and his brother stopped beside the form of a man, lying facedown in the mud. Why do they all seem to fall on their faces, I thought.

"I told you we done some hittin' of our own," Joe Mountain said. There were at least two bullet holes in the back of the man's jacket, large and ragged, and I knew these were points of exit for large-caliber slugs. He was small and his hat was gone, the short black hair plastered tight

137

against his head. Finally, I bent down and pulled him over onto his back. Moma July, who had the second lantern now, held his light close.

The man was wet and muddy and dead, but even so I recognized the puffy features. His eyes were open, and one was the color and texture of wet gauze. I felt as though someone had just kicked me in the stomach and I expelled a long breath, looking down into the face I had seen only once before, ages ago, when Mrs. Eagle John and Jennie's father and those two Choctaw workhands had still been alive.

"And that's your Milk Eye," Joe Mountain said.

Still bent over the motionless form, Moma July muttered in Creek. Then he looked at me, his eyes bright in the lantern shine.

"It's Rufus. It's Rufus, all right."

With another exclamation in Creek, he turned and ran back toward the barn, the lantern he still held bobbing through the darkness until it disappeared.

"What the hell . . ." I said, but my mind was too full and muddled to make anything more of it. I felt buffeted by physical blows, much as Big Rachael had to feel after his bout with Dirty Jake. Joe Mountain and Blue Foot were still talking, their excitement bubbling up now that they had shown me their kill. I caught enough to understand that they had gone on down the lane until it petered out and found nothing more than a lot of horse tracks.

Two of the Creek policemen each took Milk Eye by a foot and began to drag him toward the store, and the rest of us walked behind, the two Osages still yammering. Milk Eye's arms were pulled up above his head and his jacket bunched around his neck as they yanked him along the ground, and before we reached the rear of the store, his shirt, too, had pulled up, revealing his slender belly and a dark puncture that still ran blood near the navel.

Louie Low Hawk came out to meet us, swearing softly when he saw what the policemen were dragging. They dropped Milk Eye's feet with two distinct sodden plops in the mud of the yard and left him lying there. Low Hawk said something about watching the body because of the stray dogs that were always wandering around the place.

Burris Garret was still lying where I'd left him, but now the lamps had been moved back and someone had pulled a blanket over his face.

"God dammit, God dammit," I said, bending close to the body and pulling back the blanket. His eyes were open and I closed them with my fingertips. His face was still warm. Everyone stood back away from me, along the walls, watching silently. I covered his face again.

"Where's the old woman?" I asked, my voice choking. Louie Low Hawk looked at me questioningly and shook his head.

"What old woman?"

"The one in the damned rocking chair. Milk Eye's mother."

"I reckon she run when the shooting started."

"Like hell she did. She sat there through all of it, then she was gone."

He shook his head again and shrugged, and his expression told me he made no connection between the old woman and the shooting.

"I don't know where she's at. But Marshal Pay, there's something you ought to know. Burris said something just before he died."

"He said something?"

"He tried to talk right after you left. I couldn't make anything out at first. I got down close to him and he said, 'Smoker Chubee.' That's what he said. He said it twice."

My mind was so fogged, the name made no impression on me.

"Smoker Chubee? What does that mean?"

"It's a name. The man's been working for Orthro Smith at the Furnace. Burris said, 'Smoker Chubee. Smoker Chubee's voice out there.' Then he died."

"Are you sure of that?"

"I'm positive, Marshal."

"And he works at the Furnace? God damn, man, we've got to get up there with this posse." I must have sounded a little frantic because Louie Low Hawk took my arm and held me firmly.

"Moma July's already gone. If Smoker comes back to that Furnace, he'll have him."

"Did he take men with him?" I asked, looking around the room, and from the number of them still there I already knew the answer.

"No, he went by hisself. Don't fret, Marshal Pay. If Smoker goes back there, Moma July will have him."

"Yes, and probably blow his head half off with that damned shotgun."

"We can't stop it one way or another now," Louie Low Hawk said, in the tone I suspected he would use to soothe an angry child. "You'd be too late if you started now. Whatever's gonna happen has already happened, most likely, or will before you could get there. Why don't you come back in the kitchen for a cup of coffee?"

Strangely, with his mention of it, this place suddenly smelled like fresh-ground coffee. My mind darted from one thought to the next, and I seemed unable to control it. The unexpected viciousness of the night's events was pressing down on me with smothering weight. Louie Low Hawk continued to talk, but his words meant nothing to me. I could only look down at the bundled figure of Burris Garret and think that but for his last words for me to get away from him as we stood on the porch together, I might be lying there, too, riddled with bullets that came from the red flashing night.

"Mr. Low Hawk," I cut in. "Have you got any whiskey?"

It startled him and he drew back, and I sensed a tension in the room from my words, spoken too loudly and too harshly.

"That's again' the law," he said.

"I'm not trying to arrest you," I said, waving a hand impatiently. "But I need a drink and someplace to think."

With considerable hesitation he led me back into his living quarters, where a number of women were gathered around a cookstove jabbering in Creek, standing in their nightgowns. As we entered they were silent, watching us until Louie Low Hawk said a few sharp words and they withdrew into another part of the house, looking back at me as they went.

I sat at the kitchen table and Louie Low Hawk brought me a half-gallon jug and a cup, explaining this was for medicine only, and not for sale. Joe Mountain came in and said something about a bad night with two men dead and a good horse besides. Then he and the Creek storekeeper left me there alone and I tried to think of what needed doing. There was no one else left to give this thing direction, but I was immobile.

I thought of the name, Smoker Chubee, and knew we should mount a posse and go after him. I thought of the two Osages with their rifles out there in the darkness of that porch when the shooting started, and of Rufus Deer's body lying spread-eagle in the yard. And I damned Oscar

Schiller for not being here. But always, my thinking returned to the figure of Burris Garret, stiffening now in the next room but once bending across a fire toward me and telling me of his dreams for The Nations becoming a United States territory, a dream he would never see. I thought of his high, handsome forehead and his dark, penetrating eyes, and it became very difficult to control my emotions. I knew there should be bitterness and hatred because of what had happened, but somehow there was nothing but a total loneliness, an empty sense of frustration and inadequacy and loss. We had yet another of our Winding Stair killers now, but it was not worth the cost.

Twelve

BY DAWN, THE SKY WAS CLEAR AND THE SUN CAME HOT AND blistering. Before the people of the community began to gather, some of the men in our posse washed the mud from Milk Eye Rufus Deer's face and lay his body on a door unhinged from the barn. They took the rifle we had found in the lane and put it under his folded arms, and one of them with a Kodak box camera snapped his photograph. His eyes were still open.

As though by some prearranged signal, when this ceremony was completed, the people appeared. There were a few whites, but mostly there were Creeks, and they stood in a large circle, well back from the small body still lying on the door, but now without the rifle. That had been handed over to Joe Mountain for safekeeping until our return to Fort Smith.

Their young came with them, and their dogs, all held back a respectful distance. I could see no sign of mourning on their faces. It seemed they came to view some ghastly sideshow that passed only infrequently and wanted the opportunity to tell their grandchildren they had been there. Not a word was spoken. The only sounds were the bleatings of Louie Low Hawk's goats behind the barn and somewhere to the west a mourning dove making his low signal that the rain had passed. With the exception of a few men wearing red or yellow neck scarves, they were a colorless group, a study in gray and faded blue or tan work clothes bleached even more by the harsh rising sunlight.

The Creek policemen allowed the people to have their look, and then lifted the body from its resting place and wrapped it in blankets secured with heavy hemp rope.

After they had Milk Eye's body laid out on the porch, they came inside for Burris Garret. I had some inclination to protest, but decided against it, for he was after all a part of these people although of a different color. They took the cover off him and lay him on the porch near Milk Eye, and it occurred to me that one of the purposes of these long porches was for laying out the dead. Still wordlessly, the people passed by the body of the marshal and a few of the men took off their hats for a moment. Soon it was over, and they began to disappear, each going back to kitchen or barn or field to begin the day's work. The policemen wrapped Garret as they had Milk Eye.

I heard a wagon coming near and soon it drew up at one end of the porch. A small man, looking very old but somehow familiar, got down and with two policemen helping, lifted the body of Milk Eye and slid it into the back of the wagon. I knew this was Old Man Deer, and on the wagon seat, her hat off now and the shawl pulled up over her head like a heavy veil, was the old woman. She sat looking straight ahead, her face hidden under the shawl, her hands folded in her lap.

When the body was safely stowed, the old man came back to the porch and stood for a moment staring at the mummylike form of Burris Garret. Watching from a rear window, I could see no expression on his face, no sign of emotion. Then he went back to the wagon and climbed to the box and whipped his mule, driving across the backyard and leaving deep ruts in the still-wet ground.

Louie Low Hawk was writing out what amounted to a coroner's report, another of his duties in this place, where I had learned he was not only a member of the school board but mayor as well. He told me he would send it on to Okmulgee. Two men killed, he wrote in laborious English, one the result of ambush, the other at the hands of federal officers from Fort Smith in defense of their lives. After he finished, he wrote a second one for me, identical to the first, signed it and sealed it with red wax, into which he imprinted his initials.

"We don't know whether it was Burris or your Indian scouts who hit Rufus," he said. "It could have been both. But now, with the family taking Rufus home to bury, we'll never know. And it's just as good. I'd as soon not mention that maybe the ones who helped kill him were Osages. Some of my people might not like that. So I just said federal officers."

"I didn't see any signs of grief over his death out there."

"No. Our people weren't proud of him and the things he did, and a lot of them were afraid of him. But he's still one of us. I'd as soon leave it uncertain who actually hit him."

During all of this the Okmulgee doctor had arrived. He was a white man who had known Burris Garret for years and spoke highly of him as a peace officer and as a man. We discussed disposition of the body. I knew there was no money available from Fort Smith for the burial, and I gave the doctor twenty-five dollars to help with the expenses. He assured me it would be handled in the best possible manner. He would take the body back with him to Okmulgee, along with Louie Low Hawk's report of the incident, and some of the Creek policemen would ride with him as a guard of honor, more or less. My impression that Burris Garret had been well liked in this country was confirmed when Louie Low Hawk said that if Smoker Chubee was caught, he'd best not be kept around the Corners too long. Some of the local citizens might try to take the law into their own hands.

I was still hesitant about going out after the man whose voice Garret had recognized. There was a pattern of confusion in my thoughts. I wasn't sure I had the authority to mount a posse. Besides, having seen Oscar Schiller work, I had learned that one must plan ahead clearly in such dealings, and I couldn't escape the idea that for lack of that, Burris Garret had paid with his life. At any rate, my mind was not functioning clearly.

As it turned out, the matter solved itself. Shortly after the doctor and his escort of Creeks departed, someone ran in to say two horsemen were coming down the lane behind Louie Low Hawk's barn. One of them was Moma July. I felt great relief, but no personal pride, because things were developing not because of any plan but in spite of my indecisiveness.

They rode round the corner of the barn and into the yard, Moma July in the rear with his shotgun across his saddle. Leading was a dark-faced man manacled and hatless, his black hair swept back from his face. As they came up, I saw it was a deeply pockmarked face, but otherwise strikingly exotic and well formed. His skin was the color of ebony, yet his features were Asiatic with a finely formed nose, narrow and straight between prominent cheekbones and over a wide mouth and clean-shaven jaw. His eyes were black, set wide apart and slightly slanted under brows so fine they appeared to have been plucked. I supposed him to be under forty, rather heavy in body but tall enough to take the weight without any appearance of obesity. His glance swept across the yard and the Creek policemen waiting there.

As they drew rein, Moma July searched out Joe Mountain among us and nodded.

"You Osage boys hit another horse last night. This one," and he waved the muzzle of his shotgun at the man mounted before him. "He come to the Furnace riding a little bay shot all to hell. Hadn't been for that, he'd have beat me there and been gone."

Louie Low Hawk was close behind me as I waited on the edge of the porch, and he said, "That's him. That's Smoker. I told you Moma July would get him if he was there to be got."

Creek policemen moved around the horses and pulled Smoker Chubee down, roughly shoving him forward to stand in front of me. He seemed unaware of them and their hard hands on him, watching me alone now, his black eyes hot as Oscar Schiller's blue ones were cold. When I stepped off the porch, our faces were on a level. He stood there with his back straight, his head up, and a breeze that had started up from the west stirred his hair and dropped a shock of it across his face. It was longer than I had supposed and partly covered his eyes.

"Are you Smoker Chubee?" I asked.

"I am," he said, and his voice was deep and clear. He stared directly back at me.

"I arrest you for the murder of United States Marshal Garret."

A sardonic smile crossed his mouth for a moment before he spoke. "On what evidence?"

"We'll make that clear to you in Fort Smith," I said, and it was beginning to anger me.

"Have you got a warrant?"

"No, but I'm arresting you on strong probability. And it occurs to me that you are likely a man wanted for another crime in the Choctaw Nation. Done in company with your friend, Rufus Deer."

"I've never been in the Choctaw Nation," he said, still smiling.

"How long have you known Rufus Deer?" I asked. He shrugged. "Well, it's long enough for you to be known in these parts. Where were you the first week of June?"

"What authority have you got for asking me all this horseshit?"

"I'm a special deputy marshal from Fort Smith."

"Special for what?"

"That's none of your concern. Would you rather I rode off from here and left you for a Creek court?"

Smoker Chubee looked around at the men standing near us, all watching closely. He did it almost casually.

"No, I think I'll take my chances with Parker."

"All right. Where were you the first week of June?" I asked.

"I don't keep track of such things," he said. "Probably in Seminole country or maybe up in the Cherokee Outlet. How the hell would I know?"

"It may be to your best interests to prove you were somewhere other than the Choctaw Nation during that week." I took the last of the Winding Stair John Doe warrants from my jacket and served it on him and he stood listening to me, smiling, looking squarely into my eyes. His teeth in that dark face seemed the whitest I had ever seen. There was something disconcerting about his manner, something at once infuriating yet admirable. Johnny Boins had been flamboyant. Smoker Chubee was confident and direct, almost insolent. He acted as though we were all some lower form of life beneath his serious consideration.

Moma July had brought back two weapons. One was a Marlin rifle chambered for .44–40 ammunition he said Chubee had in his saddle boot. The other was a Colt single-action .45 found at the Furnace. It was a handcrafted weapon of outstanding workmanship, with walnut grips into one of which the initials SC had been carefully burned. I had never seen such an excellent weapon in this part of the country, where such things were generally taken for granted and treated like plows or empty coffee cans, thrown about carelessly on woodshed or pantry shelves. I concluded that Smoker Chubee was a thoroughly dangerous man, the most dangerous we had taken, and it amazed me that it had been done so easily by one stocky little Creek policeman.

Everything moved quickly then, because Moma July and Louie Low Hawk made it so. It was obvious that they felt to keep Chubee here long would be to invite some ugly reaction from the local citizens who had held Burris Garret in such high esteem.

"And besides," Low Hawk said, "there will be some who think he ought to be tried in a Creek court because all the people killed were members of the Creek Nation."

"But a federal marshal was murdered, and that's reason enough to take him to Fort Smith," I said.

"You let him get into the hands of a Creek court," Moma July said, "and you won't have anything to take to Parker but a dead man."

"He'll be tried in a hurry, you can count on it. Anybody who kills one of Parker's marshals gets quick attention."

"You get your subpoenas for witnesses back here, and we'll be ready to testify," Louie Low Hawk said.

"Yes, and keep your eye on this Orthro Smith at the Furnace. We want him."

"He'll be there."

Moma July rode with us a short distance, along with a number of other Creek policemen. But he said he would like to get to Okmulgee and see to it the funeral was done properly. We paused along a row of thorny hawthorn trees bordering a cultivated field, seeking such little shade as there was in the growing heat.

"Garret never had a wife," Moma July said. He took off his hat and wiped his face with a red bandanna. "But he's got brothers and sisters and an old mother. I'd like to be there. These men can ride on with you."

"That won't be necessary," I said. So long as Joe Mountain and his brother were with me, I felt confident in getting our prisoner back to Fort Smith.

"All right. Now, if I was you, I wouldn't go to Muskogee. The people there knew Burris, too. Slip around it to the north and head for Fort Gibson into the Cherokee Nation. Get clear of Creek country fast and catch your train at Fort Gibson."

"What about your horses?"

"Leave 'em at Fort Gibson. They're Creek horses and the police there will hold 'em until I send someone to pick 'em up in a day or so."

"There's a thing I wish you'd do for me," I said.

"I'll do it."

"Get a telegram off to Oscar Schiller. Send it to George Moon, at Hatchet Hill, down in Choctaw. Tell him we've killed Milk Eye and we've got another Winding Stair suspect we're bringing into Fort Smith."

"Yes. I'll do it."

"And tell him Marshal Garret's been killed."

147

"I'll do that, too."

I held out my hand to him and he took it.

"Moma," I said. "You've done a lot for us."

For a moment he stared at me, and I thought he was about to smile, but then he shrugged and took his hand away and slapped his hat back on his head. I watched him ride off and thought about him dashing out into the night alone after a man who had just proven his deadliness. It was a strange sensation, this admiration for a man with whom I had so little in common, and had he appeared at my home in Saint Louis, I suspected my mother would feed him at the back door and send him quickly away.

We rode on for a while and Joe Mountain turned to me and grinned.

"You're gonna make one damned fine marshal, Eben Pay."

"I have no intention of continuing in the work," I said. "When this is all finished, I'm going back to Missouri and take my bar examinations."

But I recognized it for a rare compliment and found myself liking it very much. And I thought of Oscar Schiller. I knew he would view the killing of Milk Eye Rufus Deer as a mixed blessing. Because the little Yuchi's family had taken the body, we would not have to pay his burial expenses out of travel money, as was usually the case. But neither would anyone collect the reward money offered by the Creek chief. There was a stipulation in that about a conviction in court, and now Milk Eye would never get his day in court.

The sun lifted before us as we rode northeast into its glaring light, headed for the Missouri, Kansas and Texas railroad bridge across the Arkansas outside Muskogee. Only a few miles beyond that would be the Cherokee Nation and Fort Gibson and the tracks of the Kansas and Arkansas Valley line into Fort Smith.

At first, there were gnats and flies whipping around our sweating faces, but soon the heat was enough to drive them to shade. We rode the edges of plowed fields and through clover pastures where cattle grazed. On the higher ground, there were patches of hop hornbeam, the ironwood trees used by the old prairie and plains tribes for lances. Along the small streams we crossed were black willows. And the red bud trees, their lavender blooms long since replaced by the delicate heart-shaped leaves. All around us were meadowlarks and quail, and above us the turkey vultures and Cooper's hawks, hunting.

We pushed the horses hard, but had to stop often to breathe them in the heat. Mostly, we were silent, each man with his own thoughts. For myself, it seemed incredible that only a few hours before, when we'd found the dead Tar Baby behind Louie Low Hawk's barn, I had despaired of ever settling the Winding Stair case. Now we were going into Fort Smith with the last member of the gang, I was sure, and it was finished. Except for the trying.

A T THE NORTH END OF THE federal courthouse was the room where Judge Isaac Parker sat in judgment. It ran the entire width of the building, with polished oak floors and a high whitewashed ceiling. To those news-papermen and other visitors from the East who came to watch this famous tribunal in action, it probably was a great surprise to find that it looked like any other federal courtroom of the era. There was nothing of the raw frontier associated with so many justices and courtrooms of the Old West. It was marked by order and formality. It was a federal court, governed in its conduct by the laws of Congress and, after 1889, sub-ject to appellate review by the Supreme Court of the United States.

As one entered from the main hall the spectator section was to the right, with high windows behind looking out onto the court-house compound, the churchlike pews polished bright from the trouser seats of those hundreds who at one time or another had sat there watching justice as it oper-ated in Fort Smith. At the center of the room was a sturdy wooden railing, setting off the official from the unofficial areas. Beyond that railing were tables for the de-fense and the United States attorney, in front of which was the clerk's desk. Along the far wall and next to a small fireplace was the jury box, its twelve swivel chairs made of oak, as were all the court furnish-ings. Before the jury box was the witness stand, and beside that, a small table used by the court reporter.

Dominating the end of the room was the judge's bench, a high bar with a green felt top, and behind that and the leather upholstered chair spread a back wall of wood that looked like a massive headboard on a four-poster bed. To the right stood a standard with the national colors. Throughout the room, placed strategically, were huge brass cuspidors polished to a high shine.

Opposite the jury box was a door that led into a corridor and thence into the jury room and the judge's chambers and finally back into the main hall. Directly across the hall at that point was the entrance to an open passage that terminated at its far end in the jail. Defendants marched along this route to their day in court. If they were considered dangerous, they were shackled and wore leg-irons. Escorted by a small army of deputy marshals, they clanked past the end of the main hall, where citizens gathered to gape at them, on past the judge's chambers and the jury room, and out into the courtroom. It was a short and dreadful walk.

Sessions of court were attended by a number of deputy marshals, one of whom acted as bailiff, and others who were charged with guarding the defendants. There were always a few in the spectator section, watching the people who were watching the proceedings. At the door were two more of them, making a second search for weapons as the people filed in, the first having been made by another pair at the outside door to the main hall.

Before court opened there was a carnival atmosphere in the spectator section, men calling back and forth to one another, laughing and joking, discussing crops and cattle in loud voices. When the defendants were brought in, the noise suddenly ceased. All knew that Parker would be close behind to mount his throne that reminded many of a pulpit in a great church. Waiting, they sat leaning forward, like obedient schoolchildren, for Parker had been known to levy heavy fines on anyone misbehaving in his courtroom.

In this hush the bailiff would rise, face the crowd, and intone with as much dignity as he could summon:

"Oyez! Oyez! The Honorable Court of the United States for the Western District of Arkansas, having criminal jurisdiction of the Indian Territory, is now in session, the Honorable Isaac C. Parker presiding. God bless the United States and the honorable court!"

Thirteen

IT WAS ALMOST AUGUST. OUTSIDE, THE SUN BEAT DOWN WITH a merciless glare on the compound and there was no breath of wind stirring. In the courtroom, people sat in shirt-sleeves or cotton blouses, busily waving before their wet faces cardboard fans with large black letters proclaiming the benefits of Indian Blend nostrum for rheumatism and neuralgia. They had come early, anxious to see the trial newspapers were heralding as the preliminary show to the Winding Stair case. Some had lunch pails or brown sacks filled with sandwiches, unwilling once they had a seat to give it up if the proceedings went beyond noon.

As yet, Evans had not gone to the grand jury with the John or Thrasher cases. We had heard twice from Oscar Schiller in Choctaw Nation, but he had not located Mrs. Thrasher. I had begun to despair that he ever would. At least, the boy Emmitt had identified Smoker Chubee as the "dark man who just sat on his horse and grinned." When we showed him the Colt .45 found among Chubee's things at Smith's Furnace, he told us it looked like the big pistol the dark man had fired at him when he ran from the scene on Hatchet Hill road.

During those long, hot days after we brought in Smoker Chubee, I had been working on unrelated cases. Evans explained that he wanted me to have no further part in Winding Stair in view of my being a possible prosecution witness. I had not seen Jennie Thrasher throughout that time, but had talked with Zelda Mores. After the Cornkiller and Grube hearings before the commissioner, Zelda said, Jennie had stayed close to the jail, seldom leaving her room on the top floor. She had asked for books and spent her time reading. I could imagine, as the days grew hotter, how miserably uncomfortable she must have been. I had, on many occasions, given Zelda money to buy Jennie ice creams from one of the Rogers Avenue shops, and had secretly hoped the girl might ask to see me. But she made no response to these feeble overtures. Twice I dreamed of her, but her features seemed to be slipping from my memory, and that made me all the more eager to see her once more.

Merriweather McRoy, the Little Rock attorney, had been in town throughout much of this time, working on his defense for Johnny Boins.

153

He had volunteered his services to Smoker Chubee for nothing more than the nominal court fee paid appointed defense counsels. It bothered me that he wanted this case, but Evans was unperturbed.

"Old Mac just wants to test me in court. He doesn't give a damn about Chubee. But we haven't been adversaries since right after the war, in central Arkansas. He wants to get the feel of me before we get into the John and Thrasher thing."

The Smoker Chubee trial would be my first opportunity to observe Judge Parker preside in court. On that sweltering July morning, only he and Evans were wearing coats. And over his coat, Parker wore the black robe of office. My first impression of him was his intensity. His blue eyes followed each witness to the stand and he seemed to listen with total concentration to every word spoken. From time to time, he pushed a pair of steel-rimmed glasses onto his nose and made pencil notes in a large pad before him. But generally, he held the spectacles in his hand, and sometimes as he became impatient he tapped them lightly on the green felt top of the bench. Now and again he lifted a gavel and seemed to fondle it with both hands as he listened to exchanges. At his side were a number of lawbooks, most of them the statutes of Arkansas. For, like most federal courts of that period, in cases not specifically covered by federal law, precedents followed were those of the old English common law and sometimes of the state in which the court sat.

Parker gave every appearance of a man accustomed to great power. Yet somehow, in his unusual position, the sense of power seemed to make him both confident and humble at the same time. No less so than Parker himself, the people were aware of the unique character of this court. And although some of them understood no nuance of the law, all sat in awe of these proceedings and of this man.

Now, the indictment charging murder had been read, and Smoker Chubee had pleaded not guilty. Evans opened with a few remarks indicating the government would prove murder and the intent to commit it, resulting in the death of United States Deputy Marshal Burris Garret in the Creek Nation at the hands of one Smoker Chubee, here charged, and his companion in the crime, Rufus Deer, deceased. McRoy waived opening and Judge Parker instructed Evans to present his case.

I sat in the spectator's section, at the wooden barrier immediately in rear of Evans's desk. When Orthro Smith was called, sworn, and took the stand, I glanced at my watch. It was 8:32.

"My name is Orthro Smith. I live at my business, which is brickmaking, at a place called Smith's Furnace, Creek Nation."

"Do you know the defendant in this case?" There was little of the dramatic about Evans's courtroom manner. He remained standing behind his desk during examination of witnesses, fully twenty paces from the witness, but his strong voice carried clearly across the room.

"Smoker Chubee," Smith said, pointing. Chubee was slouched in his chair, but he watched the proceedings with a hard, intimidating glare that unnerved Smith. "He's worked for me about four months. Off and on. He comes and goes a lot."

"Mr. Smith, do you recall any conversation you had with the defendant on July fifteenth or thereabouts?"

"I recall something he said to me on that day because I thought it was unusual. He don't talk much." Smith shifted constantly on the stand, as though his underwear were too tight. He was a nondescript man except for a waxed handlebar mustache that drooped now with sweat. He gave a visible start when McRoy rose to object.

"This is hearsay, Your Honor."

"Overruled," Judge Parker snapped. "A witness can testify to another's words to show they were spoken, so long as it doesn't go to the substance of the charge, and—"

"Your Honor," McRoy interrupted. "I object to your instructing the jury at this time."

"—and besides, you know as well as I do, Mr. McRoy, statements made by a defendant are admissible. Overruled!"

"Exception, Your Honor."

"Let it show in the record," Judge Parker said to the reporter, who was taking shorthand notes. "Go on, Mr. Smith."

"Smoker said Rufus was coming back into the neighborhood to see his folks. They got a little farm nearby the Furnace. Smoker and Rufus was friends. I'd seen them together a few times."

"The defendant made a point of telling you this?"

"Yes. I recall because at the time he told me, everybody knew the law was after Rufus."

155

McRoy was on his feet again. Even in shirt-sleeves, he was an imposing figure. A full head taller than Evans, who was no small man himself, the defense counsel wore a Vandyke beard and his thick brown hair was close-cropped and graying at the temples.

"Your Honor, I object to that statement." He spoke without effort, yet his deep voice boomed throughout the large room.

"Mr. Smith," Judge Parker said. "It is sufficient to tell what you knew."

"Thank you, Your Honor," Evans said. "Now, sir, you say you were aware that Rufus Deer was wanted by officers of this court?"

"It was in all the newspapers. He was wanted for the Winding Stair killings—"

"Your Honor," McRoy said, cutting into the testimony. "I object to any reference to matters other than those under consideration here."

"Sustained, and the jury will disregard any reference to other crimes."

"Sir, I object to the word *crimes*," McRoy said. He was completely at ease, in marked contrast to Evans, whose face had begun to grow purple. Judge Parker tapped his glasses on the bench as he calmly considered the defense counsel. Everyone in the room knew that this early bickering, although perhaps justified in substance, was largely a testing of the court by McRoy.

"Sir, it is hardly likely we can avoid the word, since our entire purpose here is to determine if there has been a crime and who committed it. Mr. Evans, please continue."

"The government is prepared to produce a warrant issued on Rufus Deer," Evans said.

"It is sufficient the witness knew he was being pursued by the law."

"Your Honor, I object to the term *pursued*," McRoy said, smiling. For a moment Judge Parker fixed the defense counsel with his eyes.

"Mr. McRoy, please sit down," he said. "Let's get on with it."

"Very well," Evans said. "Mr. Smith, when the defendant told you Rufus Deer was coming, was this his habit? Confiding such information?"

"No sir. He was pretty tight-lipped about things. I recall him saying it because it was unusual."

156

"Did it occur to you that he was giving this information for a purpose?"

"Objection," McRoy said from his seat.

"Sustained."

"Very well, Mr. Smith, what did you do after the defendant told you this?"

"That Rufus was coming? Why, I rode into Okmulgee that night and told Marshal Garret what Smoker had said."

"Had you ever done this before?"

"Yes sir. A lot of the boys are always hanging around my place and I hear things useful to the law."

"Did the defendant know this?"

"It wasn't any secret—"

"Objection." This time McRoy's voice was harsh. "This is an assumption."

"Sustained," Parker said, and he bent closer to the witness. "Mr. Smith, did you ever tell the defendant that you provided information to the deputy marshal in Okmulgee?"

"No sir, I never done that," Smith said. "But everyone knew—"

"That will be enough along that line," Parker said, an edge to his voice as well.

"Mr. Smith," Evans said. "Do you recall if the defendant told you the time Rufus Deer would come?"

"Smoker said in a few days. Then he said July eighteenth."

Evans took a paper from his desk and walked to the bench, handing it up.

"Your Honor, I introduce a Creek Nation coroner's report, a copy of which has been provided defense counsel, stating that the death of United States Deputy Marshal Burris Garret occurred on the night of July eighteenth–nineteenth, and ask it be entered in evidence."

Parker, his glasses on as he read the paper, asked if defense objected and McRoy said defense did not.

"No more questions," Evans said, and McRoy was up for cross-examination.

During his interrogations, he stood directly before the stand, his hands thrust into hip pockets as he leaned from the waist toward the witness. He reminded me of the umpires at baseball games I had watched in Saint Louis.

"Mr. Smith, the prosecution instructed you on that date, didn't they?"

"I object," Evans said.

"There's nothing wrong with the question, Mr. Evans. Go on, Mr. Smith, answer the question."

"We talked about it some, yes. But I remember that's what Smoker said."

"Mr. Smith," McRoy said congenially, as though he were having a conversation with an old friend. "You sell whiskey at the Furnace, don't you?"

Smith started to answer, glanced quickly toward Evans, then shook his head. Before Parker could instruct him in answering properly, McRoy asked his next question.

"Have you ever been arrested?"

"A long time ago, yes," Smith said, squirming. Smoker Chubee was grinning, his teeth showing white in his dark face.

"In fact, twice, you were arrested and fined for selling whiskey. Is that true?"

"Yes sir."

Evans was leaning forward in his chair but he didn't object because he knew Parker would not sustain him.

"And isn't it true that at the present time, you are free on bond from a Creek court for selling whiskey?"

"They never brought that one over here to Fort Smith. They dropped the charges."

"Why did they do that?"

"I don't know. Lack of evidence, I guess."

"Isn't this true, Mr. Smith: You are legally in The Nations on a work permit and the Creek police caught you selling whiskey; but because you are an informer for a federal officer, they dropped the charges?"

"I don't know why they dropped the charges."

"Isn't it true that federal officers pay you for information?"

"Well, yes, sometimes," Smith said. He was sweating hard now, his shirt showing in wet patches between the straps of his suspenders.

"How much did they pay you for this information about Rufus Deer?"

"Seven dollars."

"Then you are a paid informer?"

Parker broke in. "I think he's answered adequately without taking it any farther, counselor. Do you have anything else for this witness?"

"No," McRoy said, turning away and smiling at the jury. "I think not."

There was a low grumbling in the courtroom as the witness left the stand, but Parker ignored it. Evans called me next and I detailed how the two Osage scouts and I had gone to Low Hawk Corners to meet Garret, responding to Smith's information. McRoy made a great fuss over proof of Garret being a federal officer, but Evans had anticipated him. He introduced a copy of Garret's commission. When we had brought in Cornkiller and Grube, I saw Garret sign his name to a number of documents in the commissioner's office and now affirmed that the signature on the oath of office was indeed Garret's.

McRoy continued to fume over the authenticity of the document, but it was all court smoke, as Evans put it, meant only to confuse the real issues before the jury. After a moment of wrangling, I continued my story. By then a fly had begun to hum around my moist face and I waved it away repeatedly, but it kept coming back. Smoker Chubee watched all of this with obvious amusement. From time to time, when he shifted his position, his leg-chains gave off a faint clink.

I told of hearing the voice call Garret's name, of going out to the porch, of the shooting. I told of Garret's wounds as I had observed them, and of finding empty .44–40 shells, a dead horse, and Rufus Deer, along with an empty rifle. On my identification, the shells and the weapon were introduced into evidence.

It was an exciting experience, spinning out testimony of a violent crime. But cross-examination was not so entertaining or pleasant. McRoy was on me like a hog after a garden snake.

"Mr. Pay, you're an assistant to the United States attorney?"

"No sir, I have not passed the bar," I said. "I have been working as clerk in the prosecutor's office, reading law. And recently I was given appointment as a special investigator in regard to another case."

"What experience have you had as a peace officer?"

"Before I came to Fort Smith, none."

"What experience have you had in examining wounds and identifying signatures and articles to be placed in evidence?"

"None."

"Mr. Pay, how many .44–40 rifles do you suppose there are in The Nations?"

"Objection," Evans roared, leaping up, his face red. "Such a question is meant only to cloud the issue."

"It seems a rather good question to me, Mr. Evans," Parker said. "However, it calls for an opinion the witness is incompetent to answer. Sustained."

"Very well," McRoy said, pacing for a moment and glancing at the jury knowingly. Once again he resumed his half-bent posture before me. His constant smiling infuriated me. "On the shooting, Mr. Pay. Did you recognize anyone at the corner of the barn?"

"I could see the forms of men and horses, but I recognized no one. Later, I recognized Rufus Deer when we—"

"Very well, Mr. Pay, very well. You needn't enlarge. Now think carefully. Who fired first?"

"The first shots came from the night. From the barn."

"In a moment of great danger, and you flat on your face on the porch floor, how can you be sure?"

"I wasn't on my face until after the first shots were fired," I said, and the anger was rising in me. "And they came from the barn."

"You'd swear to that?" He was no longer smiling.

"Mr. McRoy," Parker said. "He has just done so."

"Mr. Pay, you went to Low Hawk Corners to arrest Rufus Deer on another matter?"

"We hoped to arrest him, yes."

"Did you have a warrant for him?"

"Yes sir, we did."

"Did you have a warrant for Smoker Chubee?"

"No, we had a John Doe—"

"I am not asking about John Does. What I'm asking is, were you after Smoker Chubee?"

"Until that night, we had not heard of Smoker Chubee."

"Then why would he have any reason to ambush a United States Marshal?"

Evans was up, but before he could object, McRoy spun and waved him off.

"I withdraw that," he said. But as he took his seat, he once more looked at the jury and smiled.

When Joe Mountain entered the courtroom after Evans called him, I was flabbergasted. I had not seen him in a number of days, and in that time he had bought a new suit and hat. The suit was yellow and brown plaid, complete with vest, and the hat was a small bowler that perched on top of his head like the purple plum atop a gigantic orange cake. As he walked through the barrier gate, he looked at me and grinned, his great eyeteeth showing and the tattooed dots along his cheek standing out like blue buttons.

He confirmed all I'd said about the shooting and what we had found in the lane afterward. McRoy crossed with a vengeance once more, claiming the big Osage was not a duly constituted officer of the court.

"They pay me," Joe Mountain said. "I go out when they ask me. With the Cap'n. That's Oscar Schiller. And Eben Pay," and he pointed toward me.

"Have you ever been sworn or taken any oath of office?"

"No. They just ask me to come. They hire me. Me and my little brother Blue Foot. We come and track and scout and shoot when we have to."

"You shoot very quickly, don't you?"

"Up to now, it's always been quick enough," Joe Mountain said, and the crowd laughed. Parker rapped his knuckles against the bench, but I could see a smile on his face.

"In fact, you shot very fast that night at Low Hawk Corners. You shot first, didn't you?"

"No, I never done that." The big Osage was completely unruffled, sitting there on the witness chair like some great yellow and brown plaid circus tent. "Them boys at the barn shot first."

"Did you recognize Smoker Chubee there at the end of the barn?"

"No. I never seen him before Moma July brought him in."

"Ha! You'd never seen him before he was brought in. Thank you, Mr. Mountain, thank you." And he strode back to his place, nodding at the jury.

Evans was up quickly for redirect.

"Mr. Mountain, that night at the back of Low Hawk Corners. Could you have recognized anyone at the corner of that barn, even if you had known him?"

"I reckon not. I could see the shapes, but I couldn't see the faces."

Louie Low Hawk came to the stand and affirmed that Burris Garret was a deputy marshal of the court and that he often used Low Hawk Corners for a posse rendezvous. Evans made a great deal of this, implying that had anyone wanted to ambush Garret, this would be the place. Then . . .

"Mr. Low Hawk, other witnesses have testified that at one point a number of men went out into the night to discover a dead horse and so on. Where were you at that time?"

"I stayed inside the store. They had carried Burris Garret back inside and I stayed with him."

"You were with him when he died?"

"Yes sir."

"Was anyone else there?"

"A number of people were standing around. My hired clerk Wendell Boggs was there with me, helping with Garret. He's a Creek citizen, too."

"Did Marshal Garret say anything?"

"Not at first. Then after the others had gone out, he tried to talk. He could only whisper and I had to bend low over his face to hear him. He was lung-shot."

"Did you hear any of his words?"

"Yes. He said, 'Smoker Chubee.' Then he breathed hard for a while. Then he said, 'They've killed me, Louie.' Then after a while, he said, 'Smoker Chubee's voice out there.' I heard him say that."

"Was that all?"

"Just before he died, he said, 'Smoker Chubee' one more time. Me and Wendell Boggs heard it."

"No more questions."

McRoy moved out from his chair quickly, taking his stance before

162

the witness. Looking at Smoker Chubee, I saw that at some point McRoy had cut him a chew of tobacco. It bulged in his cheek, but he wasn't chewing it, just letting it lodge there in his mouth.

"How well do you know Smoker Chubee?"

"Not too well. He'd been in the store a few times."

"Would you recognize his voice in the dark?"

"No. I don't know him that well."

"In fact, Smoker Chubee is little known in your part of Creek Nation. Isn't that true?"

"I'd say it was."

"Did Garret ever tell you he knew Chubee?"

"No, I don't recall he ever did."

"Did you ever see them together?"

"No, I never did."

"Then how could Garret recognize his voice?"

"Objection. Calls for an opinion," Evans said.

"Sustained."

"Let's talk about this talking Garret did before he died," McRoy said. "You said he whispered. That he was lung-shot. It must have been difficult to hear him. Is that true?"

"I've said so."

"Did he give any indication that he knew he was dying?"

"He said, 'They've killed me.' He said that."

"You're sure you heard that?"

"Yes sir, I said that I did."

"He didn't say, 'I'm dying.' He didn't say that, did he?"

"No, I told you already what he said. . . ."

"Very well, Mr. Low Hawk," McRoy said turning toward the jury with his knowing look. "We've heard what you *claimed* he said."

McRoy dropped words before the jury like pieces of tainted meat, the odor lingering in their nostrils after the meat had been dragged away. By this time, I despised him, of course, but he was good.

The store clerk Wendell Boggs confirmed Low Hawk's testimony, and then McRoy proceeded against him with great relish. I sensed that Boggs was going to be a disaster.

"Have you ever been arrested, Mr. Boggs?"

Boggs was a dark man, looking much like the other Creeks I had seen. He held his high-crowned hat on one knee, and although McRoy went at him relentlessly his only sign of nervousness was a twitching of his fingers on the hat.

"Yes, I've been arrested."

"How many times?"

"I don't remember. Maybe two."

"You were arrested twice for selling whiskey and fined in a Creek court, is that true?"

"I think so."

"You were arrested by Creek police for fighting, were you not?"

"Yes."

"What was your punishment?"

"They whipped me."

"And you were arrested for stealing a horse and were whipped again, is that right?"

"I recall it was."

"Tell us about that incident."

"I lost some money on a chicken fight. More than I had. So I took this little roan to pay my debt. I planned to make it good when I had some money together."

"And from whom did you steal this horse, Mr. Boggs?"

For a long moment it appeared the witness would not respond. Parker began to tap his glasses on the bench.

"From Smoker Chubee."

"And who was principal witness against you?"

"Smoker Chubee."

There was a shifting, muttering sound from the spectators, like a restless herd of cattle, and Parker rapped his knuckles sharply on the bench.

"And since then, you have held this grudge against Smoker Chubee."

"Objection," Evans shouted, but from his face I could tell he knew the damage had already been done.

"Sustained. But please, you needn't shout in this court, Mr. Evans." Parker turned to the jury. "You will disregard defense counsel's last comment."

Evans then called three Creek policemen, each of whom corroborated what they could of other testimony. None had heard Garret's death statement. Prosecution called a large Creek woman, attractive but fat, who said her name was Nellie Williams. Her dress was decorous, except for a large purple hat with a white feather that bobbed up and down when she turned her head.

"Where do you live?" Evans asked.

"Low Hawk Corners, in the Creek Nation." she said. As she spoke, she seemed always to be eyeing the men on the jury, a half-smile on her full lips. "My husband was a Creek. But he's dead now."

"Where in Low Hawk Corners do you live?"

"My house is alongside a lane behind Louie Low Hawk's store."

"On the night of July eighteenth—or more properly the morning of July nineteenth—did anything unusual occur?"

"I was woke up a couple hours after midnight. There was a knock on my door. There was two men there, wet from the rain. It was lightning and I saw their horses tied to my rail fence along the lane."

"Did you know them?"

"I knowed one. Rufus Deer. The other one I didn't know then. But that's him sittin' right over there," and she pointed to Smoker Chubee. By this time Chubee seemed uninterested in what was happening. He sat chewing his cud, contemplating the handcuffs on his wrists.

"What did they want?"

"Rufus asked if they was anybody at the store. I said there was a lot of law over there. A posse."

"What else did he say?"

"He never said no more about that. He asked me if I'd saw his old lady. His mother. I told him my little girl had gone to the store early in the night to get some candy. Right after dark. Mrs. Deer was over there on Louie's back porch. They got to visitin', I told Rufus, and his mother had told my girl she was gonna stay there the night because of the storm."

"That's all he said?"

"No, he said some more. He said they was gonna kill some white sons a bitches. That's what he said. I could smell they'd been drinkin'. I never thought much about him sayin' that."

Judge Parker glanced at the defense table, expecting an objection. It was clearly objectionable, but McRoy made no move. Smoker Chubee sat

165

unperturbed, giving no indication that he had heard what Mrs. Williams had said.

"What happened then?"

"They left," Mrs. Williams said. "I went back to bed. In a little while I heard this shootin'. I got up and locked my door, and went back to bed."

"Your witness," Evans said, and McRoy rose and moved forward, smiling.

"Mrs. Williams," he said graciously. "You say it was the wee hours of the morning these men came. You were sleeping and suddenly wakened. It was dark. Yet, you are positive this was one of those men," and he pointed back toward Chubee.

"That's who it was."

"These other witnesses from around Low Hawk Corner say they saw Smoker Chubee from time to time. They did not know him well, but they saw him. You claim you never saw him before?"

"I don't get out of the house much," she said, and laughed suddenly. A few of the jurymen glanced at one another.

"You were paid, were you not Mrs. Williams, for saying what you did about shooting white sons of bitches?"

Evans was up, livid.

"I object most strenuously, Your Honor. Defense counsel knows witnesses are paid their travel expenses to come here and swear under oath before this court. They are paid, just as the jurymen are paid."

"Sustained. And I'm sure the gentlemen of the jury are aware of this," Parker said.

"Mrs. Williams," McRoy said, "did the United States attorney speak with you ahead of time concerning your testimony?"

"Yes, he did."

"And when I spoke with you before this trial, as is my right as representative of the defendant, isn't it true you neglected to tell me of this phrase you used about killing white sons of bitches?"

"That's true. Mr. Evans said I didn't have to talk to you at all if I didn't want to."

"Mrs. Williams, these two men you saw. If they were indeed coming to shoot Marshal Garret, why would one of them say they had come to kill white sons of bitches when everyone knows that Marshal Garret was a colored man? Isn't that strange?"

I expected Evans to object, but he sat quietly and I could see beneath his beard a trace of a grin.

"No," Mrs. Williams said. "It ain't strange. Some of the old-line folks in The Nations still call colored people black white men."

It came like a blow to McRoy, but he quickly recovered his poise.

"The man who spoke to you on the porch, did he speak in Creek?"

"That's right. Rufus could speak in Creek or Yuchi or Seminole or English and I don't know what all else."

"What is your method of livelihood?"

The witness looked at Parker and he bent toward her.

"How do you make a living, Mrs. Williams?"

"I sew a little," she said, and laughed again. "My girl runs errands for folks."

"Aren't you known in that part of Creek Nation as Fat Nellie?"

"That's what the boys call me."

"You have a great many gentlemen callers?"

"Yes, I make good pies," she said, and this time the jury and the crowd in the courtroom laughed with her. Parker rapped his knuckles.

"Mrs. Williams, wouldn't a woman of your calling know most of the men in your neighborhood?"

"There's a few I don't think I've met," she said, and the laughter swelled again. Parker let it die of its own accord.

"Mr. McRoy, what are you trying to establish here?" Parker asked.

"I am simply trying to show that a woman of Mrs. Williams' profession would have known that second man on her porch had it indeed been the defendant," McRoy said. "But we have pursued it far enough to make the point, I believe."

He held out a hand and assisted Mrs. Williams down from the stand, bowing. As she left the courtroom her undergarments made a soft rustling sound of silk. All eyes followed her.

Moma July took the stand wearing the same thigh-length coat I had seen him in that day of the prizefight. Now as then, the heat seemed not to bother him at all. Evans guided him quickly through the events of that night at Low Hawk Corners until we found the body of Milk Eye Rufus Deer.

"When you saw the body in the lane, did you recognize it?"

"It was Rufus Deer."

"What did you do then?"

"I made a beeline for Smith's Furnace."

"Why would you do such a thing?"

"Orthro Smith had told us about Smoker sayin' Rufus was on the way back home. I figured maybe Smoker had been with Rufus when all the shootin' had took place. I figured they might have been together."

"I object, Your Honor. That's an assumption."

"Yes, but it has been stated as a reason for the witness's action at the time, Mr. McRoy. Overruled."

"Exception, Your Honor."

"The reporter will so indicate. Now, get on with your examination, Mr. Evans."

"I made a beeline for Smith's Furnace," Moma July continued. "I figured if the other man was Smoker, he might head back there. I didn't know anywhere else to look. I got there before first light and hid out in one of Orthro's barns. It was just light when I seen a man comin' along a fence row towards the barn on a horse in bad shape. The man was whippin' the horse hard. When he got closer, I seen it was Smoker Chubee and the horse was bad shot up, with blood all over his flanks and blowin' red at the muzzle."

"You recognized the defendant at once?" Evans asked.

"Yes. I've known him since we was boys together, in the western part of Creek Nation."

"And is this the same man?" Evans said, pointing to Chubee.

"Yes. That's him. Smoker come in the barn where I was hid. In a stall. He had a lever-action rifle. He got his horse stalled and started pullin' gear off it and throwin' it on one of Orthro's horses. I seen his own horse was about done with gunshot wounds. He laid his rifle down and so I stepped out and put him under arrest. The rifle was a Marlin .44–40. It had one shell still in the magazine."

The rifle was produced and identified by Moma July and placed into evidence as a prosecution exhibit.

"When you arrested him, did defendant say anything?"

"He said, 'You're up damned early in the mornin', Moma.' And I said, 'Smoker, you're under arrest for shootin' Burris Garret.' I didn't know then he was dead. So Smoker never said anything else right then, he just smiled."

"He put up no resistance?"

"No, I threw down on him with a shotgun. I told him we'd better look in his bunk place and we walked out of the barn and over to this shack where Orthro lets his hired help sleep. I looked around Smoker's bunk. He showed me where it was, which one it was. I found a six-shooter and some clothes and that's about all. Then we went back to the barn. I had cuffs on him by then. I looked at his horse, almost dead in the stall. I said, 'Smoker, what happened to that horse.' And he said, 'Some hunters mistook it for a deer.' And I said, 'Where at.' And he said, 'Back along the road a piece.' Then we mounted up, him on Orthro's horse, and come back to the Corners."

"Your witness, Mr. McRoy," Evans said.

Moma July watched McRoy advancing on him, deadly serious. I could see the jaw muscles working in the stocky little Creek's cheeks. I had great admiration for this man, and hoped McRoy would not somehow destroy his dignity.

"Did you have a warrant for the arrest of Smoker Chubee?"

"No. There wasn't time for that."

"Did you have a search warrant for his quarters?"

"No, I didn't have that either."

"Were you wearing a badge when you confronted him with a shotgun?"

"I don't recall I was wearing it."

"When he told you his horse had been shot by hunters, did you make any attempt to find those hunters?"

"No, I didn't."

The questions came like rapid-fire gunshots, and the answers just as fast.

"To your knowledge, was Burris Garret a citizen of the Creek Nation?"

"Yes, he was."

"To your knowledge, is Smoker Chubee a citizen of the Creek Nation?"

"Yes, he is."

McRoy stopped abruptly and turned to Judge Parker and held out one hand, as though in supplication.

"Your Honor, this man has testified that under all the rules of apprehension, he has made an illegal arrest and an illegal search. What's more, he has indicated that all parties are citizens of Creek Nation. I therefore move a mistrial."

I would have expected Parker to react violently to the defense counsel's statement, but the expression on his face did not change. For a moment he rapped the bench with his glasses, contemplating the man standing before him.

"Mr. McRoy, I am sure you know that your motion has been misstated. There are no grounds for mistrial here. What you have asked, and I will consider it as such, is a dismissal."

Judge Parker turned to the witness stand and bent toward Moma July.

"Mr. July, when you apprehended the defendent, were you acting as a member of a federal posse?"

"That was what I thought," Moma July said.

"Your Honor," McRoy said, becoming agitated. "I ask the jury be excused for any comments you make on my motion."

"That won't be necessary. The jury is here to decide on the indictment. Any question of jurisdiction will be determined by the court."

"Your Honor, I ask an exception."

"It will be noted in the record. Now, Mr. McRoy, let me explain that it has been found on recent appeal that Negroes who reside in Indian Territory, no matter their tribal affiliation, are under the jurisdiction of this court. Further, recently it has been the intent of Congress that all murders committed in The Nations be tried in this court. Finally, sir, when parties to such a crime committed against an officer of this court are taken into custody by officers of the court, indicted by the grand jury, and brought before this bar, they will be tried here, no matter the victim's race or complexion or former heritage. Therefore, your motion is denied."

"I ask an exception and further suggest, Your Honor, that your statements are prejudicial to my client," McRoy said.

Parker's face was rigid, his lips tight-pressed as the color rose in his cheeks. I could feel the tension in the room as we all waited for his reply to this unprecedented questioning of the court's authority. But it passed quickly as Parker said, his voice low and under control, "Your exception will be noted. Are you finished with the witness?"

McRoy took his seat and Evans was up for redirect.

"Mr. July, have you ever before arrested a man without a warrant?"

"A lot of times, when I was right in after him."

"Do you know what that is called? Being 'right in after him'?"

"No, I guess not, except it's when you haven't got time to get a warrant or your man will get away from you."

"Exactly. It is called an arrest being made in hot pursuit."

"Is prosecution making a summation?" McRoy asked, almost casually.

"Mr. Evans, hold your comments for closing," Parker said.

"Thank you, Your Honor. I am finished with this witness."

"If there is no recross, the witness is excused," Parker said.

"The government rests," Evans said.

"Mr. McRoy, are you ready to present the case for the defendants?"

"Your Honor, I move a directed verdict of not guilty."

"Overruled. Present your case, Mr. McRoy."

McRoy called Wanada Deer and she came from the outer hall escorted by a deputy marshal. As when I first saw her, she was wearing a calico dress and shawl, and the man's hat was on her head. Beneath its wide brim the features of her dark, wrinkled face were twisted. As she sat on the high witness stand, I could see she was wearing lace boots. Throughout the questioning, she kept the hat on her head.

With her came a court interpreter, and through him she was sworn in Yuchi.

"You are the mother of Rufus Deer?" McRoy asked. Through the interpreter, she said she was.

"On the night of your son's death, where were you?"

"At Low Hawk's store. On the back porch."

"In the Creek Nation?"

"Yes."

"Did you see the shooting that occurred there?"

"Yes. I saw it. My son came to the end of Louie Low Hawk's barn and Burris Garret came on the porch. My son had a friend with him from the Seminole."

"The Seminole Nation?"

"Yes. I don't remember his name. My son had been hiding with this man. He was hiding because they were after him for a thing he did not do."

Evans started to rise, but then shrugged and let it continue.

"Had you seen your son that day?"

"Yes. He was hiding on our farm, with the Seminole. My husband and me went to Low Hawk Corners to buy things and it started raining. We stayed the night. Before we left the farm, my son told me he was coming in to give himself up to Burris Garret. So he did, and I saw him when he came to the Corners."

"Did he call out to Garret?"

"No. The Seminole did."

"What did he say?"

"The Seminole helloed Burris Garret's name and when Burris Garret came out, the Seminole said my son had come in to give up. He said Rufus had come to give up."

"What happened then?"

"Burris Garret shot my son." There was a stir in the courtroom, like a faint sigh.

McRoy paused for a moment, looking down at the floor, his chin in one uplifted hand. After he had the suspenseful effect he wanted, he continued.

"At that time, had your son and the Seminole fired?"

"No. When the Seminole said Rufus had come to give up, Burris Garret shot him, and then the Osages shot and there was a lot of shooting."

"There was lightning, wasn't there?"

"Yes. I could see Rufus at the corner of the barn, and the Seminole."

"Do you know this man?" and McRoy pointed at Smoker Chubee. Chubee had begun to watch carefully.

"Yes. That's Smoker."

"How long have you known him?"

"Since he was a little boy," she said.

"Was he at the barn with your son that night?"

"No. It was a Seminole."

Evans took the witness. Her black eyes glared at him defiantly.

"Mrs. Deer, you said your son was going in to give himself up to Burris Garret. How did he know Garret was at the Corners?"

"He told me that morning he'd heard Garret would be there. I don't know who told him."

"This Seminole, when he called out, did he speak English?"

"No. He spoke Creek."

"But Mrs. Deer, other witnesses have testified whoever spoke did so in English. One witness cannot even understand Creek."

"Maybe it was English. I was excited."

"Mrs. Deer, if it was English, how did you understand it?"

"I speak English."

"If you speak English, why are you testifying through an interpreter?"

"I don't speak English that good."

"Very well. Now this Seminole. Where is he?"

"I guess he ran off, out of the country because he was afraid."

And that was all of it. McRoy rested his case on the one witness, and Evans whispered to me that he had to. There had been no Seminole nor hunters either, else McRoy would have been screaming for a continuance in order to find them. I hoped Evans was right.

When Merriweather McRoy rose to make his argument, one would have thought him the minister of a revival tent-meeting. I began to mark the times he called on God in His mercy. Before he was finished, he had done so twenty-seven times, which amounted to about once each minute that he spoke. He harped on the question of jurisdiction and returned again and again to Mrs. Deer's testimony, a mother mourning for the soul of her son and surely in that state not inclined to commit perjury. He cast aspersions on the character and credibility of every defense witness. In his words, I became the young and inexperienced thrill-seeker down from Saint Louis to dabble in the serious business of other people.

Evans confined his remarks to one sentence.

"Gentlemen, it's very hot in here and I see no reason to keep you any longer than necessary because the evidence speaks for itself."

Judge Parker's charges to the jury were sometimes long and complex, but on this day he was brief, dealing primarily with the jury's determination of whether Burris Garret knew he was dying when he spoke the defendant's name. The case went to the jury at 10:45, just a little over two hours after testimony had begun.

Fourteen

FOR MANY YEARS, THE IMAGES OF THAT MUGGY DAY WOULD come uninvited to darken the memory of my time in Fort Smith, for there was more than the murder trial of Smoker Chubee. It was the day we found the note, and the day Emmitt tried to run away from his fears, and the day we finally knew there was no longer a chance to bring anyone to the bar for the killing on Hatchet Hill road.

When the jury retired, I went into the main hallway, pressed along by the crowd that had suddenly gone noisy and high-spirited. It reminded me of an intermission at one of the Gilbert and Sullivan plays at the Opera House. At the end of the hall, before the doors marked WHITE MEN and WHITE WOMEN, there were queues of people. Almost none stood at the COLORED MEN and COLORED WOMEN doors. There were some Indians among them, but I saw only two Negro men. I pushed my way through the throng to the front of the building and had just lighted a cigarette, standing on the porch hoping for some small breeze, when a bailiff came and told me Judge Parker requested my presence in his chambers.

I found Judge Parker and Evans, both in shirt-sleeves now, and both in a high state of agitation. Parker sat at his desk, drumming his fingers. His mouth was set in a hard line and his heavy brows were pinched together in a frown. Evans was pacing, red-faced, waving about a small piece of paper. His pince-nez perched at the end of his nose, and each time they seemed ready to fall off he pushed at them with a vicious little jab of his hand. On a side table was lemonade, chunks of ice floating in it and the pitcher beaded with pearls of cool moisture. Empty glasses were waiting and I knew they had not been touched.

"Show it to him," Judge Parker said.

The paper Evans handed me had a familiar look to it but I could not at that moment place it. It was rectangular, thick, and of high quality, with a distinctive tooth. It had been folded twice. As I spread it at the front of Parker's desk, I could see a pencil scrawl and a rough sketch:

My mind still on the Chubee case, I had no notion what this message meant.

"What is it?" I asked.

"Found in one of the cells of the women's jail," Judge Parker said. "The room we've had that Negro boy in."

"Emmitt? You found this in his room?" I asked. My first thought was how the boy must have reacted to such a thing. That morning on the Hatchet Hill road, when Schiller asked him to identify the men responsible for Mrs. Eagle John's death, he'd said, "They cut my guts out." And the danger to Jennie Thrasher struck me. If someone wanted the boy silenced, surely she must be no less endangered.

"That boy told me he could read," Evans was saying, still pacing the small room from wall to wall. "But even if he couldn't read, the picture is enough to convey the meaning."

"The boy's gone, Eben," Judge Parker said. "And Mr. Evans tells me that without him your Eagle John case won't get an indictment from the grand jury."

"My God," I said, staring at the penciled skull. "My God."

Parker slammed his hand against the desk top and I jumped visibly.

"I want to know what's happening here," he shouted. "In a federal jail. Intimidating a grand jury witness. Somebody carrying off a boy in protective custody right under our noses."

"If somebody carried him off, Judge, I doubt they'd have left any note," Evans said, pushing his pince-nez up onto the bridge of his nose. "There'd be no reason for the threat if they physically took him. I suspect he ran off on his own accord, Your Honor."

"But when—" I started and Evans cut me off.

"This morning. Zelda Mores found his room empty. She'd come to see the church people about the baptizing. When she went back up, he was gone."

"The what?"

"The church people," Evans said irritably. "They're baptizing today."

"Now and again," Judge Parker said, "churches send their ministers down here to baptize any prisoners who want it. Today, it's the Baptists." He said it with some distaste, being a staunch Methodist. "And Miss Thrasher had indicated she wanted to be baptized. The whole party's down at the river now."

"Jennie Thrasher is off down at the river—" But Evans interrupted me again. Both seemed to have little concern for her situation. The boy's disappearance was all that occupied their thinking.

"Some of the deputies have been looking for him all morning," he said. "They finally decided he was gone and told us about it just now. And gave us this." He pointed to the note, still lying open on Judge Parker's desk.

"Who found it?" I asked.

"Zelda Mores. Just before she took the Thrasher girl down to the river," Judge Parker said.

"We've had no chance to talk with Zelda," Evans said. "All we know is what the deputies told us she said. She planned to take that boy with her down to the river, along with the girl. But when she went for him, he was gone. After that, she didn't want to leave Jennie Thrasher."

"Well, I'm glad *Zelda's* aware there might be some danger to the girl," I said, and Evans glared at me over the tops of his pince-nez.

"Eben, you've got four men in jail that are supposed to be the ones involved in these Winding Stair crimes. Now we've got this note. Is there any doubt in your mind about those men? Do you think there's someone else out there you've missed?"

Judge Parker's question surprised me. Everyone knew the personal interest he took in his cases. But I wasn't sure a judge was supposed to be this involved, especially even before a grand jury sat on the case. But he'd asked and I answered as surely as I could.

"With the evidence we've got and the testimony of that boy, I think any jury would agree we've got them. All of them."

"Yes, and that's just the point." He waved his hand at the note again. "That thing right there probably scared him out of testifying another word."

"If you've got them all, the note means they have friends out there," Judge Parker said. "And very close by. I want them, whoever they are."

"Sir," I said, feeling all this talk was wasting valuable time when Jennie Thrasher might be in danger. "I'm going down to the river and talk with Zelda Mores."

"That's one reason we called you in here," Evans said. "With Schiller still in Choctaw Nation, you're closer to this case than anyone else around."

"And Eben," Judge Parker said, moving around his desk and placing a hand on my shoulder. "Use your own judgment about talking to that girl. Her room is at one end of the corridor up in the women's jail, the boy's was at the other, but she may have seen something. On the other hand, we don't want to frighten her. We don't want to upset her about this thing and frighten her off."

I recalled the afternoon Jennie had slipped away and come to my hotel room, but I knew that wasn't what Parker meant. He was afraid she might balk at testifying or have a loss of memory if she thought friends of the gang were trying to silence witnesses.

"Go on and see Zelda," he said. "But use your own judgment."

That was something, anyway, but my mind was too busy with other things to be congratulating myself on the judge's show of confidence. The bailiff was hurrying down the hall, and I knew Smoker Chubee's jury was ready to come in. The crowd still milled about in the main corridor as I slipped out the rear entrance and started for the west gate of the compound. Within a few steps, sweat was streaming off my face. I crossed the railroad and came to the high west bank of the river. I saw the group at once at the water's edge, and there were a good many townspeople standing along the high ground watching.

The church people were wearing white choir vestments, in a compact bunch near the pilings for the new railroad bridge still under construction, looking like a flock of snow geese. They were singing something I didn't recognize. At the water's edge were three men with leg-irons and handcuffs, and close beside them two deputies with

Winchesters. It was an incongruous scene, this religious ceremony attended by the fire power of Parker's court.

A few paces to one side was Jennie Thrasher. They had given her a vestment, too, and she stood in the sunlight, her golden hair shining down her back, a bright, thin little figure against the background of the muddy Arkansas. Beside her was Zelda Mores, and the sight of that bulky form with her pistol-heavy purse gave me a sense of relief. Facing the bank and waist-deep in water were the minister and two young assistants, all with Moses beards. When the singing ended and the minister began to shout the opening words of his sermon, I moved closer and caught Zelda Mores's eye. She came back up the bank to me at once. Jennie Thrasher's back was toward me and I could not see her face.

"Mr. Pay," she said, puffing as she came closer, the sweat running in rivulets through her thin mustache.

"We haven't found that boy," I said harshly, ready to blame her for what had happened. "You should have brought that note to somebody right off, and you should have kept Jennie in her room."

Zelda stiffened and glared at me, and at first she had trouble speaking, her mouth opening and closing like a river catfish. When it came, it was a wrathful flood.

"I can't watch two people at once. That girl down there's my main concern. And she wanted this baptizin' and I wasn't goin' to deny it to her. It's about time she done something to save her soul. And that damned boy. Always wanderin' around in the compound and he's everybody's pet and them other deputies is supposed to watch him. When I found that note, I told them deputies and they started lookin'. They wasn't one thing Evans or His Honor could do about it then, they was already in court."

"All right, you did what you could," I said, irritated that what she said was reasonable. "But about that note. Where did you find it?"

"On the boy's bunk."

"Who's been in those rooms since yesterday?"

"Nobody," she said, still furious. "Just the old colored cleaning lady, comes in each morning."

"Then maybe you can tell me how the note got in there."

"I can. I thought about it. Last night when Emmitt was out in the

179

compound, before supper, somebody give him a sack of popcorn. They're always doin' that. Given' him things. That note was in the sack. It couldn't be any other way.''

"If he brought it up from the compound, somebody could have slipped it into a pocket.''

"He ain't got no pockets,'' she said. "He wears them slick homemade britches and a flannel shirt, no pockets in nothin'. He come back up to eat supper and he hadn't touched that popcorn yet. The sack was full, and he spilled some on the bunk and I told him he'd have to clean that up after he ate his supper. Then after supper, I could hear that sack rattlin' when he started eatin' it. The popcorn. He never left the room after supper.''

"Were you up there all night?''

"Every night. I sleep there, in the anteroom to the women's jail. This mornin' I took him his breakfast and the curtain was drawed across the door. Them women's cells got curtains so they can have some privacy for certain business. After that, I went down to talk with them church people, and when I come back up he was gone and I found that note on his bunk and the popcorn half et from last night. It was on the floor by his bunk.''

A sack of popcorn! Someone had come into that compound, somebody who knew Emmitt was often there and that people were in the habit of giving him things to eat.

"And Mr. Pay,'' she said, seeming to anticipate my next question, "Ain't nobody saw who give him the popcorn. I ast all them deputies and anybody else who might have been around. It could have been anybody. With court in session, there's always a mob there.''

At the river, they had begun to baptize the prisoners. Each of them waded into the water awkwardly, dragging his leg-irons through the mud, holding his manacled wrists before him. Each in turn was ducked beneath the surface and came up sputtering and spitting. The two young assistants with Moses beards led Jennie Thrasher out. By the time she reached the minister, the water was up to her breasts. He placed one hand at the small of her back and the other he cupped over her mouth and nose, and with a few shouted words he pushed her backward into the water. He seemed to hold her under for a long time. She came up gasping, the water streaming from her hair and face. As she waded back to the bank, the two young men still at her arms, the wet vestment clung tightly to her body.

"I've got to talk to her," I said.

"Mr. Pay, she's told me she don't want to talk to you or even see you," she said. There was no longer any indignation in her voice. She seemed close to pleading. "We don't want to go scarin' her with this note business, Mr. Pay. That girl's had enough to go through. And besides, if you done that, she might get a seizure of forgetfulness and Evans would raise cain about that."

It was true, of course. And it infuriated me. As I turned away abruptly and started up the bank, I knew the anger was not because of the note or of losing a witness nor even because of possible danger to Jennie. It was because this girl had said she didn't want to see me. And I wanted very much to see her, to tell her stories again of the city, to go back to National Cemetery and tease about cutting initials into elm trees, to sit together above the Poteau and eat meatloaf sandwiches from the Rogers Avenue shops. She had come to me once and I had put her off. With all other girls I had known, there would have been a second and a third and perhaps even a fourth chance. But it began to dawn on me now that Jennie Thrasher offered only once and my opportunity had passed.

"Zelda, you watch over that girl," I called back.

"You can bet on that, Mr. Pay," she said.

I struggled to the top of the sand and limestone river embankment, passing through the lines of people watching. Behind me at the water's edge I could hear the singing once more.

It was a dismal afternoon. The picture of Jennie Thrasher coming out of the river with the vestment plastered tight against her breasts would not leave my mind. Intruding on that was the thought of the boy, lying all night in his hot cell, awake and thinking about that death's-head note. I found Joe Mountain, still grinning in his absurd yellow and brown plaid suit, and we joined the search for Emmitt. "They cut my guts out," he'd said. I knew if we did find him, we'd likely never get another word out of him. I could understand that, and certainly the boy knew the kinds of people we were dealing with better than I did.

In midafternoon, we heard the Smoker Chubee jury had found him guilty of murder, and Judge Parker had sentenced him to hang. Date of execution had been suspended until completion of proceedings on the Winding Stair case. It left a bitter, hollow feeling in my chest. For the first time, a man I had helped bring in was going to die on the gallows.

Clouds gathered over the western horizon late in the day, but the promise of rain and some relief from the heat was never fulfilled. By the time I reached my hotel room just before dark, my clothes were wet. We had looked everywhere. We had gone through the shantytown in the Choctaw Strip alarming everyone there who was sober enough to know who we were. We had asked questions up and down Garrison Avenue and in the livery barns and saloons, and among the swarms of black children playing and fishing along the rivers. The city police had been alerted, but by darkness they had failed to find any trace either.

After the trial and the baptizing, Zelda Mores had told her story over and over again to Evans, and it had done nothing to soften his disposition. I stayed away from him, and from the courthouse. As Zelda suspected, nobody had seen anyone give Emmitt the red and white striped sack of popcorn. But someone had given it to him, and then faded into the city. Although the death's-head note might appear redundant had someone actually taken him away, there was the dread in all our minds that the next time we saw the boy, he would be a sodden lump washed up on one of the river sandbars.

My ceiling fan did nothing more than stir the hot air in my room. I was lying in the darkness in my damp underwear, trying to put it all from my mind, when I heard heavy footsteps along the hall to my door. There was a long pause before the knock came.

Seeing the large hulking form, I thought at first it was Joe Mountain. But then in the hallway's dim light, I could see the battered features, still showing the marks of the prizefight across the river. Big Rachael stood there like a trained bear, his head bowed forward and his hands held together before his massive chest, the fingers twitching nervously.

"Mr. Pay. Miss Henryetta says you ought to come down to her place."

"What the hell for?" I asked. "Have you got some railroad men who need to give somebody a whipping?"

"Mr. Pay, Miss Henryetta says we're awful sorry about that."

"You didn't do much to stop it, if I recall."

"I just do what she tells me," he said helplessly. "And she says you ought to come. It's about one of these court cases. She says it's important and she don't want nobody but you to come."

It took me less than a minute to dress. I recalled that our start on the case had been at the railyard whorehouse, and all kinds of possibilities flashed through my mind. I slipped on my shoulder holster and checked the little Smith and Wesson for loads. I had no intention of getting battered again. In my mirror each morning as I shaved, the face peering back at me looked like one of Dirty Jake's prizefighting opponents rather than my own, and I was determined it would get no worse.

Garrison Avenue was crowded with people looking for a breath of fresh air. We passed an ice wagon where children had gathered. From the tailgate, a man was chipping ice from a three-hundred-pound block, passing chunks of it to grasping hands. The children ran along the sidewalks, holding the ice in their fingers, sucking it as the cold water ran down their arms. It occurred to me that I'd like to lie naked on that chunk of ice.

It was the wrong time of month for good business at Henryetta's. There were two men lounging against the bar as Big Rachael led me to the rear, through a large kitchen and onto a screened porch. The only light was shining through two windows, and in the shadows a number of Henryetta's girls sat sprawled in rocking chairs in their chemises. One bent over an ice cream freezer, slowly turning the crank. As we came onto the porch, their chattering stopped and they watched me, the crank of the freezer making the only sound, a dry, brittle crunching like walking in snow.

"Where at's Miss Henryetta?" Big Rachael asked.

"Upstairs," one of the girls said. "Is that the new marshal you got with you?"

Big Rachael ignored the question and pulled an empty rocker over to one end of the porch in the darkness.

"Sit down, Mr. Pay. I'll fetch Miss Henryetta."

The girls watched for a moment, then went on about their casual conversation as though I had suddenly disappeared.

"Damned ice cream is gettin' stiff," the one at the freezer said. "Somebody else come crank this son of a bitch for a while. It's about ready."

"God, it's hot."

"Yeah, this is a good business in wintertime," one said. "But this kind of weather, it's a bull bitch."

"You ain't had any business for a week anyway," said another, and they all laughed.

"Well, I'm glad them two out front just came for the drinks."

Henryetta appeared at the kitchen door, her face glistening with sweat, her gold teeth flashing in the lamplight. She held one hand to her hip and with the other switched a rattan fan back and forth before her large bosom, where the buttons were loosened.

"Mr. Pay," she said, walking over and placing a small hand on my shoulder. "I'm glad you come. Listen, I sure didn't know you was such an important person until Marshal Schiller and that nigger officer come in here the night you had that little row, and explained to me. And we sure was sorry to hear that nigger man got killed at Okmulgee."

"It wasn't exactly in Okmulgee," I said.

"It was too bad. Too bad. But I hear Parker passed the one done it to the hangman today."

"He'll likely appeal."

"You was the one arrested him, I hear."

"No, it was a Creek policeman. What was it you wanted?"

She bent and peered closely at my face.

"I'm sorry about that nose, Mr. Pay."

"It doesn't matter," I said. "What was it you wanted with me?"

"Let me sit down. This goddamned heat's about to melt me down."

Big Rachael pushed a chair up behind her and she sat down with a loud grunt, the fan going again in little whipping movements. She sat close to me and bent forward when she spoke.

"Mr. Pay, I don't want no trouble," she said.

"Why would you have any trouble?"

Once more, the girls around the ice cream freezer had stopped talking and were watching us. Henryetta turned to them and bellowed, "Go on about your business over there."

On cue, the girls immediately began to talk again, and the freezer's grinding sound began once more.

"I just want you to remember that I'm helping you on this thing," Henryetta said.

"Helping on what?"

"Mr. Pay, when we first come to Fort Smith, Big Rachael would go out along the tracks and gather coal, where it had fell off the tenders," she said. "We was poor as hell then. Well, he still does that, only now he does it in daylight because the coal is easier to find and them railroaders don't give a damn."

She rocked back and forth, wheezing as she fanned herself furiously.

"If the railroaders don't care, the law doesn't either."

"No, that's not it," she said, and I could smell the talcum powder and sweat. "Today, about noon, Big Rachael was out there with his basket. He got way off down at the far end of the yards, where there's this line of empty boxcars. And Mr. Pay, he found something."

"He found that boy!" I said, and grabbed her arm. It was sticky with sweat but I held her tight as she caught her breath.

"Mr. Pay, that hurts," she gasped, pulling back. "Yes, he found that boy. Everybody in town knew about him from the newspapers, being a witness and all. Some of the Fort Smith police was in here and they told me he'd run off from Parker's jail."

"Where is he, Henryetta? Where is he?"

"He's all right," she said. "Don't get mean with me, Mr. Pay, I know you're an important man now—"

"Where is he?" I cut in, and I was still holding her fat arm.

"I don't want no trouble."

"There won't be any if that boy is all right."

"He's upstairs. I've been keeping one of the girls with him. I didn't know what to do. I could have sent him over to the jail with Big Rachael. But I wanted you to have him, Mr. Pay, to show there's no hard feelings about that night them railroaders—"

"Get him down here," I said, and I jerked her arm viciously. "Right now."

Big Rachael moved over close to us, threateningly, and I slipped a hand under my coat. But Henryetta waved him off and sent him for the boy. It took only a few minutes, and during that time, we didn't speak again. Henryetta's girls showed a studied indifference, but I knew they had been listening to every word.

When Big Rachael reappeared, he had Emmitt, holding the boy by the back of the shirt to keep him from running, I supposed. The boy's eyes were wide and shining in the light from the kitchen windows. I reached out a hand to take his but he drew back quickly with a sharp breath.

"This man ain't gonna hurt you, honey," Henryetta said. "He's from Judge Parker's court."

"I know who he is," Emmitt said defiantly. "I ain't gonna tell you nothin', mister."

"You don't have to tell me anything. I just want to take you back to the jail where we can watch out for you."

"I ain't gonna tell nothin' to you."

Another of Henryetta's girls was on the porch then, moving closer to us, and I assumed she had been watching the boy until Big Rachael came for him. As the lights fell across her face, I could see the full-lipped smile and the bad teeth.

"They told me you'd had that pretty face busted," she said. "But it don't look so bad. Makes you look like you're older is all."

"Mr. Pay, you remember Lila, don't you," Henryetta said. "She come back from Memphis a few days ago."

"I remember." It seemed ages ago that this girl had first put us onto Johnny Boins. "I'm glad to see you, Lila. You plan to stay around awhile?"

"As long as you've got my old boyfriend in that jail."

"The United States attorney may want to talk to you soon."

"I'll be here, I suspect. So long as you've got my boyfriend in jail," and she laughed.

"Good. We'll know just where we can find you then." I reached for Emmitt again and once more he pulled back against Big Rachael. "Come on, boy, let's go now. There are a lot of people over at the jail worried about you."

"Well, now, we're about ready for some peach ice cream, Mr. Pay. This boy ought to have some peach ice cream before he leaves. You like some peach ice cream, boy?" Henryetta asked.

Emmitt said nothing, pressing back against Big Rachael's belly and glaring at me, part resistant, part fearful.

"He thought I was gonna hurt him when I pulled him out of that boxcar," Big Rachael said.

My first impulse was to leave as quickly as I could, but then the ice cream was finished and one of Henryetta's girls was bringing heaping bowls of it. Emmitt hesitated at first, then took one of the bowls and stood there shoveling it into his mouth, his eyes still on me. It was a little slushy from a dash of brandy they'd put in it, but it was good.

"Honey, you could sit down," Henryetta said.

"He acts like he's sure hungry, don't he," Big Rachael said.

"You ought to come down here sometimes," Lila was saying, standing near my shoulder. "You ought to visit us more. We make ice cream all the time."

I refused a second bowl and this time moved suddenly to grab a fistful of the boy's sleeve so he couldn't get away. Henryetta and Big Rachael escorted us back through the house.

"Now, you remember, Mr. Pay," Henryetta said as we went down the front steps into the light of the switch engines working the yards. "You remember we helped."

"I'll remember."

"And you come back and see us again," she called after us as we started along the tracks toward Garrison Avenue, me still holding tight to the boy.

I looked down at him then and asked him where he had found the death's-head paper.

"In my room," he said. "I found it in my room."

"When, Emmitt?"

"I ain't gonna tell you no more, I'm done tellin' you anything anymore."

"All right. You don't have to tell my anything."

"They cut my guts out," he said, almost to himself.

Whatever sanctions Judge Parker might threaten against him, I knew then that Emmitt would never be a witness in the Eagle John murder and rape case. And without him, I knew equally well that we had no case. But there was still the Thrasher murders, and there was still Oscar Schiller in the Choctaw Nation. And just finding the boy alive made a good ending to a bad day.

Fifteen

EMMITT HAD BEEN SAFELY BACK IN HIS CELL FOR TWO DAYS when Oscar Schiller came. He came like a general leading his troops, marching at their head from the Frisco station up Garrison Avenue and then along Third Street to the federal compound. Observers said the Cap'n had brought in half the Choctaw Nation. It was understandable. For each witness he produced there were travel expenses to be collected plus a fee of fifty cents a head.

They had come from Hatchet Hill, boarding a northbound passenger train and filling one car almost to capacity, riding with the compliments of the railroad on Oscar Schiller's passes. The telegrapher at Fort Smith knew about their coming a few moments after the train had been flagged on Kiamichi River, and with that the word had spread up the avenue like a flash flood. By the time the big road-engine snaked its cars into the depot, a mob of curiosity seekers was on hand. It was as if some infamous outlaw was being brought in, like one of the Daltons or Belle Starr. The crowd stayed well back from the line of marchers, none of them willing to risk a bruised head if the Cap'n felt himself crowded. But a few waved their hats and cheered. They, like all Fort Smith crowds, were wise to the ways of the federal court and its officers. From street gossip and the newspaper columns, they knew this little cavalcade had to do with Winding Stair.

The people Oscar Schiller led through the streets that bright summer morning created a dazzling scene. They had taken their best from old trunks and cedar chests and paraded it now, the reds and yellows and purples of silk shirts and dresses brilliant in the sunlight. It was a mélange of white man's and traditional Choctaw dress. There were beads of glass or of Indian pipestem bone, bracelets of hammered copper wire or trade-store brass. Most of the men had wide-brimmed hats, some with feathers trailing from them, the vanes carefully groomed and waxed. Beneath the broadcloth coats of a few were vests, black silk or scarlet and blue patterned. Their shoes were high-button felt and leather, brushed and polished. One among them wore a turban and below it dangled

DOUGLAS C. JONES

silver earrings that swung with each step. The women were in mail-order clothes, long billowing dresses and hats drooped with imitation ostrich plumes. A few had their hair drawn back and hidden under bright scarves tied beneath their chins, and some had hair docked at the shoulders, red ribbons trailing from the nape of the neck. One of them wore eyeglasses.

Charley Oskogee was among them, and walking with him, his wife. Of all the women, she alone wore a Texas-style man's hat. There were others who had been in the Winding Stair posse and a few from McAlester. Oscar Schiller led them along the sidewalks, and directly behind him came George Moon, Choctaw police chief, and beside him a small, well-proportioned Choctaw woman of about thirty-five years, her face smooth and handsome, her eyes wide and dark. She walked with a distinctive grace, her body seeming to float above her short-striding legs. She wore a flowing cotton dress of subdued blue and a white shawl with delicate beaded designs. Her hair was cut short and it glistened in the sunlight like gunmetal. This was Mrs. Thomas Thrasher. The onlookers that day knew as well as any federal official that on the shoulders of this small woman rested the success or failure of the government's Winding Stair case.

The events of that day and those immediately following came to me later, secondhand through the words of others who were there. On the morning after I brought Emmitt from Henryetta's a telegram had come advising that my mother had been stricken with typhoid fever. Father was deeply concerned—at that time there was no effective vaccine for the disease. I took the Frisco north at once, with the blessings of Judge Parker and Evans and a fistful of Oscar Schiller's railroad passes I still had in my belongings.

Saint Louis was sweltering, almost as bad as Fort Smith, and my discomfort was not in the least lessened having to leave the border with our case still in doubt. But Evans wired me the day Oscar Schiller came in with Mrs. Thrasher and that plus the doctor's opinion that my mother was out of danger lifted my spirits for a while. Then I visited the zoo to watch the tigers and to think of Jennie Thrasher. It was a mistake.

Depression increased when I received a surprise letter from Zelda Mores, written I was sure with great effort and obviously without the aid of a dictionary. But misspellings were of little concern as I read it.

Oscar Schiller had taken his charges into the federal compound and through the crowd there—the witnesses, prospective jurors, and hangers-on. Moments after her arrival, Mrs. Thrasher asked about Jennie and the girl was brought down from the women's jail. Zelda was not present at the time and could tell me nothing of their reunion.

Around the compound at Fort Smith, there were a number of small hotels where witnesses and jurymen were housed while in town on official business. In one of these, Zelda wrote, they had taken a suite of rooms for Mrs. Thrasher. She was heavily guarded by marshals and directly across the hall were George Moon and Charley Oskogee and his wife. Mrs. Thrasher insisted that Choctaw policemen be with her, and whenever she left her quarters they were a part of her escort along with the marshals.

On that first day, when the armed men walked with Mrs. Thrasher across the compound to her rooms, Jennie returned to the women's jail. Throughout much of that evening, Zelda Mores reported, she could hear the girl crying.

The grand jury sat on the case the fourth day of August, a Monday. Witnesses and depositions were taken during the morning, and by midafternoon deliberations had been completed. Indictments were brought against the four men we had in jail, for rape and murder. It was only after this became public that the people of the city understood the magnitude of Mrs. Thrasher's reluctance to appear, for it could have been none other than herself who was victim of the first-cited crime.

The following morning, Judge Parker arraigned the four men on the charges and announced September 2 for trial. He would have moved more quickly if for no other reason than to avoid sending witnesses home only to have to bring them back again within a month, all at government expense, but Merriweather McRoy insisted on at least this much time to prepare his case. Part of this involved talking with prosecution witnesses, which meant keeping them in town for two or three days in rooms paid for by the government. It went against Judge Parker's thrifty grain. Moma July was the only Creek involved and although McRoy wanted him brought—his grand jury testimony had been by deposition—Parker refused. The court pointed out that defense counsel had spoken to the little Creek policeman before the Burris Garret murder trial, and that was sufficient.

During this time, I fretted in Saint Louis. It would never had occurred to me when I was fighting loneliness in my Fort Smith hotel room, or drinking by myself in some Garrison Avenue saloon, or riding across The Nations with a posse, that I would someday prefer that little border city to my own Saint Louis. None of my old friends had the faintest idea of what a Choctaw was, or how the Civilized Tribes had been removed from their old homes east of the Mississippi, or how law enforcement worked in The Nations. Their only concept of Fort Smith came from the sensational newspaper accounts of the bloody hanging judge. But once I had talked with Father at length about what I'd been doing, I indeed wanted to be back.

When Evans's telegram arrived, informing me of the date of trial and asking that I try to be there, I was grateful for the excuse.

I took the train on the same schedule that had first brought me to The Nations' border. The daylong trip across southern Missouri and northern Arkansas in the heat seemed endless. But finally, I was walking across the familiar Frisco depot platform, smelling the river, seeing the lights of the railyard switch engines in front of Henryetta's. I could not help but recall the first night I had walked across that platform and seen Johnny Boins and Milk Eye Rufus Deer as they passed me in the lantern light.

Evans was still in his office, working furiously over his notes for the trial. He stared at me over his nose glasses, smiled, and handed me the piece of paper we had all wanted so badly. The grand jury indictment.

UNITED STATES OF AMERICA, WESTERN DISTRICT OF ARKANSAS
IN THE CIRCUIT COURT, JULY TERM, 1890

United States
  vs
Johnny Boins
Smoker Chubee   Rape and
Nason Grube   Murder
Skitty Cornkiller

The Grand Jurors of the United States of America, duly selected, impaneled, sworn, and charged to inquire into and for the body of the Western District of Arkansas aforesaid, upon their oath present:

That Johnny Boins, Smoker Chubee, Nason Grube, and Skitty Cornkiller on the 7th day of June, 1890, at Choctaw Nation, in Indian country, within the Western District of Arkansas aforesaid, did upon Mrs. Thomas Thrasher, a Choctaw woman and wife of a white man, feloniously, forcibly, and violently commit an assault, and against said Mrs. Thrasher then and there did ravish and carnally know her.

Further, in conjunction and concomitant with aforesaid assault, did willfully take the lives of Mr. Thomas Thrasher, a white man, and John Price and Oshutubee, Choctaw Indians, contrary to the form of statutes in such cases made and provided, and against the peace and dignity of the United States of America.

E. J. Black

Foreman of the Grand Jury

William Evans

United States District Attorney, Western District of Arkansas.

Sixteen

WHEN WILLIAM EVANS ROSE TO PRESENT THE GOVERNMENT'S case that September day, the courtroom was cool. Rains driven before high winds out of Indian Territory had broken the August drought. Too late to save much of the truck-garden crop around Fort Smith, it served at least to dispel the humidity that had hung like damp cotton gauze over the Arkansas Valley for more than a month.

For days people had been coming into the city, by train and riverboat, wagon and horseback. Some walked. Hotels were full, saloons did a boomtown business, and each night the city jail was overflowing with drunks. One café on Rogers Avenue offered a Winding Stair Special consisting of spareribs and red kraut with hill-grown huckleberries and cream for dessert. By midafternoon each day, chili vendors had run out of their fiery brew and trundled their carts home to refill. It became difficult to find ice cream in the city, and late-grown watermelons were selling for as much as twenty-five cents each.

People from The Nations went to the Choctaw Strip to camp in the streets or sleep with relatives. Indian children played around the courthouse compound as though it were a schoolyard, mothers in groups seeking shade under trees along the walls, watching the small ones roll hoops or play tag along the gallows fence.

A group of lawyers upriver from Little Rock held forth each night in the Main Hotel dining room. Eastern newspapermen were in town as well, anxious to interview the Hanging Judge, but he disdained them.

When the doors to the main courthouse hall were opened that morning at 7:00 A.M., the mob surged inside like a stampede of mules. Although a good many deputy marshals had been alerted to assist the bailiff, they had difficulty managing the crush of people and keeping citizens out of the pews reserved for the press. When Judge Parker saw the throng in the hallway, with the courtroom already jammed to capacity, he ordered the building cleared of anyone not already in a seat. Some of those forced out were witnesses, and they had to be retrieved

194

from among the crowd along the front veranda and in the compound, then were herded into an assistant prosecutor's office guarded at the door by a deputy.

Johnny Boins led the defendants into the courtroom, leg-irons clanking. He looked well scrubbed and brushed, his blue eyes shining in a face freshly shaved and baby pink. He was smiling, and as they moved him to the defense table, he looked boldly about the room like an actor counting the audience. His eyes fell on me for a moment, but he showed no sign of recognition.

Behind Johnny Boins marched Skitty Cornkiller, shuffling with head down, his hair in his face. He was wearing the same duck trousers and jacket he had worn when we brought him in, but they had been recently laundered. Next came Nason Grube, looking grayer than I remembered him. He seemed in a trance, beads of sweat standing across his black forehead like chips of glass. The welts along both cheeks had a purple tint and rose from his skin like the sword scars of some Heidelberg duelist. His eyes sought Cornkiller's, but the young Creek ignored him.

The last was Smoker Chubee, almost as tall as Johnny Boins but looking more solid and heavy. He moved with grace despite the irons at his ankles, and his head was up. There was a cud of chewing tobacco in one cheek, the bulge emphasizing the deep pockmarks. His eyes met mine, and incredibly he winked. He sat a little apart from the others as though they might have some contagious disease.

The jurors trooped in and took their places in the box. They were twelve solid citizens, selected the day before from a panel of western district of Arkansas voters. It struck me once more, the unique quality of this court. Three of the four defendants were citizens of The Nations, but not a single juror came from Indian country.

Even after Judge Parker entered the room, the crowd took some time to settle down. Throughout the reading of indictments and opening statements there was the muffled noise of scuffing feet, coughs, and whispers. I glanced back through the spectators, looking for Johnny Boins's parents. I had seen them in Fort Smith a number of times, a quiet and well-dressed couple of middle age. But they were not here this day and before I could wonder at that, my attention was brought back sharply to the trial. Evans had called Jennie Thrasher. The newspapers had been calling her "The Woman in the Attic." Now everyone watched the door into the jail corridor with eyes shining, mouths agape. I have since seen the same expression of morbid curiosity many times in a courtroom. But on that day it was particularly disconcerting because the one they waited to see was Jennie Thrasher.

She wore a new gingham dress, blue with white flowers and ruffles across the front, a bow behind. Her hair was done away from her ears and allowed to fall loose down her back. On her head was a small bonnet, with a ribbon that matched the blue of her dress and of her eyes. About her long, slender neck was a single strand of tiny pearls. When she stepped to the stand, I could see black patent leather shoes with a strap across the instep.

She was calm. Her cheeks were creamy white, her curved lips a delicate pink. As she stood with her right hand raised, I had the feeling she knew exactly where I was sitting behind Evans, but her eyes never sought mine. She looked directly at the clerk as the oath was read, and when she affirmed, I hardly heard her voice. She was for all the world like a schoolgirl.

"Miss Thrasher," Evans said in a courtroom gone completely still, "are you the daughter of the late Thomas Thrasher?"

"I am."

"Do you recognize any of the accused?"

Her blue eyes moved slowly from one face to the next along the defense table, a steady gaze returned challengingly by Johnny Boins and with utter detachment by Smoker Chubee. The other two defendants sat leaning against one another, as though they were no part of all this.

"I've seen two of them before," Jennie said. Although I had been expecting that answer, when she said it I felt a hard knot growing in my belly, and my heart was thumping so, I was sure everyone around me could hear it.

"Which two, Miss Thrasher?"

She pointed deliberately to Boins and Cornkiller. The muscles along her neck worked almost convulsively.

"Describe how you first saw them."

"In late April it was. When I saw Johnny Boins." Hearing her say the name made me flinch. I thought I'd prepared myself for this, but I hadn't. I wished I was somewhere else, yet there was no question of leaving. "My papa went to Wetumka in the Creek Nation on a building contract. I went with him. He had a wagon fixed so we could live in it. I'd cook for him and wash his clothes. Papa was working one afternoon and Johnny Boins came to our wagon where I was doing something. Peeling potatoes, I think. He had a little Indian man with him who had a bad eye. It was white. While he talked to me, this Indian looked at Papa's horse, the racer. Tar Baby was his name. After a little while, they rode off."

"Was that the only time you saw Johnny Boins?"

"No sir. After Papa finished his work, we went to Saddler's Ford. That's on the north fork of the Canadian, not far from Wetumka. There were some races there. Papa ran Tar Baby in the two races and he won them both. While we were there, Johnny Boins came to the wagon again and we talked."

"Was that the last time you saw him?"

"Yes, until he was arrested and brought here to Fort Smith."

"Now about the other man, Miss Thrasher," Evans said, almost gently.

"About a week later we were home. This other man," and she pointed once more, "came by the house. Along the McAlester road. He stopped for water and him and Papa talked. He wanted to see Tar Baby and Papa took him to the barn and then they talked some more. Then Papa told him how to get down to the Kiamichi Valley without going the road. Through the woods."

"This is largely hearsay, Your Honor," McRoy said, but Parker waved it aside.

"It's all right, it doesn't go to the issue," he said tartly. "Go on, Mr. Evans."

Jennie related the events of that terrible day when her father hid her in the attic. She said she heard no voice other than her father's and stepmother's that she could recognize. She told of hearing guns firing and then the silence before the storm, and finally of the posse taking her down from the loft.

With that, Evans completed his examination.

McRoy took his time before cross-examination, pacing to the witness stand and back again to his desk to review his notes. He stared up toward the ceiling, drawing out the tension in the room. When he finally approached her, he did so gingerly, as though he were walking among a brood of baby chicks.

"Miss Thrasher," McRoy said softly, "I'm sure you understand that I need to ask a question or two. The lives of four men are at stake."

Judge Parker shifted in his high-backed chair, irritated at the comment. At the arraignment, McRoy had asked for a severance so he might defend Johnny Boins in a separate action, but Parker had denied it. Now, McRoy was showing the armor of knighthood for taking all the defendants, even though every person in the room knew his principal interest was Boins.

"At Wetumka," he said, "and at Saddler's Ford, when these men came to your campsite, why did they leave?"

"They'd finished talking, I guess."

"Did your father see them when they visited you at Wetumka?"

"No sir."

"And at Saddler's Ford, did he see them there?"

"Johnny Boins was all that came to visit me there. Papa saw him there."

"What did your father do?"

"He run Johnny Boins off. Papa always run off anybody who wanted to visit me."

"Exactly where did your father find you and Mr. Boins?"

"At the camp. At our wagon."

"But Miss Thrasher, where, exactly?"

For a moment then, she looked at me. I could see the pain for an instant in her eyes and a tear rolled slowly down her cheek. The muscles in her jaw worked, making unsightly knots in that unblemished skin.

"Miss Thrasher," McRoy said insistently, "let me refresh your memory. Didn't your father find you and Mr. Boins in the wagon?"

"Yes sir."

I couldn't look at her face. The bile was thick in my throat and I studied the floor under Evans's chair, trying to make my ears not hear what I knew must come next.

"Miss Thrasher, on your oath now. On that day, did you have intimate relations with Johnny Boins?"

Looking back, I don't recall having heard her answer. But I knew what it would be before she opened those finely sculpted lips now drawn thin and white.

"Yes sir."

"And you had relations with him before that, too, before your father caught you, at Wetumka?"

"Yes sir."

"How many times, Miss Thrasher?"

"Your Honor, for heaven's sake," Evans said.

"No, Mr. Evans," Judge Parker said, without turning his attention from the witness stand. "Go on, Mr. McRoy."

"More than once, Miss Thrasher?" McRoy asked.

"I don't know. I can't remember. He said he wanted to marry with me."

"Your memory has been excellent up to now," McRoy said. She said nothing, looking more and more like a small child being chastened by the headmaster, softly defiant yet somehow completely defeated and overwhelmed.

"On those days you spent in the wagon with Johnny Boins, did you ask him to come and take you away from your father's farm?"

Down her cheek and along the jaw and neck was the bright snail's path of that one tear, but there were no more.

"He said he wanted to marry with me."

"You told him where to come, didn't you?"

"I just told him we lived in Winding Stair. That's all. He said he wanted to marry with me before we . . ." She stopped. McRoy waited, bent toward her, but she said nothing.

"But you asked him to come, didn't you?"

"I never asked him to bring his friends."

"What friends, Miss Thrasher?"

"That milk-eyed man."

"And Miss Thrasher, you don't know if he ever came at all, do you?"

Once more, she sat silently, and although Judge Parker was leaning over the bench toward her, he made no effort to force an answer. McRoy finally shrugged and turned away. There was no smile on his face now. His eyes were hard and his lips set in a hard slash across his face. As he reached his table, he wheeled toward the stand once more, a finger thrust out like a pistol pointed at Jennie Thrasher's face.

"Isn't it true, Miss Thrasher, that you tempted Johnny Boins with your body in Creek Nation, and because your father always ran off young men who came to court you, you asked Johnny Boins to come and take you from that farm, no matter what it took to accomplish it, holding out again all those favors you had been so generous with before?"

"Is he making a final argument?" Evans shouted, on his feet, his cheeks fiery above the flowing beard.

"Sustained. Jury will disregard counselor's last statement," Judge Parker ruled.

"Let me rephrase," McRoy said. "Miss Thrasher, isn't it true you love Johnny Boins?"

Jennie's jaw set and there was an instant of defiant light in her eyes.

"Yes, and I loved my papa, too."

"Do you really think this man, this man who shared an afternoon bed with you, do you think him capable of killing anyone, with all that tenderness and love—"

"Your Honor," Evans shouted, on his feet again. "That calls for an opinion and I object most strenuously!"

"Sustained."

"Very well," McRoy said, moving around his table and sinking into his chair, his face still grim.

The courtroom crowd remained completely still, leaning forward in their seats. Then across that heavy silence one voice cut sharply.

"Little tart!"

Judge Parker jerked upright, as though he might leap across the bench. He slammed the green felt top with both extended palms.

"Arrest that man," he shouted. "Arrest him, arrest him. Take him to the cells."

There was a sudden scuffling behind me, feet scraping across the floor, and when I looked back two deputies were pulling a man from the pews, dragging him across the laps of others toward the door, spilling hats and lunch bags and a woman's purse. It was a white man, but I had never seen him before and never learned who he was.

"You'll be brought into this court on charges of contempt," Parker was bellowing. "As soon as more pressing business is complete. I warn you people, all of you . . ."

He let it trail off as the man was pushed through the door into the main hall, the two marshals handling him viciously.

I have no recollection of having watched Jennie Thrasher walk out of that courtroom. The sensation in my belly reminded me of what Joe Mountain had said: "You puke more'n any man I know." It was like my first experience with hard liquor, when a college roommate had brought a bottle of brandy to the dormitory and I had swilled down a jigger of the raw stuff on an empty stomach. I tried to block it all off in my mind, Jennie Thrasher's testimony and indeed Jennie Thrasher herself.

Evans had to call me twice before I could respond. As I moved to the railing, I thought for an instant that Judge Parker was watching me with some sympathy. Looking back on that time, I know now it was good that Evans called me immediately after Jennie. It gave me something else to do with my thoughts. I have no idea why Judge Parker had allowed me to sit in that courtroom during another witness's testimony, but I suspect it was part of the plan to convince me once and for all that Jennie Thrasher was not the girl for initials cut into trees, or ice cream sundaes or visits to the Saint Louis Zoo.

I had passed through the railing and was midway to the stand when Merriweather McRoy intercepted me and placed a hand on my shoulder. He addressed the court.

"Your Honor, I object to this witness for the government and anything he might say to the jury."

"On what grounds, Mr. McRoy?" Parker said. At least once during the Burris Garret murder trial he had lost his temper, and now he was clearly trying to hold it in close control. His voice was calm.

"This young man has been party to preparation of the case, an assistant to the United States prosecutor."

"That is no bar to his testimony if he has evidence of which he has firsthand knowledge," Parker said.

"Your Honor," Evans said, from his usual place behind the prosecution desk, "the government wants only to ask Mr. Pay a few questions dealing with the time prior to his arrival at my office."

"He can testify to anything he has knowledge of," the judge repeated.

"Very well," McRoy said, dropping his hand from my shoulder and smiling. I felt a complete fool standing in the center of the courtroom, and I hurried to the witness stand. "However, I ask an exception."

After I was sworn and identified myself, Evans asked me to relate the events of my first night in Fort Smith.

"At some point on the train between here and Seligman, Missouri, this man," and I pointed to Johnny Boins, "boarded the cars. I recall him from his appearance. He was well dressed and a handsome man. When I was waiting for my baggage at the Fort Smith station, he passed me in company of another man."

"Do you recall the date, Mr. Pay?"

"It was June third, a Tuesday."

"Describe this other man."

"He was a short man. An Indian. He had one eye that appeared to be afflicted with cataract in its advanced stages. The eye was white."

"Did you know this man?"

"Not at the time. I later learned his name was Rufus Deer."

"Did you ever see him again?"

"Only after he had been shot and killed near Okmulgee—"

"Your Honor," McRoy broke in. "This was not prior to the time Mr. Pay went to work for the prosecutor in this case."

"I've said the witness can testify," Parker said, his voice testy.

"There will be only this last question, Mr. McRoy," Evans said, pushing his pince-nez up on his nose. "Now Mr. Pay, you saw this Rufus Deer after he was killed. On that occasion, in whose company was he?"

"Objection, Your Honor," McRoy said quietly.

"Mr. Evans," Parker said, "you know as well as I do that the only reference you can make to a previous case is its result. Any of the details of that case you must present in evidence here."

"Very well, Your Honor, I withdraw it. It doesn't matter." And of course, it didn't. Anyone who had read a newspaper after the Burris

Garret murder trial knew of a connection between Smoker Chubee and
Milk Eye Rufus Deer.

Merriweather McRoy surprised me with no cross-examination and I
was left momentarily on the stand, hesitating. As I walked away McRoy
said loud enough for the jury to hear, "My best regards to your father, Mr.
Pay, a fine man and attorney."

The son of a bitch played all the chords. I reluctantly had to give
him that.

Lila Masters was dressed as any Fort Smith housewife might have
been, but her cheeks were rouged and her full mouth as well. My first
impression of her was confirmed. She was a beautiful woman until her
teeth showed.

"Miss Masters, do you know any of the defendants in this case?"

"I know him." She pointed. "Johnny Boins."

"Can you recall for the court, during the month of June, did you
see him?"

"Yeah, about midmonth he come to see me. I don't know the exact
time." She sat upright on the stand, but somehow beneath her dress she
managed to show the lacy hem of at least two petticoats and her high-
button shoes were polished to a bright shine.

"What do you recall of that meeting?"

"He wanted to have a good drunk. Then he started telling me—"

"Objection," McRoy shouted, raising his hand like a schoolboy
wanting to be excused. Judge Parker grimaced.

"Mr. McRoy, now you know what a defendant has said is admissible. Overruled."

"He got drunk," Lila continued. "He told me he'd been in The
Nations. He said him and his bunch—that's what he called it, his
bunch—had got even with this man. . . . You want me to say his words?"

"Yes, please, Miss Masters," Evans prompted.

"Well, he said they'd got even with this son of a bitch who'd tried to
keep him away from a girl he'd found. He said his bunch was meaner
than the James gang."

"Did he say anything else?"

"Just that over and over. He talked about always getting even with a
man who'd try to keep him away from a girl."

"Did he say where this had happened?"

"He said the Winding Stair. He kept saying that. The Winding Stair."

"What did you do with this information?"

"I got in touch with Deputy Marshal Oscar Schiller and he come over and I give it to him. Just like I told it now. I knew about this big killing over there in Winding Stair from all the newspapers."

Watching her, I pondered the question: After at first so vehemently refusing to take any part in the case, why had she finally decided to take the stand? Merriweather McRoy was obviously pondering the same question, in different terms. When Evans released the witness, McRoy sprang to the cross-examination, moving quickly to stand before the witness in that thrust-forward posture of his.

"May I call you Lila?"

"Most do," she said, and her bad teeth showed as she smiled broadly.

"Lila, where did you meet Johnny Boins?"

"Where I am employed," she said, seeming to make a joke of the words. "At Henryetta's Frisco Hotel and Billiard Parlor. I entertain there."

"And Johnny Boins was a regular customer there?"

"Yes. He always asked for me," and she was proud of it, it sounded in her voice.

"On the night you've described—I assume your work is done mostly at night," and McRoy paused to allow the crowd to have its laugh. "Did Johnny Boins call the name of the man he got even with?"

"No, he never told no names."

"He drank that night, you said. He drank most of the time, isn't that true?"

"Mostly, he drank a lot."

"Was he a calm drunk?"

"No, he was a little crazy, mostly."

"Drunk and crazy beyond any capability to know right from wrong?"

"Objection, Your Honor," and Evans was up, his pince-nez almost falling off his nose. "She's no expert in such things."

"I suspect she might be," McRoy said, smiling at the jury.

"Sustained," Judge Parker said, scribbling on a note pad and not looking up.

"Lila, you said he was crazy."

"Objection!" Evans shouted. "This woman may be an expert in a lot of things, but this isn't one of them."

Parker sustained it again after letting the crowd finish its laughing.

"Lila, did Johnny Boins ever hit you?"

"Lots of times, when he was crazy drunk."

"Your Honor . . ." Evans said, almost pleading, but Parker waved him down.

"It's just a manner of speaking, Mr. Evans. Let's get on with it."

"Lila," McRoy said, leaning closer to her, speaking confidentially. "Were you afraid of Johnny Boins?"

"Yes I always was."

"In fact, you told me, Lila, that at first you were afraid to testify here, isn't that true?"

"That's right."

"Then why did you change your mind?"

Lila looked at Johnny Boins, and the young man returned her gaze, smiling, his teeth showing across the pink flesh of his face. After a moment, Lila shifted her eyes, and I thought there was suddenly more color in her cheeks.

"I thought it was the right thing."

"Johnny Boins often talked of other women to you, didn't he?"

"All the time."

"What did he say about them?"

"He bragged about how good he was with them."

Abruptly, McRoy asked the question designed to fluster the little whore, but she remained unperturbed, even a little haughty.

"Do you love Johnny Boins?"

"Yes, I love him."

It was becoming increasingly clear to me that Johnny Boins had some kind of incredible way with women, and the thought of what else he was made it sickening.

"You're jealous of these other women?"

"Yes, I am."

"So despite your fear, you've come here to tell this tall tale to get revenge on Johnny Boins for those other women, isn't that right?"

"No." Excepting the slight flush, she was still calm.

"Did federal officers pay you for this information?"

Evans started to rise but before he could speak Judge Parker waved him down.

"They paid me damned little," Lila said, and the crowd snickered. She looked up to Judge Parker. "Pardon the expression."

"But you made a little money and at the same time found this opportunity to take out your jealousy on Johnny Boins."

"No, that ain't right," she said, and everyone in the room knew that McRoy would not shake her.

I heard two newspapermen in the next pew whispering together as Lila swung out of the courtroom, walking its width to the corridor door, her heels clicking.

"That one'll have more business than she can handle the next few days," one said.

"Yeah, she knows how to advertise it."

"I'd take that little chippy who was on earlier, myself."

It dumbfounded me that the remark had no power to infuriate me now, as it most certainly would have earlier. I sat and absorbed it and the only thing I felt was a deep sense of disappointment over the bitter things people did to one another. Much of it was self-pity, I suppose.

When George Moon walked to the stand, everyone in the courtroom could see that he'd just had his hair cut. Across his neck below the hairline was a strip of skin the color of parchment. The Choctaw police chief was wearing a suit with a black silk vest and a shirt without a collar.

Evans led George Moon through the events of that June day when our posse went from the Hatchet Hill road through the woods and mountains to the Thrasher farm, and the carnage we found there. The dead chickens, the dog under the porch, the milk cow, all shot with a large-caliber weapon. And of course, the men. Thomas Thrasher butchered against the well curbing, the hired man John Price dead and naked and partly eaten by hogs in the pigpen, Oshutubee found shot dead where he sat with pants down in the outdoor toilet. He told of the search for the two women, Jennie and her stepmother, and of finding the girl in the attic after the storm.

"Now, Officer Moon, would you describe the wounds you found on Mr. Thrasher's body?"

"He was bad cut up here," George Moon said, indicating his shoulder and chest. "And along both sides. They was deep cuts, right through the clothes. Right through the ribs. Up high on his shoulder, there was bone sticking out through the wound."

"Did you find any weapon that would produce such wounds?"

"Yes sir, within six, eight feet of Mr. Thrasher's body we found a single-bitted ax with a curved haft. It had blood all over it."

A deputy brought in the ax and George Moon said it was the same one because he recognized three crosshatch marks cut into the metal head with a file, a mark Thrasher put on all his tools. For the moment, Evans did not introduce the ax into evidence but had it marked for identification only. Merriweather McRoy objected to the whole business, but Judge Parker overruled him with some irritation.

"In your investigation, Officer Moon, did you find anything missing from the Thrasher farm," Evans continued.

"All the horses were gone. A black stallion racer with white socks at the rear and a T brand on the left flank where it'd be hid by the fender when the horse was saddled. Mr. Thrasher brands all his horses like that. I mean he used to."

"Have you had occasion to see that brand since then?"

"Yes sir. On a bay gelding over in the federal stables. Marshal Oscar Schiller took me over to show me the horse. It's Thrasher stock."

"Besides horses, was anything else missing?"

"Yes sir. A black Texas hat with a pearl button on the front."

The hat was brought in, the one we had found on Nason Grube's head the day we arrested him at the Cornkiller farm. It was marked for identification and George Moon said it was Thrasher's hat that he once had worn to town and to races.

In his cross, McRoy tried to show that there were any number of single-bitted axes like the prosecution exhibit, and that marking one was a simple procedure anyone could accomplish. He did the same thing with the Texas hat, asking George Moon to guess at the number of such hats he had seen since he'd been in Fort Smith for the trial. He got the Choctaw officer to admit that a button could be sewn on any one of them. It was all designed to put doubt in the jurors' minds, but it served mostly to chafe Judge Parker.

"Now about that bay gelding," McRoy said. "Have you ever seen Mr. Thrasher riding him?"

"I probably have."

"No, Officer Moon. Have you ever seen him riding that horse?"

"I can't say for sure certain, but Charley Oskogee who lives just down the road says—"

"That will be all, Officer Moon."

Evans immediately called Charley Oskogee, who identified ax, hat, and the horse in the federal stable as having belonged to Thrasher. McRoy let him go without cross-examination. Charley Oskogee left the courtroom, seeming disappointed that his time on the stand had been so short.

Before Evans could call another witness, one of the jurors raised his hand, looking embarrassed and red-faced.

"See what he wants," Judge Parker snapped.

The bailiff went to the jury box and listened to the whispers of the juror and came back to the bench, smiling. He whispered to Judge Parker, who looked more and more annoyed, scowling at the jury. Then he slapped a palm against the green felt of the bench and declared a ten-minute recess. People in the courtroom began to rise and stretch, and there was a sudden burst of subdued conversation until Parker's bellow caught them with mouths open, staring at the bench.

"You people stay seated and keep still," he shouted. "You stay right there until this jury is out of here. I don't want anyone talking to this jury or interfering with them. You marshals take this jury out to the toilets and then to the jury room and keep those halls cleared. Once they're in the jury room, you people can go do whatever it is needs doing. But I don't want anyone near that jury."

Seventeen

EACH DAY AT NOON, A MISSOURI PACIFIC PASSENGER TRAIN departed Fort Smith for Little Rock. During that first recess I very nearly left the compound to pack and take it, to turn my back on everything. But I recalled my father telling me that if I wanted a place in criminal law, there would be situations unpleasant to a degree almost beyond bearing. I determined that my repugnance should not defeat me.

Testimony had begun when I returned to the courtroom and found Joe Mountain in my seat, grinning and once more wearing that outlandish plaid suit. He shoved people along the pew, squeezing them tight together to make a place for me beside him.

"I thought you might not come back, Eben Pay," the big Osage whispered.

"You're too perceptive for your own good, Joe." His long eyeteeth gleamed as the grin stretched across his flat face.

Oscar Schiller was on the stand. He had on a seersucker suit a little too big for his small frame. On the floor beneath the witness chair was the palmetto hat. He had combed his hair with water and it lay plastered to his skull, parted carefully in the middle. There were tiny red marks on his cheeks where he had cut himself shaving. He was holding an envelope and slip of paper in his hands.

"This is a letter we found in Johnny Boins' room in Eureka Springs after we arrested him," he said. "It's addressed to him. Mailed on the KATY at Muskogee, Creek Nation, postmarked May twenty-first."

"Read the letter, Marshal," Evans said.

"It says, 'J.B. A man named C found the place. Horse and girl. Meet me F.S. on 3 day of next month.' And then there's a pencil drawing of a deer's head."

"The three day of next month. What month would that be?"

"June. The third of June."

"Do you recall that date for any reason?"

"Yes. It was the day Mr. Eben Pay got to Fort Smith to begin work with the prosecutor's office."

"Now, what do you make of all these initials? This J.B. and this C and this F.S.? And the deer's head?"

"Objection," McRoy said.

"Sustained."

"Very well, Your Honor," Evans responded. "I ask this letter be placed in evidence."

"Object," McRoy said. "Anyone could have written that note."

"A postmark speaks for itself," Evans said. "But I can show chain of custody."

"You should have done that first, Mr. Evans. Proceed with it," Judge Parker said.

"Marshal Schiller, what did you do with this letter after you took it from Johnny Boins' room?"

"I've had it with me, in my custody, until a few minutes ago when I handed it to the bailiff."

"Your Honor?" Evans asked.

"The letter is admitted in evidence." Evans passed it to the jury and they began to hand it from one to the next.

Evans introduced the brass cartridge cases we had found in the Thrasher kitchen and the flattened slug Oscar Schiller had cut from under the skin of John Price's chest after we'd carried his body from the hogpen. McRoy objected but Parker allowed all of it to be introduced, once more after Schiller testified that the items had been in his possession since leaving the scene. Evans produced the ax once more, Schiller identified it, and it was introduced over McRoy's objection. The railing before the jury was becoming cluttered with exhibits.

Then the Texas pearl hat. But McRoy won on that, explaining to the court that there were likely at least ten men in the room who owned one like it and that anybody could sew on a button. Even if the prosecution could prove chain of custody from the Cornkiller farm, where we had taken it, McRoy contended, we had not placed it at the murder scene. Parker sustained him. Once all these exhibits were disposed of, Evans returned to his direct examination.

"Marshal Schiller, when you arrested Skitty Cornkiller, did he say anything to you about this crime?"

"While we were talking, one of us accused him of complicity in the

Thrasher killings, one of them being Mrs. Thrasher. He denied it and said Mrs. Thrasher was still alive. Words to that effect."

"Had you been looking for Mrs. Thrasher?"

"The Choctaw police had."

"Objection," McRoy shouted, in hot temper from all the wrangling over prosecution exhibits.

"Marshal," Parker said. "Do you have knowledge of that fact?"

"Yes sir. We found no trace of Mrs. Thrasher at the scene. Our posse looked for her immediately after, but until Cornkiller mentioned it, we had no idea whether she was alive or dead."

"The objection is overruled," Parker said. "Move along, Mr. Evans."

"Marshal, did you conduct a search of the Cornkiller farm?"

"I did."

"And did you find anything that might connect the people there with the crimes at the Thrasher farm?"

"We found a bay gelding with a T brand. We brought the horse to the federal stable in this city, and he has been there ever since."

"And to whom have you shown this horse?"

"I took George Moon and Charley Oskogee over there the day of the grand jury hearing on this case and they identified the horse."

"Marshal, did you eventually find Mrs. Thrasher?"

"I did. And like Cornkiller had said, she was alive. We got information from Mr. Pay that during an interview with the Thrasher girl, she had mentioned Mrs. Thrasher had a brother living near McAlester. That's where I found her, in hiding."

Evans turned the witness over to the defense, and McRoy began relentlessly, still irritated by some of the judge's rulings, I suspected. It seemed a tactical error to me. I would have led Schiller along in some more friendly vein, hoping to trap him. But it was soon apparent that it probably made little difference. Oscar Schiller was a cold and calculating witness, a professional at this kind of thing and confident in that knowledge. As McRoy bent toward him, firing questions rapidly, Schiller's eyes remained calm and unblinking behind the thick glasses.

"When you talked with Skitty Cornkiller, did you warn him that anything he said might be used against him?"

"He knew he was under arrest."

"You have a reputation for bringing in your man, don't you?"

"I usually get whoever I'm after."

"And you're proud of that reputation?"

"It's what they pay me for."

"You do it so well, in fact, that no matter whether the man is the right one or not, you bring him in."

"I arrest them. The court decides whether they're guilty."

McRoy was standing well back from the witness stand, his voice deep and resonant. It was in sharp contrast to the gravelly replies of Oscar Schiller.

"Do you carry railroad passes with you?"

"I do."

"And don't you collect travel expenses for witnesses, prisoners, and your own posse that actually come to Fort Smith on those passes?"

"That's right."

"Isn't that in violation of your oath?"

"I take no money fees from anyone. That would be in violation of my oath."

"And don't you take supplies from various stores in The Nations, and use horses from various livery stables there, and take other services from people who are afraid of you, and never pay for them?"

"Your Honor, I'm going to have to object to all this," Evans said easily from his chair. "Defense counsel is giving testimony. He's not cross-examining the witness. Besides, it's all irrelevant."

"Sustained," Judge Parker said. "Now Mr. McRoy, you're allowed wide latitude in cross, but the way this is going I'll have to disqualify you and put you on the witness stand under oath. Besides, the United States prosecutor is correct. It is irrelevant. The objection is sustained."

"I have nothing more for this honorable man," McRoy spat.

"Now Mr. McRoy," Judge Parker said, thrusting his head forward and tapping his glasses rapidly on the bench. "I won't have these asides any longer, either. You know better than that."

Evans called Moma July, and the little Creek policeman testified to finding the pistol in Smoker Chubee's quarters at Smith's Furnace. When Evans produced the weapon from a brown bag that had been lying on the prosecutor's desk throughout the trial, McRoy objected.

"Your Honor, we've had a deluge of material the prosecution has introduced here. It has reached the point of absurdity. Those shell casings and that bullet, they could have been fired from any weapon, any time, any place. Now this pistol. Everyone here knows there are likely hundreds of pistols like this one within a ten-mile radius of where we sit."

"Your Honor," Evans countered, "I have been interrupted, not for the first time, before I have completed my identification of an exhibit which I introduce here to show strong circumstance."

"Then complete your identification, Mr. Evans," Judge Parker said.

"Officer July, describe the weapon you took from Smoker Chubee's room."

"Well, when I took it out of Smoker's place, I said to myself I ain't ever seen a gun like this one. It was fine tuned, like a clock, like it was hand-tooled. Easy trigger and smooth hammer action. The blue was good on it and the walnut butts were deep-checked to keep it from slipping in a man's hand. The initials SC are burned into the grip. It's a better took care of gun than any I ever saw."

"Was there anything else?"

Moma July pulled a small dog-eared note pad from a coat pocket and frowned as he leafed thrugh it.

"I took the number on it. When I took it, I read the number and wrote it down. It was 3-0-6-4-3," he said.

Evans passed the pistol to Moma July.

"Please read the serial number on this weapon."

Moma July turned the pistol butt up and read the number from the frame just forward of the trigger guard. It was the same.

"And what caliber is this weapon?"

"It's a .45," Moma July said. "A .45 single-action, a Colt."

The big revolver was placed on the jury railing along with the other items there. Evans took the note we'd found in Johnny Boins's room and handed it to the witness.

"Let me show you this letter," he said. "Do you observe the drawing at the bottom?"

"Yes sir."

"Have you ever seen this symbol before?"

"Yes sir. It's the way Rufus Deer signed everything."

"You knew Rufus Deer?"

"All my life."

"Do many people in The Nations sign letters with such symbols?"

"A few do. I've never seen one like this except when Rufus signed it."

"And when did you last see Rufus Deer?"

"The night Marshal Burris Garret was killed over in Creek Nation. Rufus had been shot dead in that fuss."

"And when did you arrest Smoker Chubee?"

"About two hours later."

Evans introduced the grand jury indictment against Smoker Chubee, charging that he and Rufus Deer, deceased, had killed Burris Garret.

"Was Smoker Chubee convicted of this offense?"

"Yes sir, in this court."

"Your witness, Mr. McRoy," Evans said.

McRoy sat at his table, rubbing his forehead with his fingertips. His eyes were closed and he was frowning.

"No questions," he said.

"Call your next witness," Judge Parker said.

Evans, still on his feet, turned toward the jail corridor.

"I call Mrs. Thomas Thrasher."

All eyes followed her small figure across the room to the witness stand. She was wearing a long, loosely fitting dress of bleached muslin; on her head, holding back pitch-black hair, was a purple scarf knotted beneath her chin. I had seen many Choctaw women wearing such scarves, and it somehow gave her the look of a Greek vineyard worker. Her face was composed and rather handsome. When she was sworn, she looked at Judge Parker with wide, dark eyes. She had come here, Oscar Schiller had told me, to relate her story to Judge Parker, and I wondered if until this moment she had fully realized it would have to be told before a room crowded with white people.

"Madam, what is your name and where do you live?" Evans asked.

"I'm Mrs. Thomas Thrasher and I live in Winding Stair Mountains, in the Choctaw Nation." Her voice was soft and the words were spoken slowly and deliberately. I suspected she had been part of those reading-aloud evenings Jennie had told me about. Wherever she had learned her English, she had learned it well.

"Mrs. Thrasher, I know it is hard for you to come here and tell of the terrible events that led to your husband's death. I know it will not be an easy task. But I ask you now to relate for us what happened that day in June on your farm in Winding Stair."

She hesitated only for a moment, her eyes going across the room, seeing the gape-mouthed faces. After that first look, she held her gaze away from the crowd, as though she might be pretending that no others were there.

"It was on June seventh," she began. "I was below the house, planting some flowers when I heard my husband call Jennie, my stepdaughter. He had a funny sound to his voice. I went up the breezeway through the house. I started along the breezeway from the back porch toward the front when my husband came out of Jennie's bedroom. I didn't see her. She'd been in the kitchen getting something ready to cook. She was a good cook. My husband had taught her when she was a little girl—"

She seemed to be wandering, her eyes gone vacant. Evans interrupted her and she gave a little start, coming back to the moment.

"Yes, Mrs. Thrasher, and what happened then?"

"I started towards my husband, there in the breezeway, and he grabbed my arm and said I'd have to hide. But before we could get into the other bedroom, this man came up on the front porch and saw us. That man," she said, and pointed to Smoker Chubee. She stopped again, looking at Chubee's face, and he sat easily at the defense table, his jaw working slowly on his tobacco. His eyes were flat, passionless.

"Yes, Mrs. Thrasher?" Evans urged gently.

"I hadn't heard any horses, but that dark man was there, and he was grinning at us and there was a big black pistol in his pants. He said to me and my husband, 'Come on out to the front, folks. You've got company.' He said it quiet, but I was afraid, the way he looked at us.

"Me and my husband went out front, that dark man behind us. They were there on horses. Four of them. Those three sitting there," and she pointed again, her finger stopping at each of the defendants, "and another one, a little man I thought was a Creek, with a white eye. I heard

215

these other men call him Rufus. I heard them call the dark one with the big pistol Smoker. I don't remember the other names."

She paused, bending her head down as she swallowed. Evans moved to his desk and poured a glass of water from a pitcher. She took the glass in both hands and sipped it slowly. When she had finished drinking, Evans took the glass from her and she turned to Judge Parker, who was looking down at her sympathetically.

"I hope I can tell it all, Judge."

"You just take your time, Mrs. Thrasher, and tell it as though only you and I are here," he said. "It's hard, but it has to be told."

"Yes sir. The men on the horses were all grinning at us. They had bottles and were drinking. The one called Rufus said their horses needed water. That's when I saw one of them was the Creek whiskey peddler that had come by the place some time before. Then my husband said they were welcome to water and they all got down. That colored man took the horses to the well and drew up a bucket. He was laughing and he fell down twice. The others just came up on the porch and stood around us, grinning, and they didn't say anything.

"Then the one they called Smoker, that one," pointing again, "he went back in the house and after a while came out with my husband's shotgun and rifle. He took 'em over and threw them in the well. I started shaking then because I was afraid, and I stood behind my husband. The man called Rufus said they'd come to buy some horses. My husband said he didn't have any for sale. So the Creek whiskey peddler, he went down to the barn while we all stood around on the porch, and when he came back he said the black was there. I knew he was talking about Tar Baby, my husband's racer. The one with the bad eye, the one they called Rufus, said he wanted to buy that horse. My husband said he wasn't for sale."

Evans had placed the half-empty water glass on the edge of Judge Parker's bench, within her reach. Now she took it and drank again and I saw her hands shaking. She brushed her lips lightly with her hand.

"So then that white man," and she pointed to Johnny Boins, "asked my husband where his daughter was at. My husband said she was in town, visiting some friends. And when he said that, this white man swore an oath. He started to come over to my husband, but the man called Rufus laughed and pushed him away and said they were hungry and wanted something to eat.

"They all went into the kitchen with us, and my husband said they were welcome to anything we had. There was some ham and sweet potatoes and some other stuff, I don't remember what. I fixed it and put out dishes on the table and they drank from their bottles and laughed and talked, mostly about racing horses. My husband they had sitting over against one wall on the floor, and the one called Smoker was standing beside him. When I had the meal on the table, I went over and sat down next to my husband.

"After a little bit, our two hired hands came in. They'd been out driving our cows to some summer pasture in the woods. John Price and Oshutubee. They sat down and ate some ham, too, and took some drinks from these other men. The one called Rufus said they ought to eat, after working so hard, but they were both a little scared, too. While they were all eating, that white man . . ."

"Johnny Boins," Evans said.

"Yes. Well, he asked Oshutubee where Jennie was at. Oshutubee looked over at my husband, and then he said he didn't know. In a little while, Oshutubee said he needed to go outside and they all laughed and said the ham was good but too greasy. Oshutubee got up from the table and went out and the one called Smoker went with him. In a minute, the one called Rufus got up, too, and went out back. When he did, that Creek whiskey peddler took out a little pistol and put it on the table and said we'd all just sit and talk while Oshutubee made his business out back in the privy, and when he got back he could tell us all about it. They all laughed at that, too. Except John Price, who was real scared by then. He looked a little sick to his stomach.

"Then I heard shooting in the backyard. I think there were six shots. Everybody just sat there real quiet then. Pretty soon the man with the bad eye and this Smoker came in, and Smoker had his pistol out. He started hulling empty cartridge casings out of his gun and reloading it. That's when my husband said they could take the horses and anything else they wanted, but not to hurt anybody. John Price had started shaking. They made us go out to the front yard again. Then . . ."

She coughed, and Evans went to his table and refilled the water glass. She drank once more, the only sound in the courtroom the low buzz of September flies. Mrs. Thrasher almost choked on the water, coughing for a moment after Evans took the glass. At the defense table,

Nason Grube was facedown on his folded arms. Beside him Skitty Cornkiller was slumped in his chair, his eyes unseeing. But Johnny Boins was sitting straight, a smile still on his lips, his eyes searching the faces of the jury. Smoker Chubee chewed slowly, his pockmarked jaws working methodically.

"They made my husband and John Price go out in the yard. The white man pushed me up against the wall . . . and started putting his hands under my clothes. He kept asking me where my daughter was, and laughing. He started unbuttoning my clothes. My husband saw it and the ones in the yard pushed him down in the dirt."

She caught her breath with a sharp, rasping intake, her face showing the strain. Judge Parker spoke to her softly, so softly I couldn't hear his words. Her breasts lifted as she took a deep breath.

"The man called Rufus told my husband and John Price to take off their clothes. They were all waving guns around then. They made my husband and John Price take off their clothes, down to their underwear . . ." She broke down for a moment, her choked sobbing the only sound now where even the buzzing flies were unheard. With a shudder, she continued, her eyes bright with the tears.

"The man called Rufus said he wanted my husband and John Price to fight. They shoved them together. That colored man was laughing, lying on the ground, and the white man was still feeling me and trying to get my clothes off. The other two, Rufus and the whiskey peddler, were standing behind my husband and John Price, shoving them together, hitting them with guns. The one called Smoker was over at the well curb, watching, just standing there rolling the cylinder of his gun with his fingers. Then the one called Rufus made John Price take off his underwear and he was naked. That whiskey peddler was shooting at the ground close to my husband's feet, yelling they should fight or he'd shoot them in the backside.

"But John Price broke and run. Toward the barn, running all naked. The one called Rufus started yelling, 'Shoot him, shoot him,' and he was making foul oaths. That's when Smoker shot John Price in the back, while he was running away."

She paused to take another deep breath and I looked at Smoker Chubee. He was still chewing, but the fingers of his hands were making little tapping movements on the tabletop.

"Then it all started happening," Mrs. Thrasher said, her voice trembling and hardly audible in the room. "Two of them carried John Price's body to the pigpen and threw it in. They were laughing about it. That's when the white man, Boins, turned me loose and him and the man with the bad eye tied my husband to the well curbing. My husband was begging them . . ." She choked on it and bent her face into her hands. But she recovered quickly. "I could hear the white man, Boins, raving about my stepdaughter. He was saying vile things about her and about my husband. He was foaming at the mouth when he ran back onto the porch and tore at my clothes and my husband was begging them to stop and take anything they wanted. They got all around me and had me on the floor on my back . . . tearing off my clothes until I was all . . . naked. They . . . held me there, and . . . each of them knew me, each one, and the others watching and my husband begging them to take anything . . ."

She stopped again, but her crying was finished. It was as though she were in a hypnotic trance, her eyes wide and glassy, staring above the heads of the spectators. This time, when Parker spoke, I could hear him.

"Mrs. Thrasher, there is nothing for you to be ashamed of," he said gently. "You have done no wrong."

"I tried to fight them," she said, the words rushing out now. "Then afterwards, they just left me lying there, except for the whiskey peddler, and he sat close to me with his little pistol and he'd point it at me and make a popping sound with his lips and then laugh. The others started shooting at my chickens. But nobody hit one, and the man called Rufus said something to Smoker, and he started shooting them, killing them with his big pistol. The colored man said there was a dog hid under the porch. He was just an old hound dog. He never even barked at anybody who came. He was old and afraid. The one called Smoker bent down and looked under the porch and then he shot under there and I heard the old dog make one little bark and that was all.

"Somebody said all this made them hungry again. They dragged me into the house, holding me where I was naked. But the white man, Boins, was yelling bad things about my husband and stepdaughter and I saw him take the ax from a chopping log at the end of the porch. I saw him running out to the well curbing where my husband was tied, and I screamed at him because I was afraid for my husband. But the others had me inside by then. They tied me to Jennie's bed with cotton line we had on the breezeway for hanging wash when it rained. Outside, I heard my husband yell once. Then they were all in the kitchen, breaking things and running through the house. The white man came in, and he was all bloody and . . . he knew me again, there on Jennie's bed. He was all bloody.''

I thought of Jennie, lying in the attic above that brutal scene. Behind me, a woman in the crowd had begun to sob.

"After the white man left me, I got loose. They were too drunk to tie me good. I was afraid to go into the breezeway. I could hear them in the kitchen. I went out one of the bedroom windows and started around the front of the house to untie my husband, but when I saw him . . . I knew he was dead. And that one," she pointed to Smoker Chubee, "was leaning against the well curbing, looking at me. I went a little crazy. I started to run, and I thought he'd shoot me like he did John Price. But nothing happened and I ran down the hill away from the house so they couldn't see me, the ones inside in the kitchen. I ran across the McAlester road and into the woods and started west towards my brother's farm.''

Her story was finished, and there was a soundless sigh in the courtroom, felt but not heard. Her hands in her lap were working together, the fingers twisting.

"Mrs. Thrasher, how long did it take you to get to your brother's?" Evans asked.

She gave a little jerk, her eyes slowly coming into focus. When she spoke, the words were shrill, almost hysterical.

"I don't know. I was naked, and then the storm came and I sheltered under a big cedar while it was dark and wet. I ran past the place where my husband had his cows on summer pasture. The bushes cut me. I slept and went on and it was daylight and I stayed in the deep woods. I hid in my brother's barn at night until he came out to do the morning milking.''

"And you stayed at your brother's farm until Marshal Schiller found you there?"

"Yes sir. The Cap'n came to my brother's house twice. The first time, I was afraid to come out. I was scared of those men finding me. The next time, he told my brother the men who did it had been caught and the one called Rufus had been killed up at Okmulgee. So I came out and he brought me here."

"Mrs. Thrasher, I know this is a terrible experience, but allow me to ask once more. These men who knew you against your will and came to your farm and killed your two hired men and your husband, are these those same men?" And he swept his arm back toward the defense table. Her eyes sought the face of each one, pausing only a few seconds on the bowed head of Nason Grube.

"Yes, they're the ones, along with the one they called Rufus, who had a bad eye."

Now, again, Evans asked for the black Texas hat, and when he placed it in her hands she broke down once more and for a few terrible long moments sat sobbing.

"Is this your husband's hat?"

Now I understand why Evans had made such a small fight of introducing the hat before, why he had not even shown it to Jennie. It would have been superfluous, at best. The impact on the jury of Mrs. Thrasher holding her husband's hat and sobbing, head down, must have been overwhelming.

"Let the record show she has answered in the affirmative," Judge Parker said. "You may enter it in evidence if you wish, Mr. Evans."

"Mrs. Thrasher, I had planned to ask you to identify other items here today, but the experience has been painful enough already. You are a brave woman."

McRoy came out of his chair with great hesitation. From his expression, I knew this trial had now become a painfully distasteful experience for him and I could not help but feel sympathetic. As he neared her, she regained control and her dark eyes met his.

"Only a few questions, Mrs. Thrasher," he said, addressing her as gently as Evans had. "You said these men were drinking. How drunk were they?"

"Your Honor, she has no way of quantifying such a thing," Evans said.

"You'll have to rephrase that, Mr. McRoy."

"Very well, Your Honor. Mrs. Thrasher, you saw these men drinking? How much drinking were they doing?"

"They had been drinking when they got there. They all had bottles and they drank all the while. Some of them couldn't hardly stand up. Except for the one they called Smoker. I didn't see him drinking."

"They were crazy drunk?"

Before he could object, Mrs. Thrasher said they were and Evans let it pass.

"Now Mrs. Thrasher," McRoy said, "you were afraid and highly excited while all this was going on. Being in that state, how can you be sure these are the men who were there that day?"

"Because I saw them."

"But can you be sure these are the same men?"

"She's said so, Mr. McRoy, she's testified to it," Parker snapped, and his glasses made their little pecking sound on the green felt.

"Mrs. Thrasher, how frequently do you see colored men down there in Winding Stair?"

"There are a few there," she said.

"But you don't see them often?"

"Not very."

"This defendant," McRoy said, and he pointed to Nason Grube. "Was there anything about his face that would make you remember him?"

Nason Grube had placed his face in his arms on the defense table.

"He was just a colored man."

"Nothing unusual about his features?"

"No. Just a colored man."

McRoy walked back to the defense table and whispered to Nason Grube. When the black face rose, the eyes were red as though he had been crying. McRoy touched the large welted scars along Nason Grube's cheeks.

"Scars so obvious as this, Mrs. Thrasher, and you failed to see them?"

"I was too scared to notice that," she said.

"Everyone in this courtroom can see these scars, Mrs. Thrasher. And are you telling us now that you saw no such scars on the face of the man who lay close over your body that day. . . ?"

"Mr. McRoy, there is no need to be that graphic," Judge Parker snapped.

"Very well, Your Honor. Mrs. Thrasher, you did not see these scars that day?"

"I don't remember. It was all so sudden and awful."

McRoy shook his head and walking around the defense table to his chair glanced at the jury.

"That's all I have."

"Mrs. Thrasher, you're excused," Judge Parker said. "Mr. Evans?"

"Your Honor, the government rests."

Eighteen

THE JURY WAS A GRIM-FACED CREW AFTER MRS. THRASHER'S testimony. Among the spectators, even the horse racers and chicken fighters were taking no bets on acquittal, at any odds. But McRoy still seemed confident when he called his first witness, a man named Philas Schafer, who identified himself as the Boinses' family doctor. He was a smallish man with a well-trimmed beard and perhaps the most expensive waistcoat in the room.

"Doctor Schafer, what has been your relationship to Johnny Boins and his family," McRoy started.

"I have been their physician. I have been the personal confidant of the family for years, and a personal friend of John Boins, Senior."

"And what has been the relationship between Johnny and his parents?"

"On the parents' part, a bit of overindulgence and a tendency to overlook what in normal children and young men is generally considered to be antisocial activity. On the boy's part, a sometimes violently manifested urge to break family ties, although this has been thwarted by the parents' overweening attention to him and his own reluctance to leave their protection."

"Your Honor, I don't see that this has any relevancy to the case," Evans remarked almost casually.

"It may well have, Mr. Evans," Judge Parker said. "I'm going to allow it for a while yet. Proceed, Mr. McRoy."

"Doctor, as a medical expert, how would you describe Johnny Boins as a boy and as a young man?"

"At a very early age, it was apparent he was different. Unlike other boys. He was wild and undisciplined, often violent to his playmates and to adults, to the extent sometimes of inflicting physical injury. This was a condition that persisted throughout his life. The most disturbing part of it was that he never showed contrition for his acts. I have never known him to display the slightest repugnance over anything he did."

Johnny Boins looked back through the crowd, arrogantly, as though proud of what this medical man was saying.

"As an expert witness, Doctor, would you say that the defendant often acted without any clear understanding of what was right and wrong?"

"I would say so, many times. Although he was brought up in a Christian home of outstanding quality, given love and affection, he seemed to rebel against all proper deportment from an early age."

"In your opinion as a medical expert, Doctor, would you say this condition has improved over the years," McRoy said. It began to be amusing, this constant reference to Schafer as a "medical expert," a term designed to impress the jury, but from their expressions having little effect.

"It has not improved. It has gotten worse."

"Would you say at this moment, Doctor, that Johnny Boins is capable of determining what is morally right and wrong?"

"No, I doubt he can make that distinction."

McRoy was trying to avoid the rope by sending his client to the asylum, and Johnny Boins seemed unaware of what was happening. Or, I thought, perhaps he knew exactly and was playing his part well. He still smirked, his eyes going boldly about the room.

"Do you think he can make such a determination before the law?"

"If he cannot determine right from wrong morally, it is hardly likely he can do so under the law. The restraints of Christian morality are more wide-ranging, it seems to me, than are those of the law."

There was an interesting point of procedure here. McRoy was having his cake and eating it, too, pleading his client not guilty yet arguing now for consideration of a verdict of not guilty by reason of insanity. Normally, he would have to plead to that effect, which is actually an admission of guilt though not culpable due to mental derangement. But he hadn't done that. It was as if he were giving the jury a choice: Johnny was either not at the Thrasher farm at all, or else if he was, he was insane. I assumed Judge Parker was allowing it due to the pressure of Supreme Court review and to ensure that no one could say the defendants had not obtained their full day in court. Evans remained silent for his own reasons.

"Does drinking strong spirits have any influence on this behavior?" McRoy asked.

"It makes it worse. The restraints of morality are lessened by hard drink, even in a normal person, and in Johnny Boins there has never been much moral restraint to begin with."

"As an expert witness, Doctor, do you think Johnny Boins has been incapable of making a determination of right from wrong over, say, the last year?"

"It is my opinion he has not had that capability."

"Your witness," McRoy said, wheeling toward the defense table with that now familiar flourish, his head up, smiling, looking pleased and sure of himself.

I suspected Evans was in unknown territory, but I was soon to learn that such an experienced prosecutor did not stand in awe of any expert witness.

"Doctor Schafer," Evans said, "what is the nature of your practice?"

"I am a general practitioner."

"In that role, how much time do you spend reading the most recent literature on the practice of medicine as it applies to mental disorders and insanity?"

"I have read some of it, certainly," Schafer said, becoming a little indignant. Evans was unperturbed, moving calmly, the best I had seen him at any time in this court.

"Are you familiar with any of the periodicals inspired by studies on mental disorders done in such places as Vienna?"

"I read German very badly," Schafer said, and laughed.

"In your practice, I would suppose that you need to keep abreast of developments in such diverse fields as surgery, obstetrics, infectious disease, respiratory ailments, constipation, falling hair, blemished skin, and other such things. Is that true, Doctor?"

The doctor flushed as the laughter spread through the crowd. Judge Parker sat with his head down, one hand over his face, and I could see the smile behind it.

"Yes, my practice is diverse," Schafer said.

"Then how do you find time, Doctor, to read so widely in the field of insanity?"

"I try to keep up with all manner of medicine."

"Doctor, have you ever studied at an institution the symptoms or the treatment for insanity?"

"Well, no—"

"But Doctor," Evans cut in sharply, "you have been presented here as an expert on the subject."

"Well, I am not what you'd call an expert on insanity."

"I could have sworn I heard the defense counsel refer to you as a 'medical expert.'" And the people laughed again, and a few of the jurors as well. "But never mind. You used the word *normal*. What is a normal person?"

"It would be difficult to provide a definition on the spur of the moment."

"You have indicated that Johnny Boins was not normal, and it seemed that was on the spur of the moment."

"I've watched him over a good many years."

"Did you watch him, or treat him, or even see him throughout the month of June last?"

"No, I don't believe I saw him during that time."

"Yet, you would come here and state that at the time of the Winding Stair crimes, which occurred in June, that he was not able to distinguish between right and wrong?"

"That is my opinion," Schafer said.

Evans startled the courtroom with a short, harsh laugh, a burst of mirthless sound, and abruptly he sat down.

When McRoy called his next witness, the crowd moved expectantly, and Judge Parker subdued them with his usual slap on the bench. Johnny Boins walked to the stand and lifted his hand to be sworn, his lips twisted into a crooked smile as though he had some dark secret about to be shared.

"Johnny, do you have headaches?" McRoy asked.

"All the time," he said, but there was no show of pain on his face nor even the flicker of its memory.

"Are you sometimes forgetful?"

"Your Honor, he's leading his witness," Evans said without rising.

"Rephrase it, Mr. McRoy."

"What is the state of your health, Johnny?"

"Not good. There are times I get these bad headaches and there are times I can't remember anything."

227

"How do you relieve this pain?"

"I take these powders the druggist gives me, but they don't do much good. Usually, I drink."

"And what happens when you drink?"

"I don't have headaches anymore," he said, and laughed. "And I don't usually remember anything."

"Now Johnny, you've heard in testimony here of a letter written to you by someone who drew a deer's-head signature. Do you recall getting that letter?"

"Sure. I met Rufus Deer in the Creek Nation a long time ago, and we sometimes went to horse races together, and sometimes chicken fights. Last May we were at Saddler's Ford on the North Canadian where they were having some races. Rufus saw this black stallion he wanted to buy, but before he could make any offer, the man who owned the horse left."

"It was at this time you met a girl named Jennie Thrasher?"

"Sure. At Wetumka I think it was a few days before, then at Saddler's Ford. Her daddy owned the horse Rufus wanted to buy. I got to know Jennie pretty well," and he laughed again. Joe Mountain, still beside me, placed a hand on my leg and patted me as though soothing a skittery horse, as though he were afraid I'd leap over the railing and assault the witness. "I told her I'd marry her and she asked me to come to her daddy's farm because she was willing. But her daddy found us together and threatened to kill me if I ever came around again, so I decided it was useless and forgot it."

"Then you received the letter?"

"Sure. Rufus knew about the girl and that I was taken with her, and of course I knew about that horse he wanted to buy. I'd gone on home to Eureka Springs and then I got the letter. He'd sent somebody to find that horse, and the girl was there, too. So I decided I'd go with him and maybe I could talk her daddy into letting us get married."

"What happened then, Johnny?"

"I met Rufus here in Fort Smith. We went across the river that night and got good and drunk. I guess we stayed drunk for two weeks. I don't remember anything until I was back home."

"Do you recall going to the Winding Stair Mountains?"

"Rufus may have, I don't know. I don't ever remember being down in that part of The Nations. A little far south of my normal range."

"Have you ever seen any of these defendants before, the ones at that table where you've been sitting?"

"I never have. Not until they brought 'em into this jail, where they had me locked up."

"Now Johnny, this loss of memory when you're drinking. Does it happen often?"

"All the time. The pain in my head gets so bad and I start drinking and then I can't remember. I was up in Missouri once for over two months, and didn't remember a thing."

"You might say your mind leaves your body."

"You might say that."

"No more questions," McRoy said. Evans sat for a long time, staring at the witness, then shook his head.

Nason Grube took the stand, his eyes still bloodshot. He sat on the edge of the chair, his hands clasped between his knees.

"Nason, have you ever been in the Choctaw Nation?"

"No sir, I ain't."

"Nason, how do you make a living?"

"I work on Mr. Cornkiller's farm," Grube said. "I work there all the time."

"Were you there during the month of June?"

"Yes sir, I ain't been off the farm since last Christmas when me and Mr. Cornkiller went into Muskogee to get drunk."

"Was Mr. Cornkiller there, too?"

"Most of the time. He went to Okmulgee once and then to Muskogee to trade horses. He goes around Creek Nation and horse-trades some."

McRoy had been holding a slip of yellow tablet paper behind his back throughout this, and now he presented it to the witness.

"Do you recognize this document, Nason?"

"Yes sir. It's a bill of sale."

"Your Honor, I ask this be entered in evidence," McRoy said. "It indicates that on June tenth, 1890, a bay gelding and a blue roan mare were sold to one Skitty Cornkiller in Creek Nation the Indian Territory, for the sum of seventy-five dollars each."

"Objection," Evans shouted. "I request His Honor instruct the jury."

229

"Sustained," Parker said. "The jury will disregard the defense counsel's statements going to the content of this paper. Let me see that thing."

He carefully placed his glasses on the end of his nose and studied the yellow paper intently, then shook his head.

"Mr. McRoy, you're going to have to show proper foundation for this. More than the testimony of the witness. It is self-serving."

"Your Honor, may I call another witness at this time?"

"Prosecution hasn't had the opportunity to cross," Parker said.

"I will recall Mr. Grube, Your Honor."

"This is all playacting," Evans said, obviously upset. "A sudden so-called bill of sale, and now this sandwiching of witnesses."

"I am going to allow it, Mr. Evans," Parker said, a dangerous edge on his voice. "But I must tell you, Mr. McRoy, your sequence of witnesses leaves a great deal to be desired."

I wondered if Judge Parker would have so ruled before his decisions became subject to review by the Supreme Court. Nason Grube clanked back to his place and McRoy called James Fentress, a man who identified himself as an operative of the Acme Detective Agency in Little Rock. He was a seedy-looking man with a face like a squirrel, running mostly to nose.

"Would you explain your involvement in the cause now in hearing?" McRoy asked.

"Yes. I was retained by your law firm, Mr. McRoy, to go into Creek Nation and search the premises of a farm occupied by two of these defendants, Nason Grube and Skitty Cornkiller."

"Did you find anything of evidentiary value?"

"We found a bill of sale for two horses. It was stuck behind a calendar tacked to the kitchen wall. I suppose it was a kitchen. There was a cookstove in there."

I tried to picture in my mind the Cornkiller farm, but too many other images intervened. I could recall nothing tacked to the walls of the kitchen except a page from a *Police Gazette*, an engraving of a woman trapeze artist. McRoy was passing the slip of paper to the witness.

"This is the paper," Fentress said.

"Would you describe the signature?"

230

"Yes, it's a drawing. The whole thing is done in pencil, and there's no proper signature. Only a drawing of what appears to be a deer's head, with antlers."

There was a grumble of sudden conversation in the crowd and Judge Parker slammed the bench with his hand. McRoy asked once more that the bill of sale be entered in evidence, and over Evans's fuming about theatrics, Judge Parker allowed it. Fentress was excused and once more Nason Grube was on the stand, hands tightly held between his knees.

"Nason," McRoy said, "have you ever killed anyone?"

"Never in my life. No sir."

"Nason, when was the last time you knew a woman?"

For a moment, Nason Grube sat silent, his fingers twitching. He drew a deep breath and swallowed, and I could not help feeling sorry for him.

"Mr. McRoy, I don't remember. It's been a long time ago."

"Nason, have you ever raped anyone?"

"God is my witness, Mr. McRoy, I ain't ever done that."

"Now Nason, you know that you are testifying here under oath and that in God's name you have sworn to tell the truth—"

"For heaven's sake, Your Honor," Evans shouted.

"All right, all right," Parker said, waving Evans back into his seat. "Get on with it, Mr. McRoy."

"Nason, have you ever been in the Choctaw Nation?"

"No sir, never in my life."

Evans was across the room in a headlong rush to begin his cross-examination. He grabbed the Texas pearl hat from the railing before the jury and waved it under Nason Grube's nose. Grube drew back quickly, his eyes going wide.

"You were arrested with this hat on your head," Evans said, and his voice shook with intensity. "Where did you get it?"

"Mr. Cornkiller give it to me. He had it one time when he come back from Muskogee or Okmulgee, I don't remember which. He'd been horse tradin' and he said—"

"Never mind what he said," Evans roared, tossing the hat in the general direction of the jury. It came to rest on the floor directly before the box. "Can you read, Mr. Grube?"

"No sir."

"Then how can you recognize a bill of sale?"

"I seen it before."

Evans darted over to the jury railing again. He snatched the yellow paper and thrust it into Nason Grube's hands.

"Read that, Mr. Grube."

There was a long pause, Grube staring at the paper in his hands. He shook his head.

"You don't know whether it says something about two horses or three pigs, do you, Mr. Grube?"

"No sir, I just seen that—"

"All right, please just answer my questions," Evans said, pulling the paper from Grube's hands. "Now you say you've never been in Choctaw Nation, is that right?"

"I never been there."

"Isn't it true that you first came into the Indian country on a work permit with the Missouri, Kansas and Texas railroad?"

"Yes sir."

"That line runs straight through the Choctaw Nation."

"But I was just workin' on the northern section—"

Evans cut in again, pressing harder than he had at any point in this trial. It was having its effect on the witness, who had begun to sweat, his black face shining and the scar welts seeming to stand out even more prominently on his cheeks.

"Didn't you watch the officers from this court searching your farm the day you were arrested?"

"I see 'em lookin' around, yes sir."

"They didn't find any bill of sale, did they?"

"Objection," McRoy said. "He's testifying, Your Honor."

"Sustained."

Evans kept boring in, keeping Grube confused as his questions jumped back and forth from one subject to another. Grube's mind seemed to adjust to each new idea and then he was asked about something else. It was a technique I wanted to remember.

"You and Mr. Cornkiller over there, you make a lot of money farming, is that true?"

"No sir, we don't make much."

"How much do you make, in say a year?"

"Not much. We sell a little garden truck."

"And those trips of Mr. Cornkiller's, they aren't for trading stock, are they? They're for selling whiskey, isn't that right?"

"We sell some. . . ."

"Don't you trade whiskey for groceries when you need them, and a pair of shoes now and then?"

"Yes sir."

"That so-called bill of sale says you paid seventy-five dollars each for two horses. That's a lot of money. Where did it come from, Mr. Grube?"

Nason Grube's eyes darted around the room.

"When's the last time you saw seventy-five dollars on that farm?"

"I don't remember. Mr. Cornkiller . . ."

"You were sitting right over there," and Evans pointed to the defense table, at the vacant chair between Cornkiller and Smoker Chubee, "when a little Choctaw woman, a brave little woman, testified under oath that you raped her."

"I never done that, I swear I never done that . . ."

"So now, you're telling us that she was lying, that she saw your face just over hers when she was lying on that porch naked and—"

"Objection, Your Honor," McRoy shouted, banging the table with his fists.

"Stop the dramatics, Mr. Evans," Judge Parker said.

"Your Honor, I was simply paraphrasing an early question of the defense counsel when Mrs. Thrasher was on the stand," Evans said, his nostrils flared.

"Mr. Evans, I repeat, stop the dramatics."

"Very well." Evans strode away from the stand and turned back, his arms extended stiffly at his sides. "Are you testifying that Mrs. Thrasher was lying?"

"Yes sir, I guess I am. I think she just got the wrong nigger."

Evans released the witness, and the fury of his attack left the crowd leaning forward openmouthed as McRoy rested his case. Once more, McRoy moved for a directed verdict and once more Judge Parker denied it.

233

Judge Parker said he would take closing arguments after a noon recess, and Joe Mountain and I went out along the river to smoke together. I had no yearning for food, and the big Osage sensed my need for solitude.

"You want me to leave you alone, Eben Pay?"

"No, I'd rather you walked with me, Joe," I said. "I just want to be away from that mob back there."

The shock of Jennie Thrasher's testimony had already begun to wear off, but the thought of it left a bitter taste in my mouth. I considered the defendants, back there in the federal building, chained and waiting now for judgment. A two-week drunk, Johnny Boins had said, and the lives of so many people changed as a result of it, damaged or destroyed forever. It had touched me only in passing, and yet I knew that at this moment, walking along the river with my friend, Eben Pay was a different man than the one who had taken the train south from Saint Louis little more than three months before.

"Going away from a trial like that, a murder trial, leaves a man empty, Joe," I said. "It wrings a man out."

"I like it," he said, his teeth showing when he turned his head toward me. The wind spread the tail of his plaid suitcoat out behind his butt like the cowcatcher on a Frisco locomotive. "I like them men up there yellin' at one another."

"You go after somebody with all the enthusiasm and ardor of justice on the march, and then when you've got them in that room, with their lives in the balance, everything takes on a new dimension."

He stopped and looked at me for a moment, only half sensing what I was saying.

"Well, I like goin' after 'em, too. But I like it near as well when they're in front of Parker. I like it all."

"It takes away all a man's dignity, having his life laid out bare before all those gawking people, sopping it up like free whiskey. Hell, even a killer ought to have some dignity left to himself."

"You worry too much, Eben Pay," Joe Mountain said.

We were standing now on the high ground of Belle Point, where the Arkansas and the Poteau flow together. The breeze off the flat floodplain to the west was cool. It was almost like October, and I half expected to smell elm leaves burning, as they would be soon along the streets of my home in Saint Louis. As soon as this was over, I would go there, to see after my mother's health and sort out my thoughts, waiting the verdict of the Supreme Court, for I knew Merriweather McRoy would appeal both the Garret and the Thrasher cases.

We watched a small Negro boy pull a three-foot catfish from the water near the new pilings of the Jay Gould bridge. I was reminded of Emmitt, still cloistered in that cell in the women's jail, still frightened for his life.

"I wonder what it feels like, being on trial for your life?" I asked. Joe Mountain squeezed the fire from his cigarette and shredded the short butt, watching the tobacco blow quickly away in the wind.

"You sure bother yourself about funny things, Eben Pay. You don't have to think about that, unless you do murder. And get caught."

"Justice tempered with mercy," I said. "That's the way it's supposed to work." From where we stood, we could see the gallows roof in the federal compound, rising above the stone wall.

"Well, if you got to think about that, just put your mind to what we found in that farmyard. Wasn't much mercy showed there, was there? Besides, maybe ole McRoy will argue them jurors into a not guilty," and he laughed.

"McRoy's good. He's a good lawyer, knows plenty of tricks." Somewhere along the river, a train whistled. "I wonder why Johnny Boins' parents weren't there?"

"They gone. I heard they left town two days ago."

"Maybe it's understandable, knowing the strong case Evans had, not wanting to be there and see their boy in that situation. But how could they just take that train out of here, and leave him alone?"

"Maybe they give up on him finally," Joe Mountain said. "Anyway, it don't matter to Johnny Boins. He don't give a damn. He don't give a damn for nothin'."

I thought of Smoker Chubee. Grube and Cornkiller seemed to me poor derelicts caught up in all this, brought into it by Rufus Deer. But there was an evil and brooding spirit about the dark-skinned man with the deep pockmarks, impossible to define. Thinking of him made a chill go up my spine, as it had so often when I watched him in the courtroom.

"What about that Chubee, Joe?"

For a long time, Joe Mountain looked across the river into the Indian country, where beginning heat was making a blue haze far out along the horizon.

"In the old days, he'd have been leading war parties," he said, and I sensed a certain admiration in his voice. "He's a deadly man, Eben Pay."

His sudden seriousness was somehow funny, and I laughed.

"You sound as though you might be afraid of him, Joe."

"Any man's a fool if he ain't a little scared of a homeless dog," he said. Then he laughed, too, showing those huge teeth. "But I tell you, I'm glad the only time we ever shot at each other, he missed. What bothers me is I missed, too, that night in Creek Nation. That bothers me, Eben Pay."

Downriver, we could see a steamboat pulling into one of the docks at the foot of Garrison Avenue. On the decks were bushels of peaches and bales of cotton, these last for the Fort Smith textile mills.

"Well, we'd best get back," I said. "We may as well see the finish of this."

"You bet," Joe Mountain said.

When Evans rose to make his argument, his hair and beard were fresh combed. All his combativeness of the closing moments of testimony was gone, and when he spoke his voice was calm and deliberate.

"Gentlemen of the jury. The evidence has shown that at the very least, this is what happened. Rufus Deer and Johnny Boins planned a vicious crime together. Having seen a racehorse and a girl they coveted, they sent Skitty Cornkiller, a well-traveled man in his occupation as whiskey peddler, into Choctaw Nation to find that horse and that girl. Then the three of them in company with two other companions, Nason Grube and Smoker Chubee, went to the farm where horse and girl had been found. Nason Grube because he was the constant companion of Cornkiller. Smoker Chubee because he was an expert with firearms, a bodyguard for these schemers.

"This massive evidence," and he waved his hand toward the pile of exhibits on the jury railing, "and the testimony of Mrs. Thomas Thrasher put them at the scene of the crimes, and Mrs. Thrasher's horrifying story revealed to you what happened there. Rape and murder! Committed by this gang of men, with malice aforethought. With vicious disregard for

236

human life and for the morality long associated with civilized societies. Done with laughter!

"The government of the United States asks that you do nothing more than your duty. Bring us a finding of guilty, on all counts of the indictment."

It was so short, the jury had hardly settled in their seats before it was finished. But it left them with few details to clutter their thinking, another point I would have to remember.

"Gentlemen," McRoy began, standing at the jury railing, his hands resting among the clutter of prosecution exhibits. "This case rests solely on the testimony of one person. A person understandably distraught when these depredations were committed before her eyes. Does her memory serve her correctly? Is there not some doubt in your mind? A woman hysterical, in hiding for days? Think of her in that condition. Think of her fear and suspicion. And then she is brought to confront a group of men and told by the prosecutor, 'These are the ones who did it!' Can you send men to their deaths on the basis of her reaction to such a situation?"

He paced to the center of the room and finally turned, facing the jury. He spoke of each defendant in turn, indicating the man with his outstretched hand. Johnny Boins, surely a madman, with a reasonable doubt that he had been in the Winding Stair anyway. Skitty Cornkiller and Nason Grube, with a bill of sale for a horse, arrested for having that horse and then thrust before frightened and confused witnesses for identification. Smoker Chubee, who had seen Mrs. Thrasher escaping and had not fired, surely unfit for the role of killer, in which he had been cast. He spent a great deal of time on reasonable doubt, moral certainty, and circumstantial evidence, repeating his points. Again and again he returned to the state of mind of Mrs. Thrasher, her fright and hysteria. Then he concluded.

"Yes, gentlemen, I appeal to your instinct for justice and to your humanity. I ask a verdict of not guilty. Thank you."

While Evans presented rebuttal, I studied the faces of the jurors. I tried to imagine what was in their minds, behind the frowns and pursed lips, the expressions of deep concentration. But it was impossible to tell how they would decide.

"And so, gentlemen, to conclude," Evans was saying, "I, too, appeal

237

to your humanity and your sense of justice. A fine woman has appeared before you, told you how she was despoiled and her husband and hired hands killed in ruthless disregard for the laws and manners of society. You must find these four defendants guilty as charged."

For a long moment, Judge Parker shuffled papers on the bench, all eyes on him. When he had them in proper order, he tapped them on the green felt cover, placed his glasses on his nose, and began to read.

"Gentlemen of the jury. You will find on three things: the evidence, the law, and reason.

"As to the evidence, which includes all you have heard and all you have seen properly introduced. You are the sole judge of its merits. Only you can determine the weight of it and the credibility of witnesses. You must take what you have heard and seen, and apply your reason to it. You must make a decision in full knowledge that the burden of proof rests on the government. These defendants are innocent until the government has proven them guilty beyond a reasonable doubt.

"Two of these defendants have elected to testify under oath. You will consider their testimony as you do all other testimony. Two have elected to remain silent. You cannot judge that choice in any way—not as an admission of guilt nor in any other way. Each of them, all four, whether they chose to take the witness stand or not, must be considered innocent until proven guilty beyond a reasonable doubt.

"Some of the evidence is circumstantial. In order to convict on circumstantial evidence alone, that evidence must clearly exclude all other reasonable hypotheses."

He continued in this vein for some time, emphasizing over and over that the burden of proof was on the government, and that the merits of all the evidence was a determination the jury alone could make, using common sense and reason. Then . . .

"As to the law in this case. Manslaughter is the crime of taking a human life when the person committing the homicide is incapable of forming an intent to do wrong while under the influence of alcohol. The penalty for manslaughter is at the direction of the court.

"Murder by reason of insanity is the killing of a person by another who has not the mental capability to distinguish right from wrong at the time the homicide is committed. The penalty for murder by reason of insanity is commitment to an asylum for a period determined by the court.

"Murder is the crime of killing another without just cause such as self-defense. Murder is killing with malice aforethought or premeditation, of no matter how short duration. Murder is the killing of another during the commission of a felony. Those who commit the crime of murder are all persons directly involved in the plan, not only the principal, but the accessories. An accessory is anyone who willingly takes part in a premeditation or felony and does not draw back and away from the crime prior to its commitment. The penalty for murder is death.

"Rape is defined as the carnal knowledge of a woman, necessarily including the penetration of her body, no matter how slight, against her will and without her consent. The penalty for rape is death.

"Gentlemen, once more. You and you alone are responsible for a finding. Base it on the law as I have described it, the evidence you have seen and heard, and your own good common sense and reason. Retire now, and consider your verdict."

At the end of it, Judge Parker looked tired and drawn. His cheeks had taken on a gray color and there was not in his movements the quickness so obvious before. He seemed anxious to be away from the courtroom.

The jury was out only long enough to select a foreman and take one ballot. The spectators stayed in their seats, and even the defendants remained at their table, contemplating their chains. As the jury trooped back across the front of the room, the only sound other than their heavy footfalls was the droning of flies, more active now in the rising heat of afternoon. Judge Parker took his place so quickly only a few in the courtroom had time to rise. He waved them back into their seats with that now familiar motion of one hand.

"Gentlemen, have you reached a verdict?"

A tall, rawboned man rose, a man with huge gnarled hands and the sunburned nose of a lowland farmer. He was holding in his fingers the paper given him by the bailiff when the jury retired, and now he looked somehow unsure that indeed a verdict had been reached.

"We have, Your Honor."

"Defendants rise," Judge Parker said. There was a rattle of iron as the four stood, Nason Grube leaning on the table with both hands. Johnny Boins was still smiling, as though it were perpetually with no meaning, no relationship to anything that was happening around him. Skitty Cornkiller stared at the jury through the shock of black hair that fell across his face. Smoker Chubee continued to chew, unconcerned, his flat black eyes roving the wall just above and behind the jurybox.

"Mr. Foreman, pass the verdict to the bailiff." The legal-sized sheet of paper was handed from jury to bailiff to Parker, everyone in the room watching it move from place to place. Judge Parker did little more than glance at it before he read. "We the jury find the defendants Johnny Boins, Skitty Cornkiller, Nason Grube, and Smoker Chubee guilty of rape and murder as charged in the indictment. Signed John T. Ferguson, Foreman."

Parker's eyes lifted and he stared at the jury over his glasses.

"Is this your verdict?"

"It is, Your Honor," Mr. Ferguson said, and sat down with what appeared to be an expression of pained relief.

Still, there was no sound in the room except the rattle of chains as the four men took their seats again.

"Because the sentence is set by law, there is no purpose to be served in taking arguments in aggravation or mitigation," Judge Parker said. "I see no reason to postpone sentencing. This trial has taken less time than I had thought it would. I see no advantage in setting sentencing forward on the docket. I assume, Mr. McRoy, that you will file for appeal?"

"Most assuredly, Your Honor."

"Then there being no objections," and he looked at both defense and government counsel, "I will pass sentence. The jury is excused."

Once more, the jury marched out in single file, still looking grim. The defendants were instructed to rise. Judge Parker looked exhausted now, and perhaps because of that his remarks were short. He called it a crime vicious in the annals of wrongdoing. He said only a merciful God could forgive them, but the law could not. He asked that they do what they could to prepare for final judgment from Him. Then he asked if any of them had anything to say.

"I want to appeal to the Supreme Court," Johnny Boins said, and I thought him about to laugh aloud.

"I don't blame you," Judge Parker said, but the snap was gone from his voice.

"I never done this," Skitty Cornkiller said, so low the people in rear of the room strained forward to hear.

"I never done it, either, Judge," Nason Grube said, and he began to cry.

For a long time, everyone watched Smoker Chubee, standing with his manacled hands before him, chewing calmly, his eyes on Judge Parker, showing no flame, no spark. Finally, he spoke.

"It's been a bad bet."

Then, Judge Parker sentenced them to be hanged by the neck until dead.

". . . and God have mercy on your souls."

Nineteen

IT HAD BEEN RAINING MOST OF THE MORNING. THROUGH Evans's open window, I could hear water falling from the long eaves of the courthouse building. Looking toward the river, I saw a blue-gray veil of water, a steady, ground-drenching drizzle. Some of the early dying leaves had been beaten off the maples along Second Street, and soon all would be turning brilliant red and gold in that most beautiful of times in the Arkansas Valley, the few weeks before winter.

The files before me held little interest. They were concerned with such diverse items as a stolen rick of firewood in the Cherokee Nation and a mail robbery on the Missouri Pacific in Van Buren. The papers were spongy and moist. It was like trying to write on wet tobacco leaves. Now and again, I could hear the murmur of proceedings in the courtroom, where Judge Parker was finishing out the docket for the summer term. Evans was there now, trying a white man, friend and lover of Belle Starr, for stealing horses in the northwest corner of The Nations, where for some years the United States government had reserved Ottawa, Shawnee, Ponca, Seneca, and a host of other peoples. The Indian names still had the power to enthrall me.

It was two days since I had sat in that courtroom and heard the sentence of death passed on the Winding Stair Four. The appeal process was already under way, Merriweather McRoy moving quickly to bring the case to the Supreme Court. He hoped to win reversal on some technicality, I assumed. Almost all of Parker's reversals had come as a result of his charges to the jury, and perhaps that was why in this case he had been brief and succinct. Now we would wait. And in the federal jail, in their high-tiered cells, the four would wait, too—on death row, where a light burned all night and a jailer walked past the barred door every ten minutes.

I was fiddling with a pencil and note pad, drawing tiny death's-heads, when I saw the covered taxi hack pull into the west compound gate, and recognized Mrs. Thomas Thrasher among its passengers. I hurried to the window and watched as the carriage pulled up to the back porch steps. George Moon was there, and Charley Oskogee and his wife. When the vehicle drew to a stop, the two Choctaw policemen leaped out and ran up the steps and into the building. I realized then they had come to take away Jennie Thrasher.

Evans had a few old umbrellas in a corner stand, and I took one and went out to the porch as George Moon appeared from the upper floors with an armload of luggage. He glanced at me but went on to stow the suitcases in the hack's boot before coming back to shake hands. By then Charley Oskogee was there, too, and the three of us said nothing, gripping hands silently as the rain murmured on the roof above us. Before he went back to the hack, I handed Charley Oskogee a package of tailor-made cigarettes, and a faint smile touched his lips, as he remembered with me that first morning in Winding Stair when he'd come up beside me and offered a smoke. He took the cigarettes without a word and turned down the steps, running through the rain to the hack.

It seemed an endless time I waited, looking at Mrs. Thrasher. Her black eyes were on me for a moment, and then she turned her face away. Jennie Thrasher came down. Emmitt was with her, and she was holding the boy by the hand. She wore a cape, tied round her long neck with a broad blue ribbon, and on her head was the same bonnet she had worn at the trial when she testified.

Her eyes widened when she saw me, and she paused in her step. I opened the umbrella.

"You mustn't get your new hat wet," I said.

"Hello, Eben." Her voice was so soft I could hardly hear her. "I didn't think I'd see you."

"I've been waiting all morning to see you off," I lied. "I wanted to say good-bye."

She moved quickly to the edge of the porch and stopped there, holding Emmitt's hand. The boy glared up at me. I knew everyone in the hack was watching us, and it made me uncomfortable.

"It's raining, isn't it?"

"It's been raining all morning," I said. "It's not a very good day for traveling, I'm afraid." I thought of that long ride up the mountains from Hatchet Hill to the Thrasher farm.

"It doesn't matter."

From the hack, George Moon called, "Hurry on, Miss Jennie. We'll miss that train."

But she stood silently, not looking at me again after that first moment. Her eyes were bright, but she didn't cry as she watched the rain falling into the muddy compound and beyond, along the lines of trees beside the railroad that marked the river line.

"Are you going back to Saint Louis now?"

"In a few days," I said. "My mother's been sick. But I'll be back when . . . I'll be back someday."

The boy tugged at her hand.

"Come on, Miss Jennie, we gotta get away from here."

"Jennie, I'm sorry about all this."

"It was just a thing that happened," she said.

"I could write you, if you'd like."

She acted as though she had not heard.

"I hope your mother gets better," she said. "I've gotta go now. We'll be late for the train."

We went down the steps awkwardly, me holding the umbrella over her and the boy pulling her along. He jumped into the hack first and I held her arm as she stepped up, the water running off the edge of the umbrella onto my head. For a second her hand clasped mine, and I started to say something more. But the hack driver whipped his team away and they curled around in a circle and across the compound, splashing mud. I stood there, the umbrella up, water running down my arm, and as they drove through the gate I saw her face once, looking back.

I stayed there until my feet were thoroughly soaked, looking at that dismal empty gate, the rain splattering around me. Oscar Schiller and Joe Mountain were on the porch. I'd no idea how long they had been there. I went up to them, and it seemed to me there was a hint of compassion on Oscar Schiller's face. The gray light gave a green cast to his unblinking eyes behind the thick spectacles.

We stood silently, for it seemed not to be a morning for talking, watching the rain, my umbrella hanging from my hand like a large broken bat, its wings partly open. We could hear the incoming whistle of the southbound Frisco passenger and the clanging of its bell, nearing the depot at the foot of Garrison Avenue. Above, crows were cawing, flying through the rain toward the Indian country. There was the heavy smell of wet clay and wet leaves and wet cotton cloth. Oscar Schiller took out his snuff can, dipped a matchstick into it, and popped the match into his mouth, chewing it slowly.

"Evans tells me you're going home," he said finally.

"Just for a while," I said. "I'll keep my room. Depends on how long the appeal takes. I may not come back until we hear from that. But I want some more time with Mr. Evans, I want to work with him some more. First, I need to get home and talk with my father and see to my mother."

"Man needs to get home now and again," Joe Mountain said. "Back to the place he come from."

"Right now, I feel as though I came from here," I said. I shook the umbrella and the fine spray showered their slickers. Joe Mountain had shed that outlandish plaid suit and was back in his field gear.

"I think I need a drink," I said. "If I worked anymore right now, I'd get Mr. Evans' papers all wet anyway."

"Me, too," Joe Mountain said. "I'm headin' for Osage country right away and a good drink would help the trip."

"You two go on, then," Oscar Schiller said. "I've got some business here. Got a case up in Cherokee Nation, so I'll be getting on with that. You sure you don't want to come along, Eben?"

"No. Not this time."

"All right. Good luck to you, and we'll see you sometime later." He made no effort to shake my hand, but turned and walked into the courthouse.

I suppose in one's misery there is a tendency to become more pugnacious than usual. When Joe Mountain and I walked into Henryetta's Frisco Hotel and Billiard Parlor, I welcomed the big woman's protest that no Indians were allowed in her place.

"Joe Mountain is with me," I said. "And he stays if I do, and if I don't, you're going to get more trouble from the local police than you're capable of handling."

She stepped back as though I'd hit her, and I saw Big Rachael looming up behind her. But then she laughed, showing the gold teeth, recovering quickly.

"You're getting more like the Cap'n every time I see you," she said, but there was no acid in it. I suspected her ban on Indians was more than anything else a concession to her white customers. "Rachael, get these men some drinks."

We sat in the same alcove where Oscar Schiller and I had first talked with Lila, behind the hanging beads. Big Rachael brought beer for Joe Mountain, gin and lemonade for me. When I offered to pay, he said Miss Henryetta had told him it was all on the house, anything we wanted. We watched the switch engines in the yard, puffing their smudgy black smoke into the gray mist. Brakemen moved among them in long rubber raincoats, carrying lighted lanterns as though it were the dark of night.

"How'd you like to go to Saint Louis, Joe?"

"No. Big places ain't good for me. Fort Smith is as much as I can handle." After each sip of beer, he smacked his lips loudly. "When you goin' home, Eben Pay?"

"Tomorrow, I think. I need to get away from here."

"Yeah, that's good. You need to get away."

He fished under his slicker for a moment and came out with a fistful of red cardboard strips. He tossed two of them onto the table before me.

"Where'd you get railroad passes?"

"Hell, you know where. The Cap'n. He says you might need 'em, to get home and back again someday. Can't have one of the officers of Judge Parker's court payin' to ride trains, he says."

I took a long drink, hoping the big Osage would not see that I was about to cry. But I suspect he knew, and understood.

The images began to come fast to my mind then. I remembered those first few days on the Thrasher farm. It had been raining then, too, with Jennie and me talking, her lying like some storybook princess on the bed, laughing and asking me questions about streetcars and electric lights and college dormitories. The gray stones among the meadowlarks and the short grass in the National Cemetery where we walked. The warmth of her lips when she kissed me, the butterfly pressure of her fingers on my arm, the golden hair blowing against my face and clinging as though it were magnetized, her eyes close to mine. And her last look back as the hack took her through the compound gate and to the Choctaw Nation and the Winding Stair, to that same farm. I saw in my mind the rain falling in those mountains, grim and forbidding and remote. The rain falling on everything now, slate gray and cold to the bone.

HE WAS A SLIGHT, SLOPE-shouldered man, standing barely five feet three inches tall and weighing 127 pounds. He had eyes deep-set under bushy brows and a long, balding forehead, and a blond beard flared out over the top of his vest like a coal scoop. He had been a police officer on the Fort Smith force and a jailer at the federal jail. His principal job now was the care of Judge Parker's gallows, and his name was George Maledon.

Under his supervision, the platform of the great machine was kept white and smooth with holystone and the hinges along the trap well oiled. He issued the tickets for those chosen as witnesses on execution days and he ensured order and good conduct at such times, being in charge of all the deputy marshals assigned to the task. In his own rooms, he kept the ropes. They were fine-grade hemp, woven in Saint Louis, six strands with a total diameter of one inch. He kept them smooth and flexible by careful applications of linseed oil and pitch.

He was an expert at the hangman's knot, thirteen coils that were always placed just beneath the left ear of the condemned, the rope then draped over the head toward the right shoulder. When the trap opened, the victim fell straight down and the rope popped taut, the knot snapping neckbone in one clean jerk. Most of those he had dropped had given a single, mighty lurch and were

249

unconscious and then dead. Only a few had strangled, taking a long time to die.

It was he who contracted for the pine coffins, always waiting beneath the gallows platform in neat rows on hanging days. It was he who chartered the black-draped wagons to haul them away, he who arranged for undertakers to clean the bodies left in such a terrible mess by suddenly relaxed anal sphincter muscles. It was he who buried those bodies left unclaimed, who took a signed receipt from the next of kin for those who were claimed. He kept the receipts in a little book, pasted in like photographs in a family album.

He was proud of the work he did for Parker. He boasted that none of his customers had ever come back to complain. Yet, there was in his face a vacant, haunted look, and some who came near him said to see his eyes was like peering through knotholes in a fence, with nothing on the other side but midnight.

Already he had plans for retiring and touring the country with his ropes and his double-action pistols. He had used the latter to personally dispatch at least three escaping prisoners. Of the former, one he was saving had hanged nineteen men. He would set up his sideshow tent and lecture on the evils of drink and the exploits of the men he had executed with a single, sharp pull of the trap lever. He would let the kiddies run their tiny hands over the huge, soft coils of rope.

In Fort Smith newspapers, he was called the Prince of Hangmen.

Twenty

CHRISTMAS HAD PASSED, AND JANUARY, BEFORE THE SUPREME Court returned the Thrasher and Garret cases to the western district of Arkansas, confirmed without opinion. Evans wired me at once when Judge Parker set the execution date of February 18, a Wednesday. Once again I made the long train ride from Saint Louis to the border of Indian country. There was snow in the Ozarks, dappling the steep slopes with white, a backdrop for the massed formations of oak and hickory and walnut. The gray and leafless ranks of hardwood were thick and largely uncut from valley to high hogback ridge. Twice, I saw deer running away through the woods. Some of the higher ridges were hidden in mist under a thick clouded sky, and from time to time flurries of white swept past the windows that had frosted over as we passed across the Boston Mountains. It was a wild and desolate country.

There was a mood of homecoming when I arrived. William Evans and his wife came to my hotel the first night and we ate veal cutlets covered with the thick cream gravy so popular in that part of the country. We discussed the cases, but I was grateful to Evans that he avoided any mention of Jennie Thrasher. At the courthouse the next day, Oscar Schiller greeted me, if it could be called that, with a curt nod and no unnecessary conversation. Joe Mountain was there, too, and he hugged me like a great grinning bear, almost smothering me. He smelled like grease and old leather and tobacco, and I found it a welcome change from the perfumed parlors of young women in Saint Louis whom I had been seeing over the holidays.

I visited Judge Parker for a few moments, giving him my father's best regards, and he seemed years older than when I'd seen him last. The dark patches under his eyes had extended all across his cheeks now and his hair was white. As I left the judge's chambers, Zelda Mores was waiting in the corridor, and at first I thought she might hug me, too. But she didn't. Instead she extended her hand like a man and gave me a firm grip. She seemed genuinely happy to see me. Over the months, her attitude of hostility toward me had mellowed. There was now gentle forbearance, as though she thought I needed forgiveness and compassion. The fondness of this large, mustached woman for Jennie Thrasher disturbed me, but it was a thing I tried not to think too much about.

It came as a surprise, even a shock, to learn that Smoker Chubee had been asking to see me. Evans suggested I make arrangements to meet with the dark killer before it was too late. And thus on the evening before the executions, I found myself in a conference stall at the federal jail. The room was one of many along the north wall of the jail enclosure where lawyers could speak with their clients. There was a single door leading out into the jail proper, with a heavy metal screen, a small table and two chairs and a clear-glass light bulb hanging from the ceiling on a tangled cord. Waiting, I paced back and forth to keep warm. Although I could hear the big coal furnace under the building bellow and huff, little of the heat seemed to reach this corner of the jail complex.

When Smoker Chubee appeared, dragging heavy leg-irons, I could see that he had gained a great deal of weight since the trial. His face was puffy, the eyes sunken in folds of flesh. But they had the same flat, deadly look I recalled so vividly. Shuffling in, he showed no sign of recognition, no flicker of emotion in his wooden face. A jailer pushed him through the door and toward the table, the chains making it difficult for him to move with his usual grace, that of a night-prowling cat. Now he reminded me more of a fat Rogers Avenue fruit merchant in summer, scowling over his bins and watchful of street urchins who might steal an apple or a bunch of grapes.

"Mr. Pay, are you armed?" the jailer asked.

"No."

"Good. I'll be just outside the door if you need me."

We settled into the chairs on either side of the table, Smoker Chubee clumsily, his leg-chains dragging across the floor. He sat with his elbows on the table, handcuffed arms before him, watching me as he spoke.

"Have you got any smokes?"

I placed a package of tailor-mades and matches on the table before him, and he lighted one before speaking again. He inhaled deeply, holding the smoke in his lungs for a long time before allowing it to roll lazily from between parted lips. His eyes took on a glazed light, which I assumed to be some expression of satisfaction.

"Don't they give you tobacco?"

"A little. But this isn't one of your better hotels in Fort Smith," he said, puffing a fog of smoke now. "But it's not too bad. They just took my order for my last meal tomorrow morning. Pork chops and steak I'm having, with apple pie and a lot of milk. Goat's milk. I'll be gut-full. They'll have a nice wad to clean up after they drop me."

He said it all with a natural calmness, as though he might be speaking of having breakfast at the Main Hotel. He held his breath, lungs full of smoke. Under the glaring light overhead, the pockmarks in his fat cheeks looked like the pits in a peach stone.

"All right, Smoker. You wanted to see me," I said.

"Mr. Pay, I want to ask a favor. I don't trust any of these other white bastards around here. Would you do me a favor?"

"That depends on what it is," I said.

"It's not much. I just want you to give some information to the newspapers after they swing me through that trap out there," and he inclined his head in the direction of the compound where the gallows stood.

"What kind of information?"

"It's just a little story. So everybody will know Smoker Chubee never raped anyone."

"You've been convicted of it," I said. "I don't know that anything I say to the newspapers will change that."

"Yes it will. I've done enough to be hanged all right, but rape isn't one of them. I've always taken certain pride in what I do, Mr. Pay. I don't want at the last to be remembered as a man who does rape. You can let me have that much, can't you?"

His speech was startling, coming as it did from the black, scarred face. He used the language as well as most college professors I had known, although his vocabulary was limited. He watched the effect of his words on me, drawing on the cigarette, burning the tip down a full quarter-inch and turning it red hot. Only half-finished with the first cigarette, he lighted a second one from it.

"These are good smokes," he said, puffing. I took one of the cigarettes, too, and we sat smoking silently for a few moments. I knew he needed no time to think of how to begin. He had gone over it all in his cell, I was sure. But he left me waiting, my feet growing colder each minute. He started slowly, at last, watching me closely, watching the impact of each word.

"My mother was a slave," he said. "She was a little girl when removal started. A Creek slave. After they got to the Territory, her folks tried to run away, to Mexico. There were a lot of those colored slaves who tried it. They didn't know it was over five hundred miles, and a lot of that through Comanche country. They'd never heard of Comanches."

As he drew on the cigarette, I could see its pinpoint of fire in his eyes. I recalled what Joe Mountain had said about this man: a dog without a home.

"Well, the bunch Mother started to Mexico with, the Comanches caught 'em. Somewhere in west Texas. She told me what she could remember of it, but she had no clear idea of locations. After they'd killed all the others, the Comanches took Mother with them. I guess then Comanches hadn't seen many colored people. They cut the skin on her arms and peeled it back to see what was underneath. She carried those scars on her arms to her deathbed. Other than that, they treated her well enough.

"As near as I can figure, she was with them for about a year. Then the band was on Red River doing some horse trading and a Seminole saw her in the band. He offered to buy her and the Comanches were willing. So she ended up back in the Territory, with a Seminole master. Near where Wewoka is now. I don't suppose you knew that Wewoka, the Seminole capital, was founded by a colored man."

"No, I didn't know that."

"It was. Anyway, this Seminole raised Mother and then married her in his old age. I was their son. The old man's name was Tub Something-or-other. I never knew him. He died of cholera about ten years before the war."

From that, I knew Smoker Chubee must be about forty years old. When I'd first seen him, he hadn't looked it, but now with the fat, he looked even older.

"I was raised like a good Seminole. Seminoles always treated their colored people well, even when they were slaves. Afterward, a woman like my mother was just another member of the tribe. Not only by law, but by treatment. We lived in one of those little towns, all colored people like you find in The Nations, where they settled and made their own life after they were freed. But we were still Seminoles and I went to one of their schools.

"I started herding livestock. I was a drover, and a pretty good one. I made some drives up from Texas to the railheads. My first drive was to Baxter Springs. I trailed a herd into Ellsworth once. After the cattle were sold and we got paid off, we went into town for hell-raising. Next day we were getting our gear ready for the ride south, not much hurry, and everybody with pop-head. About noon, a bunch of men rode out from town. They were armed to the teeth, and on serious business. They caught me up with ropes, and said they were about to teach me to leave their womenfolks alone. They dragged me off into a dry wash, where there was a tree down, and they spread me on that tree and pulled off my pants. All those white men I'd come north with just stood around and watched, afraid to do anything."

The muscles of his face moved as he recalled it, twisting and knotting, but his eyes still seemed detached, not a part of it. He smoked for a long time, watching my face.

"These people that live on deserts, in Africa," he said. "Where the chiefs have a whole herd of wives . . ."

"Harems?"

"Yeah. Harems. And they keep these men to guard the women who aren't men at all."

"Eunuchs?"

"That's the word. Eunuchs. Those Kansas men had a butcher knife, and they did that to me. I would have bled to death but the cook in our outfit dragged me back to camp and stopped the blood with a red-hot branding iron. You know, those bastards took it all. They took it all."

"They emasculated you?"

"That's the other word." And he laughed. Not from the memory, but from the effect it was obviously having on me.

"For God's sake, why didn't you tell that story on the witness stand?"

"It's not an easy story to tell," he said. "Besides, they had me on the killings. They can't hang you but once."

What he said next, I was sure he had not intended to say, had not planned. But somehow, once he was started, it all came out. He seemed to think aloud as though I was not there.

"A thing like that takes something away from a man." He seemed amused at his double entendre. "It makes him think in a way most men don't think. You take something away from him that all other men have, so he tries to make all the rest of living different than other men. Until you take his pants off, nobody knows he's different. He's more woman than man, maybe. But he's not that, either. He's nothing. There's going to be no women in all his life and there's going to be no children or grandchildren all his life.

"At first, I was just mad. But after a while, that changed. I was sorry they hadn't killed me. They left me to walk around alive, but I was really dead."

"And you started to take it all out on everybody then, with a gun?"

He gave a start, coming back to the moment and apparently only then realizing what he'd just said to me.

"Maybe. I never thought about it like that exactly. It was just a thing I started doing. But whatever I did, I wanted to do it better than anybody else. It wasn't revenge. It was something else."

"But you enjoyed it."

"There are only so many things a man can enjoy in his life. One of the best is women. When that was gone, something had to take its place. Did you ever see an old blind man, who's been blind a long time? After his eyes go, his fingers take on more feeling. It doesn't happen all at once, but after a while, his fingers take on some of the things the eyes have done."

It suddenly struck me that although in most cases a killer may not even be aware of it, here was one who recognized, perhaps dimly, that his own destructiveness was something sexual, something to replace all chance of his ever being with a woman again. What he said next made me believe that Smoker Chubee had never really blamed those Kansas men who had castrated him. He blamed women. Not just the one who had brought on the retribution, but all women.

"I watched Rufus and those other boys having their time with Mrs. Thrasher and it was almost like having the pleasure myself, just watching."

But if he hated women, why had he let her go that day when she'd slipped out of the house? He'd seen her just before she ran down across the yard and into the woods, just watched her and nothing more. I asked him why and it was as incomprehensible to him as to me.

"Damned if I know why I didn't shoot her," he said. "That was another one of my big mistakes. If I had, the rope wouldn't be waiting for me right now."

For many years, I have thought about that interview with Smoker Chubee. It has become impossible for me to assess what my feelings were at the time. Perhaps most distressing of all was that with this most violent of men, I took it all rather for granted. It was some hours later, lying in my bed, before I realized that the Kansas incident was not a part of his brutal nature, but the beginning of it.

"Now, do you think you might tell that to the newspapers?"

I had no doubt the press would be overjoyed with such a sensational story. But I had a price.

"If you'll do a favor for me," I said.

"Like what?"

"Just answer a few questions."

For an instant, what might have been a grimace of quick anger crossed his face. But those eyes remained unchanged, hard and cold. It was the most chilling thing about this man, the unchanging eyes.

"Just for your own amusement?"

"If you want to call it that. Did you do anything in Kansas that might have led those men to such a thing?"

He shrugged. "I lay with a white woman," he said. He lifted his hands to his face, the fingers touching the deep pockmarks. "Before I had the smallpox, I wasn't a bad-looking nigger. It wasn't the first white woman I'd been with. But it never was against their will or without their consent, isn't that how the judge said it?"

"That's how he said it."

"I guess you'd rather think of me as a Seminole, laying with a white woman."

"It doesn't matter to me one way or the other."

"I guess to you, a Seminole is a nigger, too."

257

"If you thought that, why did you call me in here. For somebody who's asking a favor, you're an arrogant son of a bitch."

He laughed, and I think he actually enjoyed me saying it.

"Well, it doesn't matter, does it? After they cut me and I got back home, I laid up a long time. My mother died about then. They said it was consumption. She'd always been a brave little woman. But she took the consumption and died." For the first time, he lowered his gaze. He stared at his hands a moment, squeezing them together until the knuckles were white. "She was the only person I ever had any feeling for. The only person who ever had any feeling for me."

The moment passed quickly and he seemed to shake himself as he took a fresh cigarette from the package and struck a match to it.

"I started getting into a little trouble then. A little horse stealing in Creek Nation and out west amongst the Kiowas and Cheyennes. I started working with pistols, and I got pretty good at that, too. Before long, I got to be what we call a hired shooter."

He leaned back and sighed, blowing smoke up at the bare bulb above us. I looked at his hands, long and delicate like so many Indian hands I had seen, yet they had a heavy strength inherited from his mother.

"Yeah, I hired out to kill people. For money. Sometimes I charged fifty dollars. Sometimes five hundred. There are a lot of men like that in The Nations. Go to any crossroads store and you can find one or two. Most of them aren't worth a sack of horseshit. They like to get drunk and brag. I never made that mistake. Only mistake I ever made was getting together with that wild little Yuchi."

"Milk Eye?"

"Yeah, Rufus. He was crazy. But I liked him. He paid me to shoot. He was always in trouble, and he couldn't shoot worth a damn, and I guess he didn't have the stomach for it either. So he'd hire me for that chore."

"Smoker, something's been bothering me for a long time, since we rode into that farmyard and saw all those dead chickens. Why in the world would you want to shoot those chickens, and the dog and the milk cow?"

"I killed anything Rufus paid me to kill."

He said it almost casually, as though he were speaking of chopping cotton or weeding corn, as though it meant absolutely nothing to him. I knew then, sitting in that cold little room in the federal jail, that it truly didn't mean anything to him. It was sickening, beyond my understanding.

"Smoker, you said Rufus Deer didn't have the stomach for shooting, but he was at Low Hawk Corners that night, when you killed Marshal Garret."

"I never did understand that," he said. "Rufus wanted to come along on that. He wanted to pop away at that marshal. I think that was the first time he'd ever shot at anybody, even in the dark. That was funny, when you were on the stand, telling about bullets hitting the wall and breaking the window glass. Those were old Rufus' shots. All mine went right at Garret."

"Joe Mountain says he's glad you missed him that night."

"The big Osage? Hell, I wasn't shooting at him. Rufus was going to give me that black horse for killing Garret." He sat for a moment, rubbing his cheeks with those slender fingers, the nails a pinkish white. "Those damned Osages. If they hadn't hit that horse, I'd be in Oklahoma Territory now, have traded that horse for a whole string of good Comanche stock."

"Smoker, that old woman . . ."

"Rufus' mother? That old woman, she's tough as boot leather. We had it all planned with her. Rufus did, anyway. I'd let out the word Rufus was coming and Rufus figured that would bring Garret out, to get up a posse for him. Most likely at Low Hawk Corners. Rufus was smart. He was a smart little bastard. If Garret was in that store, then the old woman would be on the back porch. It was all a signal. The storm was just luck. If it hadn't been for that, the old woman would have made some other excuse to stay the night at the Corners. But the storm gave her and the old man a good reason to stay in town. The old man, he didn't know anything about it. He didn't know what was happening. He was drunk most of the time, and Rufus never did trust him much. But that old woman. She's got all kinds of guts."

He laughed, a short burst of sound that gave me a start.

"When Rufus saw his old lady on that porch, he got so excited he couldn't talk. So I called out to Garret . . ."

He rose abruptly, dropping his cigarette on the floor and grinding it out with his toe, the leg-irons rattling. Before he could reach the door, I was in front of him, holding his arm, and we stood there face to face. He seemed smaller than he had that day I'd arrested him, a little stooped. I had to look down into his eyes.

"Smoker," I said. "Tell me. That colored man. Was he with you the day you hit the Thrasher farm?"

The smile that never reached his eyes came quickly.

"Well, Mr. Pay, you people convicted him, didn't you?"

I sensed it was useless to ask anything about the three men condemned along with him. But somehow, talking about Rufus Deer failed to qualify under the same code.

"But you and Rufus put this whole Thrasher thing together?"

"Hell, no. Rufus planned it. I went along because he paid me."

"How much did he pay you?"

"He paid me eleven dollars and a little gold watch we got off that first woman."

"Mrs. Eagle John?"

"I guess that's the one. He paid me fifteen dollars we found at the Thrasher farm. And he was going to give me the black horse."

"You shot three men for twenty-six dollars?"

"There was the horse, don't forget," he said. "Besides, I told you once. I liked Rufus. You had to know Rufus. He could talk a man into almost anything, make it sound profitable. He had half a dozen stores in The Nations paying him money just to leave them alone. And the other owl-hooters left those stores alone, too, because they knew if they didn't, Rufus would send me after them. Hell, owl-hooters over there were more scared of Rufus than they were of your federal marshals."

"Just a minute," I said, and handed him what was left of the package of cigarettes. "One more thing. That death's-head note we found in the colored boy's cell. What about that?"

"Note? I don't know anything about any note." I was sure he was telling the truth, but with that noncommittal face, who could tell?

"Judge Parker would sure like to know about that."

"Judge Parker?" He laughed again, that mirthless cough. "I wish somebody had offered to pay me to shoot him a long time ago."

"Come on, Smoker, you don't think you could come in here and shoot Judge Parker, do you?"

"Hell, I wouldn't do it here. At the Methodist church, or that hospital he's always visiting, or on the streets. It wouldn't be hard. Only getting away from here afterward would be hard."

I couldn't resist asking him the next question.

"Smoker, how much would you have charged to kill Judge Parker?"

He thought about it a moment, holding the package of cigarettes in his hands, turning them slowly.

"That job would take a thousand," he said.

He pulled away from me and slammed his handcuffs against the door. The jailer was there at once, and I wondered if he'd heard anything we'd said. He took Smoker Chubee's arm and led him out and along the hall toward death row, high in the tiered cells at the far end of the building. Smoker held back for only a moment, looking over his shoulder at me when he spoke.

"You remember that little story," he said. And then they were gone.

The courthouse compound when I stepped out into it was no colder than that cubicle had been. The wind was coming in from the southwest, blowing hard across the Winding Stair Mountains and out into the Arkansas Valley. I was glad I'd brought my heavy coat from Saint Louis. The compound was deserted and the only illumination was from gas lights along the walls. I walked before the wind, hands thrust into my coat pockets, thinking about the man I'd just seen and how alien his story would sound related in the fashionable living rooms of Saint Louis. I knew there were such things as professional killers, but I had never known one, certainly never to my knowledge talked with one. It seemed fantastic that I had sat alone with such a man in a dismal little room, chilled to the bone as he revealed calmly the extent of his viciousness. Yet, I found it impossible to despise him.

Twenty-One

UNDER CLOUDY FEBRUARY SKIES, THE LIGHT OF DAWN HAD begun to show the details of the federal compound. Many of the people there had come in darkness, to wait, and others were still arriving. A small group, about forty, were clustered around the gallows enclosure, waiting for George Maledon to open the gate. These were the ticket holders, the lawyers and newspapermen and prominent citizens of the town who had asked to be witnesses to the executions. All the others huddled along the walls of the compound, taking shelter against the wind until the condemned men appeared at the south door of the federal jail. A few were on the walls already, where they could catch some view of what would happen on the platform under the heavy oak beam. Some small boys were in the trees along the streets, hanging like raccoons, arms and legs wrapped around the bare branches. A truant officer moved along the rows of maples, pulling down those who were supposed to be in school. But most of them were Indians from The Nations, children of families who stood below, and they remained in the gray dawn light, dark lumps in the thicket of leafless limbs.

At the north end of the building, near the courtroom, lights burned in two offices. William Evans was going through briefs and drinking coffee from an old army china mug. And Judge Isaac Parker was there, even though on this day there were no hearings scheduled before him. He would receive no visitors, and even those with court business would not disturb him. It was said that on these days he was morose and withdrawn. He read his Bible and paced the worn Oriental carpet that floored his chambers, his face gray and his lips set in a hard line. It was said, too, that during these times he was likely to write one of the letters for which he had become famous, to officials in Washington city, scalding the system of law enforcement in The Nations and pleading for something more effective, something that allowed the people who lived there to have more voice in trying their own criminals. He would fret and fume until he heard the sound of the trap falling, a sound that echoed across the compound and through the surrounding streets like a boxcar door being slammed shut. Then, it was said, he would kneel behind his massive desk and pray, nobody knew for what or for whom.

Three deputy marshals came from the front of the building, with Winchesters, stationing themselves about the yard, watching the little knots of Indians along the walls. Everyone kept their hands pressed deep into coat pockets, their feet scuffling in the light film of snow that drifted across the ground in powdery wisps. Toward the river, a freight train passed, the engine whistle giving sharp warning to those coming from Choctaw Strip, west of the compound. There were crows in the elms and sycamores along the Poteau, and their raucous cawing came strongly on the wind. They were always there on hanging days, the old-timers said. Now and again, there was the yeasty odor of fresh bread as the wagons at the nearby bakeries loaded and began their morning runs through the city. Somewhere near National Cemetery a dog barked, and beyond that a mill whistle sounded the call to work. A bank clock along Garrison Avenue struck eight, the sound faint and distant.

With the last stroke of the clock, George Maledon appeared in the south doorway of the jail, coils of heavy black rope draped on each arm. With him were three men, his assistants, and they quickly made their way across the thirty yards that separated the jail from the gallows enclosure. Every eye followed their progress, and what little conversation there had been among those waiting was now stilled. The four men disappeared inside the fence, leaving the witnesses at the gate. From positions atop the walls and from the trees, it could be seen that the ropes were being attached to the oak beam above the gallows platform, the teardrop loops hanging in the wind, swaying back and forth, the thirteen coils on each knot dreadfully thick, as thick as a grown man's forearm.

Inside the jail, the Winding Stair Four had taken their baths and donned the simple black suits the court provided for men going to the rope. They had eaten breakfast and smoked cigars. Now, as they were led along the corridor toward the south door, those waiting in the yard could hear other prisoners calling farewell. As though on a single string, the people in the compound moved away from the walls and to the south end of the building so they might be near enough to see the four men pass toward the gallows. As they began to take their places along the route of this last walk, the enclosure gates were opened and the witnesses quickly ushered inside, to stand near the foot of the machine.

First came two deputy marshals, armed with rifles. Behind them, in the same order in which they had marched into the courtroom almost six months before, came the condemned four. Johnny Boins was calm, but he was not smiling now. His face was serious and pale in the early light. He wore on his left lapel a small boutonniere of hothouse lilacs. Close around him were more deputies, and walking beside him was a minister from a local church. During the time of waiting for a decision from the Supreme Court, his parents had been back in Fort Smith, and they had been allowed to visit him each day. But they had returned now to Eureka Springs.

In close order came Skitty Cornkiller and Nason Grube, with their escorts. The young Creek had used pomade on his hair, but the wind loosened it anyway, blowing strands across his face. He walked with his head up, his eyes wide and trancelike, but he showed no sign of fear. Twice in that short walk, he tried to brush the hair back from his forehead, lifting his manacled hands before his face. Behind him came Nason Grube, a Bible held between his hands, his lips moving silently. A Catholic priest moved beside the black man, telling his beads. The scars on Grube's face were almost invisible in the faint light, and he appeared serene.

Smoker Chubee looked about the compound as he walked toward the gallows, moving gracefully despite the heavy leg-irons, clearly making an effort to do so. His gaze was impersonal, lacking interest or curiosity, sweeping back and forth. His nostrils flared as he caught the scent of fresh bread coming on the wind, but there was no light in his eyes.

I stood just inside the gallows enclosure gate, behind a deputy marshal, and as they came each saw me there. Johnny Boins nodded, and the trace of a smile crossed his handsome face. Cornkiller glanced at me only once and then his eyes went to the gallows rising before him and I saw him swallow hard. I thought Nason Grube's lips formed my name, but I heard nothing. As Smoker Chubee passed me, he winked again, as he had done that first day in court.

Mounting the stairs was a difficult task. Their leg-irons dragged behind them, hanging on each step. Deputies at their elbows helped them. No one hesitated. No one held back. As each of them reached the top of the steps and moved onto the platform, he was silhouetted for a moment against the gray sky before moving under the slanted roof. They were then seated on a long bench that ran the length of the back wall, and everyone stood away from them except the Catholic priest, who knelt for a few seconds before Nason Grube. Finally, he, too, moved back, taking the Bible from the old man's hands.

On the far right of the platform, where the trap lever thrust upward like a huge locomotive throttle, was the jailer, holding the death warrant. Immediately behind him was Oscar Schiller, his palmetto replaced now with a Russian fur cap. The jailer cleared his throat with a loud rasp, and as he held the paper up to read a number of spectators removed their hats.

"On order of the United States Circuit Court for the Western District of Arkansas, the following," the jailer read, his voice loud and carrying out beyond the enclosure to the people gathered in the compound. "That Johnny Boins, Skitty Cornkiller, Nason Grube, and Smoker Chubee shall be put to death at eight-thirty o'clock on this date and at this place, Fort Smith in the State of Arkansas, by hanging, for crimes capital committed in the Indian Territory, having been duly tried before a jury of their peers and found guilty of rape and murder, and having exhausted all appeals for the sentence under the law. Signed, J. W. Mitchell, United States Commissioner for the Western District of Arkansas, February eighteenth, 1891."

He turned toward the four seated men.

"Do any of you have anything to say?"

"Could one of the reverends say a prayer?" Skitty Cornkiller asked, his voice quavering.

Now all the hats in the enclosure came off, and heads were bowed as one of the ministers on the platform moved to the front and faced the condemned men. He spoke aloud, but his words were indistinguishable to those immediately below him.

"Anybody else have anything to say?" the jailer asked.

"I was born a free man," Nason Grube said loudly, "and I will die a free man."

There was a long pause, with no sound but the wind. Oscar Schiller's harsh voice cut across it.

"All right. Everybody onto the trap."

The deputies came from the far ends of the platform again to help the four as they rose and formed a line under the oak beam. Two deputies worked with each of them. Handcuffs were removed and the men's arms pinned at their sides by steel bracelets on a heavy leather belt until now hidden under their coats. Leg-irons were removed, the long links thrown to the rear of the platform with a loud clatter, and replaced by short lengths of rope that secured their ankles tight together.

"Good-bye, Helen," Skitty Cornkiller shouted. "That's his sister," someone among the spectators whispered. The young Creek seemed unable to maintain his balance with his feet tied together, and a deputy had to stand close behind him, holding his elbows.

George Maledon started along the line, slipping a noose over each head, the knot pulled snug against the neck behind the left ear. He had to reach up and stand on tiptoe.

Then I saw the old woman. Rufus Deer's mother. She stood immediately below Smoker Chubee. He was looking down at her, and I heard him say something in Creek. She answered him in kind, holding a shawl about her head and small, stooped shoulders. Smoker Chubee spoke again, this time in English.

"It's too bad about Rufus, old mother."

"You'll see him in glory," she replied, her voice sharp and clear on the cold wind.

Maledon was going back along the line now, drawing black muslin caps down over their faces. I could hear Nason Grube, praying aloud, his voice strong but muffled under the cap.

"I'm sorry, Father," one of them said, and I was sure it was Johnny Boins.

Then Maledon was at the lever, the jailer standing well back, and Oscar Schiller with him. Using both hands, Maledon heaved and the trap fell with a heavy thump. Three of them fell with a quick lurch and after only a few seconds of jerking were still, turning from side to side, swinging like slow, grotesque pendulums. But Johnny Boins was strangling, and the spectators could hear him. His body knifed upward, bending as the fingers of his hands clawed out, trying to break away from the heavy leather belt about his waist. His knees lifted, almost to his chest, his legs bowing. Gray-faced, one of the witnesses turned and rushed from the enclosure. Johnny Boins writhed, trying to thrust his body up through the noose, trying to throw off the black rope. But after only a few seconds, his choking was stilled and then only his legs moved, still thrashing out to either side, kicking against the body of Skitty Cornkiller, who swung next to him. Then the spasms were through, and like his companions Johnny Boins hung limp, swinging in the wind.

Beneath each hanging figure there was a pine coffin, the lid still on. A man in a long coat and with a stethoscope started along the line, listening for heartbeats, standing on the coffin lids beneath each in turn. He moved quickly from one body to the next, calling up to George Maledon and the jailer peering down through the still-open trap that each man was dead. But at Johnny Boins, he listened for a long time and said nothing. The spectators shifted uneasily, waiting, and the wind seemed to freshen and turn colder. The doctor listened once more to Johnny Boins's heart, and yet again. Finally, after what seemed an hour but was only ten minutes, he reported that Johnny Boins was dead.

Quickly, the deputies hurried the spectators from the enclosure, and already the long wagon was pulling up to the south gate of the compound, to haul away the coffins. First to the mortuary and then to the grave. The only body to be claimed was that of Johnny Boins. Before leaving Fort Smith, his parents had arranged that it be shipped to Eureka Springs. But the others would go to potter's field, on the far side of National Cemetery and well removed from the heroes lying there under gray headstones.

At first, I had supposed I would stay and see it all through. But as I watched the deputies beneath the gallows platform, lifting Smoker Chubee's body while George Maledon bent down through the trap to work off the rope, I suddenly sickened and hurried away toward Evans's office. Later that day, I learned that on the wall of his cell Johnny Boins had scratched a message.

"Mother dear. I dreamed I was in heaven, amongst the angels fair."

Twenty-Two

THE LAMPLIGHTER HAD BEGUN HIS RIDE ALONG GARRISON Avenue, standing in the stirrups beneath each gas light as his mule stood with droop-eared patience. I watched from my hotel window, and as he moved away toward the Catholic church at the far end of the street, each lamp he touched grew into a white gauze puff without shape or definition in the falling snow. With the curtains drawn back, the only illumination in the room came from the street below. On my desk was a copy of the *Fort Smith Elevator*, an entire column on the front page taken up with the story of Smoker Chubee that I had given one of their reporters. Beside it lay the long-barreled pistol that had arrived in a brown paper bag from the courthouse within an hour after the first edition had gone on the street.

With the gun had come a note from Evans explaining that Smoker Chubee had asked that it be given to me if the account of his Kansas experience was ever published. Generally, all such weapons were confiscated by the court, but in this case Judge Parker himself had agreed that I might have it, although I had shown no disposition to own such a thing. There was a fascination about it all the same, and it was with considerable annoyance that I realized in myself the same morbid curiosity about such things as I had always thought abhorrent among the court-watchers around Fort Smith. I began to understand why some lawyers collected such memorabilia from their various cases, and why George Maledon would likely make a great deal of money someday going about the countryside displaying his ropes and pistols in a side-show tent.

I lifted the heavy pistol from the table, and although I was not then nor have I ever become an expert on sidearms, it was obvious that Moma July had been right. This was a finely tuned weapon. The great curved butt fit perfectly into my hand and the hammer came back under my thumb with an oily triple click, almost cocking itself. There was with the pistol a well-used shoulder holster and a half-empty box of .45 cartridges. The surface of the brutal, pug-nosed slugs had the consistency of warm tallow under my fingers. I wondered how many men had been the recipient of such slugs. Even now, with Smoker Chubee cold in the grave, he had the capacity to make my skin crawl.

I had brought up a bottle of brandy from the hotel saloon after a supper barely picked over. It had been three days since the executions, but still I had no appetite. The scene that cold morning was still heavy on my thinking—the men in a single row beneath the beam, the ropes open to receive their necks, the thunder of the trap falling. Twice I had tried to write my father, explaining my feelings. But it had been useless. I had had such a sensation once before, when I was a child and had seen a dog run over in the streets of Saint Louis by a beer wagon. Then and now, it was not pity nor loathing but rather some deep anguish unknown at any other time, without name, without measure, but overwhelming.

When Oscar Schiller came, I was still toying with the gun, and he looked at it and grunted. He was carrying his saddlebags and wore a heavy winter coat reaching to his knees, split up the back for riding, and with a fur collar that tried to match his Russian cap.

"I see you got it," he said. "I read the piece in the newspaper."

"Yes, I thought we owed him that much," I said.

"We didn't owe him a damned thing. Except the rope. And we paid that off."

He sat on the edge of the bed, sighing, the fur hat seeming to settle down over his ears. He pushed it back with a quick movement of his hand. His eyes darted about the room, taking in everything at one glance and then dismissing it. I had come to recognize his moods better than I would ever have thought possible, and I knew now he was here for a purpose.

"You sit around here every night in the dark?"

"No. I was watching the snow," I said, and turned on the desk lamp.

"Well, it's about stopped," he said. "We've got some kind of killing over in Cherokee Nation. Evans thought you might like to get out on another case."

"I think not."

"Suit yourself. Joe Mountain and Blue Foot are down at the ferry now, waiting. I've got four good horses, if you want to come. A deer hunter found some bones over near Going Snake."

"I'll stay here," I said.

"Suit yourself," he repeated. He sat silently, unbuttoning his coat to take out the snuff can and a long kitchen match. Below, a streetcar passed, the noise of its steel wheels on the tracks muffled by snow. I waited for him, knowing there was more. I poured another glass of the brandy.

"All right," he said finally, as though making up his mind. Reaching into his saddlebags, he came up with a book, well worn and with some of its pages still dog-eared to mark a place. He handed it up to me, his unblinking stare on my face. The book was the second volume of George Eber's *Bride of the Nile*, a popular novel of that day. "You remember when all those people went back to Choctaw Nation after the trial last year?"

"Yes. I recall it was raining."

"That's right. You and Joe Mountain went to Henryetta's to get drunk."

"No, we went there for a drink, but not to get drunk."

A hard lump was forming in my chest and I took a long drink of the brandy. It seemed to stick in my throat for an instant before exploding in my stomach.

"That day I went up and looked around those cells where that nigger boy and the girl had been kept, I found this book there, along with some others. In her cell."

"She had precious little else to do except read," I said. "Zelda Mores told me she took a lot of books up there."

"The others don't matter. This one does. Look at the front end of it."

I opened the book and there was no flyleaf, only a brown pastemark along the inner face of the title page where the flyleaf had been torn out. There was something terribly familiar about the paper, the distinctive tooth, the color. And the size and shape of it as well. The realization came suddenly, sickeningly.

"My God. That note Emmitt got from someone."

"Not someone. From her. He sure as hell didn't know it was her, else he wouldn't have gone off with her, back to the Choctaw. But she slipped it into his cell. Look at that book under the light."

My hands were shaking as I held the open book under the desk lamp

271

so the light slanted across the title page. There were the marks a pencil might make, pressed down hard on the page above, a few scribbled words and the unmistakable outline of a skull. The death's-head note had been written on the flyleaf, leaving an indented copy beneath, then torn out—the note that had terrified Emmitt and effectively put a stop to the Eagle John murder and rape case. Gingerly, I placed the book on the desk, still open, the lamplight showing clearly the message: "You talk you die." I felt the marks with my fingertips, but there was no erasing them.

"The boy's all right, of course. She never meant him any harm anyway. She just wanted to scare hell out of him. George Moon has wired me, that boy's with another family now, somewhere along the Kiamichi."

"So now I suppose you're on your way to arrest her?"

"Oh shit, Eben," he said in exasperation, not suspecting that in my muddled state of mind it was impossible to fit the pieces together. "I told you where I'm going. You think I'd have waited this long if I intended to do anything about it?"

"Does Evans or Judge Parker know about this?"

"Hell no! If they did, I'd have a warrant in my pocket for her right now. Long before now. I haven't told anybody. What's to be gained? So you've got the book and as far as I'm concerned, I never saw it before in my life. Burn the son of a bitch."

I was not confused enough to miss the point. He was doing this out of consideration for my feelings, not because of any sympathy for Jennie Thrasher. From the moment he had found the book and realized its implications, and withheld it from the United States prosecutor, he had been an accessory to obstruction of justice. And now he was making me part of it, too. But I knew at that moment, as surely as he had known six months before, that I would never hand it over to Evans or anybody else. I would burn the son of a bitch!

Yet, I could not help damning him for being so thorough, so good at his job. Damning him for sticking his nose into that cell where she had stayed, been imprisoned. And even more for telling me what he'd found.

"Why? Why would she do such a thing?"

"She told you on the witness stand. She loved that Johnny Boins.

When I heard her admit that, I knew damn well who'd written that note."

"Yes, but her father . . ."

"God damn, Eben," he said, impatient once again. He drew himself up as though preparing for a long speech. "Try to get it straight in your head. She wasn't one of those Saint Louis women you've known. She was a half-wild, confused little mountain girl, living all her life down there on that hill farm. Dreaming about all the things I'm told little girls dream about. And all she had was helping string fence with Indian hired hands and cleaning out stalls and grubbing potatoes. She'd never met anyone like this Johnny Boins. She told you all that, too. She said it on the stand. Her daddy ran off any menfolks who started getting glassy-eyed. And then here came Johnny Boins, slick as a frog's egg, who acted like he loved her, and who was her first man, Eben. A ruthless bastard, but she couldn't see any of that."

"But for God's sake, she had to know Johnny Boins had something to do with what happened at that farm."

"Remember, we still hadn't found her stepmother. And even if she suspected, she wouldn't let herself think about it. She'd lost one man she loved, her daddy, and she wasn't going to lose the other one. Then when we found her stepmother, the whole mess fell down around her ears."

"It's been my impression that you and Evans and everybody else around here suspected she had a great deal to do with this whole thing."

"I don't give a damn what Evans thinks. I never thought it. Listen to me a minute. After she'd been with Johnny Boins, she wanted to be with him again. Nothing like that had ever happened to her. She likely told him she'd go off with him. That's when the old man caught them in the wagon. They couldn't stand around then and make plots. The old man was ready to kill Johnny Boins. So after he got run off, somebody had to find that farm. And when the old man saw 'em coming that day, he must have had a good idea of what was about to happen. He'd lived most of his life in The Nations and he had to know Rufus Deer, or know about him anyway. He must have seen Johnny Boins and Rufus together at the races one time or another, likely right there at Saddler's Ford or at Wetumka when it all started."

"But in that attic? She had to hear something."

"That's been gnawing at you for a long time, hasn't it? Well, you can

273

forget it. You don't think the old man told her who was coming when he put her there, do you? If she'd known who it was, she likely would have fought going into that attic. He had to scare hell out of her to get her up there to start with. Remember the shape she was in when we dragged her down? Half hysterical and the other half fainted."

Once more, as it had so many times since this had all begun, I tried to imagine the things going through Thomas Thrasher's mind when he first saw those five ride into his farmyard and recognized Johnny Boins and the milk-eyed man. And when Smoker Chubee stepped into the breezeway before he'd had a chance to hide Mrs. Thrasher . . .

"Don't forget, Eben, Johnny Boins was on the stand, too. And if that girl had been involved he'd have spilled it."

"It's still hard to believe, her writing that note to frighten Emmitt."

"She was trying to protect her pretty boy. Up 'til then all we had was Emmitt. Without him, no case. It was too bad that she had to give it the first time to such a pretty boy who was also a son of a bitch."

"You put it all so delicately," I said bitterly.

"Just so you understand it. What I'm trying to say is, knowing how you feel, it's too bad you couldn't have been the first."

I poured another glass of brandy and threw it down and almost choked. He watched me with those impersonal blue eyes. The matchstick in his mouth had been chewed to splinters and he took it out and tossed it on the floor.

"I want to ask you something. The time she came up here, to this room. What happened between you two?"

"None of your goddamned business."

"No, it ain't. But it's the kind of thing a man wonders about."

"How in God's name did you know that?"

He seemed about to smile.

"It's part of my work, knowing what people do around here," he said.

The bedsprings squeaked as he rose. He came to the desk and placed something there beside Smoker Chubee's pistol. It was the little china dog. I could see the hand-printed legend on the side. *Eureka Springs, Arkansas, 1890.*

"I found this, too," he said. With that, he turned to the door, moving into the dark shadows of the room. "Well, I better get to business."

But he stood with his hand on the doorknob for a long time, watching me. When he spoke, his voice seemed not so harsh, not so brusque as it usually was.

"I'm sorry about all of it, Eben. But I figured it was better you knew everything."

He swung open the door and started into the hall.

"Wait a minute," I said abruptly. "I'm going with you."

He may have smiled then. I was too busy throwing winter gear from my trunk to notice. There was a sudden urgency to get away from here, to find some new country, some new people.

Although it was only a little after suppertime, the streets were empty when we went down. The snow had stopped, as Oscar Schiller had predicted it would, but the wind was blowing fresh from the west. We hurried along beneath the gas lights, neither speaking. I thought of a thousand other questions but each seemed only a repetition of something I had already asked. Beyond the Frisco depot and across the tracks, we moved down to the waterfront where a small ferry was waiting at one of the slips. There was a lantern swung from a pole at the bow, another at the stern where we jumped aboard. Horses were there saddled and standing heads down and close together, their steel shoes making rough thumpings on the deck as they shifted about on the gently lifting vessel.

Except that now they wore winter coats, the two Osages looked much as I recalled seeing them the first time, when we rode the Texas freight to the Winding Stair. Blue Foot stood silently, wearing a hat now, his brooding eyes watching me, a heavy Winchester held under each arm. Joe Mountain came up to me as I jumped on the ferry, his teeth showing and the tattooed dots along his cheek looking inky black in the lantern shine. When he saw I was carrying saddlebags, his grin widened.

"What you got in them bags, Eben Pay? Railroad passes?"

"No. Some sardines and tobacco."

"Yeah, I told the Cap'n you'd come. You got all stocked up, didn't you?"

I suppose it was true. I suppose that, after all, the most important thing was being here, with these men, a part of them. One of Parker's men.

"This here is gonna be a good one, Eben Pay. Murders are always the best kind," Joe Mountain said as we leaned against one railing and watched the two ferrymen throwing off stern lines and then manning the large sweeps. Slowly, we moved out into the current, away from the Arkansas shore. "I bet you got Old Smoker's Colt in them bags, ain't you?"

"Yes."

He laughed abruptly, sending a great cloud of vapor into the cold air. "By God. With Old Smoker's Colt, you're gonna be hell on the border, Eben Pay."

The ferry slipped through the water without a sound. Everything was as it had been. Joe Mountain had begun to tell of some ancient ancestor, before the war, fighting the Cherokees along the Verdigris River. Blue Foot, farther along the railing and in shadows, making no sound, was watching, the roach of hair hanging down his back beneath his wide-brimmed hat. Leaning against one of the horses, Oscar Schiller stood with saddlebags between his feet, fishing peanuts from his coat pocket and hulling them, popping the meats into his mouth in a cloud of breath vapor. The lanterns put a glaze of white across his glasses.

I slipped the china dog from my pocket. After a moment in my hand, it grew warm. Toward the south was the rising structure of the new railroad bridge and beyond that the pale ribbon of water bending back into The Nations. Faintly the limestone bluffs of Belle Point thrust into the night sky, along with the dark square forms of the old fort commissary and the federal building. In my mind, I could see the compound, and the outline of the gallows, stark and barren now, but waiting, always there waiting.

I dropped the china dog over the side and listened for its fall into the water, but the only sounds were the rushing wind and the sweeps in the oarlocks and Joe Mountain's voice, droning on about the way it once was. How the deer came down to drink along these shores and there were black bears in the hills and not so far west the great herds of buffalo, and the people would paint their faces yellow and black to go out on war parties, and then come home again to dance.

In Appreciation:

The National Archives

The National Park Service

The National Historic Site, Fort Smith, Arkansas

And Most Especially To:

Billy Ben Putman, swordsman, gourmet, counselor,
cherished friend—and the best damned
trial lawyer who ever stood to
the defense of an accused killer.